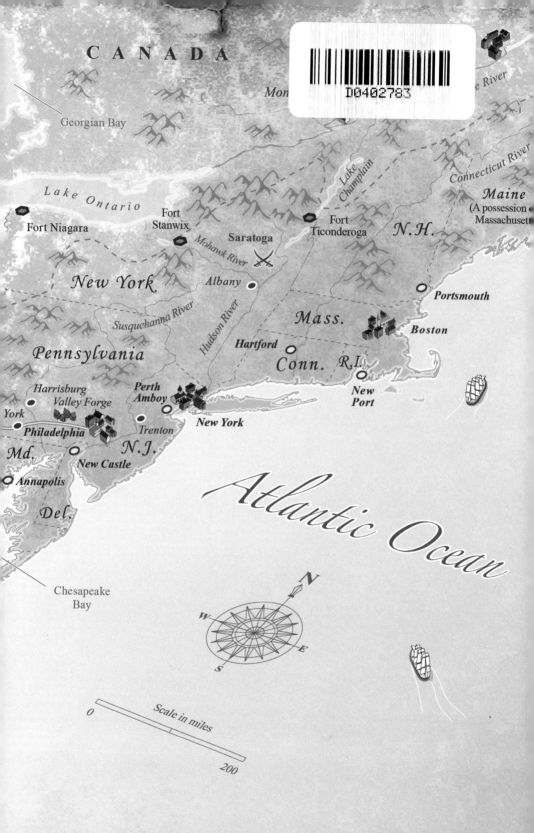

CANADA

Georgian Bay

Mon...

...e River

Lake Ontario

Fort Niagara

Fort Stanwix

Mohawk River

Lake Champlain

Fort Ticonderoga

Connecticut River

Maine
(A possession
Massachuset...

N.H.

Saratoga

New York

Albany

Susquehanna River

Hudson River

Portsmouth

Mass.

Boston

Hartford

Conn.

R.I.

Pennsylvania

Harrisburg
Valley Forge

York

Philadelphia

Md.

Annapolis

New Castle

N.J.

Perth Amboy

Trenton

New York

New Port

Del.

Chesapeake
Bay

Atlantic Ocean

N

W

E

S

Scale in miles

0

200

George Skoch

RIFLEMAN

The

RIFLEMAN

OLIVER NORTH

A FIDELIS BOOKS BOOK
An Imprint of Post Hill Press
ISBN: 978-1-64293-314-7
ISBN (eBook): 978-1-64293-315-4

Maps and end sheets by George Skoch

Copyediting by Amanda Varian

Interior design by Xcel Graphic Services - www.xcelgraphic.com

FIDELIS BOOKS Post Hill PRESS

Post Hill Press
New York • Nashville
posthillpress.com

Published in the United States of America

FOR ELIZABETH STUART

WITH WHOM I FELL IN LOVE OVER FIVE DECADES AGO

AND IN WHOSE VEINS

FLOW THE DNA OF REVOLUTION

CONTENTS

PREFACE

This is a war story. It's about real people and events before and
during the American Revolution. The central characters in this
work—Daniel Morgan, George Washington, Patrick Henry,
Charles Mynn Thruston, and Generals Arnold, Knox, Greene, Lee,
Gates, and a host of others—actually did the deeds at the places
and times described herein. So too did their accurately named
foreign and native adversaries. As you will see, our war for independence was a most un-civil, civil war.

If Daniel Morgan were alive today, he would be my near
neighbor in Virginia's beautiful Shenandoah Valley. It was while
visiting a nearby gristmill Morgan and Nathanael Burwell, a fellow Revolutionary War hero, built in the late 1700s [now restored
and operated by the Clarke County Historical Association],
I became fascinated by this unsung national hero.

The history of what Daniel Morgan and his Virginia Riflemen
endured and accomplished is recorded as accurately as a decade
of research permits. Their story is told here from the point of view
of Nathanael Newman, Adjutant to Daniel Morgan, and fictional

ancestor of Peter Newman, the protagonist in my earlier novels: *Mission Compromised, Jericho Sanction, The Assassins, Heroes Proved*, and *Counterfeit Lies*.

Though dialogue has been created to give context, the essential facts of the extraordinary events leading up to and throughout the painful birth of this nation are accurately presented. Where necessary, I have reproduced written reports, official records, and the correspondence of eyewitness participants in these dramatic proceedings.

Hopefully, by the end of this book you will be inspired—as I am—by the men and women who persevered through the brutality and privation of a vicious war to forge a new nation and create a form of government then unknown elsewhere on this planet.

They were a tough, resilient, and ultimately, very wise people. Their extraordinary courage, tenacity, and faith are exhibited by the brave young Americans with whom I served as a U.S. Marine; in the young American Soldiers, Sailors, Airmen, Guardsmen, and Marines I covered for nearly two decades at FOX News; and by the Hurt Heroes and their families aided by Freedom Alliance.

As many readers already know, I'm grateful to have spent most of my life in the company of real American heroes. I'm looking forward to spending eternity in the company of my personal American heroes and the Riflemen you will meet in this book . . .

Semper fidelis,

Oliver North
Narnia Farm
Clarke County, Virginia
January 2019

THE LETTER

At Alexandria, Virginia
Thursday, 25th August 1814

To my Sons, Henry, James, & Peter & Daughter Grace:

Please forgive this hastily composed Missive. It is most Important that you follow Carefully my Instructions below should I fail to return from this Mission Defending our Commonwealth.

For the third occasion in my lifetime, a British Monarch has Invested our shores and Invaded our Lands. In 1756 George II sent his Army here and they were occupying our lands when I was born in 1758. The lunatic, King George III, besieged us again for thirteen years starting in 1768. And now his wastrel son, the Royal Prince Regent, once more threatens our Tranquility, Safety, and Livelihood with a third British Incursion.

As you know, my unit of Virginia Mounted Militiamen was mustered to Duty in Winchester on Sunday, 21st August after a British Invasion Force disembarked from their Fleet in Maryland's Patuxent River and started moving toward our new Capital, the District of Columbia. By nightfall we assembled 103 officers and men, 115 horses and a wagon loaded with victuals, powder, and shot and headed East with dispatch to join Colonel George Minor, Commander of the Virginia Militia.

By dawn on Tuesday, despite terrible heat and the loss of a half-dozen horses, we crossed the Blue Ridge at Snickers Gap and proceeded, as ordered, East on Georgetown Turnpike. That night a dispatch rider from Colonel Minor arrived with orders directing my Rifleman to halt on the Southwest bank of the Patomack River; hold the new Finley-Chain Bridge; and await further orders.

Before first light on Wednesday the 24th there began a steady stream of panicked Citizens fleeing our Capital across the bridge into Virginia. Among them was a State Department clerk, Stephen Pleasonton, carrying orders from Secretary of State James Monroe to "Make safe and take best care of the Books and Papers of the Gov't."

We were still awaiting orders to cross the River so I dispatched 20 of my men to requisition as many horses and wagons as they could find and bring them to me. Well before noon, our loyal militiamen returned with 22 wagons, carts, and carriages. With the sound of cannon-fire from North of the city, I ordered them to accompany Mr. Pleasonton into the nearly deserted Capital.

In less than two hours all the transports were back on the Virginia side of the bridge, loaded with Government Documents sewn into linen sacks. It was then Mr. Pleasonton confided to me that he was carrying, *inter alia*, The Original Declaration of Independence and General Washington's Commission as Commander of the Continental Army.

The State Department clerk originally intended to store the records and documents at Edgar Patterson's Mill—just a few hundred yards up-river from the bridge. But I pointed out if the Redcoats succeeded in taking the Capital they would surely attack the Foxhall Foundry in Georgetown and likely force their way over the bridge to plunder and pillage Patterson's Mill.

One of my officers, Lieutenant William Binns, suggested the Precious Cargo be dispatched further West, to Leesburg for storage in the basement of a sturdy house he inherited from his father. He pointed out "the all-brick home has a spacious barrel vault in a dry basement and the place is secured by Rev. John Littlejohn, the former Sherriff of Loudoun County."

Mr. Pleasonton agreed to store our Government's Papers "in a place protected by a law officer who is a man of God." Since my Militiamen still had no orders other than holding the bridge, I directed Lt. Binns and 25 of our mounted militiamen to accompany Mr. Pleasanton and the horse-drawn vehicles conveying our Government's Most Important Documents to Leesburg.

As they prepared to sally forth at about 4 o'clock in the afternoon, a carriage and cart came racing across the bridge. In the carriage, accompanied only by a manservant and a single Dragoon of the Presidential Guard, was Mrs. Madison. The President's wife hastily informed us the American Army has been defeated at a place in Maryland called Bladensburg and British troops were now on the march into the Capital. Further, she said, "My Husband was at the fight and is now in flight, whereabouts unknown, with the Remnant of our Army."

Mrs. Madison acknowledged She departed the Executive Mansion in great haste bringing little more than some Presidential Correspondence and a Portrait of our First President, General George Washington, rolled up in a tablecloth. She also revealed a Courier, dispatched by her Husband, had instructed her to meet the President at Wiley's Tavern on the Georgetown Turnpike once he escaped the clutches of the British.

Since Georgetown Turnpike was the Route the Pleasonton expedition would be taking to Leesburg, and fearing She would be captured, I convinced Mrs. Madison and Her Escort to join Lt. Binns' Motley caravan. He placed Her carriage near the Van of his unit with four of our Militiamen as Mounted Guards and they departed up the hill in the midst of a terrible downpour.

Less than an hour afterwards there was a tremendous Explosion from East of the Capital. At dusk, a newly arrived Refugee from the City informed us the Blast had come from our Sailors blowing up the Magazine at the Navy Yard on the Anacostia River. By dark it seemed the entire City was ablaze.

My now depleted Militia unit spent the night soaking wet at the Chain Bridge on High Alert. Thanks Be To God, the British stopped their advance after looting and burning nearly all the Government buildings in the Capital. The Executive Mansion, the Treasury, the Offices of State, War and Navy and the Capitol Building are now but smoking Ruins. The only Official Structure left unscathed in the City seems to be the Marine Barracks.

This morning we have finally been Ordered into the Fight. A British flotilla is making its way up the Patomack heading for the city of Alexandria. Col Minor has directed my Virginia Militiamen to ferry over the River tonight to reinforce our Maryland Militia Brethren at Fort Warburton, across the Patomack from President Washington's home at Mount Vernon. To our great Misfortune & Dismay, we no longer have Daniel Morgan to rally more Patriots against this Vicious, Unconscionable Assault.

Now, should Misfortune befall me on this Mission, once the British have been defeated and order is restored, you must do your Utmost to retrieve two sets of Most Important papers:

First, the aforementioned Official Documents and Records Lieutenant Binns has taken to Leesburg must be recovered and preserved. If necessary, seek him out or find Rev. Littlejohn or Mr. Stephen Pleasanton of the Department of State to aid you in this effort.

Second, as you know, I have labored for nearly two decades seeking Fair Restitution and a Just Annuity for The Riflemen with whom I served during our First War For Independence. When he was in Congress, General Morgan was our advocate. But since his passing in July 1802, the task has fallen to me.

Requests for compensating Widows, Orphans, and our Incapacitated Veterans have been repeatedly submitted to Congress without result. Now, with our Seat of Government in ashes, it is likely the only Complete Record of those Appeals resides in the correspondence I have accumulated, my draft Report of Service during the War For Independence and the Sworn Testimony of others with whom I served.

To preserve said Claims for Compensation and Annuity from seizure or destruction by British Aggressors or Traitors in our midst, I sealed these files, my draft Report of Service, and my personal journals and recollections about those Momentous Days in a lead chest. Included therein is information about your Dear Mother of whom you have just the slightest memories.

When we passed over the Blue Ridge on the night of the 21st, one of my Riflemen and I secreted the lead chest in the cairn beneath Washington's Lookout atop Snicker's Gap where we often picnicked when you were young. You all know the place.

When the time is right, I urge you to do all in your power to also recover both the Official Government Records sequestered in Leesburg and the Documents I hid in the cairn.

Please Retain my journal & recollections—particularly my correspondence with your mother which is intimate. The Volumes labeled, "Record of Service of our Riflemen," are Official Documents. These & my Appeals for Restitution should be delivered to Secretary of State, James Monroe. Though a Republican, he is a Wounded Veteran, and Honorable Man and supports our appeals to Congress for Restitution.

I send this in hopes you will aid in preserving Documents precious to you and our new Nation, And I pray you will carry on my Work to Ensure the Widows and Orphans of The Beloved Riflemen, with whom I served during our First War For Independence, Not Be Forgotten.

Sic Semper Tyrannus,

Nathanael Newman

Rifleman, Morgan's Rifle Company
Lieutenant, Virginia Rifle Regiment, Continental Line
Lieutenant Colonel, Virginia Militia

TO THE READER

The original hand-written letter dated 25 August 1814 on the previous pages was delivered to my office at Centurion Solutions Group [CSG] on Monday, 2 January 2018. The document, sealed in a plastic bag, was carefully wrapped in a USPS shipping box with a postmark and tracking number indicating it had been mailed on 30 December 2017 from Morgantown, WV. It had no return address. We ran it through our screening device to confirm it contained no explosives. The inner wrapping was accompanied by an undated, unsigned note: "General Newman: This is important. Please investigate."

My company, CSG, does sensitive work for the U.S. government so it took less than three days for the FBI Lab at Quantico to provide the following information in a 5 January 2018 email:

"The only fingerprints and DNA on the USPS packaging and contents appear to be yours and that of CSG Operations Director, Daniel Gabbard.

"The computer-generated cover note—'General Newman: This is important. Please investigate . . .'—was created on a

Hewlett Packard laser-jet printer on commonly available bond paper, manufactured in 2018 by Georgia Pacific.

"A forensic analysis of the stationery used for the six-page letter dated 25 August 1814 and signed 'Nathanael Newman' indicates compatibility with that in use in the United States during the early 1800s. Each sheet bears a watermark: 'RUSE & TURNERS 1813,' indicating the paper was manufactured that year in Kent, England.

"Since this document appears to be genuine, we did no chemical, DNA, or fingerprint testing of the aging ink or paper.

"However, non-invasive, spectrographic analysis of the text indicates the ink is most likely 'Iron Gall'—a composition of Gallic acid [aka, trihydroxybenzoic acid], iron sulfate, gum Arabic, and water—a readily available, indelible medium commonly used for correspondence in the 18th and 19th centuries. Given the brown hue of the text, typical for Iron Gall ink as it ages, it appears the ink was likely applied to the paper in a time frame compatible with the date on the letter.

"Finally, microscopic examination of the script indicates a left-handed person writing with a sharpened goose quill likely prepared the document. If other documents, known to have been prepared by the person whose signature appears on the letter dated 25 August 1814 exist, our handwriting analysts will be pleased to quickly confirm authenticity."

On Monday morning, 8 January 2018, it was 18°F in the Blue Ridge Mountains when Master Gunnery Sergeant Dan Gabbard, USMC (Ret.) accompanied me to Bears Den hostel along the Appalachian Trail. Using climbing lines, we rappelled down the west face of the overlook and found the "cairn" referred to in Lieutenant Colonel Nathanael Newman's missive of 25 August 1814.

In less than an hour of digging in the frozen rocks we discovered the lead-covered chest described in Lieutenant Colonel Newman's letter. The container, apparently intact, and the document dated 25 August 1814, were delivered to Dr. Scot Marsh, Curator of the Museum of the Shenandoah Valley in Winchester, VA.

Since then, Dr. Marsh; the Clarke County Historical Association; archivists at Anderson House, Headquarters for the Society of the Cincinnati; and student scholars at Patrick Henry College; the College of William & Mary, and Shenandoah University have helped to interpret Capt. Newman's hand-written work and the signed affidavits of his fellow Riflemen. With their assistance we have discerned the following:

1. The lead-clad chest was completely intact and its contents, in good condition, are as described in Lieutenant Colonel Nathanael Newman's letter dated 25 August 1814.

2. Lieutenant Colonel Nathanael Newman, the author of the letter, was my great-great-great-great-great-great-grandfather. According to family records, he was born in Winchester, VA on 7 August 1758, and is listed on the muster rolls of those who served with Daniel Morgan in the Revolution and afterward. He was left-handed and I am directly descended from his youngest son, Peter.

3. Early on 26 August 1814, five days after he apparently deposited the lead-sealed container in the "cairn" at the foot of the overlook at Snickers Gap, Lieutenant Colonel Newman, leading a contingent of Virginia Riflemen, was ferried across the Potomac from Mount Vernon to the Maryland shore to help defend Fort Warburton, now known as Fort Washington.

4. That night, Lieutenant Colonel Newman was severely wounded in the head by shrapnel from British guns or rockets during Royal Navy Commodore James Gordon's bombardment of the Fort. The following day, after the well-documented, cowardly surrender of the bastion by Maryland Militia Capt. Samuel Dyson, the Virginians who were killed and wounded in the attack were conveyed by British seamen to the western shore of the

Potomac at Mount Vernon. Those unscathed were taken prisoner by the British invasion fleet.

5. On 29 August 1814, the unconscious Lieutenant Colonel Newman was loaded on a wagon for transport to Winchester. He never fully regained consciousness for more than a few minutes at a time. He died at his home in Winchester, VA on 8 January 1815—never knowing of the Christmas Eve Treaty at Ghent, ending what he called the "third British Invasion of our shores"—or Andrew Jackson's defeat of the "Redcoats" that day at New Orleans; and unwitting that his sons never recovered the lead chest he had carefully hidden in "the cairn beneath Washington's Lookout atop Snicker's Gap."

6. The Official U.S. Government Documents secured by Jonathan Pleasonton, including the "Original Copy of the Declaration of Independence" Lieutenant Colonel Newman had sent to Leesburg with Lieutenant Binns, were recovered by State Department agents in November 1814 and returned to Washington.

7. When Nathanael Newman drew his last breath, he was not yet fifty-seven years old. Perhaps ironically, the day we discovered his lead-clad chest full of Revolutionary War documents, was the 200th anniversary of his death.

His story—and riveting accounts of his exploits with those he called his "beloved Riflemen"—are on the following pages, all extracted and edited from the 1,837 pages of Nathanael Newman's contemporaneous journals and notes, his "Record of Service" and the "Sworn Testimony" of sixteen of "The Riflemen" with whom he served during what he called, "America's Fight for Independence."

Lieutenant Colonel Newman's journals, his "Record of Service," and the affidavits of his comrades in arms are presented herewith in chronologic sequence and dated as he intended. Though he did not do so, I have assembled them in chapters, with headings I created, and added footnotes so present-day readers can more easily place locations and events.

Though Nathanael Newman was well educated and articulate, for modern linguistic clarity we updated his grammar, capitalization, punctuation, and dialogue while trying to remain true to his original record. For your understanding as to how our language has evolved, his 25 August 1814 letter to his children is presented as written on the previous six pages.

We have not yet discovered who sent the unsigned, undated missive addressed to "General Newman: This is important. Please investigate" document to my office on 8 January 2018.

Peter J. Newman

Major General, USMC (Ret.)

Bluemont, Virginia

5 February 2019

CHAPTER ONE

A DEATH IN THE FAMILY

Winchester, Virginia
Saturday, April 22nd, 1775

It was mid-afternoon and the Shenandoah was swollen from three days of heavy rain when a single mud-spattered rider, mounted on a big bay gelding, arrived at the river's east bank. In a loud voice he hailed us to bring the ferry over from the western shore.

David Casselman, Jr., just a year older than I, opened the toll ferry service in August '74 as a means of producing revenue for his large family. The ferry was a profitable venture until this past January when an early thaw flooded the Shenandoah and sent his rafts tumbling in the torrent all the way to Harpers Ferry.

In February this year, David asked me to help him repair and run the ferry while I waited to start the autumn term at the College of William & Mary in Williamsburg. We reconstructed the pulley system and built two rafts—one small for a horse and rider and another large enough for a wagon and a team of horses or oxen. The fare was one shilling for the small barge, five for the large ferry.

We were about to tell the rider to wait until morning in hopes the river would subside overnight when I recognized him as one of the Trusted Couriers for the Frederick County Secret Committee of Correspondence and Safety. Though the river was flowing faster than safe passage could be assured, we hitched the two draft horses to their traces and I rode the ferry across while David tended the tow.

During the transit I introduced myself and asked the messenger from whence he had come, but he only replied, "This is my ninth horse and fourth day and night of hard riding."

When we arrived on the western shore, he handed David a shilling for the toll, and asked, "Where are your fathers, lads?"

David replied, "They are meeting at Glen Owen[1] with Pastor John Peter Gabriel Muhlenberg, the chairman of Shenandoah County Secret Committee, and Rev. Charles Mynn Thruston, chairman of our local committee."

As he re-mounted his steed, the weary rider shook his head and said sternly, "You should not mention the committees to those you do not know for certain. There are Tory spies everywhere."

I interjected, "We understand, sir, but I recognized you as a committee courier."

He nodded and said, "Best not mention that to others, either. These are dangerous times."

Then turning to David, he asked, "Glen Owen is the place your family bought from Colonel and Mrs. Washington, right?"

"Yes, sir, just go west on the turnpike. It's on your right, about three miles. May I inquire, why are you seeking our fathers?"

"I'm sorry lads, but I cannot speak to others about this matter. Only to them."

While David and I used the horse team to drag the ferries out of the water onto the west bank of the river, my curiosity gnawed at me like a hunting dog chewing on a knucklebone.

We arrived at Glen Owen just after dark. Our fathers were alone, seated before the fire when we entered the home. David's father immediately said, "Come with me, son," and they departed the room together with a male slave named Jonathan, leaving my very somber father and me alone.

My father, at forty-seven, was a much-respected architect and well known from Williamsburg to the Shenandoah Valley. By the standards of the day we were wealthy—with a comfortable home and stable on a cobbled street in Winchester.

Though he never spoke of it, others told me and my two older brothers, Joshua and Paul, of our father's courage, tenacity, and skill as a Virginia militiaman on Lord Braddock's ill-fated campaign to capture Fort Duquesne in the summer of 1755. Perhaps it was that experience that caused him to spend so much time teaching the three of us how to ride, shoot, hunt, and live in the wilderness.

Our father was known to be a wise and generous man, but his cheerful demeanor diminished considerably following our mother's death from Ague[2] in 1771 after returning to Winchester from visiting her sister's home in North Carolina. Father was in Charlottesville at the time, working with Mr. Jefferson at Monticello. It fell to Joshua to make the mournful ride to deliver the news to Father while Paul and I buried our mother.

Now, as he motioned me into the chair vacated by Mr. Casselman, I perceived our father was once again greatly saddened.

Without preamble he said, "Nathanael, I was just informed by the courier you met at the ferry your brother Joshua was killed on Wednesday in a skirmish with British troops in Concord, Massachusetts."

Denial is the first response to the delivery of terrible news. I recall drawing a deep breath and saying, "Oh dear God. How can this be? In Joshua's letter we received on Monday he said he was preparing for his final examinations and would be home next month after graduating in just three years from Harvard."

Father nodded and said quietly, "All true. But your brother Joshua was more than a student. He was also a secret member of Boston's Committee of Correspondence. Samuel Adams, the founder of the whole committee network, personally asked Joshua to join shortly after your brother arrived for his first year at Harvard."

"Did you know Josh was part of this?"

"Yes. Joshua told me about it when he came home for Christmas that first year. He brought with him a letter from Mr. Adams— also a Harvard alumnus—urging me to encourage members of our House of Burgesses to form similar committees in Virginia. It took six months for our legislators to bring it to a vote, but thanks to the skills of Messer's Richard Henry Lee and Patrick Henry, the measure passed and now there are near-identical committees throughout all thirteen colonies."

"But how did Josh get killed by British soldiers in this place you called Concord?"

"Because he could ride and shoot, Joshua was a Trusted Courier for a surveillance group headed by a gentleman named Paul Revere. The messenger you met at the ferry told me that very early Wednesday morning Mr. Revere summoned his couriers to alert Patriots in Lexington and Concord—two towns about fifteen miles west of Boston—700 British troops were coming to confiscate militia supplies of arms, gunpowder, and lead shot.

"There were two fights, the first in Lexington and a second that afternoon at a bridge near Concord. Joshua was apparently killed in this second engagement. Mr. Adams was kind enough to

dispatch the courier with this dreadful message that very evening."
Father then handed me a folded piece of parchment.

Concord, Massachusetts, 19th, April, 1775
To Mr. James Henry Newman, Esq.

My Dear Sir:

It is my sad duty to inform you that your brave Patriot son,
Joshua Newman, was Killed in Action today at Concord,
Massachusetts while serving as a Trusted Courier in Mr. Paul
Revere's Special Unit of my Committee. Your son was struck
in the head by a musket ball fired by the British Invasion Force
at a bridge being defended by our Minutemen.

I was there and can confirm Joshua died the instant he was
shot. He and the other Patriots who fell in Concord will be
interred with honors on the morrow at First Parish Church
Burial Ground with Rev. William Emerson, Sr. presiding.

Please know Joshua was a courageous soldier in the cause of
Liberty. He will be dearly missed by all who love Freedom.

With my prayers our Merciful Lord will assuage your grief, I
remain,

Your very humble servant,

Samuel Adams

After reading the letter, I could think of nothing to say. So I
stood and wrapped my arms around my father and we wept together.

Since it was late and raining again, the Casselmans insisted Father and I dine with them and remain overnight. When supper was finished, Mrs. Margaret Casselman hustled David's six younger siblings upstairs, leaving David Sr. and Jr. and my father and me alone at the table.

After some talk about the ground being too wet to plant and a brief discussion of plans my father drew up for an addition to their home, Mr. Casselman Sr. said, "James, in the morning, let me send a slave and an extra horse with Nathanael so he can get to Williamsburg and tell Paul about Joshua before he learns about what happened from others. Word of what transpired in Massachusetts on the 19th will spread very quickly through the committees."

Father thought for a moment, shook his head, and said, "No. Thank you, David. I will go myself. I'll leave after Rev. Thruston's service tomorrow. Paul is near to finishing his second year at William & Mary and I'm concerned this will be a distraction from his examinations. I will stay there until he completes them and we'll ride home together."

"Do you wish to have me go with you, Father?" I asked.

"No, Nathanael. We shall go together to Rev. Thruston's service in the morning and I will ride from there to Williamsburg. I want you to stay here and meet on Monday with the commander of one of our Frederick County militia companies. He was here this afternoon for the meeting with Pastor Muhlenberg,[3] and Rev. Thruston[4] when the courier arrived to deliver the terrible news of what happened to Joshua in Massachusetts."

Despite a gulp from the cup of cider before me, my mouth was dry when I asked, "Does this mean there will be a war?"

Father nodded and said, "Yes. This means war. And it will require the service of every brave Patriot good with a rifle. You are an expert marksman with a rifle. You are fit. You ride well and have grown up hunting. And now you have reason to fight beyond fidelity to cause or colors. Our enemies killed your brother."

"With whom do you want me to meet on Monday?"

"Captain Daniel Morgan."

ENDNOTES

1. The Glen Owen Farm owned by the Casselman family in 1775 was, as described here, between the Shenandoah River and what is now Berryville, the Clarke County, VA Seat of Government.

   It should not be confused with Glenowen Farm in Loudoun County, Va.

2. *Ague, and Fever and Ague:* archaic terms for what we now call malaria, transmitted by parasitic protozoa carried by infected mosquitos.

3. Rev. John Peter Gabriel Muhlenberg, ordained Lutheran and Anglican clergyman. In 1775 he was Rector of the Lutheran Church in Woodstock, VA, a Lieutenant Colonel in the Virginia Militia, and the Chairman of the Virginia House of Burgesses Secret Committee of Safety.

4. Rev. Charles Mynn Thruston, ordained Anglican minister; Rector of Frederick Parish [one church and seven chapels]; Chairman Frederick County Committee of Correspondence and Safety.

CHAPTER TWO

FAREWELL AND A CALL TO DUTY

Battletown, Virginia[1]

Sunday, April 23rd, 1775

Father and I arose early to a bright and clear Sabbath dawn. Before the sun crested the Blue Ridge, we thanked the Casselmans for their generous hospitality, saddled our horses, and were headed west for Battletown. There we watered our steeds and headed three miles south for the Chapel at Cunningham's Tavern where Rev. Charles Mynn Thruston was to preach.

We arrived a full half-hour before the service was set to begin, but the log structure was already packed to overflowing. Before we could even dismount, neighbors and others we did not know, surrounded Father and me.

Somehow, all around us had already heard about Joshua's death in faraway Massachusetts. Along with sincere expressions of condolence, the word "murdered" was oft spoken. Also in the crowd were "Loyalists" muttering that my brother deserved what happened for having joined a "rebellion" against "King George, God's appointed ruler."

Rev. Thruston, garbed in his vestments, saw the commotion and rescued us from the crowd of mostly well-intentioned, sympathetic parishioners. He escorted us to the tiny vestry just off the chapel's altar and sent one of his vestrymen to save us seats in the front row of benches.

The Chapel at Cunningham's Tavern was in those days a fairly primitive place of worship. Unlike many of the city churches in places like Williamsburg and even Winchester, the chapel did not have a pipe organ. As we entered the nave, two men with fiddles and an attractive young woman with a flute played Charles Wesley's hymn, "Love's Redeeming Work Is Done" as the congregation sang the words:

> *Love's redeeming work is done, fought the fight, the battle won.*
>
> *. . . Death in vain forbids him rise; Christ has opened paradise.*
>
> *Lives again our glorious King; where, O death, is now thy sting?*
>
> *dying once, he all doth save, where thy victory, O grave?*
>
> *Soar we now where Christ has led, following our exalted Head;*
>
> *Made like Him, like Him we rise, ours the cross, the grave, the skies . . .*

The service conducted by Rev. Thruston was unlike any I have ever attended. Here, just one week after Easter, when we celebrated the Resurrection of our Savior, he chose to remind us of "Our Christian Duty." The Old and New Testament readings weren't about forgiveness or turning the other cheek. This was both a funeral service for my brother and a call to arms against those who killed him.

For the Old Testament reading, Rev. Thruston chose chapter 1, verses 6–9, from the book of Joshua, my brother's namesake:

Be strong and of a good courage: for unto this people shalt thou divide for an inheritance the land, which I sware unto their fathers to give them.

Only be thou strong and very courageous, that thou mayest observe to do according to all the law, which Moses my servant commanded thee: turn not from it to the right hand or to the left, that thou mayest prosper whithersoever thou goest.

This book of the law shall not depart out of thy mouth; but thou shalt meditate therein day and night, that thou mayest observe to do according to all that is written therein: for then thou shalt make thy way prosperous, and then thou shalt have good success.

Have not I commanded thee? Be strong and of a good courage; be not afraid, neither be thou dismayed: for the LORD thy God is with thee whithersoever thou goest.

Then, as Rev. Thruston requested, my father read Psalm 23:

The LORD is my shepherd; I shall not want.

He maketh me to lie down in green pastures: he leadeth me beside the still waters.

He restoreth my soul: he leadeth me in the paths of righteousness for his name's sake.

Yea, though I walk through the valley of the shadow of death, I will fear no evil: for thou art with me; thy rod and thy staff they comfort me.

Thou preparest a table before me in the presence of mine enemies: thou anointest my head with oil; my cup runneth over.

111111111111

11111111

Surely goodness and mercy shall follow me all the days of my life: and I will dwell in the house of the LORD forever.

Somehow, Father made it through the reading without his voice cracking until he got to the final verse about dwelling "in the house of the LORD forever." I must acknowledge shedding tears as soon as he began to speak.

For the Gospel reading, Rev. Thruston chose Luke 22, verses 35 and 36. He began saying, "These are the words of Jesus Christ our Lord:"

And he said unto them, "When I sent you without purse, and scrip, and shoes, lacked ye any thing?" And they said, "Nothing."
Then said he unto them, "But now, he that hath a purse, let him take it, and likewise his scrip: and he that hath no sword, let him sell his garment, and buy one."

He concluded with: "These are the words of our Lord," to which the congregation replied. "Amen."

Then, to the consternation of some, particularly our Quaker neighbors and those urging submission to the British monarchy, he delivered a sermon worthy of Jonathan Mayhew, the pastor who used his pulpit in Boston to denounce the Crown for "taxation without representation."

Rev. Thruston began by quoting the first two verses of chapter 13 of Paul's letter to the ancient Christian Church in Rome:

Let every soul be subject unto the higher powers. For there is no power but of God: the powers that be are ordained of God.
Whosoever therefore resisteth the power, resisteth the ordinance of God: and they that resist shall receive to themselves damnation.

And then he pointed out that "every soul" included the king—and emphasized there was nothing in the remainder of the passage—or anywhere else in the Holy Book—prohibiting rebellion against evil. He went on to remind all in attendance "the Lord of the Universe is a Just God" Who would "punish evil doers who do not repent, just as He punished Ahab, Israel's evil king for oppressing his people."

He then quoted several verses from Proverbs 29, noting as he did, "God's word has a powerful message for rulers who abuse their power and the people they rule:"

> *He, that being often reproved hardeneth his neck, shall suddenly be destroyed, and that without remedy.*
>
> *When the righteous are in authority, the people rejoice: but when the wicked beareth rule, the people mourn.*
>
> *In the transgression of an evil man there is a snare: but the righteous doth sing and rejoice.*
>
> *The righteous considereth the cause of the poor: but the wicked regardeth not to know it.*
>
> *The bloodthirsty hate the upright: but the just seek his soul.*
>
> *If a ruler hearken to lies, all his servants are wicked.*
>
> *The king that faithfully judgeth the poor, his throne shall be established forever.*
>
> *When the wicked are multiplied, transgression increaseth: but the righteous shall see their fall.*
>
> *Where there is no vision, the people perish: but he that keepeth the law, happy is he.*
>
> *Many seek the ruler's favour; but every man's judgment cometh from the LORD.*
>
> *An unjust man is an abomination to the just: and he that is upright in The Way is abomination to the wicked.*

His sermon was interrupted by frequent shouts of "Amen!" from the congregation. Much to our father's gratitude, Rev. Thruston described Joshua as "upright, "righteous," and "just." He closed with the words of Solomon from Ecclesiastes:

> *To every thing there is a season, and a time to every purpose under the heaven:*
> *A time to be born, and a time to die; a time to plant, and a time to pluck up that which is planted;*
> *A time to kill, and a time to heal; a time to break down, and a time to build up;*
> *A time to weep, and a time to laugh; a time to mourn, and a time to dance;*
> *A time to cast away stones, and a time to gather stones together; a time to embrace, and a time to refrain from embracing;*
> *A time to get, and a time to lose; a time to keep, and a time to cast away;*
> *A time to rend, and a time to sew; a time to keep silence, and a time to speak;*
> *A time to love, and a time to hate; a time of war, and a time of peace.*

To which he added, "Now, sadly, this is a time for war."[2]

In case anyone in attendance may have missed the message, the service concluded with another of Charles Wesley's hymns, "Soldiers of Christ Arise":

> *Soldiers of Christ arise, and put your armour on, strong in the strength which God supplies through His eternal Son;*
>
> *strong in the Lord of hosts, and in His mighty power: who in the strength of Jesus trusts is more than conqueror.*
>
> *Stand then in His great might, with all His strength endued, and take, to arm you for the fight, the panoply of God.*

From strength to strength go on, wrestle, and fight,
and pray: tread all the powers of darkness down, and
win the well-fought day. . . .

. . . That having all things done, and all your conflicts
past, ye may o'er come, through Christ alone, and stand
complete at last.

Father and I stayed behind as the others departed the chapel. His eyes were dried of tears by the time Rev. Thruston, now unadorned by vestments, came from the vestry, sat down beside my father, and said, "James, how may I be of service to you?"

My father asked him to meet me in the morning and accompany me in meeting with "the Captain." The pastor agreed and said, "I know you are heading to Williamsburg, but can you stay for a few minutes? As we do when the weather permits, the ladies of the parish have spread blankets on the lawn and set out a delicious repast. You should eat some of what they have prepared before you start your journey."

Ever the gentleman he raised his sons to be, Father agreed. We accompanied Rev. Thruston outside and were immediately surrounded by ladies and plied with food and cups of cider. I must confess, I looked in vain for the girl who played the flute for the hymns during the service.

Father stayed for little more than an hour. Then, he quietly thanked everyone for their kindness and excused himself explaining, "I must hasten to Williamsburg to inform my son Paul what has happened to his brother."

Rev. Thruston walked with us as Father headed for his big bay stallion. Before mounting he turned to us and said to me, "Tomorrow morning Rev. Thruston will accompany you to the Shenandoah Store to meet the best commander in our Virginia Militia. He is seeking men with your skills, great perseverance, and courage to fight for our country. You are the kind of man he needs."

Then, as though he thought for a moment before putting his left foot in the stirrup, he turned to me, kissed me on the forehead, put his arms around my shoulders, and said, "Godspeed and good hunting."

I didn't know it then, but it would be two long years before I would see my father again.

ENDNOTES

1.   Battletown is the archaic cognomen for what is now the town of Berryville, VA.

2.   In January 1776, Rev. John Peter Gabriel Muhlenberg would give a similar sermon to his Lutheran congregation in Woodstock, VA, at the end of which he cast off his clerical robes and revealed he was wearing the uniform of a Colonel in the Continental Army. He promptly recruited more than 200 from his parish and his neighbors in the Shenandoah Valley, to enlist in his regiment.

CHAPTER THREE

LISTEN AND LEARN

Winchester, Virginia

Monday, April 24ᵗʰ,1775

In accord with my father's instructions, before retiring on Sunday night, I put out the clothing and kit he recommended and set the alarm on the pendulum clock our mother inherited from her parents. The chimes awakened me before first light. I arose, put on a linsey-woolsey hunting shirt, linen leggin's, a good pair of moccasins, and belted on my hunting knife and the steel fighting hatchet Father gave me.

Thus attired, I gathered my journal, two quills, and checked to ensure the lid on the tin travel inkwell was tight. I then collected the equipment Father prescribed: my .45 caliber William Henry rifle, a leather cartridge case with sixty hand-made, paper-wrapped, powder and ball cartridges sealed with bear fat, and a full, goatskin water bag. I also grabbed the leather case containing my bullet mold, spring vise, wiper, screwdriver, six extra flints, small file, pick, and the ball-puller Father made. All but the rifle, cartridge case, and water skin, I loaded in my saddlebags, stepped out on the porch, and locked the door with the key hanging from a lanyard around my neck.

Father taught us to never leave home with an empty firearm, for one never knew when it might be needed. So, standing on the porch in the dim pre-dawn light, I cocked the hammer on my rifle and checked by "feel" that the flint was sharp and tight in the jaws of my rifle's hammer. After placing the leather cover over the frizzen, I drew a cartridge from the case and bit off the end. In a motion that was second-nature to every hunter in the valley of Virginia, I poured a small amount of powder into the flash-pan, closed the frizzen, poured the rest of the charge down the barrel, drove home the ball and linen wad with my ram-rod, and set the hammer at half-cock.

Satisfied with my preparations, I walked to our stable, saddled my favorite mount, Midnight, a steady, sure-footed mare, tossed my saddlebags across her rump, and mounted. As we departed the stable, Casey, my faithful female spaniel—and the best pointing-flushing-retriever a hunter could ever want—started whining frightfully. I relented and turned her loose to accompany us.

We were barely out of town when Casey suddenly alerted, hunched down, and pointed into the wind toward the underbrush on the left of the path. I dismounted, cocked my rifle, checked the pan to ensure I hadn't lost any powder, and walked slowly up behind her.

Though I could neither hear nor see anything, she remained frozen in place as I crept forward. Save the slight quiver in her hindquarters and the anxious furrow in her brow, the dog might have been carved of wood. After peering into the foliage without glimpsing anything, I shrugged and said quietly, "get 'em up!"

As my little brown dog charged into the brush, I hoped she wasn't about to flush a polecat or worse, a bear. My concern was instantly dispelled by several sharp "putts" as a large tom turkey ran out on the trail with Casey in close pursuit. The big bird took flight in a rush of wings, heading straightaway down the path, high enough to give me a clear shot. The fowl dropped like a stone into the underbrush—followed by a retriever on a mission.

My satisfaction at hitting a fast-flying bird with a single ball was instantly quashed by the sound of a furious fight between fur and feathers. From the sound of things, the turkey was far from dead when it hit the ground. To further my lesson in humility, I then noticed my horse was no longer behind me. In my excitement at the prospect of fresh game, I had failed to tether her reins when dismounting and she bolted at the sound of my shot.

Having forgotten one of Father's important lessons, I wasn't about to ignore another. Before wading into the woods to learn the outcome of the dog versus turkey battle, I quickly pulled another cartridge out of my case and recharged my rifle.

As I rammed home another round, I was treated to the sight of Casey dragging the still-flapping turkey out onto the trail and a rider approaching from the opposite direction leading Midnight by her reins. The panting dog arrived first, her muzzle covered with blood—mostly from the bird but some of her own inflicted by the big tom's beak and spurs.

A quick examination and a "Good Dog!" was all it took for her to place the bird in my hand and sit—tail wagging madly—as I swung the bird by the neck to finish its misery.

Casey was licking the blood off her paws as the rider arrived with the exclamation, "Good dog indeed, Nathanael! And a good shot as well. Would this horse be yours?"

This was certainly not the way I intended to meet Rev. Thruston this morning, but he was smiling as he handed me the reins and said, "If you're going to dress that bird for dinner, please be so kind as to save me some wing feathers for quills."

"Yes sir," I replied. "I shall do so now if it won't make us late arriving at the Shenandoah Store."

He consulted his pocket watch and nodded, "We have time, if you're as good with a knife as you are with your rifle."

It took less than five minutes to tether the dog and the horse, tie the bird's legs to a sapling, cut the carcass, breast it, and wrap the two large breasts, the wings, and tail feathers in a leather sheet and stuff them into my saddlebags. As I remounted and our horses headed south, side-by-side on the path, Rev. Thruston said, "Well done. Your father was right."

"Right about what, sir?"

"He said you are as well skilled in the woods as any frontiersman twice your age."

Those were words I never heard from my father so I asked, "May I inquire when my father said this to you?"

"I was with your father on Saturday afternoon at the Casselmans' home when the Trusted Courier from Massachusetts delivered the sad news about your brother, Joshua. Captain Morgan was there as well. After hearing the Courier's report, Captain Morgan asked your father if you were 'of age to fight' and whether you can read, write, and do numbers. Your father said you were one of the best marksmen he knew and described you as the hunter and woodsman you just showed me to be. He also said you're big for sixteen and know how to read, write, and do arithmetic."

I was pleased to hear what Father said, hoped my hubris did not show and asked, "Why did Captain Morgan ask about whether I can read, write, and do numbers?"

"I will let him tell you," answered Rev. Thruston. Then he queried, "Nathanael, who taught you your schooling?"

"My mother. And after she died, my father continued teaching my brothers and me."

"And what else did your parents teach you?"

"Well, many things. Our mother certainly taught us to avoid the place where we are heading now. She told us Mr. Allason's Shenandoah Store was a 'rough place frequented by coarse men who play cards and drink too much rum.' Is it still?"

Rev. Thruston laughed, "Ah, yes. She was correct. But it's also the kind of place where Captain Morgan can recruit the coarse, rough men he is going to need in the days ahead. Tell me, Nathanael, what do you know about Captain Morgan?"

It wasn't the kind of question I expected and replied, "It seems as though everyone in the Valley of Virginia knows about Daniel Morgan. Some people seem to love him and others hate him but most everyone seems to respect him. My father told us he owes his life to Captain Morgan—"

"Go on," Rev. Thruston said when I paused.

Our mother taught us to never speak gossip so I tried to dodge the minister's question. "Well, sir, these events took place before I was born in the summer of 1758, so I can only tell what my father and mother and their friends told my brothers and me or we over-heard since we were young boys."

Pastor Thruston nodded again and said, "I understand. Just tell me what you remember from what you heard."

"Yes, sir. My father was an officer in the Virginia Militia from 1753 to 1763. He was an ensign with the 1,860-man force Governor Dinwiddie sent in March of 1754 under Lieutenant Colonel Washington with orders to push the French and their Indian allies out of the Forks of the Ohio. Until our mother was dying, Father said those five months were the worst days of his life.

"Their supplies of food, powder, and shot were inadequate. Building a road through the dense forests and steep mountain slopes exhausted the men, and only a handful of Seneca Indians joined their cause—far fewer than needed. My father was wounded at Great Meadow the day before Lieutenant Colonel Washington surrendered Fort Necessity to the French on July 4, 1754.

"According to Father's account, Daniel Morgan was then a young, almost unknown 'wagoneer' driving one of Mr. Robert Burwell's teams hired to deliver supplies on the 100-mile trip to Fort Necessity from Frederick Town which people now call Winchester.

"Our father said, after the surrender, Mr. Morgan volunteered to bring a wagonload of casualties back to Frederick Town without payment. A French musket ball broke my father's leg and he could not walk. He told us had he not gotten that ride, he would not have lived."

"As far as I know, that's all true," Rev. Thruston said. "Daniel has told me he was 'born poor' in New Jersey in 1736 and walked down the Great Wagon Road from Philadelphia to Frederick County when he was just seventeen. After working at farming and as the foreman of a sawmill for about a year, John Ashby, Robert Burwell's superintendent, hired him to drive wagonloads of produce from the Shenandoah to the seaports in Alexandria, Dumfries, and Fredericksburg and return with goods needed in the Valley.

"When Morgan transported your father to safety from Fort Necessity, he was just eighteen years old. Your father also served in the Braddock Expedition the following year, didn't he?"

"Yes, sir. By then he had been elected to command a Virginia Militia Company. They were called up in February 1755 when General Braddock arrived in Virginia with two regiments of British Regulars. In May, General Braddock and his troops arrived at Fort Cumberland with orders to drive the French out of the fort they erected where the Monongahela and Allegheny Rivers merge to form the Ohio. It's also when he again met Mr. Morgan and Colonel Washington."

"Ah, yes," Rev. Thruston nodded, "the ill-fated expedition in the summer of 1755 to seize Fort Duquesne[1] from the French and their savage allies. By then Daniel had saved enough to purchase his own team of draft horses and a sturdy wagon. He was hired to haul supplies and military equipment from Winchester to Fort Cumberland. It's ironic your father, young Morgan, and George Washington all participated in two catastrophes on the same ground—both caused by British arrogance and unwillingness to take advice from mere colonials. What did your father have to say about that venture?"

"He told us that between April and June his Militia Company was posted at Fort Cumberland and how Mr. Morgan was flogged for disrespect to a British officer . . ."

The Reverend smiled and said, "According to the oft-repeated story, a court-martial for insubordination sentenced Daniel to 500 lashes—but the drummer miscounted and he only received 499. Whatever the number, if you ever see him with his shirt off you will see the scars. That kind of beating would likely have killed a lesser man than Daniel Morgan. What more did your father have to say about the campaign?"

"He said Lieutenant Colonel Washington was unable to get a Royal commission so he volunteered to serve without pay as one of General Braddock's aides. Unfortunately, as you said, the general ignored most of his advice until it was too late. He also told us General Washington and Daniel Morgan were heroes in the midst of the disaster."

"Did your father tell you what happened?"

"Not really. He has never spoken much about it."

"Well, you should know; for the past will enlighten you about the war we are about to experience. First, the classical definition of the word 'hero' describes a person who willingly puts oneself at risk for the benefit of others. Do you understand what I mean?"

"Yes, sir."

"Good, because Washington, Morgan, your father, and your late brother Joshua are all heroes. Now, as for the disastrous campaign in the summer of 1755; Lieutenant Colonel Washington urged Braddock to keep his army together, take the time to recruit more of the natives to the British side, and move slowly enough to bring his entire force to bear against the French holding Fort Duquesne. But Braddock was too proud to take the advice.

"He was also unwilling to delay while a suitable road could be carved through the mountains enabling the whole army to advance as a single unit. So he split his force of 2,600 into a 'flying column' of 1,400 British Regulars, grenadiers, two light artillery cannons, and three companies of militia with the balance—including most of the militiamen under a Colonel Dunbar—following slowly in trail with the rest of the artillery, heavy equipment, and baggage.

"When Braddock went charging off into the wilderness toward Fort Duquesne on June 18, Washington and your father went with him. Morgan, ordered to stay with Dunbar, was placed in charge of the baggage train and lead it forward as fast as the engineers could build a passable road.

"Though Washington had far more experience in this terrain than any of the British officers, he was violently ill with bloody flux and colic[2] for most of the march. He was near the front of Braddock's column on the morning of July 9th when they crossed the Monongahela—about ten miles from Fort Duquesne and collided with a force of 800 French Regulars, Canadian militiamen, and natives dispatched from Fort Duquesne.

"Had Braddock and Lieutenant Colonel Thomas Gage, commanding the advance guard, heeded Washington's advice to send scouts out in front and on the flanks of their mile-long column, disaster might have been averted. Though the French and their vicious red-skinned allies were fewer in number than the British force, they quickly enveloped the British moving single file on the narrow path in heavily wooded terrain. The murderous crossfire turned the defile into an abattoir.

"Nearly all the senior British officers at the front of the column—including Braddock—resplendent in red dress coats and gold braid, were felled in the first hours of the fight. When the general was shot off his horse by two musket balls in the chest, Washington, your father, and one of the general's aides were the first to reach him. They carried their gravely wounded commander out of immediate danger where his surviving aides were able to shield him while a surgeon attended to his grievous wounds.

"With chaos all around him, Washington realized there would be a massacre of biblical proportions if they were unable to disengage and withdraw back across the Monongahela before dark. He brought up the two light cannons and directed them to fire grapeshot at their attackers and ordered your father to take his militia company to fight their way uphill to protect the left flank of the column all the way back to the crossing point at the river.

"In the time it took Washington to attempt organizing anything close to an orderly retrograde, he had two horses shot from under him and musket balls perforated his coat in four places without wounding him. I can assure you Colonel Washington believes in Divine intervention in the affairs of mankind.

"So too, does your father. He was wounded in his right shoulder by a ball fired by one of the pursuing savages as he and his company were guarding the ford over the river. They were the last to cross over, well after dark. Though thoroughly exhausted, they brought with them their three dead and seven wounded. Had they failed in their mission, there might well have been an even greater catastrophe.

"It took more than two and a half days for the remnants of the shattered column to traverse the forty-five miles back to Great Meadow. Along the way, your father and another militia company fought off bands of savages intent on killing wounded stragglers and scalping and looting the dead.

"As the long column made its painful way east, Washington dispatched messengers to alert Colonel Dunbar to the exigencies of their situation and asked that fresh troops be sent to assist their beleaguered comrades. But the requested help never came.

"Late on the night of 11–12 July, when General Braddock's grenadier escort arrived at Dunbar's encampment just west of the ruins of Fort Necessity, their grievously wounded commander's litter was lashed to an artillery caisson. Word quickly spread and by dawn of the 12th, panic ensued in the ranks of the British Regulars, the militiamen—and especially among drivers in the wagon train.

"Dunbar and his officers, fearing mass desertion, appealed to Morgan—the civilian they flogged just weeks before—to quell a mutiny among the 200 or so wagon drivers who began dumping their cargoes in preparation for fleeing back to Fort Cumberland.

"Morgan, from his experience a year earlier, realized many wagons would be needed to carry the wounded and dead. Armed with his long-rifle, a pistol, and a tomahawk in his belt, he climbed atop the cargo in his own wagon and bellowed out, 'Gather 'round me all you wagoneers! Now!'

"When the grumbling crews assembled around his perch he told them, 'Hear me! You may dump your loads in the five places I point out to you. But if any of you move a wagon down the trail toward Fort Cumberland before ordered to do so, I will shoot you dead for desertion and give your draft horses to your widows and orphans. Are there any questions?' There were none.

"Throughout the remainder of the day and night, as Braddock struggled in and out of consciousness, the bloody remnants of his expedition, no longer pursued by the enemy, straggled into the encampment. At dawn on the 13th, Lieutenant Colonel Washington and your father arrived with the rear guard. A quick council was held beneath the tent sheltering General Braddock and this time he took Washington's advice: retreat to Fort Cumberland.

"Under Morgan's supervision more than seventy of the sturdiest wagons were cleared of their cargo and loaded with blankets and six to eight sick and wounded apiece. The bodies of eighteen dead officers carried back to the encampment by their men were wrapped in canvas and piled in two wagons. To avoid the dust, General Braddock, struggling to breathe, was gently placed into the lead wagon, directly in front of Morgan's at the front the column.

"Colonel Dunbar was ordered to remain behind with 600 Regulars and a company of militia to cover their retreat, destroy the artillery, and burn the five mountains of cargo pulled from the wagons. Each pile had gunpowder to insure ignition of the baggage, barrels of flour, salted pork, and beef. Left for the pyre were scores of common soldiers and camp followers who perished in or near the camp. Colonel Dunbar had the decency to wait until the last of the defeated troops and wagons were out of sight before setting it all afire.

"If memory serves me right, your wounded father was riding in Morgan's wagon. The slow-moving cavalcade was but a few miles down the trail toward Fort Necessity when Morgan and your father saw Braddock gesture to Colonel Washington whose horse was aside the general's wagon. The entire procession stopped as Washington climbed into the transport and knelt beside his dying commander. Though Daniel told me he couldn't hear what was said, he watched as Braddock handed Washington his red sash—the symbol of command—and then expired.

"Colonel Washington asked Daniel to gather some men and dig a grave in the middle of the roadway so pursuing savages would be unlikely to find and desecrate the general's body. The surviving members of the staff, including Thomas Gage, Charles Lee, and Horatio Gates were quickly gathered.

"When it was discovered the chaplain was too badly wounded to come forward, Colonel Washington led a brief and apparently moving funeral service. Morgan and your father, despite his wounded shoulder, were among the men who interred the British Commanding General in an ignominious, unmarked grave in the middle of the road through the wilderness.

"All told, Braddock's expedition lost more than 570 missing, killed in action, or died of wounds. Another 422 were wounded and survived. Of the eighty-six commissioned British and Colonial officers who headed off to the Monongahela, twenty-six were killed and thirty-seven were wounded and lived, your father among them.

"Omitted from the official reports submitted to the government in London is any mention of the fifty-six women who accompanied their husbands on the expedition into the wilderness. Only four, all injured, survived. The women who perished suffered the cruelest deaths of all. After being repeatedly violated by the savages, they were scalped alive, disemboweled, and finally beheaded."

I was sickened by his description and asked, "If the women weren't mentioned in the official reports, how do you know what happened to them?"

"Good question, Nathanael. I learned about the women last year when several members of our Committee of Safety met with a secret emissary sent to Virginia by Count Vergennes, the French Foreign Minister. We met for two days in Alexandria. In our conversations he told us the horrible fate of the women in Braddock's column.

"He also informed us that in the fight along the Monongahela, the French and Canadian troops lost only eight soldiers—including their commander, Daniel Liénard de Beaujeu. Their Indian allies had just fifteen killed and twelve wounded. He claimed some of the French officers shot several of the savages in an effort to stop them from torturing the women.

"The sad caravan, led by Washington and once again headed by Morgan's wagon, arrived back at Fort Cumberland on the 17th of July, 1755. A few days later your father and Daniel returned to Winchester. When all this happened, your father was twenty-seven, Washington was just twenty-three years old, and Morgan was but nineteen."

I was totally taken by the story. When Rev. Thruston stopped talking, I shook my head, astounded by what he told me about my father and his comrades, at what happened when they were so young and said, "And now, my father is forty-seven, Washington is forty-three, and Morgan is thirty-eight?"

"Ahh," the pastor said with a smile, "you *can* do your numbers. Would you like to know more about the man you're about to meet?"

ENDNOTES

1. Fort Duquesne, erected by French troops dispatched from Canada in 1754 is the site of present-day Pittsburgh, PA.

2. "Bloody Flux" and "Colic": terms used in the 1700s to describe what we now call dysentery.

CHAPTER FOUR

PLANTING THE SEEDS OF WAR

Allason's Shenandoah Store

Winchester, Virginia

Monday, April 24th, 1775

Rev. Thruston was a font of information about Daniel Morgan and he clearly knew more than I did about my own father. I asked him to tell me more.

After checking his watch, he continued, "Within a month of Braddock's disastrous attempt to capture Fort Duquesne in July 1755, the savage tribes allied with France were raiding homesteads and murdering entire settlements throughout the Valley of Virginia. Washington, already lauded as 'The Hero of Monongahela,' was commissioned a full Colonel and made Commander of the Virginia Militia by Robert Dinwiddie, the Royal Lieutenant Governor. Washington's first order was to raise three companies of Rangers to patrol and protect the frontier.

"As you probably know, Colonel Washington asked your father to take command of one of the three Ranger companies. But your mother, proving the value of marrying a wise woman, convinced Colonel Washington her husband first needed time to recover from his most recent wound. At the time, he couldn't raise his right arm enough to hold a rifle."

"No sir, I have never been told about any of that. My mother told us he was wounded and we could see the scar in his shoulder when he took off his shirt or when Mother helped him bathe, because he couldn't reach the back of his neck, but neither of them spoke more of it and we learned not to ask . . . ."

Rev. Thruston nodded and said, "I do not have the gift of prophesy, but if things go as they seem to be heading, you will soon come to understand why real heroes like your father rarely speak of their own courage—but are quick to tell of how other heroes act in harm's way."

I knew of nothing to add, so he continued his story.

"Your father wanted to command one of the Ranger companies, but he benefitted from your mother's intervention. He returned to Williamsburg and used the time recuperating to finish his courses at William & Mary and learned the skills necessary to become a very successful architect.

"John Ashby, the man who first befriended young Morgan and taught him how to drink rum, ride a fast horse, play cards, wrestle, fight with his fists, and most importantly, drive a wagon and care for good draft animals, was appointed to command the 2nd Ranger Company. One of the first men he recruited was Daniel Morgan.

"Morgan accepted Ashby's invitation. As I have heard Daniel tell it, he knew the pay wouldn't be as good as the money he could make as a 'wagoneer.' He claims he joined out of 'loyalty to Ashby, adventure, camaraderie, and the chance to kill savages who would otherwise kill the most vulnerable of our countrymen.' Those seem to be proper motives to me.

"In October 1755, Morgan was promoted to lead a fifteen-man Mounted Ranger Patrol with the mission of building stockades and blockhouses, protecting settlers on the frontier, and escorting wagon trains loaded with supplies through hostile territory.

"The winter of 1755–56 was fierce, forcing the Indians and the Rangers to hunker down and find shelter from the snow and cold. Apparently, Ashby, Morgan, and their comrades used the weather as an opportunity to consume prodigious quantities of rum and to gamble. If the stories I have heard from others are true, Captain Morgan finished the winter's card games owing a considerable sum—at least on paper.

"With the spring thaw, fighting season resumed. On the 16th of April 1756, Morgan and a fellow Ranger were heading on horseback to one of their outposts when seven Indians, armed with French muskets and tomahawks, ambushed them.

"Morgan's comrade was killed instantly and a musket ball struck Daniel's neck from behind, passed through his mouth and out through his cheek, removing several of his teeth on the way. Though badly wounded, and bleeding profusely, Morgan somehow managed to stay mounted and spur his horse to outrun the savages before they could remove his scalp.

"He spent several weeks recovering his strength in a remote blockhouse before he was strong enough to resume full duties, albeit many pounds lighter, from inability to eat solid food. Some of those who were with him say he convalesced on 'cornmeal soup' and rum.

"The Ranger companies were disbanded in October '56 because Colonel Washington deemed them to be less effective than expected. Morgan returned to 'waggoning,' hauling cargoes of wheat, flax, hemp, and tobacco from 'The Valley,' over the Blue Ridge to Alexandria, Fredericksburg, and Richmond. On return trips he loaded his wagon with lead, gunpowder, imported grindstones, salt, rum and when he couldn't find a more valuable cargo, 'ballast bricks' for construction.[1]

"In January 1758, acting Governor Dinwiddie returned to England and Francis Fauquier was appointed Lieutenant Governor by the Crown. Fauquier immediately urged London to deal forcibly with 'the French threat' and in the autumn of 1758, a British Army and Colonial Militia force of 7,000 men commanded by General John Forbes with Colonel Washington as his appointed deputy, finally captured Fort Duquesne. The Indians, denied access to their French patrons and safe-haven, temporarily ceased their raids into Virginia. By then, Daniel owned two sturdy wagons and employed two drivers.

"Unfortunately, attaining a degree of financial success didn't change Morgan's behavior much. He was still a 'rowdy' who drank too much rum, engaged in frequent pugilistic altercations at Tavern in Battletown[2] and at the Shenandoah Store, where we're heading now. On numerous occasions between 1759 and '62 he was remanded to appear before Frederick County magistrates for charges such as 'brawling,' and 'drunken, disorderly conduct,' and 'disturbing the peace.' It was after one of those misadventures when he began to mend his ways."

"What changed him? Was it one of your sermons?"

Rev. Thruston chuckled, "Well, I would like to take the credit, but I didn't become the Rector of Frederick Parish until 1768. From what Daniel has told me, his initial change of behavior wasn't so much spiritual as it was physical. He fell in love with Abigail Curry. They now have two daughters, Nancy and Betsy."

I was immediately reminded of the pretty girl playing the flute at church. I could feel the color rising in my cheeks but asked, "Were they at church yesterday?"

The pastor laughed again and said, "I'm guessing what you're thinking because I noticed you were very attentive to that attractive musician during our hymns. But no, none of the Morgans were there yesterday. Besides, if memory serves me right, Nancy is only twelve and Betsy is just ten. They both served as maids of honor when I officiated at their parents' wedding two years ago, at Cunningham's Chapel."

At this revelation I looked hard at Rev. Thruston to determine if he was jesting. He wasn't. But he didn't make me ask.

"Don't be off put by what I just told you Nathanael. I am well aware of what the church teaches about 'living in sin.' You know what I mean?"

"Yes, sir."

"Good. As 'believers' we're supposed to hate the sin but love the sinner. Well, we're all sinners. Though I am an ordained minister, if I turned away every sinner who showed up at a church door, I would be preaching to an empty house every Sunday. Daniel and Abigail lived together out of wedlock for ten years. What undoubtedly started as a strong physical attraction, call it 'lust' if you wish, became love. Do you have a Bible at home?"

"Yes, sir. It's how my mother taught my brothers and me to read."

"Well, when next you have time, open the Old Testament to Genesis 2:24 and in the New Testament to Mark's Gospel, chapter 10, verses 7 and 8 and read what it says about how a man shall 'cleave to his wife; And they twain shall be one flesh . . .' Do you know what 'cleave' and 'one flesh' means?"

By now I was very red in the face, but responded, "Yes, sir. Our parents explained it to us and told us it is one of the ways God made for us to express love."

"Right. If your parents hadn't 'cleaved' to one another and become 'one flesh,' you and your brothers would never have been born. It's the same for Daniel and Abigail. It just took them a decade to have a minister bless their union. But I believe them when they say they have been faithful to one another throughout— and that's what really matters.

"It's no secret Abigail has been a very positive influence on Daniel. She is not only an attractive woman, she is also very wise. She and your mother define the meaning of a 'Proverbs 31 wife.' Do you know what that means?"

"Yes, sir."

Were it not for Abigail, Daniel might never have mended his ways, become as successful as he is, ever set foot in a church, or have been motivated to come to know his Lord and Savior. And had all that not happened—even before Daniel and Abigail married—Isaac Zane, Angus McDonald, and I would not have voted to commission Morgan a captain in the militia in 1771.

"In retrospect, it was good that we did because things were heading the wrong way here in this colony and elsewhere well before Daniel returned to service."

"How is that, sir?"

Rev. Thruston thought for a moment and said, "Well, whether people realize it or not, Britain is already at war with us. Your brother Joshua is one of its first casualties. But the seeds for this fight were planted in the treaty that ended the war your father, Morgan, and Washington fought—and that killed General Braddock."

"The Treaty of Paris in February 1763?"

"Yes. Well done, Nathanael. How do you know that?"

"At supper each night, our parents made us take turns reading aloud every newspaper, broadside, and pamphlet that arrived in our home."

"Well then, if I'm telling you things you already know, stop me. The Treaty of Paris ended what we call the French and Indian War. But seven years of conflict, fought here, at sea, and in Europe bankrupted the British treasury. The Crown desperately needed ways to reduce costs and increase revenues. Unfortunately, desperation often prompts people to do really stupid things.

"The first of many stupid acts by London came in October 1763—just eight months after the treaty—when Parliament issued a proclamation barring any settlements west of a line drawn down the crest of the Allegheny Mountains. They believed it would save money by eliminating the cost of protecting settlers from the savages."

"I know about the 'Proclamation Line,' but how did Parliament decide where the line would be drawn?"

"Good question. Few of the geniuses in London ever came to this continent, so they drew a line based on where water went. All land where the water flowed east, into the Atlantic, was approved for colonial settlement. Land where water flowed west, into the Mississippi River and the Gulf of Mexico, was suddenly Indian Territory and barred from Colonial settlement.

"Of course, this decision completely ignored the rights of tens of thousands of families who were already settled west of the line. Some of them had been there for forty years or more. They weren't about to move back east, so they ignored the new ruling—as did thousands more immigrants from all over Europe who were brave enough to risk starting a new life in a new land. They too continued to move west—disregarding a mere line drawn on a map.

"From then on, there was a succession of stupid things done in London to infuriate almost everyone in every colony. A year later, in 1764, in an effort to raise revenues, Parliament imposed a new tax on sugar imported into the Colonies and enforced a 'Currency Act,' compelling all colonial debts incurred during the French and Indian War to be repaid only in British pounds sterling—meaning debtors could no longer repay London creditors with currency printed in the Colonies. The rule forced many colonials into bankruptcy.

"One year later, in March 1765, Parliament passed their so-called 'Stamp Act'—requiring materials printed in the thirteen colonies—newspapers, pamphlets, broadsides, legal documents, even playing cards—to be printed only on paper imported from Britain stamped with a Royal Revenue 'water mark.' The edict was detested throughout the Colonies and revived Rev. Jonathan Mayhew's 1750, 'No Taxation Without Representation'[3] sermon.

"The phrase became the rallying cry of Patriots calling for rebellion against the Crown. Here in Virginia, Governor Fauquier dismissed the House of Burgesses from their annual legislative assembly after Patrick Henry, in a speech Loyalists called 'treason,' urged Virginia to reject paying any of the King's new taxes. In Boston, angry Patriots ransacked Royal Governor Thomas Hutchinson's mansion.

"Parliament repealed the Stamp Act in 1766 but replaced it with a 'Declaratory Act' which asserted the Colonies were 'subordinate unto, and dependent upon the imperial crown and parliament of Great Britain.' The words 'subordinate' and 'dependent' provoked boycotts of British goods in colonial seaports. The Townshend Acts in 1767—a series of measures levying new duties on lead, tin, glass, lamp oil, paper, and tea exported from Britain to the Colonies—and barring the colonies from importing these goods from other countries—only made matters worse.

"Within weeks, protests against these fees erupted in Boston, New York, Norfolk, Philadelphia, and other ports—even Charleston. In 1768, in an effort to quell dissent—and ensure collection of revenues owed to His Majesty—London dispatched 4,000 British troops to restore order in Boston. Adding insult to injury, Parliament insisted that Massachusetts Colony pay the costs of quartering the British soldiers in civilian homes.

"Demonstrations and the threat of serious violence precipitated by these onerous measures quickly became even more widespread, particularly in Boston. On the night of March 5th, 1770, a Patriot group calling itself 'The Sons of Liberty' set out to evict a Crown Revenue Officer—the official responsible for collecting Royal taxes and customs duties. British troops were called out to protect him and in the midst of the confrontation, the soldiers opened fire, killing five of the Patriots, and wounding six others.

"The incident sparked outrage throughout the Colonies. Sam Adams in Boston and Patrick Henry here in Virginia—and many others in New England, New York, and the Carolinas—denounced the event as 'The Boston Massacre.'

"It's rarely mentioned these days but Sam Adam's cousin, John, also a member of Boston's Secret Committee, served as defense attorney in the trial of the British officer charged with murder for what his troops did. A jury of Bostonians exonerated the young British Lieutenant and he was quickly shipped back to England—along with the king's revenue officer—to avoid threats of 'vigilante justice.'

"From that point on, I think a break with Britain was almost inevitable, though it didn't seem that way here in Virginia. John Murray, a Scot nobleman who liked being called 'Lord Dunmore,' was appointed Royal Governor in September 1771. He immediately began encouraging westward expansion and settlement— a policy popular here in Virginia—but not in financially strapped London.

"Many, including me, believe Lord Dunmore did this to increase his own power. The further west he could push the borders of Virginia, the greater his territorial authority and population—and therefore his wealth and influence in Britain. If it hadn't been for events in other colonies, like the burning of the British revenue cutter, *Gaspee,* off the coast of Rhode Island, he might have succeeded in becoming the most powerful man on this continent.

"Unlike most other Royal Governors, John Murray—Lord Dunmore—actually took to the field last year, leading militiamen against the Shawnee tribes on the Ohio in what he cheerfully called, 'Lord Dunmore's War.' It was a magnificent distraction for those of us here in Virginia. While the New England Patriots were contending with the Crown in London for their rights, Virginians were fighting Indians on the frontier for their lives.

"But I'm getting ahead of myself. After Massachusetts Governor Hutchinson narrowly escaped being lynched by a mob, he petitioned Parliament for relief —which was partially granted late in 1771. As a conciliatory gesture, some British troops were withdrawn from domiciles in Boston proper and sent to Castle William: a fortress island guarding the sea approaches to the harbor.

"A few of the most egregious regulations and taxes were repealed or held in abeyance—but not the tax on tea. The effect should have been predictable: posters, handbills, and broadsides appeared all over the Colonies: 'Patriots don't drink British Tea.'

"The boycott was so successful by 1772, the British East India Company, the preeminent purveyor of tea to the Colonies, was soon in financial duress. Several members of the Royal family and a good number of members of Parliament owned shares of this enterprise. So, in May of 1773, in legislation obese with chicanery, Parliament passed the Tea Act granting the British East India Company a monopoly on importing any and all tea to the American colonies.

"The result of this blatant attempt to save the company—and the shareholders in London from bankruptcy—could have been foreseen by anyone not blinded by arrogance, greed, and self-interest. The harbor pilots, seamen, and dockworkers essential to berthing, loading, and unloading ships simply refused to handle any cargoes of British East India Company tea arriving in American ports on British ships.

"During November 1773, three British merchant ships— *Beaver, Dartmouth,* and *Eleanor*—arrived in Boston Harbor, carrying loads manifested as 92,000 pounds of British East India Company tea. The vessels languished at anchor, awaiting towboats and oar-men to be dispatched by the harbormaster to tug them into berths so their cargoes could be offloaded. The 'tugs' never came.

"The captains finally convinced their crews, if they wanted any shore leave before Christmas, they would have to lower their own longboats and pull the ships to Griffin's Wharf themselves. The sailors did so. But the 'dockers' refused to unload the vessels—or allow collection of the mandatory Crown Customs Duty.

"Colonial officials urged Governor Hutchinson to send the ships back to Britain with the tea still aboard. He refused, a standoff ensued, and the 'Sons of Liberty' posted a watch on the pier to ensure the cargo was not unloaded.

"On the afternoon of December 16th, Samuel Adams called for 'a meeting of Patriots' at Old South Meeting House—a Puritan congregation's place of worship and the largest building in Boston. More than 6,000 gathered for what began as a peaceful civil protest.

"But shortly before midnight, by which time most of the merchant sailors were ashore whoring and drinking voluminous quantities of rum in the port's taverns, a band of about 140 Sons of Liberty sortied from the meeting house and headed for Griffin's wharf.

"While thirty or so stood watch at the shore end of the pier, the rest of the 'Sons,' many garbed as Mohawk Indians, boarded the three vessels and unloaded the entire shipment of tea—into Boston Harbor. By dawn on the 17th all 342 chests of ruined tea were floating out to sea on the tide.[4]

"Infuriated by what he called 'wanton destruction of private property,' Governor Hutchinson ordered British troops to commence house-to-house searches of every domicile and commercial building in Boston believed to be hiding the perpetrators. Dozens of suspects were rounded up, but no witnesses could be found to testify that any of the accused participated in the crime.

"Word of what the Patriots did in Boston spread quickly through the Colonies—and reached London shortly after Christmas. Immediately after the holiday, Parliament convened 'in emergency session' and decided they must suppress any further 'criminal violence' with far more stringent measures than those already in force.

"Lieutenant General Thomas Gage—you remember, he was a Lieutenant Colonel with Braddock, Morgan, and your father in the disaster on the Monongahela in 1755—was summoned to Parliament to provide advice on what to do. Gage suggested a draconian prescription and Frederick, Lord North, the prime minister, and a favorite of King George III, accepted the recommendations.

"Since General Gage came up with the plan, he was given the privilege of implementing it. Gage was ordered to prepare 2,000 fresh troops for deployment to Boston and told he would replace Thomas Hutchinson as Royal Governor of Massachusetts Colony when he arrived. He was also given the authority to impose martial law if he deemed it necessary.

"On 13 May 1774 when General Gage arrived in Boston aboard *HMS Lively,* a twenty-gun British warship, he came armed with the additional soldiers and extraordinary punitive powers authorized by Parliament. His mission was to bring Massachusetts Colony and the rest of us 'to heel' like you did with your hunting dog earlier.

"The new General-Governor didn't waste any time carrying out Parliament's wishes. In London they called these measures 'Coercive Acts.' Here in the Colonies we called them 'The Intolerable Acts.' But no matter their name, General Gage in Boston—and Lord Dunmore—here in Virginia—carried out King George's orders with zeal worthy of a despot's acclaim.

"Gage immediately enforced the Boston Port Act—completely closing the port of Boston to all commercial shipping and placing the harbor under martial law. A week later, on May 20, the elected Massachusetts colonial government—which traced its lineage to the 1690s—was abolished by an edict issued by General Gage.

"On the same day—in what London cynically called the 'Administration of Justice Act,' all British authorities were exempted from prosecution in colonial courts. And two weeks later—on June 2nd, the Quartering Act made it mandatory for colonists to pay all costs for billeting and feeding British soldiers whether in their barracks or housed in private homes.

"Here in Virginia, Lord Dunmore wanted the House of Burgesses to act on funding his plan for a military campaign against the Indians in the Ohio Valley. Instead, the oldest elected legislative assembly in this hemisphere—dating back to 1619—began debating resolutions opposing the Crown's tax and regulatory authority. The Governor simply dismissed them from their annual session and locked them out of their chamber.

"Instead of leaving Williamsburg for home, the Burgesses reconvened at Raleigh Tavern and, among other things, selected from their number seven members to represent Virginia at the Continental Congress, which convened in Philadelphia last September.[5] Are you following me on all this?"

"Yes, sir," I replied. "Since my two older brothers went away to college, my father has often spoken to me about what you have described. When we lived in Williamsburg, Mr. Patrick Henry was often at our home.

"Two years ago, I went with Father to the gallery of the House of Burgesses on the day Mr. Patrick Henry, Mr. Richard Henry Lee, and Mr. Thomas Jefferson all spoke in favor of forming a Committee of Correspondence in Virginia.

"And last October, just a few days after the Continental Congress adjourned in Philadelphia, Mr. Henry visited us in Winchester on his way back to Williamsburg. If I remember correctly, you were among the group of men who joined the discussion the following morning."

"That is correct. You have good recall, Nathanael," Rev. Thruston said. "Do you know why we were meeting at your house?"

"After you left, Father said all seven of Virginia's representatives to the Congress were sent to different regions of the colony to explain what was accomplished in Philadelphia."

"And did he say what was achieved in Philadelphia?"

Once again, I was uncertain how to reply to Rev. Thruston's probing. Often after meetings at our home—or others elsewhere I was allowed to attend—Father would admonish me not to talk about who was there and what was said because, "There are Loyalists everywhere and not all of them make their sympathies known."

When I hesitated to respond, Rev. Thruston said, "I respect your loyalty and discretion, young man. You have maturity beyond your years. You are wise to keep your father's counsel to yourself.

Let me tell you my assessment—and it's the same as Patrick Henry's.

"The Continental Congress didn't do as much as many of us hoped. But they did agree to a total boycott of all British goods—which went into effect on December 1st last year in every colony except New York. The Congress also informed Parliament that if the 'Intolerable Acts' are not rescinded by September this year, the American colonies will ban all exports to Britain. And finally, the Congress unanimously agreed to meet again next month in Philadelphia."

Before I could ask any more questions, we rounded the bend in the road and could see a crowd of about 250 men—and perhaps four-score womenfolk—gathered in small groups talking among themselves on the meadow in front of the Shenandoah Store. There must have been 100 horses tethered to hitching posts and several dozen wagons and several fine carriages being tended by servants and slaves who were carrying water buckets to all the animals.

As Rev. Thruston and I dismounted, one of Mr. Allason's Negro servants came up, took the reins of our horses, and said to the pastor, "Captain Morgan wants to see you inside as soon as you arrive, if you please, sir."

As we waded through the crowd with my dog at heel, I noticed most of the men were tall, "rangy" fellows, dressed in hunting clothes like my linsey-woolsey blouse, leather leggin's, and moccasins. There were a few in fine shirts and trousers and wearing shoes and stockings. Those I could see were all armed with muskets or rifles and everyone appeared to be considerably older than I. Though I had never seen any of these fellows in church, they all seemed to know Rev. Thruston.

We were escorted into the "great room" of the tavern and as my eyes adapted to the darkness, I could see a very tall, powerfully built man seated at a table near the fireplace talking quietly with three others. They were all wearing hunting attire. As Rev. Thruston walked to the table, the big man stood, smiled, shook the pastor's hand, and said to the others, "The reverend—he pronounced it 'rev-ar-end'—is here, let's begin . . ."

The group stood and spoke quietly among themselves for a few moments while Casey and I waited out of earshot as my father taught me to do. At one point, Rev. Thruston pointed toward me and my dog and everyone glanced in our direction, then everyone chuckled. I was glad it was dark enough the others couldn't see the color rise in my cheeks.

As they began to file out onto the porch, I noticed the big man had a tomahawk and a pistol in his belt. He grabbed a rifle propped by the door, put his hand on my shoulder, and said, "So you are Nathanael, James Henry Newman's youngest son."

I nodded and said, "Yes, sir."

"Good. You look like your father, only bigger. I'm Captain Daniel Morgan." He smiled and I could see the scar on his cheek wrinkle as he did so. Then he said, "That's a good-looking dog. Stay near me, outside on the porch. We'll talk later, but first, I have some news for everyone."

ENDNOTES

1. Bricks were often used as ballast in the bilges of wooden sailing vessels. If a ship was deemed no longer seaworthy, before it was broken up the bricks were removed and used to cobble streets and for constructing "fine buildings."

2. The town at the intersection of the Winchester Turnpike and Charlestown Road is part of land first granted by the Crown to Captain Isaac Pennington in 1734. George Washington surveyed the property in October 1750. In 1754 Pennington sold it to Colonel John Hite who operated a tavern at the intersection. By 1765 when Hite sold the tract and the tavern to his son-in-law, Major Charles Smith, the little settlement was called "Battletown," a sobriquet reflecting the behavior of many of the tavern's rowdy patrons, one of whom was Daniel Morgan. In 1797 Major Smith's son John sold twenty acres of the property to Benjamin Berry who

divided it into lots for a town. He changed the name of the settlement to "Berryville" the following year. In 1836 Berryville was designated as the county seat of Clarke County.

3.   Rev. Jonathan Mayhew, the Congregationalist Pastor of Boston's Old West Church, first used the phrase "No taxation without representation" in a sermon in 1750. The discourse was subsequently widely printed in the Colonies, London, and Paris.

4.   The "tea dumping" in Boston Harbor on the night of 16 December 1773 was not referred to as "The Boston Tea Party" until after the war of 1812.

5.   Virginia's seven representatives to what we now call the "1st Continental Congress" were: Richard Bland; Benjamin Harrison [5th governor of Virginia; father of U.S. President William Henry Harrison and great-grandfather of President Benjamin Harrison]; Patrick Henry [1st elected governor of Virginia after independence]; Richard Henry Lee [drafted and moved the resolution for independence from Britain during 2nd Continental Congress in 1776]; Edmund Pendleton; Peyton Randolph [presided over the 1st Continental Congress]; and George Washington.

CHAPTER FIVE

A CALL TO ARMS

Allason's Shenandoah Store
Winchester, Virginia
Monday, April 24th, 1775

As we moved into the sunlight, while the others were greeting people in the crowd, Rev. Thruston whispered, "Do you know the three men who were seated at the table with Captain Morgan when we came into this place?"

"Not really, sir. I have seen them at our home for meetings with my father but I have never been introduced."

He nodded and continued, "The oldest of the three is Isaac Zane. He's a 'fighting Quaker' who is also a Burgess and serves on our Secret Committee of Safety. He built Marlboro Iron Works and works with your father on forging iron used in Mr. Jefferson's home near Charlottesville. He is a Patriot and we can trust him with our lives. I hope he will someday marry his mistress, Miss Betsey McFarland, so their son won't be known as a bastard."

This statement made me wonder how many more of my father's associates were not married to the women with whom they lived. But I didn't have time to dwell long on the matter, for Rev. Thruston was intent on continuing his *post hoc* introductions.

"The one with the Scottish accent, on Captain Morgan's right, is Militia Major Angus McDonald. He first fought the British Crown in Scotland during the Jacobite Rebellion in 1745 at about your age. He came here to Virginia a year later when the Stuart and McDonald clans lost to King George II. If memory serves me right, Angus McDonald was an officer with Colonel Washington on the Forbes expedition to capture Fort Duquesne in '58 and was Daniel Morgan's commanding officer last summer during Lord Dunmore's expedition against the Shawnee out west on the Ohio.

"Captain James Wood, the youngest of the three, is the only one who was born here in Virginia. His father was a surveyor for Lord Fairfax and helped Jost Hite found Fredericktown, which we now call Winchester. Young James is also a veteran of Lord Dunmore's war against the Shawnee and served under Major McDonald. Captain Wood is a member of the House of Burgesses and is part of our Secret Committee of Safety. He's also the only member of our group who owns no slaves."

Rev. Thruston completed his descriptions of the men I met briefly inside while we waited on the porch for three of Captain Morgan's Negro slaves to push one of his heavy freight wagons up to the front of the store. On the back of the wagon was a half-barrel and stacks of wooden and tin cups. It must have been taken from an icehouse, for the barrel was coated with condensation from the moist air.

When the wagon was in place, the Captain leapt from the porch onto the wagon. Towering over everyone, he bellowed, "Friends, neighbors, and fellow Patriots, gather 'round for I have news . . ."

There was an immediate hush as the throng pulled closer to the wagon. He began with a brief preamble: "You have been invited here this morning because you are Patriots. Your loyalty to our country and our people is unquestioned. Everyone here has been 'vouched for' by me and the men you see behind me. I have fought beside many of you in battles against our enemies. You have likely noticed some of our neighbors are not here. That is because their loyalty is not certain and we cannot risk having Tory spies betray us.

"We asked you here because we are all in great danger. Last Wednesday, British Regulars murdered fifty-five of our countrymen and wounded forty-one more in an unprovoked attack on two towns in Massachusetts Bay Province. Five of our countrymen from this act of war are still missing.[1] The Redcoats were on a mission to seize gunpowder and weapons from the local militia and capture two Patriot leaders.[2] One of those killed in the defense of our liberty was the oldest brother of this young man—"

At this he turned and gestured for me to come forward. I grasped my Henry rifle, told Casey to "Stay!" and jumped from the porch onto the wagon to stand beside Captain Morgan. I must confess my first thought was *Thank You, Lord, that Father urged me to wear hunting garb to this occasion and not my "Williamsburg finery."*

The captain put his arm on my shoulder and continued, "This is Nathanael Newman. Many of you know his father, my friend, James, who was twice wounded serving with great courage as an officer in our militia.

"Nathanael's brother Joshua was among those killed by his Royal Majesty's Redcoats last Wednesday in Massachusetts Bay Colony. Nathanael is here because he has vowed to avenge his brother's murder!"

At this there were several "huzzahs"[3] from the men in the crowd. But as I nodded my head, some of the womenfolk in the crowd who were at church on Sunday, gasped. One of them said, loud enough to be heard, "Oh dear, no!"

The captain motioned for me to resume my place with the three men on the porch and as I did, he said quietly to the women, "Don't worry about this lad, dear ladies. He will be with me. This 'Old Wagoneer' always brings his soldiers home."

After a brief pause Captain Morgan resumed his stentorian tone: "The King of England is no longer our protector. The British Crown many of us fought for in battles against the French and the bloodthirsty Indians is now waging war against us. It's not just in Boston or New York. His agents, the Royal Governors, including our own Lord Dunmore, are showing their true colors.

"Just last year, Major McDonald, Captain Wood, and I, and a good number of you, marched all the way to the Ohio to fight the savage Shawnee for Lord Dunmore. But now the Royal Governor has turned against us.

"Last month his Lordship locked the members of our House of Burgesses out of their hall in Williamsburg. They convened anyway at St. John's Church in Richmond, where our Patriot friend, Mr. Patrick Henry, introduced a measure putting all of Virginia 'in a state of defense' and directing every county to form companies for military service.

"In urging the Burgesses to vote in favor of the motion, Mr. Henry pledged, 'Give me liberty or give me death.' Well, I believe we deserve liberty and *life*!"

This prompted another round of "huzzahs" from the crowd. Several men in the back began to shout, "Liberty and Life!" In a matter of seconds, others picked up the chant and soon nearly every man in the meadow was shouting the slogan.

Never before had I witnessed the power of oratory to raise the passions of a large group of people. It was suddenly clear to me why the men beside me on the porch chose Daniel Morgan to deliver this message.

When the cheering died down, Captain Morgan continued, "On Thursday, April 20th, the night after the murders in Massachusetts, Lord Dunmore, the governor we willingly fought for, sent British Marines to break into the Williamsburg magazine to steal our gunpowder—the property of our Virginia militia—and transport these supplies, kept for our defense, to a British warship, *HMS Magdalen*, now at anchor in the James River.

"Mr. Patrick Henry is also Colonel-Commander of the Hanover County Militia. Yesterday he sent us a message, warning us to take necessary action to guard our powder supply so what happened in Williamsburg won't happen here should Lord Dunmore send Redcoats to seize our powder, our supply of lead, and the weapons for our defense.

"Our Committee of Safety has directed us—Isaac Zane, Major McDonald, Captain Wood, and me—to come up with a plan to protect our county and send reinforcements to Williamsburg if Colonel Henry needs help recovering the powder and shot seized by Lord Dunmore in the dark of night.

"Our first task is to secure our own gunpowder and shot, presently stored in the stone powder magazine at Lewis Stephens's place on Cedar Creek. We need nine men to re-build the palisade around the magazine and post three sentinels, day and night, inside and on watch. Captain Stephens has volunteered to supervise the construction and the watchmen.

"Second, we must re-establish the 'Alarm and Muster Network' we had in place during the war against the French and the savages. As before, we will need men and boys who have swift, sure mounts and who know the county well to serve as Reliable Messengers. Because the county now has many more families than in the past, we will need at least fifteen 'Reliables.' Captain Wood will command the messenger unit.

"Third, we are forming a company of 100 Rifleman who have proven themselves to be excellent marksmen, fit for marching great distances, and ready at a moment's notice to fight. Volunteers for this unit must sign-on for not less than six months of duty. Mr. Patrick Henry has told us the Virginia Convention will pay privates six Milled Spanish dollars per year; sergeants will receive eight dollars; Ensigns will be paid ten dollars; Lieutenants will get fifteen and Captains, twenty.[4]

"Every volunteer must provide his own rifle, tomahawk, hunting knife, bullet-mold, canteen, and maintain his own 'ready kit' of two hunting shirts, two pair of leggin's, four pairs of shoes or moccasins, a hunting hat, and a cloak or blanket. Major McDonald will take your names today. We will select members of this unit Friday on the green at the Battletown Tavern. If it rains we will hold the selection on the first fair day after Friday.

"The Committee of Safety has appointed me to command this company of Riflemen and I have accepted the appointment. Once we have selected the members of the Rifle Company from the list of volunteers, we will hold a vote for the officers.

"We all know this is planting season for tobacco and corn. We also know volunteering for these duties will work a hardship for all of us who are about to move plants from seedbeds to our fields. Therefore, other than the Rifle Company selection on Friday we will not commence training, drills, and inspections until two weeks from today.

"Those of you with whom I have served know I have never asked others to do that which I cannot or would not do. I have never asked others to venture where I would not go. My tobacco fields are ready for planting as are yours. If we are called out for any length of service or sent a distance from home, we may not be here when it's time to pull suckers, top the plants, or harvest the leaves.

"If that happens, Isaac Zane, Major Angus McDonald, and I are offering to lend you some of our slaves and indentured servants to assist your families. And finally, Thomas, Lord Fairfax, has renewed the pledge he made during our expedition to the Ohio, of a bounty of fifty acres to every man who completes one year of service."[5]

At this, there was another loud "huzzah" from the crowd. Captain Morgan waited for the cheering to subside and pointing to a table on the far side of the porch, he shouted, "Those who wish to volunteer today, line up here, give your name to Major McDonald, put your mark on the muster roll, and have a cold cup of cider on me!"

There were more loud "huzzahs" as scores of men rushed to get in line. I could not help but notice there were a good number of women and girls in the crowd clinging to their husbands, brothers, and fathers. Not a few of them had tears flowing down their cheeks.

Captain Morgan watched the tumult for a few moments until Major McDonald gruffly shouted to restore a semblance of order. The Captain then motioned for Rev. Thruston and me to follow him back into the store's great room. Pointing to a three-legged stool at the table where I first met him, he pulled up a seat across from me. Casey parked herself beside the rector at the end of the table as an unexpected interrogation commenced.

"I am told you can read and write well and do well with numbers. Is that correct?"

I nodded and replied, "Yes, sir."

"Your father told me you are also a skilled marksman and hunter. Rev. Thruston said on the way here you hit a turkey 'on wing' with a single ball from your rifle. Is that all true?"

"Yes, sir," I responded, instantly glad the rector had apparently not informed Captain Morgan of my failure to tether my horse before shooting at the bird.

"I'm also told you know how to navigate and can use a sextant, surveyor's transit, and a circumferentor.[6] How did you learn all that?"

"My father taught me how to use these devices so I could help him map property boundaries and building sites."

"So you can find your way in the wilderness and know how to shoot. What's the biggest game you've bagged?"

"Last spring, while Father and I were surveying a plat for Mr. Jefferson near Charlottesville, I shot a charging bear."

"At what range was the bear?"

"About seventy yards, sir. Thankfully my one shot felled her for I had no other weapon but my hunting knife. She had two cubs and we had nowhere to run."

"What did you do with the cubs?"

"They were too young to survive—not yet weaned. Father and I brought the meat to Mr. Jefferson. His slaves had them for dinner."

The Captain nodded, leaned across the table, and quietly asked, "Have you ever shot another person?"

"No, sir. But I would gladly shoot the person who killed my brother."

He stared as me for a moment and asked, "How old are you, son?"

"I will be seventeen in August, sir."

He nodded again and said, almost to himself, "Not much older than I was when I arrived here." Then, "If you march with me you will likely see action by your birthday. Is that what you want to do?"

"Yes, sir."

"Do you have any duties here other than the work you do at Casselman's ferry over the Shenandoah?"

"No, sir. My father's indentured tenants, Pieter Van Buren and his wife, Lotte, live behind our house. They have a key to our home and will tend to the livestock and crops."

"Do you trust them?"

"Yes, sir, my family trusts them. They have been with us for over a year. They are Dutch and they hate the British."

"What crime did they commit to become indentured?"

"I do not know all the facts, sir, but it is my understanding they are both bound by a seven-year sentence that began in December

1774. I believe Pieter and his wife, Lotte, were accused and convicted of importing Dutch East India Company tea into Virginia in violation of the 1773 Tea Act. Father purchased their sentences from the Royal Customs and Revenue Court in Norfolk."

When Captain Morgan smiled, the scar on his cheek wrinkled. It did so now, "They must be good people. The usual sentence for that crime is three years. If the Van Burens got seven years, they must have slipped a fair amount of good Dutch East Indian tea under His Majesty's big nose."

Rev. Thruston added, "Since he was caught here in Virginia, we likely enjoyed some of that tea ourselves and may well be judged to be their co-conspirators."

Both men laughed for a moment but Captain Morgan suddenly became serious and turned toward the rector, "Ahhh, you're right, Charles. The Crown will certainly accuse us of crimes. But if we fail in what we're about to do, the British won't sentence us to seven years of servitude. They will hang us all."

He turned to me, stared for a long moment, then said, "Nathanael, if you are willing, you shall be my Adjutant, with the rank of ensign. The Adjutant keeps the muster roll and pay roster, maintains our equipment list, keeps an accurate journal of all we do, records all the orders our company receives and issues, and has the account book of what we purchase and spend. Can you do all that—and fight when we must?"

"Yes, sir. But I must have my father's permission."

"Your father is in Williamsburg. He and your brother will likely be with Colonel Patrick Henry's Hanover Militia unit until they recover the powder, shot, and arms Governor Dunmore has stolen. You will need to write your father a letter."

At that he nodded to Rev. Thruston. The rector reached into the leather pouch slung over his shoulder, pulled out a sheet of paper, an envelope, a small "traveler's inkwell," and a quill. Smiling, he handed it all to me and said, "This is why I need those turkey feathers."

While he and Captain Morgan spoke quietly, I wrote my father a brief message:

At Allason's Store, Winchester
24ᵗʰ, April, 1775

Dear Father,

Captain Morgan has offered me the opportunity to serve as Adjutant for his Rifle Company.

Though it is uncertain when we shall be called to service, I ask for your permission to accept this appointment.

Please keep me in your prayers, as you and Paul shall be in mine.

Most respectfully, your son,
Nathanael

I blotted the note with the sleeve of my hunting shirt and handed it to the captain. He read it, nodded, and gave it back to me with instructions: "Address the envelope to 'Captain James H. Newman, care of Col. Patrick Henry,' and give it to Rev. Thruston."

As the rector packed my letter and the writing tools in his pouch, Captain Morgan explained, "Rev. Thruston is the Chairman and Secretary for the Frederick County Committee of Correspondence and responsible for our Trusted Courier service. He has a messenger riding to Williamsburg this afternoon. Your father should have your letter tomorrow. Hopefully, you will have his answer before Friday when we hold our Rifle Company selection at the Tavern in Battletown.

"Unless your father objects to your appointment as my Adjutant, you should arrive at the Battletown Tavern by dawn.

Rev. Thruston will meet you there with our Rifle Company supply wagon. He will bring with him several leather-bound journal books, a small travel desk, a supply of ink, quills, and waxed oil-cloth to protect the records of our Company.

"He will also have a supply of candles, field lanterns, and oil. You will need these since much of your work as my Adjutant will be done at night. During daylight we will march and fight. Do you have any questions?"

By this point my heart was racing and I had so many questions I didn't know where to begin so I said, "Yes, sir. But it might be best if I wrote them down and we spoke after Rev. Thruston and I meet Friday morning at the Battletown Tavern."

Rising, the captain said, "Very well. Before you leave here today, I suggest you speak with Mr. Casselman. I saw him and his wife outside. You should inform him I have need of your services and for the time being you will no longer be available to help him at his ferry on the Shenandoah."

It was the second time he mentioned the Casselmans and I wondered how my new commander knew so much about the menial occupation of a very young person in our county, so I blurted out, "If I may inquire, sir, how is it that you know about my work at the ferry?"

Captain Morgan put his hand on my shoulder and said, "It is my responsibility to know many such things. These are dangerous times and they are about to become much worse than most people understand. Not everyone who claims to be a 'Patriot' can be trusted. Those who are not with us are against us. It is good to know friends from enemies—and deal with them accordingly."

As I had a few moments before when he spoke of being hanged, I felt a sudden chill—as if one of my brothers shoved a handful of snow down the back of my shirt during a winter snow-ball fight. Only this time, nobody was laughing.

As my mother taught me, I said, "Please excuse me, gentlemen. I must speak with Mr. Casselman." I grabbed my Henry rifle, told Casey to "Heel!" and went outside to find my former employer.

I found them as they were preparing to depart in their carriage. Mr. and Mrs. Casselman were in the seat and David, Jr. was hunched glumly in the bed of the tram.

"Mr. Casselman, sir. A brief word with you if I may?"

"Yes, Nathanael," he replied, gently pulling on the reins to halt the two spirited horses.

After the warning I just heard about "friends and enemies," I was unsure how to describe my new duties so I said, "Sir, I won't be able to work with David on the ferry for the near future as Captain Morgan has asked me to be of service to him for an uncertain duration."

Mrs. Casselman suddenly wailed, "Oh no!" She leapt from the carriage, rushed around the rear of the transport, and put her arms around me. With tears streaming down her face, she implored her husband, "David, tell him he cannot do this! I won't hear of it."

Mr. Casselman said nothing and simply stared at his horses. In the back, David, Jr. drew up his legs and rested his head on his knees, his face turned away.

She looked up at me, grabbed my elbows at her arms' length and said, her voice choked with emotion, "Nathanael, you must not do this. Your mother was one of my closest friends. She is gone. Now you have just lost your brother, Joshua. Your father is not here. You are too young. You must have your father's permission for such a decision. Taking up arms to avenge your brother's death is wrong!"

At this, her husband finally spoke. With great distress evident in his countenance, he said quietly, with formality, as though I was not even present, "Mrs. Casselman, young Nathanael is not a Quaker. You have had your way with our son, but Nathanael is not your responsibility. Please take your place beside me. We must be off."

She released her grip on my arms, reached up, pulled my face down to hers, kissed me on the forehead, and said barely above a whisper, "May Almighty God protect you."

Without another word spoken, I walked her around the tram and helped her into her seat. When she was situated, Mr. Casselman gently slapped the reins and they headed off through the meadow toward the road. As they pulled away, David Jr. glanced up for a moment and I could see tears streaming down his face.

ENDNOTES

1.   In the days immediately after Lexington and Concord, Morgan and most members of the Colonial Secret Committees throughout the Colonies had only the information they received from Trusted Couriers dispatched from New England. Many of these reports varied widely as to the number of casualties and what had actually happened in the engagements.

      To this day, the true number of combatants and the totals of killed, wounded, and missing on both sides in the 19 April 1775 engagements in Lexington and Concord and during the British retreat back to Boston remain in dispute. While Morgan erred in numbers, there is no doubt about the outcome of which he spoke at the Shenandoah Store on Monday 24 April 1775.

      We now have available copies of the official "after action" reports submitted to Royal Governor-General Thomas Gage and the Parliament in London by British Brigadier General Hugh Percy, his subordinate officers, Lieutenant Colonel Francis Smith, commanding the 10th Regiment of Foot [infantry], and Major John Pitcairn commanding the Royal Marine Detachment.

      Colonial Militia leaders and militiamen present during the engagements of 19 April 1775 also provided contemporaneous depositions to the Massachusetts Provincial Congress. British and American accounts differ as to numbers involved and the question of who fired the first "shot heard 'round the world."

      The American narratives credit the secret "Alarm and Muster Network," in which Paul Revere, William Dawes, and Samuel Prescott served to be crucial in alerting local militiamen to the British expedition. The courage and tenacity of these messengers on the night of 18–19 April saved John Hancock and Samuel

Adams from capture and resulted in nearly 4,000 armed militiamen and "Minutemen" rushing to Lexington, Concord, and engaging the British Regulars on their retreat to Boston.

A review of the surviving records yields a "best estimate" of these events as follows:

Only seventy-seven militiamen were assembled on the green in Lexington when the lead elements of 700 British Regulars and Marines arrived at the town just after sunrise on 19 April 1775. After a brief skirmish, during which eight of the militiamen were killed and a dozen were wounded, the outnumbered Patriots dispersed and 400 British troops [Regulars and Marines] proceeded to Concord with the mission of seizing colonial munitions—weapons, powder, and shot—and capturing John Hancock and Samuel Adams.

In Concord, and at the two bridges north and south of town, 375–400 militiamen initially engaged the British Regulars and Marines with minor effect. But as the day progressed, nearly 4,000 Patriot militiamen and Minutemen reinforcements arrived to fight the British during their retreat.

British search parties found small quantities of gunpowder, lead shot, a few muskets, two heavy siege cannons, and gun carriages in Concord and the surrounding farms. The Regulars set fire to most of this "war material" and battered the trunnions off the cannons with sledgehammers, rendering the artillery pieces unusable.

Shortly after noon, the King's troops, exhausted from marching through the previous night and the skirmishes in Lexington and Concord, set out on the seventeen-mile return hike to Boston. For the British, it was an unmitigated disaster.

From Cambridge, Brigadier General Percy sent forward another 1,000 Regulars as reinforcements but the British were still outnumbered by more than two to one and constantly fired upon from their flanks and rear throughout the retreat to Boston. By the time the British finally reached Charlestown on the outskirts of Boston at dawn on 20 April, seventy-three British Regulars were dead [including twenty-eight officers], 175 were wounded, and fifty-three were MIA.

Among the 3,971 Patriot Militia and Minutemen engaged in the fight, forty-nine were killed, forty-one wounded, and four were MIA. By noon on 20 April 1775, the siege of Boston was underway and the American Revolution had begun.

Seven days after the Lexington and Concord engagements, Major Pitcairn, Commanding Officer of the Royal Marines during the expedition submitted the following "After Action Report":

April 26th, 1775, Boston Camp
To: General Thomas Gage

Sir,

As you are anxious to know the particulars that happened near and at Lexington in the 19th Inst agreeable to your desire, I will in as concise a manner as possible state the facts, for my time at present is so much employed, as to prevent a more particular narrative of the occurrences of that day.

Six companies of Light Infantry were detached by Lt Colo Smith to take possession of two bridges on the other side of Concord, near three in the Morning, when we were advanced within about two miles of Lexington, intelligence was received that about 500 men in arms were assembled, determined to oppose the King's troops, and retard them in their march. On this intelligence, I mounted my horse, and galloped up to the six Light Companies. When I arrived at the head of the advance Company, two officers came and informed me, that a man of the rebels advanced from those that were assembled, had presented his musket and attempted to shoot them, but the piece flashed in the pan. On this I gave directions to the troops to move forward, but on no account to fire, or even attempt it without orders; when I arrived at the end of the Village, I observed drawn up upon a Green near 200 rebels; when I came within about 100 yards of them, they began to file off towards some stone walls on our right flank. The Light Infantry, observing this, ran after them. I instantly called to the soldiers not to fire, but surround and disarm them, and after several repetitions of those positive orders to the men, not to fire, etc. some of the rebels who had jumped over the wall fired four or five shots at the soldiers, which wounded a man of the Tenth and my horse was wounded in two places, from some quarter or other, and at the same time several shots were fired from a meeting house on our left. Upon this, without any order or regularity, the Light Infantry began a scattered fire, and continued in that situation for some little time, contrary to the repeated orders both of *me and the officers that were present. It will be needless to mention what happened after, as I suppose Colo Smith hath given a particular account of it.*

I am, Sir, Your Most Obedt Humble Servant

John Pitcairn, Major of Royal Marines

2. Loyalists in Boston convinced General Thomas Gage that John Hancock and Samuel Adams should be arrested, charged with treason, and sent to London for trial. Days before the British Regulars were dispatched into the countryside on the night of 18 April 1775, the pair slipped out of Boston to Lexington. Early on the morning of the 19th, Revere and Hawes alerted them of the approaching Redcoats. Well before the first shots were fired on Lexington Common, the Patriot pair reached Concord. From there they took flight to Bedford and finally to Burlington.

3. *Huzzah:* archaic word to describe cheering. Same as "hooray!" in modern English.

4. In the 1700s the most accepted monetary instrument in the Western world was the Spanish dollar, specified as "a coin containing 387 grains of pure silver." By the time hostilities commenced in the American colonies in 1775, only "Loyalists" or "Tories" would take payment for goods or services in British pounds sterling. Until the 2nd Continental Congress directed the formation of a Continental Army on 14 June 1775, each colony—including Virginia—set rates of pay for their soldiers—often using the Spanish dollar as a standard.

   In today's money, a private in Morgan's Company of Riflemen "signed on" for less than $30 per year. But when it came time to be paid, the troops rarely received coins. Instead, they were usually given "Promissory Notes" issued by their respective colonies—and eventually by the new U.S. Congress.

5. Thomas, Baron Cameron, the sixth Lord Fairfax, [b. Oct 22, 1693; d. Dec 7, 1781] was the only member of the British aristocracy to take up permanent residence in the American Colonies. By 1774 he had claims to more than five million acres of land and was known to be a close friend of one of his former surveyors, George Washington.

The proffer of a "50 Acre Bounty" to those who volunteered for a term of service in "Dunmore's War" [May–October, 1774] was never consummated because "The American Rebellion" intervened. There is no written record of Lord Fairfax offering such an incentive to those who served in the Rifle Companies and militia units being raised by Capt. Morgan and Major McDonald who was later promoted to Lieutenant Colonel in the Virginia Militia. Whether they had such an assurance, written or verbal, is unknown. What is certain is that Lord Fairfax remained close to Washington, corresponded regularly with him throughout the revolution, and resided unchallenged in his Shenandoah Valley home until he died shortly after the American victory at Yorktown in 1781.

6.   *Circumferentor:* archaic term for a brass-encased magnetic surveying compass with perpendicular sights. It can be hand-held or mounted on a "Jacob's staff" or tripod for determining bearings for boundary lines, estimating elevation, and locating structural foundations.

CHAPTER SIX

SELECTING THE BEST RIFLEMEN

Major Charles Smith's Crossroads Tavern

Battletown, Virginia

Friday and Saturday, April 28th and 29th, 1775

In the days since Captain Morgan's "recruitment" at Allason's Shenandoah Store, I have been far busier than any time I recall since my mother died. When I returned home on Monday evening, I immediately began preparing for what little I knew of my duties as Adjutant for a Rifle Company and the possibility of an imminent departure for parts unknown.

Early Tuesday morning I sought out Pieter and Lotte for their help. Though they are indentured to my father, not to me, his youngest son, they were most agreeable to aiding my preparations.

While I sharpened my ax and hunting knife, Pieter fired up the forge next to our stable. Then, using the cast iron crucible, ladle, molds, and sprue-cutters Father designed, we poured and finished 250 perfect .43 caliber lead bullets for my .45 caliber Henry rifle.

I spent the balance of the daylight hours carefully wrapping each bullet, a beeswax coated patch, and a carefully measured amount of powder into waxed paper, forming cartridges for my rifle—something commonplace for a person carrying a smooth-bore musket—but very rare for a Rifleman.[1] I placed twenty-five each in leather cartridge boxes and wrapped them all in oilcloth to keep them dry.

On Wednesday, while Pieter went to assist several neighbors with a barn-raising, Lotte helped me prepare clothing and equip-ment. She washed and dried four linsey-woolsey hunting shirts and three pairs of linen leggin's while I searched through several large chests in our house and the hayloft over the stable. It was a reminder of how my mother never gave or threw away anything that might be useful in the future.

Father often described our mother as "a wise and frugal Prov-erbs 31 wife." My quest for clothing and equipment proved he was correct. My search yielded two pairs of good heavy shoes and three pairs of moccasins made from sheepskin with wool inside and a half dozen pairs of wool stockings.

I also discovered the heavy hemp linen cloak my dear departed brother Joshua purchased in Boston during his first student winter at Harvard. Lotte insisted on carefully washing the garment and coating it with a beeswax compound she promised would make it waterproof. When it was dry, I wrapped it around my sextant and circumferentor in their leather cases and stuffed it all into my canvas backpack.

On Thursday afternoon, Pieter and I rode out to Father's tobacco, corn, and forage fields just north of Winchester. We agreed he would make a first-cut of hay in early June in hopes for a second cut in September and in between he would tend the tobacco and harvest the corn in late autumn.

On our way back home Pieter said, "Master Nathanael, there is much talk among the farmers and merchants about the likeli-hood of war with Great Britain. If that happens, it's probable the market for Virginia tobacco will be *beknot*—in English I think that means curtailed—or—restricted—and the price for tobacco will likely be very low. Perhaps it would be wise to consider planting more wheat, oats, corn, or even orchard grass for forage instead of tobacco. What do you think?"

I already knew growing and harvesting tobacco is one of the most labor-intensive crops in the world. In the spring young plants had to be gently pulled from their seed-beds and set out in rows in a plowed field—a back-breaking, sunup-to-sundown task. Then, it had to be hoed, suckered, fertilized, and, if the parasites, worms, drought, or too much rain didn't destroy the fragile plants, it would finally be ready for harvest in the autumn.

Harvesting, like everything else with tobacco, was arduous. The leaves had to be picked by hand at just the right moment, one at a time, strung on sticks, then hung in a barn—or on a fence—to be cured and finally "graded" by some arbitrary person who would decide what our entire crop should be worth, based on how he felt that day.

No one in London or the Colonies could honestly deny that tobacco was Virginia's most profitable crop. Nor would anyone dare admit tobacco could not exist as a profitable commodity but for slaves and indentured servants.

It suddenly occurred to me, Pieter and Lotte were far more astute than I realized. Guessing the future price for tobacco before new plants were even in the ground was a challenge every tobacco planter faced. But forecasting the consequence of a possible war on the value of a crop was, to me, extraordinary.

As though he read my mind, Pieter smiled and said, "Master Nathanael, I can hear you thinking, *How does this Dutchman know these things?* Well, you may wonder. But I'm sure you are aware, Lotte and I were convicted by the King's Revenue Officers because we were very good at predicting a profitable market price for smuggled Dutch East India tea from Java that would beat any price set by the not-so-honorable British East India Company?"

I nodded and said, "Yes."

Smiling, he continued, "Well, we came by this skill from birth, our Dutch grandparents did the same with delft porcelain and coffee. You have some of both in your house. So, it seems to us—if there is to be a war—grains, corn, and forage are likely to be in greater need than tobacco, sell at a higher price, and require less labor to plant and harvest."

I could only nod in agreement and reply, "That sounds like very good advice. I will write to Father and recommend it to him."

We arrived home just at dusk. As Pieter and I were watering our horses and putting away the saddles and tack, a Trusted Courier, mounted on a lathered stallion, arrived at our gate and shouted, "Halloo!"

Pieter grabbed one of the two lit lanterns and hastened to the portal. I heard the rider inquire, "Is this the residence of James Newman, the architect?"

"Ya," Pieter replied, "why do you ask?"

"I have a message for his son, Nathanael. Is he here?"

I tethered my horse over the water trough so she could continue to drink and rushed to the gate. "I am Nathanael Newman, sir."

The rider reached into the pouch slung over his shoulder, drew out an envelope, and handed it to me. "A relay rider from Richmond brought this to our station on the north side of the Rappahannock in Falmouth this morning. He said it was from Williamsburg and it was for urgent delivery to you."

It occurred to me how strange it was to be sending and receiving correspondence by such means. When he was a Crown Postmaster, Mr. Benjamin Franklin visited Winchester and promised to build a post office. Unfortunately, it was not yet constructed when the authorities in London dismissed Mr. Franklin for seditious activities.

I took the letter. By the lantern's dim light, I could see it was my father's hand on the envelope and a red wax seal with the imprint of his wedding ring; an ichthys.

Our mother had an identical ring and they told us their rings were a reminder to one another they were both Christians. She told us a bedtime story about how the symbol was used as a secret signal by ancient followers of Jesus to mark safe meeting places and discern friend from foe when Christians were being hunted and killed by Roman soldiers.

More than once, Father showed us how a Christian, encountering a stranger on the road, would draw the top arc in the dust with a stick. If the stranger drew the bottom arc, intersecting at the mouth and crossing at the tail, in the shape of a fish, they both could be certain they were in safe company.

Before rushing into the house to read it, I said, "Thank you, kind sir. Will you come in? It is nearly dark. Have you eaten?"

"Not yet but thank you. I have one more message to deliver before I rest tonight. May I water my horse?"

"Of course," I replied as Pieter opened the gate.

The dispatch rider dismounted and as I handed him a ladle of cold well water, Pieter led the horse to the trough. After man and beast drank their fill, I held the reins while Pieter gave the rider a leg-up to remount.

It was only then I noticed he had a British .54 caliber Sea Service pistol shoved into his belt. As we walked to the gate, he noticed my stare, patted it, and said, "Don't worry, lad. I'm not a Tory. I came by this honestly."

"Sir?"

"I stole it from Lord Dunmore's armory in Williamsburg. Since he stole our powder and shot, it seemed like a fair trade."

Pieter closed the gate behind him and as the courier rode off, said, "A fair trade indeed. The only question is which was stolen first, the powder or the pistol?"

I took one of the lanterns, went into the house, sat down at the table, and used my hunting knife to open the envelope and preserve the seal.

With the Hanover County Militia

Near Williamsburg, VA

April 26th, 1775

My Dear Son, Nathanael,

Please know how pleased I am Captain Morgan has invited you to serve as his Adjutant.

If it be your want, you have my blessing to accept the appointment. You are bright, brave, and fit. You know responsibility and accountability and possess all the skills, acumen, and tenacity necessary to the task.

These are challenging times. Some of our countrymen are just now trying to decide what to do. I am grateful that my sons are Patriots who have answered the call to duty. The three of you will be forever revered by all who love Liberty.

Be assured Paul and I shall keep you in our prayers and are grateful for being in yours.

I remain your loving father, James Newman
Sic Semper Tyrannis

On Friday morning I arrived at the Major Charles Smith's Crossroads Tavern in Battletown before dawn. The sun was just a golden glow atop the Blue Ridge when Rev. Thruston appeared out of the mist aboard one of Captain Morgan's heavy transport wagons, accompanied by Josiah, one of Captain Morgan's slaves.

After dismounting, he greeted me with a handshake and a smile and said, "Nathanael, you have to see this."

While Josiah watered the two draft horses, the reverend walked around to the rear of the wagon and threw back the canvas cover.

The contents were far greater than Captain Morgan described on Monday. I counted seven half-barrels stenciled "poudre à canon," ten stacks of thin lead sheets for casting bullets, four casks labeled "nitre,"[2] three marked "sulfur," five full barrels labeled "salt-pork," six large cooking kettles, stacks of tin dinner plates, and ten sacks of cornmeal. Bolted to the bed of the wagon was a small anvil. Beside it, open wooden boxes held a small leather bellows, casting ladles for melting lead, and the assorted tongs, hammers, and tools used by blacksmiths.

I was stunned by the quantity of supplies and how well it was packed. "Where did all this come from?"

"Captain Morgan has had it hidden in a shed on his farm," Rev. Thruston replied. "You may recall, before he became a soldier-farmer he was a 'wagoneer.' He carried hundreds of cargoes east, over the Blue Ridge to the ports in Alexandria, Falmouth, and Richmond. He once told me he never returned with an empty wagon."

"But the gunpowder—those are French military markings. How did he get that?"

"Ahh," the reverend began, dropping his voice nearly to a whisper. "Last year, after the British banned importing firearms and gunpowder into the thirteen colonies, Captain Morgan asked me to write three letters for him.

"The letters were addressed to Dutch, Spanish, and French merchant captains with whom Daniel did business over his years as a wagoneer. I delivered the letters to them when their ships called at Falmouth.

"All three captains agreed to take the risk of being caught breaking the royal embargo and each have now delivered shipments of powder hidden in their cargo holds. There are eighteen more kegs just like these still hidden on Captain Morgan's farm. These powder kegs were delivered three weeks ago in Alexandria. Josiah and I picked them up."

I wondered aloud, "You trusted a slave?"

Rev. Thruston smiled and said quietly, "Yes, Nathanael, with my life—certainly more so than some of our neighbors who support the Crown. Josiah is a good Christian man. He and his family are loyal to Captain and Mrs. Morgan and their daughters. And God-willing, someday he will be a freeman."

At this he pointed to two rectangular packages, carefully wrapped in waxed linen, and said, "The rest of this cargo is for use by all the members of the Rifle Company, but these two are for you. Open them."

I did as ordered and unpacked two small, sturdy, teak campaign chests with brass handles, hinges, and drawer-pulls. Taking two small keys from his waistcoat pocket, the rector unlocked the largest and unfolded it, revealing a well-crafted field desk containing several leather-bound books. He opened one to the first page where an inventory of the equipment on the wagon was already listed.

"All the pages are lined parchment," he began. "This one is for equipment. There is one labeled, 'Muster Roll,' another for 'Accounts,' a third for 'Orders' and a fourth labeled 'Log' in which you will keep a journal of the unit's activities at the end of each day."

He opened the second chest and pointed to an ample supply of quills, ink, candles, four collapsible lanterns with mica-isinglass "windows," and tins of lamp oil. There were even wax tapers, flint, and steel strikers for lighting the candles and lamps.

Awed by the contents, I said, "This wagon looks as though someone has thought of everything needed for an expedition. Who paid for it all?"

Rev. Thruston chuckled, "Well, payment was made in Spanish dollars from Isaac Zane, a Quaker; Major Angus McDonald, a Scot; a donation from my flock of fellow believers, and a loan from a British peer, Thomas, Lord Fairfax, at Greenway Court. He provided most of the funds to purchase unspecified militia supplies to defend the county. He said he would petition our once-beloved Royal Governor Dunmore to honor the debt. I doubt he will ever be repaid."

By then, the sun was fully over the eastern ridgeline. I watched as Major McDonald and a crew of boys marked out a shooting range on the broad open field south of the tavern. My father taught my brothers and me to shoot accurately on a similar but much smaller range set out on the largest pasture of our farm.

We used a bow saw to cut nine one-inch thick discs from the trunk of a five-inch diameter pine sapling Father felled with an ax. We used small hand-made iron nails to fasten each wooden disc to hand-cut wooden stakes—two, three, and four feet long—and painted the discs with granulated lead white mixed with linseed oil. After the white paint dried, we tacked a thin, round, one-inch diameter lead "bull's-eye" to the center of each target.

We then took the targets, three apiece, down range and drove the stakes into the ground at 200, 250, and 300-yard intervals from the firing line. Each boy was allowed three shots at each of our targets.

The winner was the brother who had the smallest cumulative total inches from the center of the target after firing nine shots. By the time I was fifteen, I won nearly every time.

The major difference today is the number of shooters. The rosters Captain Morgan ordered me to prepare has 160 names, alphabetically listed. That meant someone had to prepare at least 480 targets.

And sure enough, a wagon, filled to overflowing with hundreds of targets, pulled up in front of the tavern next to the supply wagon as a crowd of competitors began flooding into the area in front of the tavern. I wondered who did all the work to prepare for this day.

At 7:30 a.m. Captain Morgan climbed atop his supply wagon and bellowed, "All those who want to compete for the privilege of joining my Rifle Company, gather here and listen carefully!

"We are going to start in thirty minutes. Today's evaluation consists of two events: how fast you can run a mile and then shoot three rounds at 200, 250, and 300 yards. Accuracy with your rifle counts the highest. But how long it takes you to run a mile and then shoot three rounds at each of your targets also matters. We are going to do this alphabetically in groups of ten.

"When I finish with these instructions, every competitor will draw three targets and line up, ten across, in sixteen ranks behind the firing line. On my order, the ten contestants in the front rank will go down-range, place a target on the 200, 250, and 300-yard lines, and return to their place on the firing line.

"I will then give the command, 'Right face' and the ten contestants in the front rank will turn right, go twenty yards to the right, and line up between those two flags. That is the start and finish line for a one-mile course, marked in lime, on the field around the tavern.

"Behind each one of you at the starting line, there will be an evaluator with a pocket watch. The evaluator will write down your name on a sheet of paper and be responsible for keeping your elapsed time. When I fire my pistol, everyone on the starting line will start the one-mile course.

"Once you finish the run, don't dawdle. Proceed immediately to your position on the firing line and start engaging your three targets down-range.

"The evaluator will record how long it took you to complete the run and fire your nine shots. When everyone in your rank has fired nine shots, you will proceed down-range to pick up your three targets and report here to Major Angus McDonald. He will tabulate your final score. As each rank moves off the firing line, the next rank will move up and repeat the process.

"This is not complicated. If each of you pays attention to what's happening in front of you, and everyone moves with alacrity, it should take about a half hour for each rank to complete the one-mile run and fire nine shots. That means we can all be headed home by four o'clock this afternoon."

That estimate proved to be wildly optimistic.

Captain Morgan's orders were clear enough, but no one anticipated the inevitable delays. Though every shooter brought with him his rifle, powder, shot, tomahawk, and hunting knife, no one anticipated the crowd of family, friends, and supporters who brought with them victuals and ample supplies of wine, cider, and prodigious quantities of rum.

The first seven ranks went off without a hitch, but as the day wore on, the crowd of "observers" became increasingly boisterous.

As the eighth rank took off on their run, a cousin of one of the contestants decided to aid his relative by tripping the lead runner. This outrage prompted a melee involving close to 500 of the contestants and observers. It took nearly an hour for Major McDonald, Rev. Thruston, and Captain Morgan to restore order and get on with the competition.

By 4:00 we had completed only eleven ranks and a brief rain shower caused another delay. Some of those who were yet to compete began to grumble they would be at a disadvantage as darkness descended. After a quick parley, it was decided to run the final fifty through the course starting at 8:00 Saturday morning.

Though the competition was suspended, the crowd remained, much to the pleasure of Major Charles Smith, the tavern owner. He and his wife were still serving tin cups of rum and cider to a large group of paying customers when Casey and I departed for home.

When we arrived at the gate, Pieter came out with a lantern. He took the animals to the barn and I went into the house to write a note to my father.

At home in Winchester,
April 28ᵗʰ, 1775

Dear Father,

At the invitation of Captain Morgan, and with your blessing, I have accepted the post as Adjutant for his Rifle Company. Though it is uncertain when we shall be called to service, if I am not at home when you and Paul return, it means we have been called elsewhere.

Please keep me in your prayers, as you and Paul shall be in mine.

Most respectfully, your son,

Nathanael

When the competition resumed on Saturday morning, it proceeded flawlessly, in large part because Captain Morgan barred the consumption of any liquids other than tea, coffee, or water until the competition was over. By noon, all fifty remaining candidates completed the course and Major McDonald, Rev. Thruston, Captain Morgan, and I retired to a table in Major Smith's establishment with the ten evaluators. A guard was posted outside the door with instructions to prevent anyone from entering without permission.

Our task was made simpler by eliminating any competitor who took more than ten minutes to complete the mile run and any who missed a target. That process winnowed the competitors to one hundred and twelve. The final dozen were determined by measuring the accuracy of their three shots on each target.

By 4:00 we had our roster of one hundred Riflemen. Captain Morgan told me to list them in alphabetical order on a single sheet of paper and make a single copy. Once I did so, he signed them both, then folded one sheet, and placed it in his pocket.

At this point, Rev. Thruston stepped up and said to all in the room, "Nathanael, when I give the word, Major McDonald will take the other copy, label it as 'Captain Morgan's Rifle Company,' tack it to the board outside, and post a guard so no one removes it."

Muster Roll of Captain Morgan's Rifle Company

1. Adams, Mosby	17. Churchill, Robert
2. Alford, John	18. Clay, John
3. Anderson, Daniel	19. Clay, Steven
4. Anderson, Paul	20. Cochran, John
5. Anderson, Robert	21. Colbert, Richard
6. Armstrong, Porter	22. Curtis, Adam
7. Baker, Stuart	23. Dalton, Christopher
8. Ball, William	24. David, Martin
9. Bramingham, Curtis	25. Davis, Daniel
10. Boykin, William G.	26. Donaldson, John
11. Brown, John	27. Dooland, Patrick
12. Brown, William	28. Durst, Daniel
13. Bruin, Peter	29. Eisenbach, Robert
14. Burns, John	30. Enders, Conrad
15. Cackley, Benjamin	31. Feely, Timothy
16. Chapman, Thomas	32. Fickhis, William

33. Fitzpatrick, Solomon
34. Flood, William
35. George, Spencer
36. Gordon, Jeremiah
37. Greenway, George
38. Greenway, William
39. Griffith, David
40. Grim, Charles
41. Grubb, Benjamin
42. Harbinson, Matthew
43. Harbison, John
44. Hayes, Mark
45. Heiskill, Adam
46. Heth, William
47. Hoffman, Henry
48. Humphrey, William
49. Hunt, Oliver
50. Jacobs, Rowland
51. Katz, Martin
52. Kilgannon, Thomas
53. Killian, Patrick
54. Kurtz, Adam
55. Kurtz, Frederick
56. Lauck, Solomon
57. Leibendgut, Jacob
58. Leibendgut, James
59. Leibendgut, Joseph
60. McCord, Arthur
61. McGowan, Henry
62. McGuire, John
63. McGowan, Henry
64. McIntire, Benjamin
65. McIntosh, Walker
66. Mead, John
67. Merchant, George
68. Michaels, Timothy
69. Mitchell, Robert
70. Moore, John
71. Morris, Gerald
72. Newman, Nathanael
73. Norris, Cornelius
74. Porterfield, Charles
75. Rhodes, Armstrong
76. Riddle, Jeremiah
77. Roderick, Benjamin
78. Rogers, John
79. Rothroe, Benjamin
80. Rutledge, William
81. Sanders, George
82. Schultz, John
83. Secrest, Charles
84. Seedes, Edward

85. Simmons, Thomas

86. Smoot, John

87. Sperry, Jacob

88. Stephens, John

89. Stratton, Seth

90. Stuart, Michael

91. Sullivan, Brendan

92. Tait, Caperton

93. Tochterman, Peyton

94. Ware, Jacob

95. Wheeler, Jesse

96. White, Elijah

97. White, Robert

98. Williams, Thomas

99. Wilson, David

100. Wolfe, Peter

Then, to all in the room—including the ten "evaluators"—he said, "Thank you, Major McDonald, Rev. Thruston, and all of you who helped make this effort a success. I truly believe we have selected the best Riflemen in this region of Virginia to fight for our liberty in the coming war against the British Crown. I recognize many of those on this list from having served in combat with them.

"There is no way to test a man for what he will do in the midst of great danger. Courage cannot be taught. Neither commitment nor tenacity can be evaluated before it is tested in the face of privation. But from what I have seen in the last two days there is a full measure of these virtues in the Riflemen we have selected."

Turning to the ten evaluators, Captain Morgan said, "Thank you for the time you have spent here for the past two days. As you leave, remember to protect the names of those we have selected. Mr. Newman, my Adjutant, and I have the only copies. We will post a single copy out front. Do what you can to discourage anyone from copying the list because they and their families may be in jeopardy from Loyalist Sympathizers when our Rifle Company is called to service."

As they exited, Major Smith entered the room from behind the bar and said to Captain Morgan, "Sir, you have a visitor at the back door who asks permission to enter."

The captain, never an admirer of the tavern or its owner said, "Who is it?"

"It's Mr. Patrick Henry."

Morgan instantly said, "Please sir, admit him immediately," and we all rose.

Mr. Henry, entered the room and said, "Please forgive me for interrupting. I watched from afar what you have been doing and I wanted to commend you."

"Please be seated, sir," said Major McDonald, the senior officer in the room as I went to fetch a cup of cool cider to set before our unexpected guest.

"May I ask, sir, what brings you here?" Captain Morgan asked.

"Congress has been called to convene in Philadelphia in a few days and I am hastening to meet with those who will decide on our Virginia delegation. Today I am on my way to Berkley County to confer with Horatio Gates. Tomorrow I will meet with Colonel Washington at Mount Vernon in hopes he will go to Philadelphia, for I cannot."

"But you are one of our Virginia representatives," interjected Major McDonald.

"Yes," Mr. Henry replied with a nod, "but for now I must remain in command of our units pursuing the thief Lord Dunmore."

After a few more minutes of conversation, Mr. Henry rose, turned to me, and said, "You are Nathanael Newman?"

"Yes, sir."

"I must tell you, your father and brother are two of my most loyal and effective officers. When I see them later this week, I will tell them how pleased I am you are serving with Captain Morgan."

As Mr. Henry headed for the back door by which he'd entered, Rev. Thruston said, "Sir, if you are amenable, let us pray for you and the members of our Continental Congress."

Rev. Thruston prayed, "Lord of all, we beg You to protect Mr. Henry and all of us in the desperate days ahead. And when the coming contest is over, let us have our God-given rights restored and that future generations will say of us, we fought the good fight, finished the contest, and kept the faith."

Mr. Henry replied, "Thank you, Reverend, and my thanks to all of you." Then, turning to Captain Morgan, he said, "I heard your warning about protecting the identity of those who have qualified to become members of your Rifle Company. Your admonition is appropriate. Every Patriot on that list will be hunted, hounded, and hung by the British if we lose."

ENDNOTES

1.   Paper-wrapped cartridges containing pre-measured amounts of black powder, a "wad" and a lead ball were commonly used by soldiers carrying "smooth bore" muskets. Pre-wrapped cartridges could be loaded and fired from muskets every 15–20 seconds because the shooter could quickly reload. Since muskets were only lethal out to 60 to 75 yards, accuracy was less important than how quickly a formation of soldiers could deliver "volley fire" into enemy ranks.

    Rifles with "lands and grooves" inside a four-foot-long barrel—required nearly four times as long to load—or "charge" as a musket. A Rifleman had to measure an amount of gunpowder [based on the caliber of his rifle and range to the target]; pour the powder down the barrel; press a tight-fitting lead ball down the barrel atop a cloth "patch" and the powder; ram the ball "home"; cock the rifle; sprinkle some black powder into the rifle's frizzen pan; cock the weapon and fire. Riflemen rarely used paper-wrapped cartridges because the lands and grooves inside the barrel made loading so much more time consuming.

    James Newman had shown his sons how to make paper-wrapped rifle charges containing enough powder to send a lethal bullet 300 yards down-range, hit a target 200–300 yards away, inflict lethal damage on an enemy soldier [usually an officer], and reload in less than a minute.

2.   *Nitre:* archaic term for saltpeter or ammonium nitrate, an essential ingredient for making black powder when mixed with sulfur and charcoal.

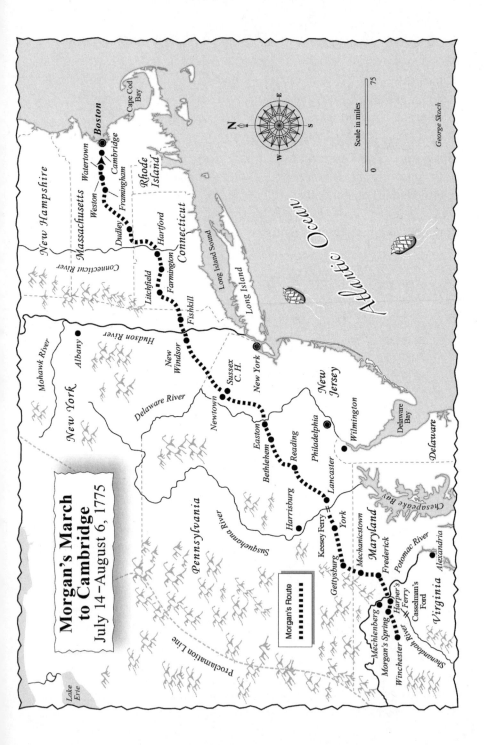

Morgan's March to Cambridge
July 14–August 6, 1775

Morgan's Route

Scale in miles
0   75

George Skoch

Massachusetts: Boston, Watertown, Cambridge, Weston, Dudley, Framingham

New Hampshire

Rhode Island

Connecticut: Hartford, Farmington, Litchfield

Connecticut River

New York: Albany, New Windsor, Fishkill, New York, Sussex C. H., Newtown

Mohawk River
Hudson River
Delaware River

Long Island Sound
Long Island

Atlantic Ocean

Cape Cod Bay

New Jersey

Pennsylvania: Easton, Bethlehem, Reading, Harrisburg, Lancaster, York, Gettysburg

Susquehanna River

Philadelphia
Wilmington
Delaware
Delaware Bay

Chesapeake Bay

Maryland: Keesey Ferry, Mechanicstown, Frederick

Potomac River

Virginia: Mechlenberg, Morgan's Spring, Winchester, Harper's Ferry, Casselman's Ford, Alexandria

Shenandoah River

Proclamation Line

Lake Erie

CHAPTER SEVEN

THE LONG MARCH TO BOSTON

The days since Mr. Henry's April 29th warning about being "hunted, hounded, and hung by the British if we lose" have been full of preparations to prevent that very outcome. Much of May and June 1775 has been spent getting seed in the ground in what appears to be a very dry planting season and the very strong likelihood of war against what many of us call "our mother-country."

Herewith, the most relevant entries in the journal Captain Morgan ordered me to keep:

Thursday, May 4th, 1775: A Trusted Courier delivered a message to Rev. Thruston, the Chairman of our Frederick County Committee of Safety from Mr. Patrick Henry, dated Tuesday, May 2nd. Capt. Morgan instructed me to record it in our Rifle Co. Journal:

To my Dear Patriot friends in Frederick County,

Lord Dunmore has pledged to pay £330 for the gunpowder
and weapons he seized from our Williamsburg Armory on the
night of 20–21 April. I regard this to be a wholly inadequate
response to our demand that he return the seventeen barrels of
powder, twenty-three muskets, and fifteen pistols he stole and
placed aboard *HMS Magdalen*. We need our gunpowder and
firearms more than His Majesty's money.

Members of the Williamsburg Committee of Safety have
informed me Governor Dunmore has fortified his palace in
Williamsburg with Royal Marines and two naval cannons. It
is also suspected he has secretly dispatched his family to refuge
at his personal estate, Porto Bello.[1]

According to these reports, he is also fortifying this place and
has surrounded it with Royal Marines and a large contingent
of armed Royalists.

I initially planned to call on Captain Morgan's new Frederick
County Rifle Company for support in capturing the Governor
and his Royal officials. That will no longer be necessary for
nearly 800 Patriot volunteers from neighboring counties now
reinforce my Hanover County Militia. We are now in a
comfortable encampment less than a day's march from
Williamsburg. Correspondents and messengers indicate
another 2,500 Patriots are prepared to join us if needed.

While I still believe it would be preferable to seize the
initiative, I am being counseled by Messrs. Thomas Nelson,
Richard Henry Lee, and Thomas Pendleton to break off this

*engagement and proceed to Philadelphia as a Virginia delegate
when Congress convenes on May 10th.*

I shall keep you apprised,

Patrick Henry

Sunday, May 7th, 1775: At Sunday morning service, Rev. Thruston read Governor Dunmore's Royal Proclamation dated May 6th in which he declared ". . . a certain PATRICK HENRY, of the county of Hanover and a number of his deluded followers have put themselves in a posture for war . . ." He then directed ". . . all persons, upon their allegiance, not to aid, abet, or give countenance to the said PATRICK HENRY or any other persons concerned in such unwarrantable combinations; but, on the contrary, to oppose them, and their designs by every means . . ."

After reading the entire proclamation, Rev. Thruston continued, "This is an illegal death warrant issued by John Murray, Lord Dunmore, the Royal Governor against Mr. Patrick Henry. Our governor hereby forfeits any authority over the people of the Commonwealth of Virginia."

Then opening his Bible, he said, "As for Mr. Patrick Henry, his refuge is in David's Psalm 26:

Judge me, O LORD; for I have walked in mine integrity: I have trusted also in the LORD; therefore I shall not slide.

Examine me, O LORD, and prove me; try my reins and my heart.

For thy loving kindness is before mine eyes: and I have walked in thy truth.

I have not sat with vain persons, neither will I go in with dissemblers.

I have hated the congregation of evildoers; and will not sit with the wicked.

I will wash mine hands in innocency: so will I compass thine altar, O LORD:

That I may publish with the voice of thanksgiving, and tell of all thy wondrous works.

LORD, I have loved the habitation of thy house, and the place where thine honour dwelleth.

Gather not my soul with sinners, nor my life with bloody men:

In whose hands is mischief, and their right hand is full of bribes.

But as for me, I will walk in mine integrity: redeem me, and be merciful unto me.

My foot standeth in an even place: in the congregations will I bless the LORD.

After reading the Psalm, Rev. Thruston concluded, "I urge you to pray for all who stand against tyranny. I am able to let you know a piece of good news. Mr. Patrick Henry is now on his way to Philadelphia, accompanied by ten armed Patriot horsemen. There, he will join Virginia delegates, Messer's Richard Bland, Benjamin Harrison, Francis Lightfoot Lee, Richard Henry Lee, Thomas Nelson Jr., Edmund Pendleton, Peyton Randolph, Col. George Washington, and George Wythe who were already there when Continental Congress re-convened on the 5th."

Monday, May 8th, 1775: Capt. Morgan and I were inspecting the reconstruction of the powder magazine at Cedar Creek, when Rev. Thruston rode up to inform us that one of the first measures passed after Congress re-convened was a plan to improve the Trusted Courier Service throughout the thirteen provincial capitals. In keeping with the idea Mr. Benjamin Franklin had before the British dismissed him as Colonial Postmaster General, the

Congress agreed each colony would establish and maintain a "station" every twenty-five miles on the 1,600 miles of "post roads" Mr. Franklin surveyed back in 1763. Each station is to have "a stable, not fewer than eight swift mounts, forage, water, a farrier, a place of rest, and victuals for couriers." The goal, as the Reverend explained it, is to be able to deliver mail 200 miles each day. Then, he added with a smile, "They also intend to make Mr. Franklin 'Continental Postmaster General' as soon as they can find the funds to pay him."[2]

Friday, May 19th, 1775: The drought is hard upon us. Not a drop of water has fallen from the sky in weeks. This afternoon, Mr. Isaac Zane, owner of Marlboro Plantation and the Marlboro Iron Works stopped at our home. Though he was raised and educated as a Quaker, he is also a member of our Frederick County Secret Committee of Safety. He came to thank Pieter for his advice on planting forage instead of tobacco.

Saturday, May 20th, 1775: Shortly after dawn this morning, Captain Morgan's Negro slave, Josiah, appeared at our door bearing a note from the Captain summoning me to a meeting at his farm at noon with Rev. Charles M. Thruston, Isaac Zane, Maj. Angus McDonald, Samuel Beall, Alexander White, and George Rootes.

My curiosity was piqued by the instruction, clearly in a different hand (I later learned was Mrs. Morgan's), "If possible, please bring your father's copy of Spilsbury's 1763, 'New Map of North America.'"

Perhaps because he is a surveyor and an architect driven by curiosity, my father has a large collection of maps all carefully labeled and catalogued by date, rolled, and stored on shelves here in his office. I quickly found the requested map sheet, noted its very fine scale, and took it, along with a magnifying glass, to the meeting.

Rev. Thruston and I arrived at Captain Morgan's home just north of Battletown together, followed by Major McDonald and

Messer's Zane, Beall, White, and Rootes. These latter three I met at various times—or was at least introduced to by my father. But I was stunned when Rev. Thruston explained, "These gentlemen are the members of our Frederick County Secret Committee of Safety of which I am the Chairman. You may not speak of them as such without my permission or that of Captain Morgan."

We gathered on the porch to take advantage of the light and Mrs. Morgan served us tea as Rev. Thruston read to us a missive he received this morning from Thomas Nelson, in Philadelphia:

> "Congressional Dispatch, May 18th, in the Year of Our Lord, 1775:

> "Our Virginia Congressional Delegation has asked me to report to you the following news for prompt dissemination far and wide:

> "On May 10th and 11th in this the year of our Lord, 1775, Patriot forces commanded by Col. Benedict Arnold of Massachusetts and Col. Ethan Allen of Connecticut and his Green Mountain Boys militia captured Fort Ticonderoga and Fort Crown Point, two strategically important and supposedly impregnable British-held bastions on the shores of Lake Champlain in New York.

> "The entire British garrisons of both fortresses on the direct route to Montreal surrendered and all their heavy artillery (cannons, howitzers, and mortars) along with gunpowder and other valuable military stores are now in Patriot hands.

> "Please disseminate word of this great victory throughout the Commonwealth so our fellow Patriots will be encouraged and the loyalists consorting with our former governor turned despot will be disheartened.

> //signed// Thomas Nelson, Congressional Delegate from the Commonwealth of Virginia."[3]

Immediately after reading the message, Rev. Thruston added, "Now, the reason for this meeting; Who here knows where these Forts Ticonderoga and Crown Point are located?"

We all looked at one another until Mrs. Morgan said quietly, "That's why I asked Nathanael to bring the map his father showed us last year when he described the mail routes Mr. Franklin devised as Royal Postmaster before he was dismissed by the authorities in London."

With the aid of the magnifying glass, we found Lake Champlain and both forts on the map. Capt. Morgan's only comment, "This Colonel Arnold may be just the kind of stout fellow I should have beside me in a fight."

Saturday, June 10th, 1775: Williamsburg, Virginia's capital, is now surrounded by Virginia Militiamen. But the best news was in the letter I received today from my father:

June 8th, 1775

My dear son, Nathanael:

Please accept my apologies for not writing more often. I am now commanding a contingent of Rifle Militiamen deployed in the thick forest surrounding Governor Dunmore's hunting lodge, Porto Bello. Your brother Paul was elected by our unit to be my deputy.

Before being ordered here, we were part of the perimeter controlling access into and out of Williamsburg. While there, Paul and I safely made several trips into and out of the capital and even walked by our home where you and he were born. Unfortunately, a British or Tory officer, judging by the Union Jack hanging in front of the house, has apparently commandeered it.

Several weeks ago our cowardly Royal Governor, accompanied
by a contingent of Royal Marines, fled his palace and joined
his family here at Porto Bello.

The manse is now surrounded by a recently dug earthen wall
and a wooden stockade, defended by more than a hundred
Tories and about 30 Royal Marines. They initially sent
patrols into the forest but no longer do so because our
Riflemen, operating in two or three-man teams, have killed at
least seven of them from long range.

Four days ago, *HMS Fowey*, a 24-gun, 3-masted, Royal
Navy frigate, dropped anchor in the York River, abreast of
Porto Bello. Corporal Jeremiah O'Leary, one of our best
Riflemen, hidden near the shoreline, spotted Lord Dunmore on
horseback and five bodyguards about 250 yards away heading
toward the river to greet a long-boat as it was being rowed
ashore from the British Man-o-War.

Knowing the sound and smoke of a shot would surely give
away his position, Cpl. O'Leary decided to fire anyway in
hopes of hitting our nemesis. He did. His bullet struck
Dunmore in the left leg but, sadly, was not fatal except to his
Lordship's horse. The Governor's bodyguards quickly drew
their swords and pistols and put an awful end to Corporal
O'Leary whose lovely widow Sarah and their son David now
mourn the loss of a brave Patriot husband and father.

Our grief is tempered by knowing Cpl. O'Leary's marksmanship
and courage were not wasted. In darkness early this morning,
Lord Dunmore and his family were observed stealing away from
Porto Bello, boarding *HMS Fowey* and setting sail down the
York River toward the Chesapeake Bay. Good riddance.[4]

Please know Paul and I pray daily for your safety. Until we see each other again, I remain your loving father,

James Newman

Sic Semper Tyrannus

Sunday, June 18th, 1775: Shortly after returning from Sabbath services this afternoon, the bell rang at our gate. Moments later Pieter knocked, entered the house, and informed me the visitor was a Trusted Courier with a message for urgent delivery to Rev. Thruston from Colonel Benjamin Harrison, one of our Virginia delegates to the Continental Congress in Philadelphia.

Curious as to why a courier was delivering a letter destined for Rev. Thruston to me, I went out where he was watering his horse and immediately recognized him as the messenger who delivered the letter in late April from my father approving my appointment as Capt. Morgan's Adjutant.

As I approached he smiled, handed me his .54 cal. British Sea Service pistol and ladled water over his head, saying, "My apologies, Mr. Newman, but I was instructed by a servant at Charles Thruston's home to bring this letter to you since you are Capt. Daniel Morgan's Adjutant and he and the 'the Rev-e-rant' are dining at Capt. Morgan's home this evening."

I nodded and the courier handed me the letter, and as I returned his pistol, asked, "Have you had to use it yet?"

He shook his head, shoved the pistol back in his belt, and said, "Not yet. But the time is surely coming. Be careful, young fellow."

As soon as he headed off, I went into the house, changed into hunting garb, grabbed my rifle and kit, summoned Casey, and walked outside to find Pieter had already saddled my black mare, Midnight. Giving me a leg up to mount he asked, "Will you be returning this evening, sir?"

"Pieter, you don't have to call me 'sir.' I'm still Nathanael."

"Yes, I know you are still Nathanael. But you are now an ensign in the Virginia Militia, Adjutant to the legendary Captain Daniel Morgan. I just saw you entrusted to carry what must be a very sensitive message from the Continental Congress to two men likely to be very important to the future of *our* country in a war against the most powerful nation on earth.

"Your family has been very kind to Lotte and me. We pray she is now pregnant with our first child. By the time our sentence is served in December 1781 we want our Van Buren family to be lifelong friends of the Newman family in a free country. Because Lotte and I are under indentured sentence for violating British law, I cannot *yet* serve the Patriot cause. Your father, brother, and you are already doing so. I do not say 'sir' to be subservient. I say it out of respect."

Pieter's words were much on my mind on the ride to Capt. Morgan's home. On arrival, Mrs. Morgan immediately brought me to their dining room where Capt. Morgan, the Morgan daughters, Rev. Charles Thruston, Isaac Zane, and Major McDonald were already seated. There, she announced, "Please allow me to introduce a very welcome guest, Ensign Nathanael Newman, my dear husband's Adjutant. He has agreed to accept our invitation to dinner."

As the household staff set a place for me and uncertain how to proceed, I said, "Please forgive my untimely arrival, but I am bearing an urgent message from the Congress in Philadelphia addressed to Reverend Thruston."

As though expecting the letter, Rev. Thruston held out his hand, opened the envelope with his dinner knife, and read:

"From Col. Benjamin Harrison, Congressional Delegate
of the Commonwealth of Virginia to Rev. Charles
Thruston, Chairman, Frederick County, Virginia

Committee of Public Safety, Saturday, 17th June in the year of our Lord, 1775:

"This letter is to inform you Congress voted on Wednesday the 14th of this month to form a Continental Army and the following day appointed Colonel George Washington of Mount Vernon, Virginia, as Commander-in-Chief of the Continental Army.

"Congress has now also granted, at Gen. Washington's requests, the following:

"Colonel Horatio Gates, resident of 'Traveler's Rest' in Berkley County, Virginia, is offered the post of Adjutant General of the Continental Army to serve as such with the rank of Brigadier General.

"Ten Rifle Companies are to be raised immediately for Continental Army Service from Pennsylvania (six companies), Maryland (two companies) and Virginia (two companies).

"The Commander in Chief specifically requested, and Congress has approved, the two Virginia Rifle Companies shall be commanded by Captain Daniel Morgan of Frederick County and Captain Hugh Stephenson of Berkeley County.

"I have been directed to inform you the individual officers identified above (Messer's Gates, Morgan, and Stephenson) will be notified of their appointments and commissions by Congress and personal correspondence from Commander-in-Chief Washington. The only public announcement of acceptance for these (and any other appointments or promotions) will be made from Congress in Philadelphia."

"I remain your humble, obedient servant, //signed// Benjamin Harrison."

After reading Col. Harrison's letter, Rev. Thruston raised his glass and said, "Dear Heavenly Father, we beg You to bless our cause. Shower Your Grace and Protection on Captain Morgan and all who are called to protect our God-given liberty. In the name of Your Son, our Savior, we ask the decisions we make, the leaders we select, and the events ahead be those which grant us victory over tyranny in ways that honor You, Your Son Jesus, and the Holy Spirit in the days ahead."

All at the table responded, "Amen."

Those of us who dined at Capt. Morgan's home on June 18th expected we would immediately receive orders for where and when our Rifle Company would deploy. We should have known better.

Thursday, June 22nd, 1775: This morning a Trusted Courier delivered another "Congressional Report" from Col. Harrison in Philadelphia. The message, dated June 20th, informed our Committee of Safety that thousands of fresh British troops under the command of General William Howe launched an attack on Colonial forces besieging the city of Boston.

According to Col. Harrison: "The eighteen-hour long battle on Saturday, June 17th resulted in Patriot forces being withdrawn from Charlestown peninsula, but at great cost to the British. During four frontal assaults to take Breed's Hill and Bunker's Hill, the Royal Army and Marines lost 19 officers killed, 62 officers wounded, 207 Regulars killed, and 770 Regulars wounded. A report from the Massachusetts Provincial Congress, states Patriot losses were 115 killed, 305 wounded, and 30 captured. The British would not have succeeded had Our Courageous Soldiers not run out of ammunition."

Sunday, June 25th, 1775: A Trusted Courier delivered from Philadelphia a document dated June 22, 1775, addressed "to Daniel Morgan, Esquire," commissioning him as "Captain of a company of Riflemen in the army of the United States, raised for the defense of American Liberty, and for repelling every hostile invasion thereof . . . By order of the Congress" and //signed// John Hancock, President.

Wednesday, June 28th, 1775: Troubled by the assessment that adequate supplies of ammunition could have changed the outcome of the June 17th Battles on Breed's and Bunker"s Hills on Charlestown Peninsula in Boston Harbor, Captain Morgan wants to alter our deployment equipment list before our orders arrive.

After conferring with Rev. Thruston and the other members of our Frederick County Committee of Safety, the Captain used his own funds to purchase a second wagon and team of draft horses from Isaac Zane at Marlboro Ironworks. When I delivered the wagon and horses to Capt. Morgan, he carefully examined them and pronounced all to be "fit and sturdy" but sent me back to Marlboro with a note, "Isaac, for what you charged me for the wagon, I should have been provided with two spare wheels and brass bearings!"

For the next three days, Pieter, two of the Captain's Negro slaves, and I loaded the wagon with barrels of gunpowder, salted pork, and beef, lead sheets for casting bullets, and covered it all with canvas.

Thursday, July 6th, 1775: A Trusted Courier delivered a message from Col. Benjamin Harrison with our Virginia Congressional Delegation in Philadelphia. The letter informed us:

On Monday, July 3rd, General George Washington arrived in Cambridge, Massachusetts, and has taken command of the Continental Army.

The Virginia Rifle Companies comprised of no less than sixty-eight men each and commanded by Captains Daniel Morgan of Frederick County, and Captain Hugh Stephenson of Berkley County, are hereby ordered to depart Virginia no later than Sunday, July 16th and hasten to Continental Army Headquarters in Cambridge, Massachusetts.

Sunday, July 9th, 1775: I accompanied Capt. Morgan to a meeting this afternoon with Capt. Stephenson and members of their respective County Safety Committees at the Golden Buck Tavern on Cameron Street in Winchester, Virginia. The two captains and their committees agreed to muster the two Virginia Rifle companies at Morgan's Spring, about one-half mile south of Mecklenburg[5], Virginia at 8 a.m. on Sunday, July 16th and parade together to Harpers Ferry.

Monday, July 10th and Tuesday, July 11th, 1775: In two days of hard riding, Captain Morgan, Lieutenant William Humphrey, Lieutenant William Heth, Ensign Charles Porterfield, Ensign Peter Bruin, Sgt. William Fickhis, and I contacted all of the one hundred volunteers who qualified to join "Morgan's Rifles." We ordered them to muster before dark on Thursday, July 13th at the old Hollingsworth Farm just outside Winchester.

This created a bit of a problem for Sergeant Fickhis who asked Capt. Morgan, "Sir, if we're not heading north from Mecklenberg until Sunday the 16th, why are we going to muster in Winchester on the night of the 13th?"

The Captain smiled and replied, "Well, Sergeant, we may just need to leave a little early. I don't want to make the Redcoats in Boston wait for me to pay 'em back for those stripes they put on my back."

Thursday, July 13th, 1775: Well before dusk this evening, all 100 members of Morgan's Rifle Company were "present and accounted for at the Hollingsworth Farm," just outside Winchester. I arrived early enough with my Supply Wagon #1 to write a letter to my father and brother informing them "we are on our way to join Gen. Washington" and "Rev. Thruston has pledged to keep you apprised as to where we are as best he can."

Friday, July 14th, 1775: At dawn this morning we marched north in a column of twos, with two heavily laden supply wagons headed for Morgan's Spring, just south of Mecklenberg in Berkley County, Virginia. We made the thirty-mile hike in less than twelve hours and were fed and under our tents before dark.

Saturday, July 15th, 1775: We arose before dawn. No sign of Capt. Stephenson's Rifle Co. We were underway for Harpers Ferry by the time the sun crested the Blue Ridge. Good thing we left when we did because the twelve-mile hike took less than three and one-half hours, but ferrying first the wagons and then 100 men, fifteen at a time, across the Potomac and Shenandoah confluence took us far longer than expected. We bivouacked just five miles up the turnpike toward Frederick, Maryland. It has been so hot and dry, only a few of the men bothered to set up their tents.

Sunday, July 16th, 1775: The eighteen-mile, mostly uphill, hike to Frederick, Maryland, would have been a breeze—had there been one. The men are doing fine, in good spirits and cheerful, but the draft horses are really feeling the heat. Ensign Bruin and I have developed real empathy for these great animals. Each time we cross a small stream, the men help us fill buckets of water to let the horses drink and wet them down. As we passed through Frederick this afternoon, scores of townspeople came out to cheer us on. We camped for the night at a farm about five miles north of the town, near a flowing stream.

Monday, July 17th, 1775: We're more than sixty miles from York, Pennsylvania. Capt. Morgan told the men this morning he wants us to be north of York by Thursday, the 20th of July and offers to have us stop there to put on a brief "sharpshooter show" if we're on schedule. The Riflemen promise they will give him no less than twenty-five miles a day. He orders Ensign Bruin and me to "have your wagons on the road not later than 5 a.m." We pulled out onto the dusty turnpike at about 4 a.m. but the half moon is waning to nil by the 27th, so leaving camp before sunrise isn't going to be an option for long. We stopped after twenty-six miles tonight at Mechanicstown,[6] because it's been an "uphill day" and a local militiaman told Lt. Humphrey they might have some gunpowder to sell us. They didn't.

Tuesday, July 18th, 1775: We logged twenty-eight mostly uphill miles today and hiked to the north side of the borough of Gettysburg, Pennsylvania, just before dark. This is a little "crossroads" town with several taverns, one of which is operated by the Getty family. They came out to our encampment with a barrel of cider and generously offered every Rifleman more than a mouthful.

Wednesday, July 19th, 1775: It's thirty miles from here to York, Pennsylvania. Still no rain and the temperature has to be over 90 degrees. For the Rifleman slogging along on the dry, dusty turnpike, it's tough. For the horses pulling the heavy wagons, it's brutal. We set out shortly after dawn at a blistering pace. Just as we entered York, the skies opened. It's the first rain we have felt in over a month.

Thursday and Friday, July 20th and 21st, 1775: The route on the turnpike from York to Bethlehem, Pennsylvania, is ninety-eight miles. But the road is now a three-inch-deep muddy quagmire. After conferring with the York Co. militia commander, Captain Morgan calls off the shooting competition and orders the men to "stay as dry as you can." It's the first time we have stayed in the same place more than one night on the march. It's still raining as we bed down for the night.

Saturday, July 22nd, 1775: The rain stopped before dawn. Captain Morgan told us to hustle packing up because even though it's only thirty-five miles from York to Lancaster, crossing the Susquehanna by ferry was sure to take more time than he wanted. He was right.

Based on information from the York County Committee of Safety, the Captain ordered us to head for the Keesey Ferry crossing from Accomac to Marietta on the eastern shore. According to the intelligence, the operator is known to be a Patriot and several other ferry operators are not.

When we arrived at Accomac, the normally placid river was raging from two days of heavy rain and there was a long line of waiting crossers. Captain Morgan had a hasty conference with the flat-bottom pole boat operators. Money changed hands and we moved to the front of the line at about noon. Though uneventful, each crossing took over an hour and the sun was setting by the time we were back on the turnpike headed for Lancaster. It was nearly midnight when we stopped to bed-down in a farmer's field for a few hours' rest just south of Lancaster.

Sunday, July 23rd, 1775: We broke camp at dawn and headed through town on the way to Reading, thirty-five miles up the turnpike. I had hoped to stay in Lancaster long enough to visit the William Henry Rifle factory to visit the man who made my long rifle, but after a brief "sharpshooter show" we were on our way in hopes of making it to Reading before dark.

Monday, July 24th, 1775: Our thirty-five-mile trip to the western banks of the Schuylkill River across from Reading was the toughest hike yet. Though we arrived just as a tiny sliver of moon broke through the clouds overhead, the Captain and Lt. Humphrey convinced the ferry operators to pole us across the now placid stream even though it was well past their usual quitting time. The operators may have been Tories or Quakers because they charged us £3 for their efforts.

Tuesday, July 25th, 1775: Before dawn, while the men were packing up, Capt. Morgan summoned all the officers and sergeants to gather 'round the rear of Wagon #1 where he tacked the maps showing our route from Reading, PA, to Cambridge. Pointing to the map he said, "We're not quite halfway to Cambridge, Massachusetts, which is about 340 miles from here. We've been on the road for eleven days. If we're going to get to General Washington's Headquarters by the 6th of August—twelve days from now—we're going to have to average about thirty miles a day. That means no more 'sharpshooter shows' for our boys. It also means we may need to buy a couple more draft horses to rotate them in the harnesses. Tell the men. Let's go."

Wednesday, July 26th, 1775: Remarkably, we made forty miles yesterday and camped under a moonless, starlit sky for seven hours just south of Bethlehem, Pennsylvania. We were up early again this morning and moving in haste to get across the Delaware River at Easton. The Martin Ferries—six large flat-bottom boats—are the most efficient Ferry Service we have seen yet. By dark we made camp just south of Newtown, NJ, not far from the Sussex County Courthouse where we were quartered at a Trusted Courier station.

Thursday and Friday, July 27th and 28th, 1775: The two-day, sixty-mile hike from Sussex Court House, New Jersey, to New Windsor, New York, was unremarkable but for the apparent novelty created by our linen leggin's, hunting shirts, deerskin caps, leather belts holding close-quarter weapons of tomahawk and long knife, long rifles—and of course our speed of walking.

Saturday, July 29th, 1774: It was a good thing we left at dawn for the short walk from the town of New Windsor to the Colden Ferry landing on the west bank of the Hudson River. Thankfully, the tide and winds were right for our west-to-east crossing of the nearly two-mile-wide river. We were all across and mustering in the town of Fishkill by shortly after noon.

Captain Morgan and I crossed over early to meet with Captain Jacob Griffin, a Fishkill tavern owner and chairman of the Dutchess County "Committee of Observation." Griffin was so much taken with the mission of our Rifle Company and our leader he invited to the gathering crowd a Mrs. Moira Flemming, the widow of a sea captain. She brought with her an obviously well-cared for, round leather case about a foot long. She opened it and announced, "Captain Morgan, this three-draw brass Dollond spy-glass was made for my late husband in 1758. It extends to thirty-two inches in length. If he'd had it with him last year when his unarmed cargo vessel was attacked and sunk off Nova Scotia by a Royal Navy revenue cutter, he might well have seen the threat coming and avoided the enemy. I want you to have this and use it to kill as many of the accursed lobster-backs as possible."

At the end of her brief soliloquy, the crowd erupted with cheers and tears. Captain Morgan took the case, extended the tube to its full length and said, with emotion I had not yet heard in his voice, "I see his name engraved here and will every time I use it. I assure you, madam, your generous gift will be put to good use."

We departed Fishkill at a rapid pace and were more than halfway to Litchfield, Connecticut, before dark.

Sunday, July 30th, 1775: We made our way through Litchfield and half the distance to Farmington, about forty miles total without incident by sunset today. The terrain is flatter and the roads are in better shape in Connecticut than most of the terrain we have covered. Amazingly, we have not had to wade through mud since the downpour in Pennsylvania.

Monday, July 31st, 1775: The twelve-mile hike from Litchfield to Farmington went without incident but as we covered the ten miles to Hartford, Capt. Morgan began urging us to "pick up the pace" to get across the Connecticut river before nightfall. We arrived at the Hartford Ferry at dusk but with only one boat in service, it was well after dark before all our troops were at the bivouac Lt. Humphrey found for us on the north side of town.

As soon as the men were bedded down, Capt. Morgan told me to assemble the officers behind the #1 wagon where he placed a lantern on the tailgate. The young waxing moon was still just a sliver in the east, and the captain's countenance in the shimmering lantern light was as dramatic as anything I have yet seen.

He spoke quietly, "We have a little more than 100 miles and five days to get to Gen. Washington's Headquarters. Let the men rest until sunrise. Allow them to get some food and assemble at 8 o'clock so I can talk to the entire unit. Have them bring all their gear and sit down, facing south so the sun will not be in their eyes nor mine. You will stand behind them; do not sit. I want them to see you have their backs. Now, get some rest."

Tuesday, August 1st, 1775: The troops were there as ordered. This time he spoke in a tone that could be heard by all: "You have done well. We are almost where we are wanted. The next few days will be easy compared to the many miles behind us. But from this day forward you must be on alert.

"Every night—starting tonight, we will set up camp in a perimeter, with the wagons and horses in the center. We will have no fewer than four men at a time on watch in four-hour shifts from sunset to sunrise—that means eight men per night since it's summer. When the days get shorter, we will increase the number of watches.

"Beginning tonight we will have a challenge and password that will change every night. If a person approaching our camp fails to give the proper password when you shout the challenge, tell him to 'halt' and blow one blast on the whistle I gave you when we left Virginia. If there is an attack, the signal for everyone to turn to will be three blasts on the whistle. When we get where we are going, there will be many more rules on things like field sanitation, and many more soldiers. I, and your officers standing behind you, insist on you obeying them. Are there any questions?"

There was only one: "Cap'n, sir. Where are we going?"

The Captain smiled and said, "We're going to join General Washington in Cambridge, Massachusetts. We're going there to help him defeat our enemies, free our country, liberate our families, and create a new country. When we're done with that, we will go home to our loving families, and you will have made world history."

We stopped for the night south of Dudley, Massachusetts. At dark, wagons were inside a perimeter of canvas tents, the first watch was set as ordered and every man knew the challenge: *Apple*; and the password: *Butter.*

Wednesday, August 2nd, 1775: We passed through Dudley and held up for the night west of Framingham where we observed a supply train of quartermaster wagons headed south. Lt. Humphrey asked one of the mounted officers where they were heading and he replied "We're Rhode Island Militia. We're going home but we'll be back if you need us."

At dark, the routine was apparently already becoming, routine. Wagons inside the perimeter; watch set; challenge: *Virginia*; password: *Creeper.*

Thursday, August 3rd, 1755: We had an easy march today through Framingham, Weston, and were heading into Watertown, Massachusetts, when we were met by a gentleman who identified himself as Capt. Samuel Barnard, a Minuteman and member of the local Committee of Safety.

As he has done so often on this long march, Capt. Morgan consulted a list he kept in his pocket and said, "Bring him to me."

The two of them spoke for a few minutes and the Captain turned to Lt. Humphrey and said, "Tell our company, Capt. Barnard is a hero of this revolt against tyranny. He has already fought the Redcoats. He has arranged for us to bivouac on a green less than a mile east of Watertown along the road to Cambridge. He says it has clean water and good forage for the horses."

Everything Captain Barnard said about the Watertown campsite was true. What he didn't announce at first greeting, he told us on the way to the bivouac: "Dr. Joseph Warren, killed in the battle of Breed's Hill on June 17th, was my best professor at Harvard Medical School. He was also for several years in correspondence with Mister, now General George Washington, Dr. Benjamin Rush, Dr. Benjamin Franklin, and others about how to prevent the deadly spread of smallpox which kills more soldiers in every war than enemy fire.

"In General Washington's last missive to my professor and friend, Dr. Warren, he wrote he had just undergone variolation— a process in which material from smallpox sores pustules of living victims is given to people who have never had smallpox. The inoculation process involves scratching the smallpox material into an arm or inhaling it through the nose. General Washington wrote he will also ensure any new units added to the rolls of the Continental Army must have had the treatment within a year or they shall be turned away immediately.

"Capt. Morgan, yours is the first Continental unit to arrive here in Cambridge from outside the 'New England Provinces' since this edict was handed down. How do you wish to proceed?"

Captain Morgan didn't pause a second before saying, "We will all do whatever smallpox prevention General Washington wants tomorrow." And we did.

Sunday, August 6th, 1775: We spent Friday and Saturday, August 4th and 5th in smallpox Isolation on the Watertown Village green, waiting to see if there were any adverse reactions to the smallpox variolation procedure. There were none.

This morning, Capt. Barnard arrived at our encampment with three horses in tow. He then escorted Capt. Morgan, Lt. Humphrey, and me to General Washington's Headquarters on Cambridge Heights. General Washington was not there at the moment, but we were graciously welcomed by Brigadier General Horatio Gates, the Army's new Adjutant General. He instructed one of his aides to take Capt. Morgan, Lt. Humphrey, Capt. Barnard, and me to "see the sights" and choose a place to billet our company not far from the British lines at Roxbury.

We found a perfect spot. We were just a few hundred yards from an excellent "sniper hide."

Monday, August 7th, 1775: Captain Morgan was lying on his stomach in the wet grass, still as a stone, peering through his new spyglass into the haze rising from Boston Harbor. There were three of us—the Captain, Corporal Brendan Sullivan, the best Rifleman in our company, and me.

Without moving his head, a twig or a blade of grass, the Captain put his trigger finger in his mouth then slowly held it in the air to test the wind. Without seeming to move his lips he whispered, "Sulley, the breeze is directly behind us. Do you see the officer on the gray horse, about 350 yards down the hill, beneath the maple tree?"

"Yes sir, I have him in my sights."

"Good. Kill him."

Without taking my eyes off the target, I heard the muted click as Corporal Sullivan cocked the hammer on his rifle. He took a deep breath and started to exhale. The snap of the flint striking the powder pan on his rifle was followed an instant later by the crack of a bullet leaving the barrel with a flash and a puff of white smoke.

The projectile struck the British officer in the throat. He suddenly dropped his reins and pitched backward out of the saddle. As he fell, the horse bolted, dragging the Redcoat by his right leg, caught in the stirrup.

As four or five of the officer's troops jumped up in an attempt to catch the terrified horse, Corporal Sullivan readied his second rifle for another shot. Captain Morgan shook his head and said, "Hold your fire. Good shooting. One is enough for this morning."

It was the first time I saw a person killed by another human. It would not be my last. It was my 17th birthday.

ENDNOTES

1.   Royal Governor Dunmore's hunting lodge, Porto Bello, is located on the banks of the York River and on the grounds of Camp Peary, a 9,000-acre U.S. Army facility that serves as a CIA training facility. Though listed on the National Register of Historic Places, access to Porto Bello is limited to those with "a need to know."

2.   On 26 July 1775, Congress appointed Benjamin Franklin Continental Postmaster General with an annual salary of $1,000 and appropriated an additional $340 for a comptroller—with responsibility for hiring and firing postmasters to deliver mail and dispatches from Maine to Georgia.

3.   For reasons lost to history, Mr. Nelson omitted from his report on the great victories Colonels Arnold and Allen achieved at Ticonderoga and Crown Point were over garrisons totaling fewer than fifty British troops. Also unmentioned was the bickering between Arnold and Allen over who should get the credit for the conquests. Perhaps that's because including either fact would have diminished the propaganda value for the Patriot cause.

4.   Unfortunately, Lord Dunmore was not yet done with Virginia. Throughout the remainder of 1775 he ordered dozens of mixed raiding parties consisting of Royal Navy, Royal Marines, and Tories

ashore to plunder and burn "rebel" plantations, homes, fishing boats, and businesses along the James, York, and Potomac rivers, and the Chesapeake Bay. In nearly every case the raiders stole horses, cattle, even hogs—and killed the livestock they could not ride or carry back to their Royal Navy ships.

The depredations continued unabated until December 1775 when Patriot Militiamen defending Norfolk soundly defeated a Dunmore raid force. The battle cost the former governor the loss of four Royal Marines and a dozen Tories with no Patriot losses. On New Year's Day 1776, as Captain Daniel Morgan was being taken prisoner in Quebec, Lord Dunmore finally set sail for England.

5.   Now called Shepherdstown, WV.

6.   Now called Thurmont, MD.

CHAPTER EIGHT

1775: THE CONTINENTAL ARMY— FROM DEFENSE TO OFFENSE

Captain Morgan's determination to be the first of the Rifle Companies Congress raised to arrive at General Washington's Headquarters here in Cambridge, Massachusetts, has served us well. Our Captain was able to choose undisturbed terrain in defilade from British naval cannons in the waters below us, yet a short walk to overlook the British redoubts at Roxbury, just outside Boston. The site he chose here on the heights has trees for shade, forage for our draft horses, a spring for water, our "field sanitation station" is downhill and downwind, and our Company Assembly Area is on dry, level ground. But all that may be about to change.

Roxbury Heights, overlooking Boston

Friday, August 11th, 1775

Before dawn each day since we arrived, Captain Morgan has sent out at least three two-man sniper teams to engage British troops—preferably officers wearing epaulets on their shoulders. Our Riflemen fire from 50 to 100 yards behind Patriot lines. Every morning, at least one Redcoat was felled—often followed by loud cheers from the New England militiamen manning the American trenches, usually less than seventy-five yards from the British entrenchments.

This morning, it was immediately evident that overnight the British have abandoned their forward Roxbury and Dorchester redoubts and re-built them further from the Continentals' front lines. While we regarded this as consequence of our long-range rifle accuracy, it also means new American fortifications dug, closer to the new British entrenchments.

Apparently, a contingent of Massachusetts and Connecticut militia officers complained, "The Virginia Riflemen are the only ones among us having any fun. Our troops are tired of digging new lines every few days."

Whether that's what prompted Brigadier General Horatio Gates, General Washington's Adjutant General, to issue new orders we don't know but at noon today, General Gates's aide delivered a message to Capt. Morgan:

August 11th, 1775
Continental Army HQ, Cambridge, Massachusetts

Dear Captain Morgan:

Please know Capt. Stephenson's Rifle Company has arrived at Watertown and is now undergoing Smallpox variolation. His Rifle Company will soon be billeted near yours. Since your and his Virginia Rifle Companies are the first of the Ten Rifle Companies authorized by Congress to arrive, the Commander-in-Chief desires both Companies to Parade for His Excellency and our Senior Officers at Cambridge Headquarters at Noon on Monday, August 14th.

Effective immediately, all Rifle Company sharpshooters will be deployed to engage enemy targets only when under attack by our enemy or authorized in advance by this Headquarters.

Rifle Company personnel not otherwise engaged in contact with our enemy or authorized sniping duty shall henceforth assist our Continental soldiers in digging protective revetments and preparing field fortifications including abatis, fascines, and gabions.[1]

//signed// Horatio Gates, Brg Gnr'l., Adjutant General of the Army

Roxbury Heights, overlooking Boston

Tuesday, August 15th, 1775

Yesterday's parade of our two Virginia Rifle Companies—led by Captain Morgan—included a "pass in review" accompanied by fifes and drums before General Washington and his mounted staff.

It will always be memorable to me because it was the first time I ever laid eyes on General Washington and the parade was held on the campus of Harvard College where my brother Joshua was a student when the British killed him at Concord, just four months ago.

After the parade, Captains Morgan and Stephenson were invited for "refreshments" with the Commander-in-Chief and his staff. The rest of us in the two Virginia Rifle Companies were treated to a gill of diluted rum, which helped relieve any lingering angst Capt. Stephenson's Riflemen may have over Capt. Morgan's "early departure" from Virginia on July 14th.

This morning, two sharpshooters of Capt. Stephenson's Company killed two British officers as they were inspecting their Redcoat Regulars on Boston Neck. In the aftermath, ships of the British Fleet anchored around Boston fired at least 100 rounds of every possible artillery caliber toward our lines without inflicting a single casualty. Apparently, very few of the cannons aboard the British warships in the harbor can be elevated high enough to reach our position.

Roxbury Heights, overlooking Boston

Monday, August 28th, 1775

In the two weeks since our parade for General Washington, the additional Rifle Companies—two from Maryland and six from Pennsylvania—have arrived and been assigned to picket duty around Boston. The newer arrivals, apparently less disciplined than our Virginia Riflemen, have spent their first few days sniping at targets of opportunity—and each time a Redcoat falls, the British fleet anchored in the Boston Harbor responds with rarely effective cannon fire.

Capt. Morgan takes time every day to inspect the men and speak with each one, and I accompany him on these rounds. This morning, he walked up to one of our Riflemen who was busy constructing a gabion and asked, "How are you today, Private Kilgannon?"

"Well sir, I'm glad you asked. I thought I was coming on this expedition to fight the enemy. I've only fired my rifle once since leaving Virginia, but this is the twentieth wicker basket I've made since we arrived."

The Captain nodded, then replied: "The fighting will come soon enough. If the Redcoats sally forth from those ships down below and charge out of their garrison in Boston, when that basket you're weaving is full of rocks, it could save the life of a Patriot— maybe yours."

As we walked back to his tent he said, "Have Lt. Humphrey inform Adjutant General Gates's aide that I desire a meeting with the general."

Late this afternoon, Captain Morgan was informed General Gates would see him at 8 a.m. tomorrow.

Gen. Washington's Headquarters, Cambridge, Massachusetts
Tuesday, August 29th, 1775

As Capt. Morgan, Lt. Humphrey, and I were walking to Continental Army Headquarters this morning, one of Captain Stephenson's lieutenants informed us, "My Captain was supposed to go with you to a meeting with General Gates this morning. Unfortunately, Captain Stephenson has been taken to the hospital. The doctor believes he has Camp Fever[2] and has quarantined him and the four Riflemen who carried him there. Please keep them in your prayers."

We agreed to do so, but as soon as the messenger was out of earshot, Capt. Morgan turned to Lt. Humphrey and said, "I thought this meeting with General Gates was just for us, evidently Capt. Stephenson was invited, are there others?"

Lt. Humphrey said, "I don't know, sir."

"Now, regarding Capt. Stephenson's malady, I do not know how Camp Fever is transmitted. I have been told it could be by rats. But I do know many of our men have friends in Captain Stephenson's company. As soon as we get back to our encampment, tell all our officers and sergeants to quietly inform our Riflemen to stay away from Stephenson's troops and keep them out of our billeting area. And separately, issue an order that every Rifleman who brings Ensign Newman a rat killed by anything other than a rifle or pistol shall be issued an extra gill of rum."

At this, Lt. Humphrey replied, "Aye, sir. May we also let it be known to the men that effective immediately, Ensign Newman's nickname is officially changed from 'The Boy' to 'Rat Collector'?"

Even I laughed with them at the suggestion, but was gratified when Captain Morgan said, "No."

On arrival at Continental Army Headquarters, a large, attractive, three-story brick house once the home of a prosperous Loyalist, Major George Baylor—General Washington's aide—greeted us at the front door. He escorted us into a library to the left of the entry portal and said, "Please excuse me for a moment, I'll be right back."

Less than a minute later, Brigadier General Horatio Gates entered, shook Captain Morgan's hand, and said, "Captain, so good to see you again. Please come with me."

We followed him across the entry hallway and as we entered a large meeting room he said, "Your Excellency, gentlemen, please allow me to introduce Captain Daniel Morgan of Frederick County, Virginia. As has become his habit, he is the first to arrive for our meeting."

General Washington rose, as did the other three men at the far end of the table. The Commander-in-Chief held out his hand to our Captain, shook it, and said, "Daniel, thank you for joining me in another fight. Lord willing, this one will turn out better than when we served with General Braddock."

He then introduced the others, "This is Major General Charles Lee, Brigadier General Nathanael Greene, and Colonel Benedict Arnold. While we await the arrival of others, Captain Morgan please introduce your officers."

While Capt. Morgan was doing so, the process began all over again as seven other officers arrived. Colonel Arnold did the introductions:

"Lieutenant Colonel Christopher Greene of Rhode Island and his deputy, Major Timothy Bigelow of Massachusetts;

"Lieutenant Colonel Roger Enos of Vermont and his deputy, Major Return Meigs of Connecticut;

"Captains William Hendricks and Matthew Smith, commanding their Pennsylvania Rifle Companies, and Captain David Jones, commanding our artillery detachment."

The introductions complete, General Washington bade everyone to sit while he stood and spoke.

"Gentlemen, it's clear our British adversary in Boston is unwilling to emerge from behind their buttresses to confront us. Though they cannot break out, we cannot break in. Congress has therefore decided to end the stalemate by launching a campaign to Quebec in hopes of bringing Canada into this contest on our side."

At this he moved to uncover a map of the northern colonies tacked to an easel. Pointing to the map, he continued, "This is to be a two-pronged offensive, the primary force moving north from Albany, up Lake George and Lake Champlain to seize Montreal under the overall command of General Philip Schuyler. With Montreal secured, General Schuyler will proceed northeast to Quebec.

"A second force, commanded by newly promoted Colonel Benedict Arnold, consisting of ten infantry companies, three rifle companies, a light artillery detachment, and necessary logistics and medical support will depart here and proceed to the northern coast of Massachusetts where it will embark on vessels to a port in southern Maine. There, Colonel Arnold's men will disembark and proceed overland to the St. Lawrence River, opposite Quebec. The two Patriot forces, united under the command of General Schuyler, will then subdue the British garrison in Quebec, liberate the populace and, as Congress hopes, and Providence wills, succeed in encouraging our Canadian neighbors to become our allies.

"Since you are going to be taking more than a thousand men into harm's way, I order your particular attention to two very important matters.

"First, security is paramount as you prepare your men for this mission. What I have just shown you on this map and your ultimate destination may not be divulged to your men until you have arrived in the backwoods of Maine. If British spies learn of this plan, between now and your departure, their fleet could destroy this entire force at sea before it even begins.

"Second, you must strictly enforce my General Order prohibiting harm to any of the local population on your way to or in Canada. This includes any Indians you encounter. As you know, any of our soldiers charged with rape, looting, plundering, desertion, or harming any inhabitant who is not threatening our soldiers shall be immediately court martialed and if convicted, immediately sentenced to death by hanging. Do I make myself clear?"

There was an immediate chorus, "Yes, sir!"

"Very well. Colonel Arnold, I yield the remainder of this briefing to you."

At that, General Washington and his staff exited the room. We all stood as they departed but not a word was uttered until the door closed.

Colonel Arnold moved to the head of the table, sat, and motioned for us to do so. It was then I noticed General Nathanael Greene remained behind. He nodded and Arnold began, "You are all volunteers, that is, except for Captain Morgan and me. We are both commissioned officers in the Continental Army. But if any of you choose not to go on this expedition, speak now."

Everyone in the room knew of Benedict Arnold's well-publicized exploits in seizing Fort Ticonderoga in May. And I recalled having to bring one of my father's maps to Captain Morgan's home so a group of Virginians could see where Ticonderoga is. This morning, no one said a word about not accompanying the "The Hero of Ticonderoga" to Quebec.

Colonel Arnold continued, "Gentlemen, as of now, I plan to organize as follows: Captain Morgan will command a 250-man Advance Guard comprised of his Virginia Rifle Company and volunteers from the two Pennsylvania Rifle Companies commanded by Captains Hendricks and Smith.

"Lieutenant Colonel Greene and his deputy Major Bigelow will command our 1st Infantry Battalion, which will consist of three companies of one hundred Massachusetts volunteers each.

"Major Return Meigs will command our 2nd Infantry Battalion comprised of three, one-hundred-man companies of Vermont and Connecticut volunteers, and Captain Jones's artillery.

"Lieutenant Colonel Roger Enos of Vermont will command our Reserve and Rear Guard Force comprised of three, one hundred-man, New England infantry company volunteers and our teamsters, engineers, carpenters, pioneers, logistics support, and medical personnel.

"When we meet tomorrow, bring with you a roster of volunteers who have enlistments that do not expire until year end or later. Though you cannot tell the men our mission or objective, Quebec; you may tell them we are going to take the fight to the enemy, we shall return victorious and I will be their commander.

"We will meet again tomorrow morning at eight o'clock at the yellow house next door. Adjutant General Gates has generously allowed us to use it as our headquarters since we have a very short-term lease." The humor was missed. I immediately sought out my counterparts in the Pennsylvania Rifle Companies to get their rosters.

Colonel Benedict Arnold's Headquarters,
Cambridge, Massachusetts

Wednesday, August 30th, 1775

As everyone now knows to be Daniel Morgan's habit, the Captain, 1st Lt. Humphrey, and I arrived a half-hour early at the yellow house on "Tory Row" at 7:30 this morning. A young guard, armed with a musket and wearing leather shoes, white britches, a white vest, blue jacket, and a matching cocked hat[3] greeted us: "Halt! State your name and business."

"I am Captain Daniel Morgan, Commander of the Virginia Rifle Company. These are my officers. We're here to see Colonel Arnold."

"Stand where you are, sir. I will return in a moment."

The guard disappeared inside and just seconds later, came out the door followed by Col. Arnold and two other men; one very young, short, thin, and dressed in a Continental Army uniform and another; older, heavier, and garbed in what we Virginians would call "Williamsburg Finery."

In a grand gesture, the colonel said, "Gentlemen, this is Captain Daniel Morgan, Continental Line, a legendary hero of many frontier fights in Virginia and the commander of the Advance Guard on our upcoming expedition. Captain Morgan, please meet Lieutenant Aaron Burr and Mr. Reuben Colburn, an experienced and much admired boat builder from Maine. Both men are Patriots committed to the success of our mission. It's likely you will see a good bit more of each in the days ahead."

With that, Messer's Burr and Colburn said, "Good to meet you," while shaking our hands. They then saluted Colonel Arnold and departed. Colonel Arnold waved us to follow him into the house and we entered a room not much different than the one we were in yesterday.

Spread out on the large dining room table were maps, sea charts, and sheets of paper with lists of equipment, supplies, and sketches, which appeared to be fortifications. Colonel Arnold sat at the end of the table, motioned for us to do so as well and asked, "Captain Morgan, what brings you here a half-hour before the others?"

Though our Captain is six years older than Col. Arnold, our commander is usually deferential and polite to those who outrank him—particularly if the person with whom he is conversing is a commissioned officer of the Continental Line. Such was the case here this morning.

Capt. Morgan immediately responded, "Thank you for seeing us, Colonel. I, like you, want this mission to be a success. I want to help you in any way I can in planning this victory. The more I know now, the more helpful my Riflemen and I can be to you on this expedition."

"What is it you want to know?"

"Well, sir, if we were not about to embark together on what appears to me to be a very hazardous mission, I wouldn't ask this question since it would not be appropriate. If you do not mind, let's start with, who are the two gentlemen we just met?"

Col. Arnold nodded and replied, "There is no reason why you should not know this. General Washington introduced Mr. Colburn to me several weeks ago. He is, as I said, a boat-builder from Maine. He is familiar with the kind of boats we need to safely make the sea and river transit from Newburyport, Massachusetts, to Fort Western, and up the Kennebec River in Maine."

"Excuse me, sir," Captain Morgan interrupted. "Can you show me the route on one of your maps or charts so we all have a sense for the distance and time it will take?"

"Certainly," the colonel said, as he pulled out a naval chart and a terrain map labeled:

Samuel Goodwin copy (with Corrections) of Lt. John Montresor's
1760-61

MAP of the SOURCES of the

Chaudiere, Penobscot & Kennebek

RIVERS

Col. Arnold continued, "I am assured this naval chart is very accurate since it is used by Patriot smugglers to evade British

Revenue Cutters. The route we will be taking from Newburyport to the mouth of the Kennebec River is about seventy-five miles. According to Mr. Colburn, with favorable winds and tides we should get upriver to Gardinerston in another forty-eight hours."

Turning to the terrain map, he continued, "From Gardinerston to Fort Western, to the south shore of the St. Lawrence opposite Quebec, we will follow the route I have sketched on this map provided by Mr. Samuel Goodwin, a friend of Mr. Colburn's. Goodwin estimates it's about 200 miles. I'm planning about twenty days to traverse the entire route—about ten miles per day."

"We will use shallow-draft batteaux[4] to transport our heavy equipment and supplies up the Kennebec, portage across the 'Height of Land,' to Lake Mégantic, and proceed downstream on the Chaudière to the St. Lawrence, directly across from Quebec."

At this point, Captain Morgan said, "Sir, all this begs the question, when will we depart here? Winter is coming soon in these latitudes."

Colonel Arnold nodded, paused, and said quietly, "I do not yet know our departure date. General Washington is waiting to hear from General Schuyler. All I have is this"—he handed Capt. Morgan a tiny piece of paper and an opened "Courier Ball."[5]

"This was delivered to me late last night, by an Express Messenger from Albany. I opened the Courier Ball—thankfully he had not needed to swallow it—but I do not know this code."

Captain Morgan looked at the tiny piece of paper:

THE EIGHTH MONTH OF THE YEAR OF OUR LORD, 1775

1T 3A 5T 3U 4A 5T 4U 3G 5T 2A 4S 5T

4A 1G 2U 4G 5A 2T 1S 3T 5T 1A 3U 3U 3T 3G 4U 1S 4A 5T

3U 2T 1A 3U 5T 1U 4G 4U 5T 2G 4A 5T 4U 3G 3G 5T

2G 2T 2T 5T 4U 3G 5T 4U 3T 1A 4U 1S 2T 5G

3A 3G 3U 4U 2A 3G 3A 1S 3T 5A 5T 4U 3G 5T

1G 3G 3A 3A 1A 3U 1U 5G

Then he said, "This is what we call a 'calendar code.' The key is the first line. The eighth month of the year is August. Our Committees of Safety have been using these codes for more than a year—too long in my estimation. Here's how this one works." With Col. Arnold looking over his shoulder, Capt. Morgan took a blank sheet of paper and explained:

"To create an 'August code,' write the letters of the month across the top line and beneath each letter of the month, place sequential letters of the alphabet like this, five rows and six columns. A number and a letter represent each letter of the coded message. So, the first letter of the message, 1T is F. The second letter, 3A is M. The third entry, 5T is a space. 3U is P, 4A is S, and so on . . .

	A	U	G	U	S	T
1	A	B	C	D	E	F
2	G	H	I	J	K	L
3	M	N	O	P	Q	R
4	S	T	U	V	W	X
5	Y	Z	.	?	,	■

"Now, see how quickly young Nathanael can decrypt this message." I began to write . . .

FM PS TO GW [from Philip Schuyler to George Washington?]

SCHUYLER APPROVES

PLAN BUT IS TOO

ILL TO TRAVEL.

MONTGOMERY TO

COMMAND.

As I was decoding the message, Col. Arnold asked, "Captain, why do you say the Committees of Safety have been using this type of code too long?"

"Well, sir, first, the British are better than we are at code-making and breaking. You may recall it was the intercept of a coded French message that alerted General Forbes about the deplorable conditions at Fort Duquesne in November of '58. The French code was broken by the British nearly a year earlier, but the French were still using it. That's why Forbes pressed on, despite Col. Washington's advice, and the French garrison burned Fort Duquesne and fled.

"Second, our 'calendar codes' are simple to use. They can be encrypted and decrypted quickly and neither the sender nor recipient needs a codebook. Unfortunately, six of the 'month codes' have repeat letters like August's two U's. December is impossible with three E letters. 'daily codes' are somewhat better because they change every twenty-four hours but 'Wednesday' with two letters 'D' and 'E' is impossible. Given how many of these 'calendar coded' messages have been dispatched by our various Committees over the last two years, I have to believe the British can break them as fast as my young Adjutant."

As Captain Morgan finished, I handed the decoded message to him. He quickly read it and handed it to Colonel Arnold, saying, "If I may be so bold, sir, it seems this message—and the silver 'Courier Ball' in which it was delivered to you—belong next door in General Washington's Headquarters, where we met yesterday."

Colonel Arnold, looked at it, nodded his head, and said, "Captain Morgan, you are correct. If the other commanders arrive while I am gone, please inform them I shall return in short order." With that, he hastened out the door leaving the three of us alone in the room.

As soon as he departed, our Captain said, "Nathanael, I want you to write a letter today to your father, care of Rev. Thruston. Do not reveal where we are going. Ask your dad if he recalls the name of the British officer who caused me to be flogged while your father and I were on the ill-fated Braddock expedition in the summer of '55. Not the officer I struck. He couldn't speak for his broken jaw, but the engineer officer who testified falsely at my court martial. If memory serves me right, his name was Ensign John Montresor."

"The same name that's on Colonel Arnold's map?"

"Yes. And if it's not just the same name, but the same man, the scars on my back tell the tale of his perfidy. If that man had anything to do with the map that's supposed to guide us through the Maine wilderness to Quebec, we better pray now for our Lord to do for us what He did for Moses: send us a pillar of cloud to guide us by day and a pillar of fire to guide us at night."[6]

At that point, Col. Arnold re-entered the room and said, "Thank you, Captain Morgan, for your advice on the encrypted message. Adjutant General Gates is most grateful and said he will immediately deliver the message and your Adjutant's translation to General Washington.

"While we await the arrival of our fellow commanders of this expedition, let me ask, Captain Morgan, how is it you know all these things?"

Our Captain shrugged and replied, "I do not know 'how,' sir. All I do know is our Good Lord has blessed me with 'situational awareness'—the ability to realize what is happening around me and granted me the wisdom and experience to determine what needs to be done about it. That's what has kept my Riflemen and me alive in some very challenging circumstances.

"Second, I have learned to keep company with the right kind of people. I now expect—as I did not when I was younger— those with whom I associate to admonish me when I need it, encourage me when I do what's right, and hold me accountable if I fail to do my duty. I never ask others to do that which I cannot do. If we need a 'Forlorn Hope,' I will lead it and be in front of all the rest."

"So Captain, you now know more about our mission to Quebec than any of the others will know until we get to Maine. What does your situational awareness—and all your experience—tell you about our upcoming expedition?"

Our Captain looked him straight in the eye and said, "Colonel, the sooner we leave here for Quebec, the better. The days are getting shorter. The nights are getting longer. And most assuredly, the days and nights ahead will get much, much colder."

Their conversation was abbreviated by the arrival of the seven commanders and four other men who were not at yesterday's meeting. Lt. Humphrey and I retired to the outer row of chairs while the Lieutenant Colonels, Majors, Captain Jones, and the four strangers took seats at the table with Col. Arnold and Captain Morgan.

The colonel began by introducing the four strangers: Capt. Christian Febiger, his Adjutant; Capt. Benjamin Catlin the expedition's quartermaster; Dr. Isaac Senter, our physician; and Rev. Samuel Spring, our Chaplain.

He then directed all attendees to give his Adjutant the rosters of their respective units, insisting, "Every name on your list must be a volunteer who has either had smallpox or been inoculated within the last twelve months and have an enlistment that expires at year end or later or they cannot go with us."

I gave our roster of the "Advance Guard," which included all 100 of Capt. Morgan's Virginia Rifle Company, names from the two Pennsylvania Rifle Companies and a handful from Capt. Stephenson's Virginia Rifle Company—268 names in all—to Capt. Febiger. I watched as he began to assemble a stack of different-sized pieces of paper and whispered to him, "Sir, if you need any help with this, let me know and I will do so."

Col. Arnold adjourned the meeting shortly thereafter with the command: "Each one of you, post a reliable, trusted aide or messenger here at our headquarters, by three o'clock this afternoon so

I can notify you quickly of any new orders from General Washington. Have your messengers report here to Capt. Febiger and he will billet them in tents behind this building where there is a 'latrine.'

"They need not bring water or victuals. We will feed them two good meals a day and we have 'good water.' Unless I inform you otherwise, we will meet here again at eight o'clock, Sunday morning, September 3rd."

After conferring quickly with Capt. Morgan and Lt. Humphrey, I stayed behind to help Capt. Febiger assemble the rosters. By noon we had compiled an alphabetical list for every unit in the expedition, a total of 1,373 names.

Among the four units: Advance Guard, 1st Infantry Battalion, 2nd Infantry Battalion, and Rear Guard, there were 169 duplications —meaning at least that many men volunteered to serve under different commanders at least twice—some, three times!

By dark, thanks to the messengers who arrived at Col. Arnold's Headquarters as ordered, we winnowed the roster to 1,207 men. Or so we thought.

ENDNOTES

1.   During the American Revolution, abatis, fascines, and gabions were used by both sides as hasty, defensive field fortifications. An abatis is an obstacle consisting of tree branches laid in a row with sharpened tips facing outwards toward an expected enemy approach. Fascines are rolled bundles of generally straight trunks of small trees which could be rolled into place providing defensive cover and shoring for trenches, revetments, and ramparts. Gabions of the day were cylindrical, wicker-type wooden baskets open at both ends. Turned upright, they are filled with hand-dug earth and/or stones and used to protect defenders from enemy fire.

2.   "Camp Fever," now known to be typhus, is a highly contagious bacterial disease transmitted by lice, fleas, and human contact. Symptoms include severe headache, a sustained high fever,

cough, rash, severe muscle pain, chills, stupor, delirium, and death. Colonial-era doctors often mistook the onset of the rash as smallpox. The disease is treated today with antibiotics. In the 1770s the patient was bled, given water-diluted compounds containing ground dogwood and mustard, sassafras tea, and a lotion made from tulip poplar leaves.

3.   The "cocked hat," became a favorite in the Continental Army because it was the kind of head covering most often seen on General George Washington in the field and during battles. By early in the 19th century, this style of headwear was often described as a "tricorn hat" since its most distinguishing characteristic was having all three sides of the brim turned up (cocked) and either pinned, laced, or buttoned in place to form a triangle around the crown.

4.   "Batteaux" [the plural of "batteau," spellings extant in the late 18th century] of low freeboard, flat-bottomed, double-ended, shallow-draft boats used for ferrying freight and/or passengers on the interior waterways of North America. The size [length and beam] of the craft varied from 20 to 50 feet long and 3 to 6 feet wide depending on the nature of the water [calm or rapids] to be traversed.

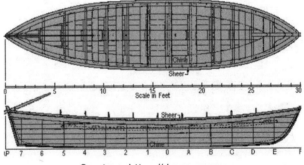

Courtesy: https://dmna.ny.gov

5.   "Courier Balls" were small, hollow, threaded silver balls, usually less than ½ inch in diameter, carefully crafted to be separated at the center and inside which, very brief messages could be enclosed.

During the American Revolution, both sides used these devices to transmit very sensitive intelligence, orders, and reports. If a courier, messenger, or spy was intercepted by the enemy, he was instructed to "swallow the ball." By 1775, Express Messengers and Trusted Couriers could only pray their feces would not reveal a silver container if they were captured. The penalty was death by hanging.

6.   Morgan was referring to Exodus 13:21. In the King James Bible of the day, the verse reads, "And the LORD went before them by day in a pillar of a cloud, to lead them the way; and by night in a pillar of fire, to give them light; to go by day and night."

CHAPTER NINE

1775: THE ORDER IS GIVEN

Colonel Benedict Arnold's Headquarters,
Cambridge, Massachusetts

Saturday, September 2nd, 1775

We have spent nearly every waking minute since the meetings on
Wednesday, preparing for what everyone in the Patriot forces
surrounding Boston now call "The Arnold Expedition to Canada."
So much for security. If the British don't know about what we're
up to, they must all be blind, and most certainly, deaf.

Both our wagons are now packed with all the powder, shot,
and lead sheets we brought from Virginia, plus locally acquired
barrels of salted beef, pork, fish, corn, beans, salt, flour, coffee,
several baskets of oranges, lemons and limes, a farrier forge,
charcoal, medical equipment and supplies, cold weather clothing,
canvas for tentage, candles, lanterns, fuel, heavy carpenter and
engineer tools, my meticulously stocked field desk, and seventeen
half-barrels of rum.

At 8:00 this morning we were informed Col. Arnold has called
a "Commanders Meeting" for 11:00 a.m. at his headquarters. As

usual, Captain Morgan, Lt. Humphrey, and I arrived a half hour early.

Capt. Febiger, Col. Arnold's Adjutant, saw us coming and greeted us at the door before the sentry could detain us. He waved us into the house saying with a great smile, "Welcome, Virginians! Good news. We have our orders. The Colonel is next door making final arrangements."

He escorted us into the dining room and offered us coffee and tea and a small, flat, circular confection he called a "pancake." It was coated with a sweet liquid he described to be "maple syrup." I had never eaten anything quite so delicious and proceeded to devour three of them before Lt. Humphrey scowled when I reached for a fourth.

As we waited for others to arrive, our Captain asked Colonel Arnold's Adjutant, "Can you tell us when we're leaving here for Maine?"

Capt. Febiger's response was both direct and diplomatic, "Colonel Arnold deserves that privilege, sir. And in truth, we do not know for certain our departure date since much depends on British sea-borne patrols, tides, winds, and ship availability to transport us from Newburyport to Gardinerston, Maine, where we shall disembark from sea-going transports to batteaux for transport further up the Kennebec River."

At this point the door opened and in trooped Colonel Arnold, our fellow "Arnold Expedition Commanders," and the remainder of Colonel Arnold's staff. We all rose immediately and remained so as Colonel Arnold said, "Chaplain Spring, let's begin with a prayer."

The Reverend responded immediately: "Almighty God— Father, Son, and Holy Spirit—we bow down before You and no other. We beg You to bless our endeavor, protect us in carrying out our mission, and pray You will deliver us from harm and return us to our families. Amen."

Col. Arnold, said, "Take your seats, gentlemen," and as soon as we did, he stated, "General Washington has ordered us to depart here on Monday, the 11th of September and proceed to a Massachusetts seaport where we will board vessels to commence offensive operations against the forces of Great Britain."

There was an immediate shout, "Huzzah!" Those at the table slapped it with their palms while those of us seated against the wall applauded as though we had just heard a great oration.

The colonel held up his hand to stop the celebration and there was immediate silence as he resumed more quietly, "All of us— you and your men—are about to make history. We are part of the first offensive operation conducted by the new Continental Army. We will be taking the fight to our oppressors, the most powerful army and navy on earth. It is important you impress upon our men how important this mission is to them, their families, and to our freedom."

After a long pause he continued, "When we leave Cambridge, every man is to carry on his person, five days of rations and sufficient powder and shot for fifty discharges of his rifle, musket, or pistol. A special allocation of powder, shot, and flints for our units will be made at this headquarters one week from today, Saturday, the 9th of September, beginning at eight o'clock in the morning. Units will report on the following schedule:

"Advance Force: Eight o'clock to nine thirty.

"1st Battalion: Nine thirty to eleven o'clock.

"2nd Battalion: Eleven o'clock to twelve thirty.

"Rear Guard: Twelve thirty to two o'clock.

"All your soldiers will bring with them all of their equipment. After drawing fresh ammunition, we will establish a temporary tent-bivouac, with your units intact, in a field one mile east of here so we will all be together after we draw ammunition and are ready to deploy. No one will be allowed to return to where you are now billeted.

"When you return from this meeting, in addition to what I have just said, tell your men the following:

"First, we will likely be at sea less than three days.

"Second, the smallpox epidemic now sweeping through Boston and several other communities near here has not yet infected the port where we will embark. But on the way to our ships, we will pass through several places that are quarantined. Officers and sergeants must insist our soldiers avoid any contact with residents of these neighborhoods.

"In the days ahead, I shall provide additional information as it becomes available. Unless I direct otherwise, the order of movement to our port of embarkation will be in the same sequence as we draw ammunition next Saturday. Are there any questions?"

There were some, mostly, very practical.

"Will there be sanitary facilities at our new bivouac here in Cambridge?" Answer, "Yes. Each of our four units will dig one. Make sure they are downhill and downwind."

"Whenever we get new powder and shot, our officers and men always test fire their rifles, muskets, and pistols. Given the General Order against wasting ammunition, will this be allowed?" Answer, "Good question. I will try to make it so and let you know?"

"Many of our men are farmers, watermen, merchants, storekeepers, clerks, and laborers from this area. Will they be allowed time between now and departure to say 'good-bye' to their families?" Answer, "Each unit Adjutant, give Captain Febiger a list of names of those so affected and I will try to make that happen."

And this question from Major Return J. Meigs, "No one in my Battalion has ever been where I suppose we are going. Will we commanders be issued maps?" Answer—after a long pause, "I will do my best to make that happen."

On our way out the door, Capt. Febiger took me aside and said, "Nathanael, I may have the answer to the map question, but I will need your help. Do you mind if I ask Captain Morgan if he will make you available?"

"No, sir."

As we all exited the room, I noticed Capt. Febiger was circled with Col. Arnold, Capt. Morgan, and 1st Lt. Humphrey. When our commander and his deputy came outside and we began walking back to our bivouac, Capt. Morgan began, "Nathanael, you recall some days back when your friend William here, suggested your nickname should become, 'Rat Collector'?"

"Yes, sir, and I am most grateful you rejected Lt. Humphrey's ill-advised, mean-spirited suggestion—since as you both know, I shoot better than he."

They both laughed at my light-hearted riposte and the Captain said, "Well, based on the last meeting, William now wants your new nickname to be 'Map Maker.'

"Sir?"

Lt. Humphrey interjected: "Colonel Arnold's Adjutant claims your help was very important to getting the rosters for this expedition straightened out. He says your handwriting is better than anyone's in this organization—though he has yet to see mine. Now Captain Febiger wants you to help make copies of the only map we have for our overland course through Maine to Quebec."

"Is this the map about which I wrote to my father?"

"Yes," said Capt. Morgan. "The map may not be accurate, but it's the only one we have. I and the other commanders have urged that we and our deputies, like William, need copies.

"Why this fellow Colburn didn't arrange for this with his pal Goodwin is beyond me, but if you can work with Captain Febiger to make copies of that map, it may prove very helpful to me and our Virginia Riflemen since we are to be the vanguard for this entire expedition through the wilderness."

"Sir, I am here to serve you and, as you direct, my friend 1st Lt. Humphrey. I will do whatever you order—but I would ask, in spite of William's suggestion, I now be entitled to the nickname, 'Virginia Rifle Cartographer.' When do I start?"

"Now, Ensign Newman," replied a grinning Capt. Morgan. "Report to Colonel Arnold's Adjutant, Captain Christian Febiger as the 'Chief Cartographer of Virginia's Riflemen.' And when you are finished, bring me the best two copies of the maps you make."

"Aye, sir," I said with a smile and a salute as I turned about and headed back to Colonel Arnold's headquarters.

Arnold Expedition Bivouac,
Cambridge, Massachusetts

Saturday, September 9th, 1775

As directed, the movement of all our units to draw fresh powder, lead shot, waxed patches, and establish new bivouacs this morning actually went flawlessly. Well before dark all our Advance Force was together in two-man shelters, latrines were dug, and watches were set.

Best of all, I am back to being Adjutant for Capt. Morgan's Rifle Company and the Advance Party.

For nearly every sunlit moment of the past week, Capt. Hans Christian Febiger and I sat wherever the light was best, tracing copies of a map no one believed to be accurate. In a drawer of the Tory house being used as Col. Arnold's headquarters, Capt. Febiger found fifteen sheets of remarkably thin, almost transparent foolscap and two magnificent silver bodied, gold-nibbed pens.

Over the course of the week, as we dipped our pens and blotted every mark we made on each copy of the map, I learned Hans Christian Febiger was born on an island off the coast of Denmark in 1749, lived for a time on St. Croix, an island in the Caribbean where his uncle was a Danish government official, and came to Massachusetts in 1772.

As our week wore on, he told me how he joined the Sons of Liberty and Mr. Samuel Adams's Committee of Safety with some Harvard College students in 1774. When I asked if he knew my brother, he answered, "No, but we all knew of him being among the forty-nine killed by the Redcoat bastards on April 19th."

He also shared, "The fight at Lexington and Concord was what motivated me to join the Massachusetts Militia just a few days later. I volunteered to join Lieutenant Colonel Arnold's expedition to Ticonderoga but on Monday, May 1st, two days before he and his volunteers left to cross the Berkshires for Ticonderoga and link-up with Ethan Allen and his Green Mountain Boys, a British patrol caught my militia unit fortifying Patriot houses and barricading streets in Charlestown. A Redcoat bayonet wounded me in my left calf and I was prevented from accompanying Colonel Arnold to Ticonderoga.

"On June 17th, when the British decided to break out of Boston, I was still on Charlestown Peninsula, on the southeastern slope of Bunker's Hill, serving as Adjutant for Militia Col. Samuel Gerrish, commander of the 25th Massachusetts Militia Regiment—who revealed himself to be a less than bold leader.

"As the Naval bombardment increased and the Royal Marines and British infantry started coming ashore, Col. Gerrish sent me forward with a company of fifty men to the southwestern slopes of Breed's Hill to discern whether the two companies of Massachusetts Militia—one from the 9th Regiment and the other from the 24th—would be able to protect the only six Patriot artillery field pieces on that side of the Charlestown peninsula.

"We took up positions to the left of Captain Nutting's Company from the Massachusetts 9th. The Patriot artillery pieces were less than fifty yards to our left—and what is now known as 'Warren's Redoubt' was less than 100 yards left of the artillery—which the British did everything in their power to destroy—and finally succeeded, only because we ran out of ammunition."

"Is this the same 'Doctor Warren,' the medical teacher at Harvard, who was actually a Brigadier General, but who fought as a common soldier?" I asked.

"Yes. I saw him fall," Capt. Febiger replied. "The British assaulted our positions on the southeast side of Breed's Hill, twice in the space of two hours. But when they came at us the third time, we had no powder or shot remaining. Dr. Warren's bravery that afternoon—and that of my men—is something I will never forget. The Redcoats not only had ammunition, they had bayonets. We had neither."

"What did you do?"

"I led my thirty-five survivors back to our original position on the southeast side of Bunker's Hill. But by the time we got there, Colonel Gerrish had run . . . I'm sorry, he retreated.

"Before nightfall I led what was left of my little company to positions with the remnants of General Putnam's Connecticut militia and Colonel Prescott's Massachusetts men to keep the British from crossing Charlestown Neck and reaching any further onto the mainland.

"By dark we were re-supplied with powder, shot, and water. On Breed's Hill, I lost six killed in action, eight wounded, and one taken prisoner who died of wounds. My little company had no further contact with the enemy. But no one deserted."

"How did you end up as Adjutant for Colonel Arnold?"

"He knew I volunteered for his Ticonderoga expedition back in May. He heard stories from others about what happened at Breed's and Bunker's Hill and sought me out."

This afternoon, as I made my way to our new "Advance Party Bivouac Area," I brought with me three things for Capt. Morgan.

First, the background on Colonel Arnold's Adjutant, Captain Hans Christian Febiger; and his humble description of his own, experience, and courage.

Second, Capt. Febiger's and my conclusion—the Montresor/ Goodwin map we faithfully copied—was hopelessly inaccurate. The scale, routing, and obstacles depicted simply could not match the estimated "200-mile River & Overland" route forecast in Good-win's notes. We estimated it might even be twice that distance.

Third, as directed, I brought with me the two best tracings of the original map, "Certified by Capt. H. C. Febiger as, 'A True Copy of The Original, however inaccurate map, as Prepared by The Virginia Rifle Company Chief Cartographer, Ensign Nathanael Newman.'"

Colonel Arnold's Headquarters,
Cambridge, Massachusetts

Sunday, September 10th, 1775

At 8:00 this morning, Rev. Spring, the Expedition Chaplain, held a prayer service in the center of the encampment. To my surprise, more than half the members of the Expeditionary Force attended. It lasted a little over a half hour and he focused on the courage of Paul in Acts of the Apostles, chapters 22 and 23 of the New Testament—ending with two words from Acts 23:11— "Take Courage!"

To which the crowd responded with a loud, "Amen!" And then, "Huzzah!"

Capt. Morgan, 1st Lt. Humphrey, and I were on our way back to our part of the perimeter when a young messenger, attired in the blue jacket and white leggin's of the Continental Army, caught up to us and announced, "Sirs, Adjutant General Gates asks that you gentlemen join him immediately for a brief meeting at Col. Arnold's Headquarters next door to General Washington's."

Once again, Capt. Febiger welcomed us and escorted us into the dining room where General Gates was seated next to Col. Arnold. Both men rose and the Adjutant General motioned for us to take seats and began, "Thank you for coming on such short notice. There are three matters that precipitated this meeting.

"First. His Excellency, General Washington, has instructed me to remind all the commanders and Adjutants that this first offensive against our enemy is a historic event and it's every Adjutant's duty to carefully document all orders received and given, to maintain a precise record of all personnel, an accurate chronology of events, and the names of all persons—friendly and enemy—killed, wounded, too sick for duty, missing in action, or taken prisoner. He also wants a careful record of all interactions with members of the local populace whether American, British, French, or Indian. Colonel Arnold and I will conduct this briefing this evening.

"Second. Several weeks ago, His Excellency and I met with an Abenaki tribal chieftain who assured us the French-Canadian population and most of the Canadian Indians—not Mohawks, who are allied with the British—will support our endeavor or at least not act against us.

"Early this morning, this same chief unexpectedly arrived here with four young Abenaki Indian braves who have volunteered to serve as scouts and guides for the expedition. They all speak some French and one of them is almost fluent in English. Colonel Arnold has agreed to have them accompany the force. Captain Morgan, if you agree, three of them will be assigned to your Advance Force."

"That's fine with me," our commander replied, "but I would like to have General Washington's orders on what kind of disciplinary measures I am allowed to use if we have problems. . . ."

"Of course," General Gates replied. "You will have those instructions in writing before you depart for Newburyport in the morning."

"Thank you, sir."

"Now," the General continued, "There's one final matter. His Excellency is very concerned the British may already be aware of our plans. If so, the British fleet may try to blockade Newburyport—or worse yet—intercept the ships required to transport the expedition to Maine—on the way into the port or even more devastating—attack the fully loaded transports with more than a thousand brave Patriot volunteers and all their supplies aboard.

"He has directed Colonel Arnold to dispatch a small reconnaissance party to Newburyport within the next three hours. I will let our Expeditionary Force Commander explain."

Col. Arnold got straight to the point, looking directly at Capt. Morgan. "Daniel, I want my Adjutant, Captain Febiger and yours, Ensign Newman, accompanied by six mounted Patriot Dragoons, to ride immediately to Newburyport and ascertain whether there is adequate shipping available for us to start moving from here to the port.

"If all is ready, we will be able to carry out our plan. Your Advance Force will depart here tomorrow and the entire expedition will be embarked in Newburyport by Saturday, September 16th and set sail that night.

"The gentleman in Newburyport who has been arranging for our shipping is Mr. Nathanael Tracy, the Chairman of the secret Sons of Liberty Committee in Newburyport. I know him well, but I have not heard from him for three days, creating great uncertainty for there are many Tory sympathizers in the area.

"What is certain are the falsehoods being spread by Tory Loyalists in the area. One is that the British fleet is planning an ambush as we sail for Maine. The second 'rumor' is that Patriot sea captains already tied up or anchored at Newburyport will not get paid to carry out their mission of transporting our expedition to Maine. That may be why many of the vessels we need have apparently not shown up there.

"To counter these lies, I am prepared to send in the saddlebags of both Adjutants, Febiger and Newman, hard currency—not paper—British pounds sterling and Spanish dollars—my own money, sufficient for half-payment of the promised fee for transporting our expedition from Newburyport to Gardinerston, Maine."

Turning to Captain Morgan, he said, "I know your Adjutant, Ensign Newman, is responsible for mustering your entire Advance Force. Can you spare him to accompany Captain Febiger on this mission?"

Capt. Morgan looked at 1st Lt. Humphrey who said, "We know the Riflemen in our company well. If Nathanael gives me a copy of the muster rolls for Captain Stephenson's company and the two Pennsylvania rifle companies along with the names of the three Abenaki Indians who will be joining us, I will get an 'All present or accounted for' report from each commander. We can make this work, sir."

At that, it was decided. Capt. Febiger and I—accompanied by six Continental horsemen—were ordered to proceed post-haste to Newburyport with 1,000£ in sterling silver coins and 1,500 Spanish silver dollars. Once there, we were to immediately find Mr. Nathanael Tracy, and start handing out "half-pay" to every Patriot merchant captain who signed on to transport the Expedition to Maine. Finally, we were directed to send a messenger back to Colonel Arnold with a daily report on developments.

That's why I was absent from the new Cambridge encampment on Monday morning—and why we didn't find out we had two extra "Riflemen" in our Advance Force until we arrived in Maine.

Newburyport, Massachusetts

Monday, September 11th, 1775

Sergeant Steven Cady, the man Adjutant General Gates placed in charge of our Armed Escort is a very big man built much like Capt. Morgan. Atop a bay stallion of at least seventeen hands, he and five well-mounted dragoons rode into our encampment precisely at 12:30 Sunday afternoon.

Each dragoon was armed with a British "Brown Bess" musket, a bayonet, a pistol, and a sabre. They were all attired in what was fast becoming—at least in Cambridge—the Continental Army uniform: a dark blue cocked hat, a matching blue wool jacket over a white shirt or vest, light tan trousers and—for these horse-back soldiers—polished riding boots.

I wore the same "uniform" of all our Riflemen—a homespun linen hunting shirt, deerskin leather trimmed linen leggin's leather half-boots, and a deerskin cap. I had my long rifle, hatchet, hunting knife, powder horn, cartridge box, and a water bag instead of a canteen. In my back-pack I carried my "mess kit," three tins of salted beef, a small lantern, a tin of lamp oil, three candles, twenty wax tapers a flint, steel, and tinder fire-starter kit, a traveling inkwell, a leather-bound journal, my dead brother's cloak—and the gold-tipped pen Capt. Febiger gave me after we finished tracing the notoriously wrong maps.

To my surprise, Col. Arnold's Adjutant was dressed like me. He admitted to cajoling 1st Lt. Humphrey into raiding one of our supply wagons for the gear that made him look like one of our Virginia Riflemen. To properly equip Capt. Febiger with a hatchet, knife, and rifle with all its accouterments, William convinced his counterpart in Capt. Stephenson's Virginia Rifle Company to "loan" him the weapons of one of their company mates who died of Camp Fever.

Sgt. Cady and his five Continental Dragoons brought with them three additional steeds—two good-looking, obviously fit geldings for Capt. Febiger and me, and a "spare mare" carrying the heavy leather saddlebags full of British and Spanish coins. We were underway a half hour later and covered the thirty or so miles to Newburyport well before sunset.

We rode most of the way, with Sgt. Cady leading—at a steady posting trot. It was instantly obvious to all eight of us—and our mounts—we were very comfortable at this gait for long distances. Our only delay was finding a decent ford across a fast-flowing tributary just south of the Merrimac River.

Only twice did we canter—through Medford and Danvers—both places where quarantine signs warned of smallpox. As we entered Ipswich, a militia guard warned the community was enduring "an epidemic of The Pox, and Yellowing Fever." It was the only time we galloped on the trip.

On arrival in Newburyport, Sgt. Cady led us directly to the very attractive home of Mr. Nathanael Tracy where we discovered why Col. Arnold has not heard from Mr. Tracy for three days. His wife explained, "This is the fourth day he has been suffering from a terrible case of gout. He has taken to bed and is medicating himself with large doses of rum and laudanum."

"Laudanum," Sgt. Cady said shaking his head, "where did he get that?"

"I never asked," she replied with a shrug, "but it probably came from Mr. Arnold's apothecary when it was open here. My husband used to manage it for Mr. Benedict."

"Madam, is your husband awake?" asked Captain Febiger.

"Barely."

"May I speak with him?"

"You are welcome to try. Come, follow me upstairs."

They were gone less than three minutes. When Captain Febiger returned, he said, "Sgt. Cady, please escort us to the waterfront. We are looking for the sloop *Machias Liberty*, mastered by Captain Jeremiah O'Brien. We need to speak to him before dark."

It took us fewer than five minutes to find the ship. She was tied up closest to the tavern at the foot of the wharf.

Mr. O'Brien invited Capt. Febiger and me aboard, and I carried the two heavy saddlebags over my shoulders to the Captain's cabin. In less than fifteen minutes, we were countering British concocted falsehoods about the Continental Army being unable to pay for transporting the expedition to Maine.

In short order, Mr. O'Brien summoned one of his mates to arrange stabling for the horses, billeting for the dragoons, and lodging at the Wolfe Tavern for Captain Febiger and me, saying, "It's the best place in this port and we will put all this on Nathanael Tracy's tab. He can afford it."

As we prepared to depart, he said, "I told my first mate to procure a fresh mount for one of your dragoons to carry a message to Colonel Arnold so he will not be concerned about not having enough vessels."

Capt. Febiger had me use the gold-nib pen to write in very fine print on the corner of a sheet of paper:

COL A. PROCEED AS PLANNED.
SHIPPING ARRIVING. NO BRITS.
FEBIGER & NEWMAN SEND

After blotting the note and waving it to dry, he used a pen-knife to trim all the margins off the note, rolled it tightly, reached into his pocket, pulled out a silver "courier ball," unscrewed it, pressed the note inside and screwed the halves together. Mr. O'Brien watched all this and said, "Hope your messenger doesn't have to eat that."

"Come here to see me at eight in the morning and I will let you know how we're going to get this to work. Now, let's take care of your men."

As we disembarked from *Machias Liberty*, Captain Febiger handed the little silver ball to Sgt. Cady, saying, "Send your best night rider who knows what to do with this, back to Colonel Arnold tonight.

"There is a waning three-quarter moon and a clear sky, so he should be able to make it to Colonel Arnold's headquarters before dawn. But remind him of two important matters.

"First, the Advance Force is scheduled to depart Cambridge for here on Monday morning. Since Captain Daniel Morgan is leading it, it's entirely possible they may be underway at one minute past midnight. Riding toward a contingent of 250 Riflemen in the middle of the night could be a life-threatening experience.

"Second, if your dragoon does encounter the Advance Force, be sure to have him inform their vanguard about the ford we used to cross that stream flowing into the Merrimac. It will save them some time.

"Captain O'Brien has made arrangements for those of us staying here. He will brief you. You and your four remaining men rest well. Ensign Newman and I will meet you here in the morning at 7:45."

On Monday morning as we walked to the pier from Wolfe's Tavern, toting our backpacks, rifles, and the saddlebags full of British and Spanish coins, the air was as cool and clear as we could wish. The harbor was pristine—and not a single British warship was in sight.

As we turned the corner toward *Machias Liberty*'s berth, we could see the five dragoons, standing beside their mounts and a crowd of a dozen or so sailors and dockworkers gathered around them, plying them with fresh baked biscuits, coffee, tea, and questions.

Sgt. Cady, seeing us approaching, detached himself from the crowd and said, "Gentlemen, Captain O'Brien suggests the first thing we should do this morning is reconnoiter where we're going to bivouac the Expedition outside of town. He has arranged with Mr. Nathanael Tracy for us to be accompanied by his Sons of Liberty deputy. He will be here on horseback in a few minutes.

"Captain O'Brien has offered to safeguard the saddlebags and coins in his cabin aboard the sloop and have one of my men stand guard over it. The other four of us will accompany you."

Thankfully, Capt. Febiger agreed, and I went aboard the vessel with one of the dragoons and deposited the saddlebags, with fresh wax seals over each pocket, in Capt. O'Brien's cabin.

As I headed back on deck, Captains Febiger and O'Brien were coming up the gangway with a third gentleman who introduced himself as Anthony Davenport, Deputy Chairman of the secret Newburyport Sons of Liberty Committee.

We spent the next four hours riding around farmland outside the port, looking for a suitable bivouac site for a thousand or so soldiers. Several of those we saw had what we needed—level ground, sufficient space for tentage in a perimeter, good water, and room for sanitary facilities—but Mr. Davenport waved us off those properties because they are owned by Tory sympathizers.

Finally, about a mile west of the port, not far off the north-south post road, he took us to just what we needed and declared, "If this works for you, it will work for all. The owner is the widow of a Patriot killed during the fight for Breed's Hill on June 17th. She and her three young children are now residing in town with her sister. If you can spare a few coins for the crop damage that will most certainly occur, I will ask her to let Colonel Arnold use the farmhouse as his temporary headquarters."

Capt. Febiger agreed immediately.

We rode back into town and went immediately to *Machias Liberty*'s berth to find at least a half dozen more ocean-going transports in the harbor and several men sitting atop the *Machias Liberty* pilothouse talking with Captain O'Brien. He welcomed us aboard and introduced them to us as "Patriot merchant masters" and us to them as "Colonel Arnold's Riflemen paymasters." He then announced, "These seven Captains want to see the color of your money."

I went below to the Captain's cabin, brought the saddlebags on deck, checked to ensure the wax seals were intact and opened one of the flaps to show the coins within. Their eyes widened as Capt. Febiger said, "There are three more pockets with an equal amount in them just like what you see here. What we have brought is more than enough to compensate you for half the sum you each agreed to with Mr. Tracy. As all agreed, the balance will be paid when we arrive in Gardinerston. We need you to tell your fellow sea-farers, they must be here no later than sunset on Friday, September 15th."

They all agreed to do so and departed.

When they were gone, Captain O'Brien and Mr. Davenport commended us for the way in which we handled the briefing and agreed to meet again in the morning. As Captain Febiger and I were shouldering our rifles, gear, and the saddlebags to head back to Wolfe's Tavern, Mr. Davenport said, "There is something I should tell you. In 1762, my father, William Davenport, built the tavern where you are staying. During the last war—he served as a captain under General Wolfe in the campaign against the French. He was with Wolfe when the general was killed. The sign in front of the tavern is a poorly rendered image of the general my father revered. And we are now at war against descendants of General Wolfe."

Capt. Febiger and I walked in silence back to Wolfe's Tavern. As we stood in front, looking at the painted sign, he said, "All war is terrible but this one may be the strangest of all. It's pitted old allies against one another, Tories against Patriots—even family members against each other. It is a most uncivil civil war."

An hour later, shortly before sunset, Sgt. Cady arrived at Wolfe's Tavern and summoned us back to duty. "Mr. Davenport asked me to inform you, one of his Sons of Liberty Trusted Couriers from Cambridge arrived a short while ago and advised that Captain Daniel Morgan's Advance Force is crossing the ford on that stream flowing into the Merrimac. He wants to know if you want to greet him and lead them to the bivouac site we picked out."

We both said together, "We will go."

The Sergeant smiled and said, "I thought you would, so I brought your horses and my four men. May I suggest, we post one of my men in the room where the saddlebags are sequestered to guard the money and the rest of us will ride out to meet the Riflemen."

As we grabbed our rifles, backpacks, and gear, Capt. Febiger said, "You are a wise man, Sergeant Cady." As we proceeded out of port at a canter, I checked my pocket watch. It was precisely 7:00 p.m.

It took us just fifteen minutes before we sighted the van of the Advance Force column coming toward us. We were not surprised to see Capt. Morgan striding out in front of the long column. He greeted us with a smile and said, "We have a few stragglers—but none from Frederick County."

We led them the last mile or so to the bivouac site we selected. After testing the light breeze with an upraised wet finger, Capt. Morgan picked a place along the tree line close to the farmhouse for his headquarters and a perimeter for our Rifle Company. He then pointed out to 1st Lt. Humphrey where the others should ground their gear, set up tents, post night guards, and dig sanitary pits.

While all he directed was being done, we had a few minutes to talk. I asked, "What time did you leave Cambridge this morning, sir?"

"General Gates said we couldn't depart until this morning so we marched out at 1:00 a.m."

I did the math in my head. Eighteen hours to walk thirty-one or so miles. Nearly two miles per hour. He added, "It's much easier than our hike from Virginia. Pretty flat, good road. The wagons had a tough time getting across that ford a few miles back but they will be here soon. What have you learned?"

As dusk settled over the encampment, Capt. Febiger and I filled him in on all we experienced and were told—particularly about the assurances we received about the shipping and the saddlebags full of British and Spanish coins. We then offered to return to town, gather our gear and the money, and return.

He thought about it for a moment, then said, "You two and the dragoons go back to the port. Tomorrow morning at 9:00, be here with two saddle horses for 1st Lt. Humphrey and me and we will ride into Newburyport, meet the gentlemen you have spoken of, and start planning to launch this expedition. I am increasingly concerned about how late it is in the season."

By now, it was dark and the three-quarter moon was just rising over the harbor. We saluted, mounted our horses, and headed toward the port. As we rode, the offshore breeze picked up a bit. And for the first time in five months, I could feel just the slightest chill in the air.

Newburyport, Massachusetts

Tuesday, September 12th, 1775

At precisely 8:30 this morning, Capt. Febiger, Sgt. Cady, his detachment of dragoons, and I arrived at the Advance Force bivouac outside Newburyport with two extra steeds for Capt. Morgan and 1st Lt. Humphrey. We spent the balance of the day meeting aboard *Machias Liberty* with Captain O'Brien and a dozen merchant captains. We also ordered fresh beef, pork, fish, and vegetables from local merchants for delivery to our encampment on Wednesday to feed our Advance Force.

On the way back to the bivouac, Capt. Morgan met with Mr. Nathanael Tracy, now nearly recovered from being down with gout.

Mr. Tracy, thanks to being Chairman of the local Sons of Liberty Committee, was a font of information about the activities of Tory spies and the British fleet—still in Boston. He assured us he would know about a Royal Navy threat to our convoy at least twelve hours in advance.

"How?" asked Captain Morgan.

"Because, the British aren't the only ones who know how to spy."

CHAPTER TEN

1775: A SORTIE DELAYED

Newburyport, Massachusetts

Wednesday, September 13th, 1775

Captain Febiger and I have twice volunteered to vacate our comfortable lodging at Wolfe's Tavern and move out to the Advance Force bivouac. Captain Morgan ordered us to remain where we are "because the money is safer there, being guarded by one of Sergeant Cady's dragoons and I want someone I know and trust to be in town with their eyes and ears open."

This morning our day began with a quick visit with Captain O'Brien aboard *Machias Liberty*. He reported there are now ten large sea-going transport vessels tied up or anchored in the harbor and there is still no sign of any nearby British warships.

We then visited with Mr. Tracy who informed us, "Not one British man-o'-war has departed Boston Harbor since the report of a very damaging hurricane that struck the North Carolina coast on Sunday, August 27th. According to my sources, the Admiralty in London has instructed Admiral Samuel Graves, commanding the Royal Navy squadron in Boston, not to risk one vessel at sea during hurricane season."

At this, Capt. Febiger said, "Sir, I would like to have our commanders hear those reports directly from you. When you are feeling well enough, would you come out to our encampment and brief them?"

"Certainly. Let me know when Colonel Arnold and his commanders have arrived and I will gladly do so."

By the time we arrived back at the bivouac, the 1st Infantry Battalion, commanded by Lieutenant Colonel Greene, was streaming into their portion of the bivouac area under the direction of 1st Lt. Humphrey. To me, some of the 300 Massachusetts men were looking pretty ragged.

Captain Febiger and I dismounted, wrapped the reins of our borrowed horses around the wheel of one of our Virginia Rifle wagons, and approached Capt. Morgan who was talking to Lieutenant Colonel Greene and his deputy, Major Bigelow. We could hear my commander say, ". . . The sooner we get underway, the better . . ." so we turned away to water our horses from a trough someone constructed for the draft horses.

When the two Militia officers departed to supervise their troops getting settled in, Captain Morgan motioned us over and we debriefed him on what we learned from Captain O'Brien and Mr. Tracy.

1st Lt. Humphrey joined us a few minutes later and advised, "Major Bigelow just told me 'about' fifty-seven Militiamen from their battalion were issued passes to visit with their families in this neighborhood. I asked if he had a roster of their names and he said he would 'try' to make one."

Captain Febiger rolled his eyes and said, "That could be a problem. Did he tell them when to be back here?"

"Yes, sir. He told them to be back before we departed."

Barely covering his frustration, Capt. Morgan said, "Let's go into town and order some more fresh food. Lieutenant Colonel Greene just informed me Colonel Arnold wants us to purchase enough fresh meat, fish, and vegetables—and eggs—to feed the entire Expeditionary Force on Friday afternoon, September 15th. Let's go see Mr. Tracy. Hopefully he knows enough Patriot farmers around here who can feed more than a thousand soldiers."

"Did Colonel Arnold tell Lieutenant Colonel Greene how we are to pay for this?" asked Capt. Febiger.

"Same question I asked," replied Captain Morgan. "The answer was 'no.'"

By the end of the day, we had commitments from about a dozen farmers to feed about half our troops. And every farmer had the same question.

What was worse, the fresh food we ordered yesterday for the Advance Force was being prepared as this conversation ensued. Everyone in the encampment downwind of us had to be salivating at the scent. Captain Morgan ordered the cooks to feed the privates first, then the corporals, sergeants, and the dragoons. The officers were ordered to eat last.

Our little group billeted in town arrived back at Wolfe's Tavern at 9:00 p.m.—just as the moon rose over the harbor. It was a bit smaller than the night before—and the air was slightly cooler.

Newburyport, Massachusetts

Thursday, September 14th, 1775

I arrived at our encampment at 7:30 a.m. with two dragoons and an extra horse. As I dismounted, Captain Morgan said, "You are early this morning, Ensign Newman. Does that feather bed you are sleeping in have lumps in the mattress? Is it keeping you awake?"

1st Lt. Humphrey was already chuckling but I wasn't sure the Captain was joking.

"No, sir. Captain Febiger sent me out here to inform you he, Sergeant Cady, Mr. Nathanael Tracy, and several members of his Sons of Liberty Committee are presently out asking every Patriot family in this region to donate whatever they can to feed the whole Expedition tomorrow afternoon. They sent me here to see if you want to accompany them."

Captain Morgan turned to 1st Lt. Humphrey and said, "Major Meigs and our 2nd Infantry Battalion should be here with the artillery detachment today—probably earlier than the 1st Battalion arrived yesterday. His Vermont and Connecticut boys seem to be in better shape. I'll be back this afternoon."

It took us a half hour to link up with the Febiger-Tracy-Cady party and there began a great experience in American generosity. By the time we stopped at the third little farm, I was captivated.

So too was Captain Morgan. The people we were talking to aren't wealthy—they're yeoman farmers. There are no large plantations like we have in Virginia. There are no slaves or paid helpers working the land, tending gardens, planting and harvesting crops, repairing barns, feeding livestock. Families—mothers and fathers and their children—were doing all the hard work.

Most, if not all, were known by Mr. Tracy or Sgt. Cady—who it turned out—is a hero of the fight at Lexington in April and Breed's Hill in June. We didn't hear that from him. We heard it from many of those who volunteered to help us with food for our troops.

Though nearly everyone who offered, asked for nothing in return, Captain Morgan began telling him or her, "If you can be at our encampment by 2:00 p.m. tomorrow afternoon, my brave Riflemen will demonstrate how accurately they can shoot. Tell your neighbors. It's quite a show."

When I asked the Captain about the "shooting show," he reminded me of the commitment Colonel Arnold made to Major

Meigs about allowing everyone to test-fire the new ammunition we were issued before leaving Cambridge.

By the time the sun was setting, over 100 families promised to be at the encampment tomorrow with something fresh and good to eat. And nearly everyone said as we departed, "God bless you."

When we arrived back at the perimeter, it was dusk. Major Meigs's 2nd Battalion and Capt. Jones's Artillery detachment were already in their bivouac.

By the time Capt. Febiger and I arrived at Wolfe's Tavern with our dragoons, it was completely dark because the sky was overcast. I ran in, relieved the dragoon guarding the saddlebags, checked the wax seals, and went back out to thank Sgt. Cady.

As we parted, he said, "Good night, Ensign Newman. We shall be here at seven in the morning with two spare mounts. Tomorrow looks to be a very busy day. Pray it doesn't rain."

Newburyport, Massachusetts
Friday, September 15th, 1775

During the night a rainsquall passed quickly over Newburyport but by dawn the sky was clear. We left the tavern together and went first to see Captain O'Brien aboard *Machias Liberty*. As he did every day since we arrived, he reported "no British warships." He went on to note, "We now have twelve transports. That should be more than enough. Do you know how many wagons Colonel Arnold plans to take along?"

Capt. Febiger replied, "I do not, sir. But he should be at the encampment this evening. Since we hope to sail tomorrow, I will find out as soon he arrives and send an answer with one of the dragoons."

We then proceeded to Mr. Tracy's impressive home where both of us thanked him profusely for what he did yesterday to ensure the troops would all have a good fresh meal before departing for the wilderness.

His answer was a revelation. "It wasn't my idea—it was Sergeant Cady's. And Captain Morgan's offer to put on a 'shooting show' was icing on the cake—simply brilliant. You know very few folks in this part of the country have ever seen anything like you frontiersmen with your long rifles, fighting knives, and hatchets.

"After you were here at our home the first time—while I was under the weather—my wife asked, 'Why do they carry hatchets and big knives in their belts? Do they chop down a lot of trees?'

"When I told her you all carry hatchets and big knives because it takes longer to load a rifle than a musket or a pistol and you may need the hatchet and knife to kill an enemy trying to kill you. She pretended to be horrified at the thought. But she wants to come with me this afternoon to see the show."

By the time we returned to the encampment, Lieutenant Colonel Roger Enos and his Reserve/Rear Guard Force had arrived and were setting up their tents and digging latrines. Capt. Febiger and I joined Captain Morgan and told him what we learned from Messer's Tracy and O'Brien.

Capt. Morgan said, "I'm glad you are back. According to Lieutenant Colonel Enos, Colonel Arnold should be here by 3:00 p.m." Reaching into his jacket pocket, he pulled out a large key, handed it to Capt. Febiger, and said, "This is the key to the front door of the farmhouse. Mr. Tracy gave it to me yesterday. Please give it to Colonel Arnold when he arrives."

He looked at his watch and said, "twelve-thirty. We're going to have a lot of company here very soon, bringing all manner of food. I have Captains Hendricks and Smith and their two Pennsylvania Rifle Company contingents preparing targets over there," he said, gesturing to the open field to the west.

"Our company working parties are setting up the range, measuring distances and preparing, with the help of the carpenters, places to stage the food prior to cooking and serving it after it's prepared. As you know from Wednesday night, our Advance Guard has some very good cooks posing as Riflemen. I asked for volunteers to assist our cooks this afternoon and fifty men from other units volunteered. I also turned down the idea of opening one of our barrels of rum. We only have sixteen left to last us all the way to Quebec."

It was a spectacular event. Nearly 400 Patriots—over 100 families—showed up with food. They brought everything from freshly butchered beef, pork, lamb, turkey, and quail to scores of just-caught fish, oysters—even several dozen lobsters. There were potatoes, tomatoes, cabbage, cucumbers, corn, and squash. People brought freshly baked cakes, apple pies, and countless loaves of bread. One of the cooks made a half-barrel of delicious beef gravy.

Colonel Arnold and an eight-man detachment of Continental Dragoons rode into camp just as the cooks began preparing the feast. Capt. Febiger rushed over to him and escorted him into the farmhouse. Captain Morgan and I joined them in the dining room.

The Expedition commander was clearly agitated. His first questions were, "How much did all this cost and who is paying for it?"

His anxiety was instantly relieved by the answer, "It is all donated by generous Patriots." When Captain Morgan told him the Rifle marksmanship competition was about to begin and reminded him about the "test fire" question from Major Meigs back in Cambridge. Colonel Arnold nodded and said, "Just one round each, right?"

Capt. Morgan's reply was spot-on: "Yes, sir. I have already placed a wager. Would you care to bet?"

"When does it start?"

"As soon as you get to the firing line, sir."

Now smiling, he said, "Let's go."

Firing his one shot at a 300-yard target, Corporal Sullivan won hands down.

After the Riflemen, the infantry companies—all nine of them—each did an impressive demonstration of 3-rank volley fire with their muskets. Thankfully, they were downwind of the camp, for each volley created an immense plume of dense white smoke that would have made cooking or eating impossible. It was during the volley firing when Nathanael Tracy and his wife came up to see their old friend. Colonel Arnold turned, embraced them both, and they retired to the farmhouse.

The crowd loved it all. Several youngsters brought kites and ran across the hay field trying to launch them in the faint onshore breeze. Capt. O'Brien and several of his crew from *Machias Liberty* said it was all like an enormous family picnic. By 6:00 p.m. the visitors were heading home, the troops were policing up the area, and like Jesus with the loaves and fishes, there were lots of leftovers.

As the camp began to quiet, Capt. Morgan came to me and said, "This is likely your last night at the Tavern. Tomorrow morning, bring all your gear and the saddlebags full of money to give to Colonel Arnold. If our original plan holds, we will all move from here to the harbor around noon and set sail after dark tomorrow night. You and Capt. Febiger will have to keep manifests of each vessels' passengers and a list of equipment taken aboard each ship. When you see Captain O'Brien in the morning, it looks like we will have five wagons total."

I said, "Aye, sir," saluted, mounted, and rode back to the Tavern with Sgt. Cady and two of his dragoons.

Newburyport, Massachusetts
Saturday, September 16th, 1775

When the knocking on the door awakened me, it was too dark to see my watch. I struck a match, lit the candle on the table next to my bed, noticed it was 4:30, and opened the door to see Sgt. Cady and one of his dragoons. Both were holding lanterns.

"Sorry to bother you, sir. But Captain O'Brien sent one of his mates summoning us to meet him aboard *Machias Liberty* as soon as possible. If you wish, I can leave Corporal Thompson here with the saddlebags."

I slipped on my shoes, lit my small windproof oil lantern with the candle, put on my backpack, grabbed my rifle, knife, hatchet, powder horn, and cartridge box, and followed Sgt. Cady downstairs and out the front door. The fog was so thick we couldn't see the cobblestones beneath our feet.

Instead of a five-minute walk to the harbor, it took us a quarter hour to arrive at *Machias Liberty*'s gangway. Through the mist we could barely see a flicker of light emanating from the porthole in Captain O'Brien's cabin.

One of his mates escorted us below, knocked on the hatch, and announced us. There was a gruff "Just a minute . . ." as a key turned and the portal opened. The captain turned up the wick on the lantern to give us better light, motioned us to the stools next to his desk, and sat on the only chair in the cabin. He wasted no time getting to the point.

"With this dead calm and heavy fog, there is no way we are going to be able to load this little flotilla today and get underway tonight. Unless we get a good steady offshore breeze, this fog could be with us for days. The sun will burn some of it off by noon, but we still need a steady wind out of the west or south to sail northeast from here to the mouth of the Kennebec.

"Tell your commanders out there, this kind of weather rarely lasts more than two or three days. The good news in all this is the British Navy patrols and Revenue Cutters won't be casting off their lines to hunt us down.

"As soon as you safely can, get to your encampment and tell Colonel Arnold to start sending wagons and other heavy equipment down here so we can load it, but the troops should not strike their tents until we know we can sail.

"By the way, that was a great show and wonderful chow yesterday. My sailors loved it. Now, one last item: how many wagons will we have to load?"

"Five, sir."

It was 10:00 a.m. before the fog thinned enough for Sgt. Cady and me to mount up at Wolfe's Tavern and head out to the encampment accompanied by one of his dragoons and an extra saddled mount for Capt. Morgan. We put the saddlebags on the spare horse.

The trip, at a slow walk, took a half-hour longer than usual. Once inside the perimeter we proceeded directly to the farmhouse so we could give Colonel Arnold the saddlebags full of hard currency.

Captain Febiger was standing on the porch and said, "Nathanael, your timing is impeccable. Colonel Arnold has just called for a commanders meeting. As usual, Captain Morgan is already here and very agitated we're not already loading the transport ships. As you know, he is very concerned about the delay."

"Oh yes, I know. The approach of winter is paramount on his mind."

While we were talking, Sgt. Cady tethered the horses, removed the saddlebags full of cash, placed them on the porch, and asked, "Captain, are the dragoons who accompanied Colonel Arnold from Cambridge still here? If so, I should speak with them to see if there is any change in our orders. When my detachment came here with you and Ensign Newman, I was instructed to stay with you until the Expedition sails."

The captain motioned and said, "The dragoons are in the white canvas headquarters tent directly behind the farmhouse. They have water for your horses."

As we picked up the saddlebags and walked into the farmhouse, Captain Febiger said, "The meeting starts in fifteen minutes. As I walked out on the porch, Colonel Arnold and Captain Morgan were talking and you were the subject of their conversation."

During the hour-long meeting, I was asked to report on what Captain O'Brien told me about how long it might be before we could sail. I could see from the expression on his face Captain Morgan was very upset.

The only ones in the meeting happy about our delayed departure were Lieutenant Colonel Greene and his deputy, Major Bigelow. The fifty-seven infantrymen given passes to visit their families in the vicinity of Newburyport were to have returned to the encampment before dark on Friday, September 15th. Only four were back in camp.

At the close of the meeting, Colonel Arnold announced, "According to Ensign Newman's report, Captain O'Brien wants us to move our wagons to the wharf as soon as possible because they will take the longest to load when we embark. As soon as the fog lifts sufficiently, the wagons will proceed from here to where Captain O'Brien directs. Two dragoons will escort and post guard on each wagon and its contents until we deploy for Maine. The officer in charge of this movement is Ensign Newman."

Hearing this, I looked at Captain Morgan who responded with a very subtle nod of his head.

Colonel Arnold concluded, "One final note, if we are still here tomorrow night, we have been invited to dine with Mr. Nathanael Tracy and his wife at their beautiful home in Newburyport. Mr. Tracy is Chairman of the local secret Sons of Liberty Committee. It is he who arranged for the ships which will take us to Maine."

At 3:00 p.m., a slight northeast breeze dissipated enough of the fog to see about a half mile. 1st Lt. Humphrey and I agreed we should take the opportunity to move the wagons. He set out to inform the teamsters to harness up their draft teams and I sought out Sgt. Cady and told him we would be leaving in a quarter hour with the ten dragoons he chose to escort and post watch on the wagons. He bellowed, "Dragoon detachment! In fifteen minutes, be saddled and mounted!"

By 5:30 p.m. the five wagons were lined up on the wharf abreast *Machias Liberty*. The draft horses were all in a paddock with plenty of hay and water behind the barn where the dragoon horses are stabled.

Each wagon is being guarded by a dragoon while his relief rests until he takes over the watch at midnight. I repaired back to my room at Wolfe's Tavern.

Newburyport, Massachusetts

Sunday, September 17th, 1775

Sgt. Cady met me at 8:00 a.m. in front of Wolfe's Tavern with a single dragoon holding the reins of two saddled horses. The fog is gone. The sky is clear. The sun is bright yellow. A crisp steady breeze is rattling the halyards on every ship in the harbor.

As has become our custom, we headed down to *Machias Liberty* to get a sail report from Captain O'Brien. It wasn't what any of us wanted to hear.

"Tell Colonel Arnold we won't be going anywhere today. The wind is at least fifteen knots straight out of the nor' east—precisely the direction we must sail to reach the mouth of the Kennebec River. There are two pieces of good news though. The Royal Navy 'square rigs' in Boston can't sail into this wind either. And we will have these five wagons loaded on five different vessels before noon."

Hearing that, I asked, "Do you have any white paint and a brush aboard?"

"Yes, how much do you need?"

"Not much. Just enough to paint a number on the sides and rear of each wagon."

In less than a half hour each wagon had a number, and I recorded it in the log I carried in my backpack. Beside each number, I made a notation: #1 – Virginia Rifles; #2 – Penn. Rifles; #3 – 1st Inf. Bn; #4 – 2nd Inf. Bn; #5 Rear Guard.

Then I asked, "Captain O'Brien, when the wagons are loaded, would you be so kind to make a list of which wagon is loaded aboard which vessel?"

"Certainly. That's very wise young man."

"Thank you, sir. If I may, I will retrieve that list this evening."

"Of course," the Captain replied. He then posed a question of his own: "Will you be taking all twenty draft horses?"

"I don't know, but I will find out."

"Good. I need to know before we load the wagons aboard the transports. Some of the ships have holds large enough for both horses and a wagon. Others do not."

"I will send a messenger back as soon as I have an answer."

I found Capt. Febiger as soon as I arrived at the encampment, delivered Capt. O'Brien's sail report, and asked him the question about the draft horses. He went into the farmhouse and swiftly returned with the answer: "Yes. Take both."

Rather than risk a garbled message, I found Capt. Morgan and 1st Lt. Humphrey sitting on camp stools outside our headquarters tent to let them know I was heading back to the *Machias Liberty* to inform Captain O'Brien that Colonel Arnold wants to take both the wagons and the horses.

The captain looked at me and asked, "When are we leaving here?"

I told him exactly what Captain O'Brien told me. When I finished, he said, "Thank you," stood, and walked off toward the tree line.

William looked downcast, so I asked him, "What's wrong?"

He looked around to ensure no one could hear us and said, "Captain Morgan is deeply concerned about the delays. He told me this operation has far too many moving parts, too little intelligence about the terrain and enemy, and the constant delays put everyone at risk from what he believes will be a fierce winter.

"He's not concerned about himself or his reputation—but for our men. An hour ago, Lieutenant Colonels Greene and Enos informed him the enlistments of over half their Militiamen expire on December 31st. "

I was alarmed at what I was hearing and said, "I must deliver Colonel Arnold's decision about the draft horses and will return immediately. When I get back, let's try to cheer him up."

The "cheer him up" part didn't work but we did convince him to ride with us to the dinner on horses provided by Sgt. Cady. Their home and gardens are certainly beautiful. The food was very good. The rum, cider, and wine flowed freely. A three-piece string ensemble played music throughout the meal. They invited to the party several very attractive young women who were virtually surrounded throughout the evening by young men dressed far more appropriately for the occasion than our Rifle officers.

But like so many people on the periphery of actually fighting in this war, Mr. Tracy took pains to describe how close he is to General Washington and of his importance to our Expedition. He even passed around the table copies of a letter from the Commander-in-Chief as proof of his significance:

To Nathanael Tracy Esq. Newbury Port

By His Excellency George Washington Esq

Commander in Chief of the Army of the United States

To Nathanael Tracy Esq.

You are hereby authorized and impowered to take up for the Service of the sd. Colonies so many Vessels as shall be *necessary for the transporting a Body of Troops to be detached from this Army on a secret Expedition: Freight of such Vessels to be paid in such a Manner and at such a Rate as is indorsed hereon: And in Case of Loss or Damage to such Vessels or any of them such Loss or Damage to be compensated by the Publick according to an Estimation to be made before the sd. Vessels proceed in the above Service.*

Head Quarters, September 2, 1775. G. Washington

After dessert, Mrs. Tracy urged us all to join her husband in the lantern-lit garden for brandy and cigars. I watched as Colonel Arnold flirted with our hostess and then recalled he lost his wife to some terrible malady[1] just three months ago.

At 9:30, Capt. Morgan signaled with a look and a tilt of his head that it was time to go. With all the gracious civility of a well-polished gentleman, he took Mrs. Tracy's hand gently in his great big paw, bent, kissed it, stood erect, looked her in the eye, and said, "Thank you, Mrs. Tracy, for a wonderful evening. We shall forever recall your gracious hospitality. We would very much like to stay longer but duty calls my officers and me back to our encampment."

She was still blushing when, as my mother taught me, I took her hand, bowed slightly, and said, "Thank you, Mrs. Tracy, ever so much, for inviting me to this wonderful evening."

William must have said something similar because she continued to smile and even curtsied. We followed Captain Morgan out the front door, found Sgt. Cady, mounted our horses, and were in the encampment in fewer than thirty minutes.

As I drifted off to sleep, the side panels and roof of the headquarters tent were flapping in the steady wind. But it had not changed direction.

ENDNOTE

1. Benedict Arnold's wife, Margaret, mother of their three sons, died on 19 June 1775 of what was described at the time as a "deadly tumor." It is today believed to have been cancer.

CHAPTER ELEVEN

1775: RIVER-READY BATTEAUX?

Newburyport, Massachusetts

Tuesday, September 19th, 1775

Monday was yet another lost day to the nor'easter. I spent much of it reconciling our Advance Force rosters and manifests with those maintained by Captain Febiger and information on troop and cargo capacities of each vessel. By the time I retired, at 10:00 p.m. the wind was beginning to shift to the left. At 5:00 this morning when Sgt. Cady awakened me carrying a windproof lantern, it was strong and steady right out of the west.

He said, "One of my dragoons just came up from the wharf. Captain O'Brien wants us to start moving immediately to embark."

While still somewhat protected from the wind inside the tent, I pulled a waxed taper out of my pocket, lit it from Sgt. Cady's lantern, and then lit mine.

"Thank you, Sgt. Cady. Now, please go to the farmhouse and awaken Captain Febiger. We need to get everyone in this encampment up and moving."

Amazingly, shortly after sunrise, the entire Expeditionary Force—all 1,207 of us—was up, packed, and ready to march to the wharf in the sequence they would board their assigned vessels.

By 8:00 a.m. Capt. Morgan's Advance Force was boarding. I arranged with our two Pennsylvania Rifle Company Commanders, Captains Hendricks and Smith, to mark the manifest for the names of each person boarding. The same process was used for every ship.

Advance Force: *Machias Liberty* and *Polly*

1ˢᵗ Battalion & Expedition Force HQ: *Broad Bay, Eagle,* and *Betsy*

2ⁿᵈ Battalion & Artillery: *Britannia, Juno,* and *Conway*

Reserve & Rear Guard: *Houghton, Abigail,* and *Swallow*

Spare/Rescue: *Dublin*

When each vessel took aboard its full complement of soldiers and equipment, the man with the manifest shouted out the name of the vessel and the words "ALL PRESENT OR ACCOUNTED FOR!" At that point the ship's crew cast off the lines and a long boat with six oarsmen tugged the ship away from the pier to anchor in the Merrimack River, bow upstream, out of the way of other vessels, and still properly sequenced.

Despite the west wind and a flood tide trying to push the transports out into the Atlantic, none of the vessels collided or dragged anchor more than a few feet. By 5:00 p.m. loading was complete and Captain O'Brien hoisted to the top of his mast, the Red and White striped Sons of Liberty Flag, the pre-arranged signal to "Follow Me!"

Within seconds, every transport raised their anchors, set sails, and sortied behind *Machias Liberty* toward the Atlantic. Once out of the harbor, they all turned northeast behind us on the course Capt. Obrien set, straight to the mouth of the Kennebec River.

The wind was perfect and throughout the night, lookouts on the bow and stern kept watch on the lights of the vessel ahead and behind, trusting Capt. O'Brien would not lead them all onto the rocks.

By dawn, *Machias Liberty* and *Polly* were on the approach to the center—and widest passage of the Kennebec channel. Each vessel trimmed sails to slow and the twelve-ship column, now stretching almost two miles long, began negotiating the twisting course upriver to Gardinerston.

Gardinerston, Maine

Friday, September 22nd, 1775

Just before dark on Thursday evening, September 21st, Captain O'Brien's bow lookout sighted the pier at Gardinerston. Because it would soon be dark with only a sliver of moon, he signaled the column of transports to close up in proper order aft of *Machias Liberty* and anchor for the night.

At dawn this morning Captain O'Brien again hoisted the Sons of Liberty flag and our little fleet raised anchors, set reefed sails on a port tack, and headed up the Kennebec River to Gardinerston on an ebb tide that went slack as we pulled adjacent to our goal. Captain Morgan, 1st Lt. Humphrey, and I were on deck, fascinated at the activity aboard, and glad the first leg of our expedition was completed without incident.

By 10:00 all twelve vessels were berthed in a row with bow and stern lines along the town's quay. Ashore, dockworkers helped secure lines while the crew and passengers aboard each vessel stowed sails and began opening hatches to expedite unloading cargo.

As soon as a gangway was set on the rail of *Machias Liberty*, two gentlemen we met in Cambridge bounded aboard, Mr. Reuben

Colburn and the diminutive Aaron Burr—still in a Continental Army uniform.

"Captain Morgan!" Mr. Colburn shouted. "So good to see you again, sir! Welcome to Gardinerston, Maine, a thriving place named for its founder, Doctor Sylvester Gardiner, a medical doctor, the fellow who built the water-powered sawmill and gristmill here—and perhaps the Colonies' largest importer of laudanum to apothecaries like Benedict Arnold's.

"Dr. Gardiner has but one serious flaw—his affection for mad King George. For that reason, Sylvester is not here to welcome you. In June, after the battles for Breed's and Bunker's Hills, he fled to Boston. Now, sir, we must greet Colonel Arnold. Where is he?"

Captain Morgan, until now mute, quietly replied, "Good to see you again, as well, Mr. Colburn. Colonel Arnold is on the schooner *Broad Bay*, the third vessel aft of us. May I inquire, sir, where are the 200 batteaux into which we are to transfer the cargo and personnel of this expedition?"

"Ahh, yes," replied Mr. Colburn. "The 200 completed batteaux are staged at my boat yard, near my home, just upriver from here. We shall proceed there immediately as soon as Colonel Arnold and I conclude some business."

At that, Mr. Colburn feigned some sort of salute, spun about, and departed down the gangway with Mr. Burr hurrying in trace.

Captain Morgan watched them go and then said, more to himself than William or me, "Lord, that man can talk. I pray he managed to build two hundred batteaux with the same alacrity."

While Colonel Arnold and Mr. Colburn were closeted aboard *Broad Bay*, we offloaded our two wagons and draft horses, formed up the entire Advance Force and moved two miles upriver on good road to Mr. Colburn's place.

On arrival, we learned Mr. Colburn was a better talker than batteaux builder.

A crew of more than forty men were hard at work on a large field close to the Kennebec. Some were sawing green lumber—aspen, birch, beech, fir, pine, spruce, even some maple and oak into boards of various lengths and boat-framing parts. Another group carried the cut boards to an area where a third crew, wielding hammers, were nailing the boards to rough-cut frames in the approximate shape of a flat-bottomed, double ended boat.

After a quick walk-through the "boat yard," with 1st Lt. Humphrey, Captains Hendricks and Smith—our two Pennsylvania Rifle Company commanders—and me, Captain Morgan called us into a circle. "Move our men over to that open field. Each company take a muster to ensure we are all present or accounted for. Set up our usual perimeter and dig some sanitation pits but don't set up tents yet.

"Captain Smith, post three of your Riflemen down by Mr. Colburn's house to guide the rest of the Force up here to bivouac so they don't interfere with the boat-builders. I am going to take Ensign Newman with me to find Colonel Arnold and let him know we need to move the Advance Guard to Fort Western today. All of us must do whatever it takes to get this expedition underway.

"While we're gone, I want the three of you to select twenty-five men from each Rifle Company. Take them to the boat ramp where we saw the finished boats. Find the best thirty-five of the batteaux and set them aside. 1st Lt. Humphrey, find the boatwright in charge here and tell him we need a barrel of oakum—that's a mixture of pine tar and hemp fibers. Use the oakum to double seal the inside and outside of the hull seams along the bottoms and between the strakes on the sides of every one of the thirty-five batteaux you have chosen. Post a guard on the boats you finish so no one else can claim them."

He consulted his watch and continued, "It's just noon. If at all possible, our entire Advance Guard ought to be headed upstream on a rising tide toward Fort Western by 4:00 p.m. It's just ten miles north of here. William, we need to know whether the track between here and Fort Western is passable for wagons. Ask some of these boat workers. They are more likely to tell the truth than some others around here.

"If those you ask, say 'no,' tell the teamsters on our wagons to remove all the hitching gear, shafts, traces, axles, wheels, brakes, seats, and associated leather and hardware from both wagons. Have them set all that equipment neatly inside our Company perimeter. Make sure the horses have forage and water.

"When all the hardware is removed from the wagons, drive bungs and oakum into the holes. The bottoms and sides of both wagons are already sealed; I had them built that way just in case we might need to use the wagons as cargo barges. Remember, every boat should have on board four long towing lines, six long, strong poles—ash, if possible—and six paddles. Any questions?"

"Yes, sir, just two," said 1st Lt. Humphrey. "If we turn our wagons into cargo barges, what will become of our draft horses?"

With a smile that wrinkled the scar on his face, Capt. Morgan replied, "William, you and Nathanael here will recall, I built the wagons and paid personally for those magnificent Virginia draft horses, better than anything seen up here.

"You should be able to auction the horses and hitching gear for much more than I paid back in Virginia. If you do so while Nathanael and I are gone, I will give you a 10 percent commission."

"If you can't get more for the horses than I paid, we will take 'em with us, because if we don't get this expedition moving soon, we will have to eat them."

We borrowed two saddle horses from the boat-builders, saddled up, and headed toward Gardinerston. A half-mile down the road we encountered the 1st and 2nd Infantry Battalions and the Rear Guard walking toward Mr. Colburn's house at an easy pace. I told the leader of each unit, "A Rifleman just ahead will guide you to tonight's encampment."

Ten minutes later, we found Colonel Arnold, Mr. Colburn, Mr. Burr, and a host of "Patriot Admirers" enjoying beverages in a tavern near the quay. I could tell from his demeanor, Captain Morgan was struggling to control himself, so I waited outside.

I cannot record the conversation for I was not there. But when Captain Morgan emerged from the tavern twenty minutes later, he said, "Let's get going to Fort Western."

Fort Western, Maine
Saturday, September 23rd, 1775

Much to my amazement, the ten-mile long trip up to Fort Western was free of any unexpected danger or drama. Thanks to the leadership and ingenuity of 1st Lt. Humphrey and Pennsylvania Rifle Company Captains Hendricks and Smith, all thirty-five of the Colburn-built batteaux and both our former wagons—turned cargo barges—were water-worthy and ready to go at 3:30 p.m.

There were a few hilarious moments as the Riflemen in each craft experimented with rowing, "pole-pushing" and steering their "riverboats" in "slack water" without capsizing. But in short order they were all headed north up the Kennebec in a long line behind our former lead wagon, now re-christened as "Rifle Cargo #1."

Local watermen advised Captain Morgan the tide would shift to ebb off Fort Western at 8:30 p.m. He wanted us to be ashore at Fort Western before that happened. We made it by 7:15.

In the deepening dusk it took an "all-hands" effort of ten men on each loaded batteaux—and at least twenty for our two large "Cargo-boats"—to drag the heavy craft out of the water and high enough up the riverbank not to be swept away if the river suddenly flooded.

We were in a perimeter under tents outside the crumbling remains of Fort Western with shallow sanitation ditches dug and watches set for each Advance Guard Company by 8:00 p.m. The challenge for this moonless night: "Sons of!" The password: "Liberty!"

I arose this morning in twilight, well before sunrise—and went to relieve myself in the nearest sanitary ditch, just outside the lines of Capt. Smith's Pennsylvania Rifle Company. As I turned back toward the perimeter, I tripped and fell over a live creature hunkered low to the ground.

Thinking it was likely an enemy Indian who crept up behind me, I grabbed the figure, pinned him face-down beneath me, pulled out my knife, and said, "Sons of . . ."

There was no response but a light groan. I repeated the challenge: "Sons of . . ." then added, "If you don't tell me the correct password, I will kill you with this knife."

At this, a distinctly feminine voice pleaded, "Please sir, don't kill me. I'm a Patriot. My husband is a member of this Expedition."

I jumped up, shoved my knife into its scabbard, helped her to her feet, apologized, and told her to accompany me back into the perimeter. She agreed to do so but asked, "May I first do what you just did? I was coming out here to pee and did not know you were already here."

At 8:00 a.m. Captain Morgan, 1st Lt. Humphrey, both Pennsylvania Rifle Company Captains Hendricks and Smith and I were on camp stools in Capt. Morgan's tent. By then all attendees knew the young woman I tripped over was Eliza Grier, wife of Sgt. Joseph Grier, a respected member of Captain Smith's Rifle Company.

"You are certain they are married?" asked Capt. Morgan, looking directly at Capt. Smith.

"Yes, sir."

"Why shouldn't I send her back to Newburyport today on the vessels that brought us to Gardinerston?"

Capt. Smith's response was as surprising as my early morning encounter. "You shouldn't send her back sir, because you will also have to send back her cousin, Jemima—who is wed to Private James Warner, in Capt. Hendricks Company."

Capt. Morgan looked at Hendricks who nodded and said, "Sir, both couples married the day before we left Pennsylvania. Both women walked the whole way from Pennsylvania to Cambridge with our companies. They are both aware this is going to be an arduous campaign, but they are both fit and have nursing experience. That's more than some of the other women in this Expedition have."

"What other women?"

At this, 1st Lt. Humphrey responded, "Sir, I do not know of any other women in the Advance Guard. . . ."

Looking directly at William and me, he interrupted, "Did you or Nathanael know about these two?"

We both said, "No, sir."

"Well, what other women are you talking about?"

William continued, "Sir, there are three or four women accompanying Colonel Arnold's Headquarters. I have seen at least three with the Infantry Battalions. I believe there are two with Major David Hyde's Quartermaster detachment. It's likely less than a dozen, total."

Captain Morgan said nothing for a moment and then, staring out the tent doorway, said very quietly, "I will never forget what happened to the women on the Braddock expedition. . . ."

He drew a deep breath, shook his head as if to clear it and proclaimed, "For now they can stay. I will talk to Colonel Arnold about this when he arrives."

At noon, Colonel Arnold, his staff, all the Expedition commanders, and Mr. Colburn arrived at our bivouac next to the humble trading post beside the crumbling ruins of Fort Western. They came in a little flotilla of canoes for what was described by the Expedition Commander as a "Final planning conference before we depart for Quebec." It was good to see Capt. Febiger again and we stood next to each other during the meeting.

Colonel Arnold began by ordering two scouting parties prepared immediately, one led by Lt. Archibald Steele of Pennsylvania to gather intelligence on the route we will take to Lake Mégantic, and the other led by Lt. Church to confirm the most direct track to The Great Carrying Place.

He directed the two scouting parties to mark Indian trails and places where portage of the batteaux will be necessary and once past Height of Land to plot a safe course down the Chaudière River to the St. Lawrence. The Colonel specified the scouting parties will depart tomorrow and the Advance Guard will follow on Monday, September 25th.

A disagreement then arose when Col. Arnold announced Lieutenant Colonel Greene of the Rhode Island Militia to command the Advance Guard of the Expedition. This was contrary to what we all heard back in Cambridge when he named Captain Morgan as commander of the Advance Guard.

The first to object were Captains Hendricks and Smith, commanding the two Pennsylvania Rifle Companies. They were very frank in expressing their unwillingness to take orders from a militia officer and pointed out the Rifle Companies were the first forces raised by an Act of Congress—and the only Commissioned Continental Army officers on the Expedition were Colonel Arnold and Capt. Morgan.

Rather than create a confrontation in front of Arnold's staff, subordinates, and the contingent of "Civilian Volunteers," which was unlikely to end well, Capt. Morgan rose and said, "This is a matter which Colonel Arnold and I will discuss and resolve before we depart Fort Western. For now, I suggest we focus on what must be done to get the "Arnold Expedition" moving to Quebec. Winter is barking like a wolf at our door."

For the balance of the meeting, all hands were engaged in discussing the particular challenges of moving 1,100 men up a river, across a trackless wilderness, down another river, and then capturing a fortified enemy-held city.

Col. Arnold began with the most obvious challenge. Without demeaning Reuben Colburn, Col. Arnold said, "We must deal with the batteaux problem.

"First, they are smaller than we wanted. But these vessels weigh 400 pounds empty. Larger boats would be impossible to carry over the portages on the Kennebec and Chaudière Rivers.

"General Washington and I contracted with Mr. Colburn to build 200 batteaux. With these smaller boats, that's not enough to transport our entire force. To solve that problem Mr. Colburn has agreed to build twenty more batteaux.

"He will do so as fast as possible but that means we will have to move from here over the course of several days—not all at once as I had hoped. By tomorrow we will have worked out a new departure schedule and sequence.

"Second, some of you have pointed out the rough construction and green lumber used in building the boats. That is true but I want everyone to consider—these batteaux are making a one-way trip to Quebec. But, to address these concerns, Mr. Colburn and two dozen of his best-boat builders will come with us as far as possible to make repairs as necessary."

The meeting adjourned at 3:00 p.m. and as the others began boarding their canoes to head back down the river to the Colburn boatyard, Col. Arnold held back to talk privately with Capt. Morgan.

When they stopped, Capt. Febiger, 1st Lt. Humphrey and I remained about five yards behind so the two men could have some measure of privacy, but I could still hear them conversing for the breeze was blowing slightly toward us off the river:

Arnold: "We brought with us, three well-built canoes for you and the other Rifle Company commanders."

Morgan: "Thank you, I will inform Captains Smith and Hendricks. They may come in very handy."

Arnold: "Now, what are your plans for those two cargo barges?"

Morgan (smiling): "Why? They are too heavy to portage."

Arnold: "Well, if you are amenable, we can use them to ferry cargo from Reuben's place to Fort Western. Since he paid your deputy, 1st Lt. Humphrey, for all the wagon parts, axles, wheels, brakes, and assorted hitching gear, he could fairly easily turn them back into wagons."

Morgan: "Sure. Tell him to make Lt. Humphrey an offer he can't refuse. I paid out of my own pocket to build two very good wagons—and apparently, very good barges."

Arnold: "Good. Please bring Lt. Humphrey and your Adjutant, young Newman, with you at 7:00 tonight for dinner at the Colburn's house."

Morgan: "Yes, sir. If at all possible, we must resolve this 'Chain of Command' issue and the matter of the women this evening."

Arnold: "I agree. On the matter of 'Chain of Command,' you know His Excellency has taken a very firm position on this matter?"

Morgan: "Yes sir, I do. But I believe I have a solution that will be amenable to all."

Arnold: "Good. I want to hear it. Now what's this about women?"

Morgan: "This is about 'camp follower' women now accompanying the Expedition. I have great concerns for their safety if they continue on with us from here."

At this point the two commanders proceeded to the river's edge and we could no longer hear what they said. But as we watched, they shook hands and Colonel Arnold deftly boarded his canoe and paddled downstream.

As usual, Capt. Morgan, 1st Lt. Humphrey, and I arrived for dinner at Reuben Colburn's comfortable home a half-hour early. He greeted us at the front door with a hearty, "Welcome, gentlemen. Thank you for joining my wife and me for dinner. As I'm sure you understand, in these days we do not have the opportunity to entertain very often.

"Colonel Arnold and Captain Febiger are in the library where I have lighted some lanterns and candles. My wife or I will knock when Dr. Senter arrives and our meal is prepared."

When the door closed, Colonel Arnold got right to the point, "Daniel, what is your solution to my 'Chain of Command' problem?"

"Simply this, sir. When we were still in Cambridge, we all agreed the three Rifle Companies would serve as the Expedition's Advance Guard under my command. But after the Advance Guard departed for Newburyport, someone on His Excellency's staff issued a new organizational arrangement, adding two musket companies to the Advance Guard, thus reducing the number of divisions in the Expedition from four to three and justifying the assignment of Lieutenant Colonel Greene as Advance Guard commander.

"Since then, we have learned much more about the terrain and river conditions we must traverse. We now know a 'three division' organizational arrangement will slow the movement of our entire expedition. The Riflemen are fit. They know how to move quickly and quietly in rough country. Rifle Company baggage is a fraction of what the Musket Companies are carrying.

"The Rifle Companies ought to be well out in front of the main body of the Expedition to prevent ambuscades by Indians loyal to the British.

"I suggest the best organization for rapid movement should be along the lines of your original idea: Four divisions, leaving Fort Western one day apart:

"First Division: Three Rifle Companies as Vanguard; departing on the 25th under my command;

"Second Division: Three Massachusetts Musket Companies commanded by Lieutenant Colonel Greene departs Fort Western the following day;

"Third Division: Three Vermont and Connecticut Musket Companies commanded by Major Meigs head upriver on Wednesday the 27th;

"Fourth Division: Three New England Musket Companies as Rear Guard, plus Captain Reuben Colburn's boat-repair unit, the engineers, pioneers David Hyde's quartermasters, the commissary, Dr. Senter and his medical personnel and 'extras'—such as the cattle, all under the command of Lieutenant Colonel Enos. By Thursday, the 28th the twenty additional batteaux now being built should be finished for the fourth division to commence moving north."

Colonel Arnold said nothing for almost a minute, then turned toward the three of us junior officers and said to his Adjutant, "Christian, what do you think of this idea? Is it the right thing to do and will it pass muster when we communicate it to Adjutant General Gates in the missive I must send to Cambridge when we depart here?"

Captain Febiger paused but a second or two and replied, "In my opinion, Colonel, Captain Morgan has a brilliant solution. The Commanding General and his staff in Cambridge must respect your perspective as Expedition Commander for the best way to organize for rapid, secure movement from here to our objective given winter will soon be upon us.

"Captain Morgan's proposal also avoids altogether the 'Chain of Command' issue since this is simply an organizational matter for how to best move from here to Quebec. Personnel who have been together for some time ought to remain together for unit cohesion in this arduous terrain so soldiers can look after one another."

Colonel Arnold nodded, said nothing for a moment then asked, "And what about the women?"

I noticed color rising in Captain Febiger's cheeks as he considered his response: "Only a few of us heard what Captain Morgan said quietly this morning when this matter was raised at your commander's meeting." I heard what he said about the women who perished in the disaster that befell the Braddock Expedition in July of 1755. Captain Morgan was there when it happened. I have only read about it. Since Dr. Senter is to join us for dinner, I suggest we seek his advice before a decision is made."

Before Colonel Arnold could render a judgment on either matter, there came a knock on the door and Mr. Colburn announced, "Gentlemen, Dr. Isaac Senter and Mr. Aaron Burr are both here and dinner is served."

We followed them into the dining room where Mr. Colburn introduced us to the absolutely stunning Mrs. Elizabeth Colburn, our host's very beautiful wife.

I could not take my eyes from her. She was dressed in a light blue gown of great finery, displaying in her ample, alluring cleavage a jewel pendant to which every man's eye was immediately drawn.

Standing beside her husband she said, in the voice of a nightingale, "Please let us bow our heads as my husband asks a blessing on our meal and the accomplishment of the mission on which you and he are about to embark and during which I shall miss him dearly."

I must confess to have been so enamored by Mrs. Colburn's pulchritude I did not record her husband's invocation.

The meal—roast leg of lamb, mashed potatoes, gravy, squash, peas, green beans, and a slice of apple pie with sharp cheddar cheese for dessert—was accompanied by scintillating conversation stimulated by Colonel Arnold, Doctor Senter, Lieutenant Burr and, surprisingly Mrs. Colburn.

The "Chain of Command" matter never came up, but the issue of whether women should be allowed to accompany the Expedition was the topic about which everyone had an opinion.

As dessert was being served, Colonel Arnold said, "With the permission of our host and hostess, by a show of hands, how many of you believe women should be allowed to accompany our Expedition to Quebec?"

Capt. Morgan, Lt. Humphrey and I were the only "no" votes.

After dinner, Colonel Arnold, Captain Morgan, and Dr. Senter spent a half hour alone in the library. It was nearly midnight when Captain Morgan, 1st Lt. Humphrey, and I arrived back at Fort Western.

As we climbed up the slope from the riverside to our encampment, I asked, "Shall I let our commanders know what was decided tonight?"

"Do not awaken anyone now. We will let everyone know in the morning."

Fort Western, Maine

Sunday, September 24th, 1775

Shortly after sunrise, Rev. Samuel Spring, the Expedition Chaplain, arrived at our encampment and all our Riflemen were ordered to muster in the center of our perimeter.

After the brief prayer service, Captain Morgan motioned for everyone to gather 'round and take a seat on the dew-damp grass.

"Colonel Arnold has decided to reorganize our expedition to liberate Quebec into four divisions. Our three Rifle Companies are the First Division. We will depart here tomorrow morning and serve as vanguard for the Expedition.

"Second Division, commanded by Lieutenant Colonel Greene is comprised of three Massachusetts Musket Companies. They will depart here on Tuesday, September 26th.

"Third Division, Three Vermont and Connecticut Musket Companies commanded by Major Meigs will follow on Wednesday the 27th.

"Fourth Division, the Expedition's Rear Guard, bearing our extra provisions, powder, ammunition, the boat repair unit, medical personnel and engineers is commanded by Lieutenant Colonel Enos. They will depart here starting on Thursday the 28th and close up as fast as they can as additional batteaux are completed.

"Our Rifle Companies will screen in front of the main body, engage any hostiles and cut trails and foot-paths where necessary.

"Every Rifleman will carry on his person sufficient powder, wadding, and shot for fifty rounds. Every man will have no fewer than five flints, a warm cloak or blanket, and five days' rations. Each company will have ten batteaux to carry forty-five days of provisions including kegs of powder, food, cooking gear, tentage, and additional clothing.

"Each of the boats will be manned by no fewer than four men and no more than six. The rest of us will walk on the riverbanks. When it is necessary to portage, all hands will pitch in to help carry the boats and their contents.

"The order of march tomorrow morning will the Virginia Rifle Company first, Captain Hendricks Pennsylvania Rifles second and then Captain Smith's Riflemen. We shall rotate the order of march as necessary.

"As soon as we finish this meeting, start packing your batteaux. Try to wrap everything in the boats to keep it as dry as possible.

"Are there any questions?"

"Yes, sir." It was Sergeant Grier. "What about our wives?"

Captain Morgan shook his head but said, "I strongly recommend against it, but Colonel Arnold has ordered that wives may accompany their husbands on the Expedition."

Captain Hendricks stood and asked, "Sir, who is our commanding officer?"

There was total silence. Everyone in the semi-circle was staring at Captain Morgan as he replied, "You're looking at him."

There was an immediate cheer as the Riflemen bounded to their feet, waving their weapons over their heads, yelling "Huzzah!" and slapping each other's backs.

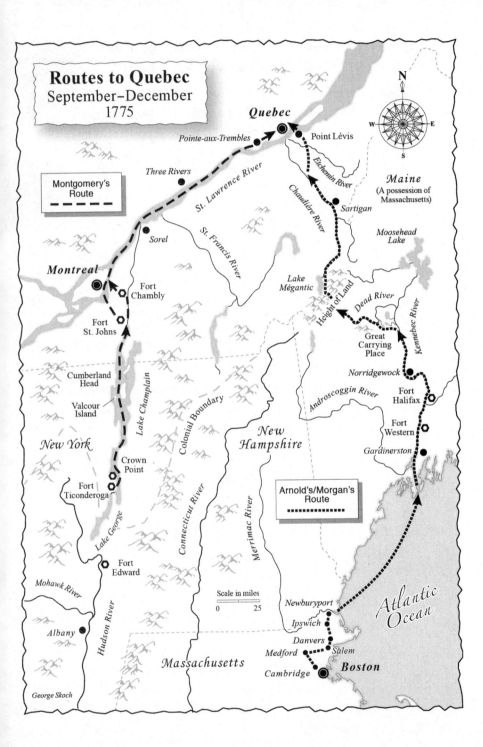

Routes to Quebec
September–December
1775

N
W E
S

Quebec

Pointe-aux-Trembles

Point Lévis

Maine
(A possession of
Massachusetts)

Three Rivers

St. Lawrence River

Etchemin River

Montgomery's
Route

Chaudière River

Sartigan

Moosehead
Lake

Sorel

St. Francis River

Montreal

Fort
Chambly

Lake
Mégantic

Height of Land

Dead River

Kennebec River

Fort
St. Johns

Great
Carrying
Place

Cumberland
Head

Lake Champlain

Norridgewock

Fort
Halifax

Valcour
Island

Androscoggin River

New York

Colonial Boundary

*New
Hampshire*

Fort
Western

Crown
Point

Connecticut River

Gardinerston

Fort
Ticonderoga

Arnold's/Morgan's
Route

Merrimac River

Fort
Edward

Mohawk River

Scale in miles
0   25

Newburyport

*Atlantic
Ocean*

Hudson River

Ipswich

Danvers

Albany

Medford   Salem

Massachusetts

Cambridge   Boston

George Skoch

CHAPTER TWELVE

1775: WINTER IN THE FOREST PRIMEVAL

Fort Halifax, Maine, on the Kennebec River

Wednesday, September 27th, 1775

Our Advance Force—250 Riflemen, three Indians, and two women—departed Fort Western early on the morning of the 25th with three canoes, thirty-one batteaux—ten for each Rifle Company and one for Captain Morgan's Headquarters equipment—including my field desk.

Six Riflemen, two from each Rifle Company, have augmented our "Vanguard Headquarters" to assist in moving our one canoe, our single batteau, and in setting up and taking down tentage while serving as messengers, and protectors of Captain Morgan in close combat with the enemy. Corporal Sullivan, the non-commissioned officer in charge of this little detachment, reports to me.

Each heavily laden batteau, containing about a thousand pounds of gear, is being rowed, "poled" (pushed), and sometimes pulled, up the Kennebec River by our Riflemen. In "good water"— calm, gentle current, deep enough for our batteaux to avoid rocks and shoals—the four men responsible for each boat are sufficient.

Unfortunately, the Kennebec River seems to have very little "good water."

The rest of us—124 Riflemen and the two women—are walking beside the slowly moving flotilla on the now overgrown but still passable military road built in the 1850s between Fort Western and Fort Halifax. Captain Morgan expected to make the eighteen-mile trip from Fort Western to Fort Halifax in just one day. We certainly could have done so by walking single file on the old path beside the river. But by dusk on the 25th we traversed just six miles upstream because moving the heavy batteaux against the current on this part of the Kennebec often requires men to wade into the water and help manhandle the boats across shallows and around rocks.

So the men would have an opportunity to warm their rations and dry their clothing—at 6:00 p.m. on Monday the 25th, Captain Morgan ordered the column to hold up at a small clearing on the west bank of the river. He directed each Rifle Company to set up a perimeter and pull their loaded batteaux close as possible to the shoreline—a task demanding at least a dozen men lifting, pulling, and pushing each boat.

By the time all thirty-one batteaux were at least partially on the riverbank, more than half the Riflemen in the Advance Guard were wet—some of them for most of the day. Capt. Morgan was one of them. He told me to go back down the column and "Instruct every company to gather tinder, kindling, and firewood sufficient to keep a large bonfire lit through the night to heat food, dry wet clothing, and warm the men."

He also began the practice of giving every Rifleman a gill of what he called "grog," a small quantity of rum, much diluted with lemon, fruit juice, or even water each night whenever possible. When he announced this policy, he said, "We will do this every evening until we run out of rum or liberate Quebec. Whichever comes first is up to you!"

Tuesday, September 26th, was generally a repeat of what we endured the day before with some new wrinkles in what the

Kennebec has to offer its visitors. Shortly after noon we encountered a place where the river broadened and the current diminished. But instead of making the task of propelling the boats upstream easier, it became even more difficult.

For more than a two-mile stretch of river, the water is so shallow, all the batteaux ran aground. In order to move forward, each of our boats had to be lifted by eight men on each side, and four more men in front, pulling towropes. For the better part of four hours this is how we dragged all thirty-one vessels across the shoals. It was an incredibly time-consuming, exhausting endeavor which left every one of us thoroughly soaked and chilled.

By 6:00 p.m., we were back in deeper water but too weary to press further. As the night before, Capt. Morgan ordered the Rifle Companies to pull the batteaux close to the eastern shore of the Kennebec, set up perimeters, and build large bonfires.

Early this morning, Wednesday, September 27th, as we were preparing for our third day on the Kennebec, one of our sentries alerted us to what he described to be "a caravan approaching from the north."

Captain Morgan immediately dispatched 1st Lt. Humphrey and three, five-man ambush teams up the old 1750's-era military road toward Fort Halifax with the mission of intercepting anyone intent on doing us harm.

I sent Corporal Sullivan south along the river to alert Captains Hendricks and Smith of a possible threat from the north. Our little "Headquarters unit" charged our rifles and proceeded to take down our HQ tent and pack our baggage for loading on our batteaux.

While all this was going on, Captain Morgan pulled his spyglass out of his backpack and calmly moved to gain a clear view to the north. After resting the fully extended telescope against a tree and observing the approaching "caravan" for several minutes he said, "They are harmless. Pass the word to let them enter our lines."

I did so and fifteen minutes later, a rough-clothed gentleman aboard a two-horse drawn light wagon pulled up and said, "I am Calvin Coolidge. I am a Patriot. So are the good people behind me. We saw your bonfires last night.

"Three days ago, a Lieutenant Steele came through here and told us Colonel Arnold's Expedition to liberate Quebec would be coming to Fort Halifax from Fort Western. There are ten wagons and carts behind me. We have come to help you on this part of your journey. Because we are very poor, we hope to be paid for our service."

Within a half-hour Captain Morgan and Mr. Coolidge consummated an agreement to compensate Mr. Coolidge and his neighbors one eighth Spanish dollar[1] for every 500 pounds of cargo they delivered from Fort Western to Fort Halifax. I wrote two copies of a "contract" to that effect and both Captain Morgan and Mr. Coolidge signed them.

I gave one copy to Mr. Coolidge. The other I placed in an envelope with a brief note, a sketch map describing the places where we camped, spots found to be challenging, and addressed the wax-sealed envelope: "Please pass to Captain Febiger, Expedition Adjutant."

I then handed the package to Corporal Sullivan with instructions to take another of his Riflemen and one of the Indians in the canoe, paddle back down the river and pass the package to Lieutenant Colonel Greene with a request he relay the message downstream to Colonel Arnold's Expedition Headquarters.

While I was doing this, the Riflemen in each Company were removing gear from each batteau and loading it aboard the wagons and carts accompanying Mr. Coolidge. As this was being accomplished, he shared with Captain Morgan, 1st Lt. Humphrey, and me how his nineteen-year-old son was killed on Bunker's Hill in June and his hope this sacrifice would not be in vain.

Mr. Coolidge also gave us some good advice for the rest of our journey. "There is no road north of Fort Halifax, and the rapids upstream will require portaging the cargo and the batteaux. If you are not receiving reports back from Lieutenant Steele (we are not), I recommend you send some of your Indians and a few of your men to reconnoiter three or four miles ahead so you know what to expect. The few remaining Indians in this part of the country will do you no harm but are unlikely to be helpful."

After looking at the copy of the map Captain Febiger and I made back in Cambridge, he told us, "The distances on the route you have chosen seem to be way off. For example, the notation you have here indicates ten days to move from Fort Halifax to Lake Mégantic. That might be possible by foot, but with all the batteaux and cargo, it could be twice as long."

Tracing the route marked on the map with his finger, he continued, "I see here your final leg of movement to the St. Lawrence is down the Chaudière River. That would be challenging for canoes. Descending in heavy batteaux this time of year will be extremely dangerous. The English translation of the French word Chaudière is 'cauldron.' It is appropriately named."

By mid-afternoon we were all safely ashore on the east bank of the Kennebec, north of the confluence with the Sebasticook River, beside the decaying ruins of Fort Halifax.

Though moving roughly half our cargo up the old military road on the carts and wagons of Mr. Coolidge and his friends allowed the batteaux to float higher, the currents and wind conspired against our still inexperienced boat crews. Most of us spent hours in the water pushing and pulling the boats along. Mr. Coolidge's wheeled transports beat the batteaux to Fort Halifax by nearly two hours.

We spent the remaining hours of daylight emptying the batteaux, packing what oakum we have left into leaks already apparent in the hulls and bottoms of our boats, and then re-packing and lashing down our cargoes.

When 1st Lt. Humphrey ordered a group of our Virginia Riflemen to start gathering tinder, kindling, and firewood for yet another bonfire, one of them replied, "No need, sir. Let's just burn the damnable 'battoes' and walk to Quebec!" He wasn't joking.

Ticonic Falls, Maine, on the Kennebec River

Thursday, September 28th, 1775

At dawn this morning Capt. Morgan dispatched Captain Hendricks, four Pennsylvania Riflemen, and an Indian guide in a canoe up the Kennebec to reconnoiter what the locals said would be our first portage. They were back in less than an hour to confirm the prognostication.

"It's a half-mile long cascade just a half mile north of here," Hendricks reported. "But the only decent portage around it is on the west side of the river and the footpath for our men who are walking is on the east side of the river. That means the 'walkers' will have to go up, beyond the portage, cross at a ford to the west side, and come back down to help move the boats and cargo up above the falls."

On the advice of a local, Captain Morgan ordered the augmentation of each four-man boat crew with two additional "pole pushers" and sent everyone else in a single-file foot column up the narrow east-side trail behind an Indian guide who claimed to know the way to the ford.

Capt. Morgan, 1st Lt. Humphrey, and I got in our canoe with two of our "Headquarters Team" and paddled across the fast-flowing stream ahead of the batteau flotilla to determine where we could beach the boats on the west side of the Kennebec and unload them. There is no such place.

The closest we could get was ten yards from the riverbank. All thirty-one batteaux must be offloaded by hand in waist-deep water. The cargo is passed from one Rifleman to another in the same fashion as firemen pass water buckets to put out a fire.

When each 400-pound vessel is finally empty, ten to twelve Riflemen drag it over the rocks to the riverbank. There, it is turned upside down and a six-man team carries it on their shoulders, staggering and stumbling, more than a half-mile up the portage where it can be put back in the water, and reloaded.

Thirty-one times we did this. Every Rifleman in our three companies was soaked in the bone-chilling water and exhausted carrying the boats and cargo uphill for more than a half mile. I saw both women from the Pennsylvania Rifle Companies struggling up the slippery rocks with canvas-wrapped provisions. They did not stop until the men did.

By the time the sun was dipping below the towering pines around us, we were encamped above Ticonic Falls close enough to hear the roaring water over the crackling of three huge bonfires. As I was lighting a lantern to make an entry in our official journal, Corporal Sullivan and his courier team arrived at the river's edge.

He jumped out of the canoe, walked over, and said, "Message delivered to Lieutenant Colonel Greene, sir. Does Captain Morgan want me to have our men set up his tent?"

Out of the twilight we heard, "Not tonight, Sully." It was Captain Morgan, accompanied by 1st Lt. Humphrey. "The Reconnaissance party we sent up the river a few hours ago just returned. They report our next challenge is just ahead. The Indians call it 'Five Mile Ripples.' The white men call it 'Five Mile Falls.'

"Whichever it is, we need to get through it tomorrow. That means we need to be moving at dawn."

Five Mile Falls, Maine, on the Kennebec River

Friday, September 29th, 1775

There was just a sliver of waxing moon when the "boatmen" reported to their batteaux this morning. The "walkers" were granted an extra half hour of rest, for the narrow path they are following along the riverbank is dangerous enough in daylight but treacherous in the dark.

Captain Morgan, 1st Lt. Humphrey, the Indian we call "Luke" (because he can write), Corporal Sullivan, Privates Kilgannon and Eisenbach, and I loaded our rifles and haversacks into our canoe. The seven of us led the thirty-one batteaux to the base of the watercourse. The reconnaissance party we sent out yesterday afternoon recommended we try going through the rough water rather than around it because Thursday's portage took all day to go little more than a half mile.

It worked, but still required a herculean effort—and meant once again every one of us spent the entire day soaking wet. It was mid-afternoon by the time we had all the batteaux through the five-mile-long "Ripples." Once we arrived at the top, the Kennebec was like a broad, smooth lake. For the first time since leaving Fort Halifax, the batteaux moved in the autumn splendor faster than the "walkers."

We poled and paddled for several miles, past two small settlements and some single structure farms until we could hear water roaring over the rocks of our next major obstacle—Skowhegan Falls. We pulled off for the night and set up a bivouac next to the river.

Anticipating the challenge tomorrow would bring, Captain Morgan ordered the three companies to break out their tents and use batteaux hauling lines strung among the trees to dry our wet clothing. It was good he did because as the sun was going down, the air temperature dropped with it. By 9:00 p.m., when 1st Lt. Humphrey returned from a walk around the perimeter to check on security, the water bucket outside our tent was frozen solid.

Skowhegan Falls, Maine, on the Kennebec River

Saturday, September 30th, 1775

If anything, this second portage is even worse than our first.

The "walkers" were up and moving in early twilight, aided by a one-eighth waxing moon and a cloudless sky. Captain Morgan held the thirty-one batteaux with five crewmen apiece downstream of the narrow defile churning with white water until thirty "walkers"—now designated "haulers"—fifteen on each side of the narrow gorge—are in position, ready to toss forty-foot long lines down to the boatmen as they enter the raging torrent below.

On each batteau, the lines are quickly cleated to the rails of the vessel so it can be held in place while the boatmen enter the icy, chest-deep water to push and pull the vessel close to shore where the cargo is off-loaded and carried up above the falls by a working party of fifty Riflemen and two women.

As soon as each 400-pound boat is emptied, the "haulers" drag it up the rocks for the hard part: hoisting it twenty feet straight up the falls to an island along the western shore of the Kennebec.

It took us more than an hour to get the first batteau up to the island. But as my mother taught my brothers and me: *Uses promptos facit.*[2] By noon we were moving four of our boats an hour through the Skowhegan gauntlet.

Because it was nearly dark and bitter cold by the time the last of our thirty-one batteaux arrived at our encampment, Capt. Morgan decided to send our reconnaissance canoe forward in the morning. Once again, we built huge bonfires to dry our clothing, set up our tents, and huddle close to share body heat as the temperature dropped so low, ice formed on the soaking wet cargoes in our batteaux.

Norridgewock Falls, Maine

Sunday, October 1ˢᵗ, 1775

This ascent—our third portage since leaving Fort Western—is only a mile or so long, but very steep. At dawn, Captain Morgan dispatched 1ˢᵗ Lt. Humphrey, Corporal Sullivan, Private Kilgannon, and "Luke," our Indian guide, to portage the canoe past the falls and offer to pay any settlers available to help haul our cargo around this cascade.

While awaiting the return of our reconnaissance team, Captain Morgan ordered us to chip the ice off our batteaux, check all provisions for damage, and use the last of our oakum on vessels with the most serious leaks.

What we discovered in this brief inspection was frightening. At least half our food is already spoiled by water leaking into improperly sealed casks. The salted beef, pork, mutton, venison, and fish we brought all the way from Virginia is still edible— because Captain Morgan bought and paid for it and ensured it was properly preserved and packed before we departed Virginia in July.

That is clearly not the case with the meat, fish, beans, peas, and bread we bought in Cambridge, Newburyport, and Gardinerston.

Worst of all, nearly all the powder kegs provided for us at Cambridge in the so-called "special allocation" are soaked through. We know the French powder kegs we brought with us from Virginia are still tightly sealed. But it appears that's the only good gunpowder we have available to us in the Advance Force.

As the boatmen commenced disposing of the spoiled and rotting provisions, Captain Morgan had me reduce this information to a note, which I sent back by relay to Captain Febiger. He then sent me to notify all three Rifle Companies we will be on "half rations" until we are re-supplied.

It was nearly 10:00 a.m. by the time 1st Lt. Humphrey and Corporal Sullivan came climbing down the steep rocks beside the falls. They reported engaging the services of seven settlers upstream with wagons and teams of horses and oxen, now on the way to help us.

We immediately began unloading the batteaux and hauling their now smaller cargoes almost a half mile so the wagoneers can load for the uphill portage. The first of the wagons arrived shortly after noon.

It quickly became apparent the two-hour round-trip for the wagons meant we were going to run out of daylight before all the

First Division boats and cargo could be above the cataract. By 4:30 p.m. only eighteen batteaux and roughly half our gear was transported to calm water above the waterfall.

Captain Morgan summoned Lt. Humphrey, Captains Smith and Hendricks, and me to a quick meeting. "Ensign Newman, Corporal Sullivan, and I are going to climb up and inform everyone who has already made it to hold in place and encamp. We will then take our canoe and try to find more wagons. We will remain on top overnight. You three set up an encampment with the men here. Remind everyone about 'half-rations.'

"It will be very cold again tonight. Unfortunately, much of our tentage has already been moved up top. Have the Riflemen build good fires to dry out and stay as warm as possible. Have them ready to move right after first light in the morning. If you hear gunfire from up above, come running. Any questions?"

There were none.

Norridgewock Falls, Maine

Monday, October 2nd, 1775

It was a bitter cold night. I wrapped in my deceased brother's cloak, but by dawn this morning I am colder than I have ever been. The good news is recorded in my journal:

6:40 a.m. Sunrise.

7:15 a.m. Four more sturdy wagons appear at our encampment above the waterfall shortly after sunrise.

8:30 a.m. All eleven wagons have descended the rough track to load the remainder of our provisions. Six more batteaux are being manhandled up the slope.

9:45 a.m. All wagons have arrived atop Norridgewock Falls. Gear is being re-packed in the batteaux.

10:30 a.m. More good news. Eight of the wagons are sturdy enough to carry an empty 400-pound batteau, properly tied in it and supported by two Riflemen walking behind.

11:10 a.m. 1st Lt. Humphrey, having climbed up the rocks from our downstream encampment, informs Captain Morgan, "Colonel Arnold has just arrived below in a canoe."

11:15 a.m. Captain Morgan challenges me to race him down the steep, mile-long portage to meet with Col. Arnold.

Capt. Morgan won because I slipped on a moss-covered rock only a few yards from the bottom of the waterfall and landed on my haversack containing three volumes of our Rifle Company's official journals and correspondence carefully wrapped in water-proof oilcloth.

Capt. Febiger saw it all, found it very amusing, and said I let Capt. Morgan win. I didn't, but I did get to pass the journals to him for relay back to Fort Western.

Colonel Arnold told us, "I have been paddling my canoe up and down the column since we left Fort Western. We're now spread out for twelve miles or more. Once we get the other three divisions to the top of this portage, I'm going to hold up here for a day or two and have Captain Colburn's boat-repair crew fix the batteaux most in need. Do you have any boats that have to be repaired?"

Captain Morgan's response was surprising, "None that we can't fix ourselves if we have more oakum and screws instead of nails."

Colonel Arnold promised to send some of each forward and they spoke for a few minutes about the spoiled provisions and the effect on the Riflemen of Captain Morgan's decision to go on half-rations for the entire First Division. The colonel also stressed the urgency of getting to The Great Carrying Place where we are to widen a twelve-mile-long Indian path so all the Expedition's batteaux can be portaged around a completely unnavigable stretch of the Kennebec River.

While the two commanders talked about the possibility of buying provisions and acquiring powder from French settlers once we arrived in Canada, Captain Febiger told me two good pieces of news: his official promotion to Major in the Continental Army was included in dispatches from General Washington's headquarters, and he found both the messages I relayed back to be helpful and he encouraged me to relay messages and correspondence back to him more frequently.

It was not yet noon when Captain Morgan and I saluted Colonel Arnold and Major Febiger and began our climb back up to the top of the waterfall.

Carritunk Falls, Maine

Wednesday, October 4th, 1775

Had it not been so cold, yesterday would have been a perfect day. The late autumn foliage was in full color. The river was wide and without a ripple. For more than ten hours we rowed the batteaux almost effortlessly up the Kennebec.

Ashore, the terrain revealed not a hint of human habitation. It occurred to many of us we might be the first white men to traverse this part of our planet. This morning, as we approached Carritunk Falls—our fourth portage—we realized why that could well be true.

Lt. Humphrey, leading our reconnaissance party, walked back around the falling water to report, "We got out of the canoe and tried to push through these rapids. About fifty feet upstream, we stepped into a deep hole, the canoe flipped over, nearly killing Luke who cannot swim. I can swim, but I barely made it out alive. We lost two paddles and I nearly lost my rifle. Don't try that with the batteaux. We will lose someone.

"After recovering our nearly submerged canoe, we dragged it to the west side, emptied it and portaged around on the west side. It's about a quarter-mile 'carry' and far safer than trying to push through these devilish falls."

We took his advice and by mid-afternoon we had all thirty-one batteaux above the rapids and were again paddling north toward the twelve-mile long "shortcut" trail between the Kennebec and the Dead River known to the Indians as "The Great Carrying Place."

The Great Carrying Place, Maine

Saturday, October 7th to Monday, October 18th, 1775

It was nearly dark last night when we located the trailhead where we are to begin the longest portage we have made since departing Fort Western.

For the three Rifle Companies, it's not just a matter of carrying our batteaux and much diminished provisions twelve miles west and uphill to the Dead River. From here on, we are to widen this narrow path so 220 twenty-six-foot-long, three-foot-wide batteaux, weighing 400 pounds each can be transported over terrain heretofore used by small parties of Indians carrying lightly loaded, slender canoes.

This morning, Saturday, October 7th, it is alternately snowing and raining so Captain Morgan told Captains Smith and Hendricks to rest their men while our Virginia Rifle Company pressed forward carrying our batteaux and using our hatchets and some limited pioneer equipment—axes, saws, spades, pick-axes, and a few adzes—to broaden the two-foot-wide footpath to ten feet in width. We managed to progress little more than a mile by nightfall.

Sunday, October 8th the weather was equally bad. Despite the continuing rain and snow, our company managed to cut and clear another two miles. Near dusk the two Pennsylvania Rifle Companies moved up to our position to encamp for the night. When they arrived, Captain Smith reported an ice-coated falling tree killed one of his Riflemen early this morning. It was our first casualty since leaving Cambridge on the 11th of September.

Monday, the 9th of October the air is cold, the sky is clear, the moon is full, and Captain Morgan has us up and cutting brush before the sun tinted the eastern horizon. Despite the early start and improved weather, we only manage to advance three miles. We do little better on October 10th.

On Wednesday, October 11th, shortly after we were underway, Lieutenant Colonel Greene's 2nd Division overtook us from behind. He had with him Colonel Arnold's order relieving the Rifle Companies of our "road building" duties and directing us to proceed "by the most expeditious means possible to secure a rendezvous site for the entire force at Lake Mégantic."

By noon on Thursday the 12th, all three Rifle Companies have gladly surrendered most of our "road-building" tools to Lieutenant Colonel Greene's Massachusetts "Musket-men" and the pioneers[3] sent forward from Col. Enos's Fourth Division.

In order to help mark the way forward and provide security for Lieutenant Colonel Greene's "road builders," Captain Morgan ordered our Virginia Rifle Company forward of them—dragging our batteaux with us up the narrow Indian trail.

We started out early Friday, October 13th, about a mile ahead of the pioneers and nearly to the second of the three "ponds" on the route. As we trudged uphill in heavy rain, a messenger from our lead security element was sighted running toward us. He breathlessly reported, "possible enemy movement ahead."

Captain Morgan quickly ordered 1st Lt. Humphrey to alert the rest of our Rifle Company and told our little Headquarters team, "Grab your rifles, fighting gear, and follow me."

We ran up the path for about a quarter mile where we discovered the "possible enemy" is actually Lieutenant Steele's twelve-man scouting party. They are a pitiful sight; ragged, filthy dirty, and exhausted. Four of them carried no packs or equipment, and only six were carrying rifles.

Lieutenant Steele, clearly overjoyed, told Captain Morgan they were heading south to report to Colonel Arnold they had made their way to the Height of Land above the Dead River but all are now near starvation. Hearing this, Captain Morgan ordered Corporal Sullivan, "break out some of our good rations and feed these men."

As his men ate their first real meal in nearly a week, Lt. Steele briefed us on our path ahead. Some excerpts from my journal entries:

"We made it all the way to the Height of Land and found no evidence of British patrols or hostile Indians."

"The 'ponds' between here and the Dead River are navigable lakes for canoes and given the recent snow and rain, likely for batteaux."

"However, the deceptive terrain connecting the remaining two 'ponds' between here and the Dead River is really a series of bogs and knee-deep swampland. It sucked shoes, boots, or moccasins off our feet when we were carrying little more than two light-weight canoes, rifles, and haversacks. God only knows what it will do to six men carrying a 400-pound batteau."

"The Dead River only appears to be dead. There are parts of it where it is broad and gentle. Other sections are a swift-moving, very narrow stream in deep ravines during dry weather. But after heavy rains like we have been having, it quickly becomes a raging torrent. It rose so quickly in last week's rain and snow as to destroy both our canoes. Nearly all of our provisions and equipment were swept away."

"Since running out of food five days ago we have subsisted on wild game and fish, but too little of either."

"The route between here and the Height of Land increases in elevation by at least one thousand feet. Every inch is brutal—and we weren't carrying batteaux."

In early afternoon we sent them on their way south with two days' worth of our scant rations, instructions to follow all the blazed trees we left behind and advice that Lieutenant Colonel Greene's Second Division is closing on our heels.

For the remainder of the 13th through most of the 16th we moved forward with most of the Pennsylvania Riflemen trailing Lieutenant Greene's reinforced Second Division and Virginia Rifle Company providing advance security.

Late in the day on Monday, October 16th, a messenger came forward to advise us Lieutenant Colonel Greene is in desperate need of food and intends to hold up awaiting Lieutenant Colonel Enos and Fourth Division to arrive with more provisions.

Early on Tuesday, October 17th we learned it would be several more days before the "Reserve Supplies will catch up," so Captain Morgan ordered Captains Smith and Hendricks to bring their Pennsylvania Rifle Companies forward.

By dark on Wednesday, October 18th all three of our Rifle Companies are again in the lead of the expedition and encamped on the banks of the Dead River.

Ascending the Dead River, Maine
Thursday, October 19th, 1775

Despite non-stop wind, bone-chilling cold, and scant food, our entire First Division began to advance up the Dead River shortly after dawn on Thursday, October 19th.

That night the low-hanging clouds opened on us and, thankfully, Colonel Morgan held us in place waiting to see what the Dead River would do with all the "new water."

Shortly after noon on Friday, October 20th, a messenger from Lt. Col. Greene's Second Division caught up with our slow-moving column inquiring if we had any food to spare. We don't.

All the edible food we have left are nine barrels of properly prepared, packed, and sealed flour, salted beef and pork we brought with us from Virginia. At half-rations, this was deemed to be enough to feed our one hundred Virginia Riflemen and the two Pennsylvania Rifle Companies for just five days.

Unfortunately, there is no longer any wild game to be seen around us and it appears the recent floods have flushed all the fish downstream. Though Greene's messenger tells us they have been reduced to boiling the leather tongues of their shoes in order to subsist, Captain Morgan tells the messenger, "Please inform Lieutenant Colonel Greene, I regret we have no food to spare."

At dawn, Sunday, October 22nd, we awakened to find the supposedly placid Dead River rising so fast we have to scramble to higher ground for safety.

On Monday, October 23rd, as we were getting underway, we discovered water rushing down the Dead River has already inundated the land on both sides of the river and the surrounding countryside. A half dozen of our First Division batteaux were lost in the maelstrom this morning, including the boat being poled and rowed by 1st Lieutenant William Humphrey. He nearly drowned when his vessel capsized and all their gear was lost.

The near tragedies prompted Colonel Arnold to summon his nearest officers for a "Council of War" at noon the same day. Captain Morgan, 1st Lt. Humphrey, Corporal Sullivan, and I paddled our canoe less than four miles downstream on the Dead River where Colonel Arnold has co-located his headquarters with Lieutenant Colonel Greene's Second Division.

There, we were joined by Major Return Meigs, commanding officer of the Third Division, Captain Reuben Colburn heading the "Batteaux Repair Unit," Doctor Isaac Senter, our Expedition Medical Officer, our chaplain, Rev. Samuel Spring, and Lieutenants Steele and Church, leaders of our Scouting Parties.

Colonel Arnold began by asking, "Who here believes we should abandon all hope of liberating Quebec?"

No one did.

By the end of the meeting it was decided:

1. A small scouting party led by Lieutenants Steele and Church will proceed immediately to reconnoiter the fastest route to Lake Mégantic which the three Rifle Companies will follow to secure a rendezvous site for the Expedition on the shores of Lake Mégantic.

2. The scouting party will then proceed across the Height of Land and down the Chaudière River valley to the French settlement, Sartigan, to buy any cattle, hogs, chickens, sheep, fish, and all available corn or flour the French inhabitants are willing to sell and return with the food supplies to the secure rendezvous site.

3. Those who are too weak or sick to press on to Quebec will be assisted in returning to Fort Western by fifty men of Lieutenant Colonel Enos's Fourth Division.

4. The rest of the Expedition Force will proceed as fast as possible to the selected rendezvous site at Lake Mégantic.

We set out thereafter with Major Meigs and his Third Division close behind us.

On Wednesday, October 25th Lieutenant Colonel Greene sent a messenger forward to inform us Lieutenant Colonel Enos and the entire Fourth Division voted to quit and return to Fort Western with the Expedition's sick and injured.

Captain Morgan, Lieutenant Colonel Greene, Major Meigs, and Colonel Arnold are outraged. Worse still, Enos claimed to have only one barrel of flour to give to those of us remaining on the mission. No wonder some of our Riflemen began referring to him as "Colon Anus."

As we struggled through the muck below the Height of Land and the Canadian border late on Thursday, the 26th of October, I noticed our Virginia Rifle Company is the only unit in the Expedition still carrying seven batteaux. Some of the ones we lost on the 23rd have been replaced with those the "Enos Cowards" left behind.

Each of the two Pennsylvania Companies brought one batteau apiece, but none of the New England Musket Companies took any. It was during the exhausting struggle through the swamp below the Height of Land that Pennsylvania Rifleman Private James Warner succumbed to fatigue, the cold, and hunger.

His wife, Jemima, nursed him for nearly a week before he expired. After enlisting some of his friends to help her bury her young husband in a shallow grave, she picked up his rifle, hatchet, scalping knife, powder horn, and shot pouch and rejoined his comrades in arms as they labored uphill toward the Canadian border.

Our exhausted Virginia Rifle Company arrived at the Height of Land late on Thursday, October 26th. By late Saturday the 28th we were encamped less than a mile from the southern shore of Lake Mégantic. The challenges our starving force endured in hauling our nearly empty batteaux this far made all the previous hardships we endured seem pale by comparison.

The following day, Sunday, October 29th, our excitement at reaching the Height of Land and the Canadian border was tempered when six of our seven batteaux crashed into the rocks of the Chaudière River rapids, throwing Captain Morgan and me into the cascade.

We lost nearly all our remaining provisions, equipment, our doctor's medical kit, and my field desk. Thankfully, all but one of the rifles was saved as were four well-sealed French powder kegs and the last half-barrel of rum.

Cold, starving, and demoralized, our Expedition now totals fewer than 650 men of the original 1,100. Only Captain Morgan's resilience and belief in God's providence keeps us moving. Though suffering as much as any man in our company, Captain Morgan constantly moves up and down our ranks, helping, encouraging, and assuring us Col. Arnold will have provisions awaiting our arrival.

By the first days of November, our starving men are eating soap, beeswax candles, hair grease, oiled moccasins, shot pouches, and even a company commander's dog. Yet, our Riflemen stagger on, many supported by their rifles.

Thanks be to God, on Friday morning November 2nd, the Steele-Church scouting party dispatched by Colonel Arnold to buy provisions from French settlers in Sartigan at the bottom of the Chaudière River valley returned, driving before them a herd of cattle and aided by an Indian named Natanis.

Our officers had to force their starving men to start fires and cook the beef so they would not eat it raw as the animals were being butchered.

Revived by the food we so desperately needed, on Sunday, November 5th, Colonel Arnold had our Virginia Rifle Company resume our Advance Security mission and lead our much depleted expedition out of the Chaudière valley and head for Pointe Lévis on the south side of the Saint Lawrence River, directly across from Quebec City.

We moved at night, attempting to avoid detection from lookouts on the walls of the city and aboard two recently arrived Royal Navy combatants, the frigate *HMS Lizard* and the sloop *Hunter* and four other armed British vessels anchored in the St. Lawrence.

On Thursday, November 9th we arrived at Pointe Lévis where we were joined by a band of thirty-seven Indians and twenty-three French Canadians who professed their desire to join our fight against the British.

By the time we ended our eight-week, 380-mile march and set up camp at Pointe Lévis, across the St. Lawrence River from Quebec, the Expeditionary Force numbered just 597. We lost sixty-three men from privation, drowning, injury, and freezing. Seventy-six turned back because of illness or injury. Eleven were charged with desertion, and the treachery and cowardice of Lieutenant Colonel Enos cost us another 353. But our Virginia Rifle Company has lost only one man drowned and suffered no deserters, unique among all the units which set out from Cambridge, Massachusetts on September 11th.

With no accurate information on the whereabouts of General Montgomery's Northern Army, Colonel Arnold dispatched Lieutenant Aaron Burr and five of Lieutenant Steele's scouts up the St. Lawrence toward Montreal to guide General Montgomery to where we are preparing to assault Quebec City. While we await their return, Colonel Arnold and Captain Morgan have us busy collecting birch-bark and dugout canoes to replace the batteaux lost on the long journey.

Of equal importance we are slowly buying replacement muskets, powder, and shot for weapons lost aboard crashed batteaux and manufacturing scaling ladders and iron-tipped pikes for when we strike.

ENDNOTES

1. During the late eighteenth century, the most widely accepted coin circulating in the American Colonies was the Spanish silver dollar consisting of 387 grains of pure silver. The dollar was divided into "pieces of eight," each consisting of one-eighth of a dollar. From the sixteenth to the nineteenth century, the Spanish dollar was the most stable and least debased coin in the Western world.

2. *Uses promptos facit;* Latin for "Use makes perfect." The modern idiom, "Practice makes perfect."

3. "Pioneers" in eighteenth-century armies were soldiers equipped for specialized engineering and construction tasks such as field fortifications, military camps, roads, and bridges.
    At Fort Halifax, Colonel Arnold directed Lieutenant Colonel Enos to designate fifty members of the Fourth Division to serve as pioneers for the Expedition and acquire appropriate equipment—a significant challenge in the remote Maine wilderness.

CHAPTER THIRTEEN

1775: QUEBEC— SETTING THE STAGE FOR BATTLE

Thus far in this chronological record, I have relied only on my own contemporaneous notes. In short, it reflects what I knew at the time I wrote it down. Activities and events prior to my appointment as Captain Morgan's Adjutant are from entries in my personal diaries. All subsequent information—from Monday, April 24th, 1775, the day I became Rifle Company Adjutant— through Thursday, November 9th, 1775 are from Official Rifle Company Journals and Logs (numbered 1–15). These official records were preserved by passing them initially to Charles Mynn Thruston and later to Captain (and subsequently, Major) Hans Christian Febiger, the Arnold Expedition's Adjutant. He, in turn, relayed my journals and logbooks numbered 1–15 (along with official documents from the Adjutants of other expedition units) back to Fort Western and thence to Continental Army Headquarters in Cambridge, Massachusetts.

On Friday, November 10th, 1775, I began making entries in Journal #16. Due to the terrible tragedy on the night of December 31st, 1775 volume #16 of our Official Rifle Company Journal has never been recovered. Therefore, the chronological record of events below is derived from my recollections and the testimony of other eye-witness participants, compiled, in some cases, months or even years after the activity being chronicled.

Whether this makes the record below more or less accurate than my sole contemporaneous note-taking, I leave for others to decide. What's certain is the record from Friday, November 10th, 1775 forward, has been shaped by others' memories and supplemented with *ex post facto* knowledge.[1]

Pointe Lévis, Canada

Friday, November 10th, 1775

By dawn on Friday, November 10th, 1775, Colonel Arnold has assembled all our ragged, weary, and formerly famished survivors of the expedition in and around Pointe Lévis. The local population consists of about 150 French settlers, farmers, and now out-of-work ferryboat and gristmill workers. Nearly 100 Indian families are in the neighborhood.

Some of our New England officers have expressed concerns about having lost the element of surprise and being bivouacked in full view, within cannon range of the enemy looking down on us from the formidable walls of Quebec City. Captain Morgan isn't one of the critics.

He, Col. Arnold, Major Febiger, and Natanis, the English-speaking Abenaki Indian sub-chieftain who befriended the American cause, chose this riverside settlement on the south bank of the St. Lawrence as our encampment for five very good reasons.

First, Colonel Arnold, Natanis, and his brother Sabatis have all been to Quebec City and Pointe Lévis numerous times—Arnold as a merchant, and the Indians as hunters, trappers, traders and warriors. They all know the British are unlikely to shell the Pointe Lévis ferry landing, gristmill, and trading post from the citadel because it would infuriate the wealthy French and British owners. And the casualties among the civilian and Indian families caused by such a cannonade would make General Guy Carleton, the British Governor, the most hated man in Canada.

Second, the French-speaking inhabitants and nearby Indians at Pointe Lévis are friendly and actively helping us acquire—in exchange for hard cash—essential equipment: birch-bark and dugout canoes, paddles, pikes, cooking pots, utensils, and provisions we will need to attack the fortress across the river. Natanis sent seventeen young Abenaki braves up the Chaudière River and brought down to us tentage and personal equipment recovered from our many wrecked batteaux. Our only regret: The locals have few shoes, boots, or warm clothing to share or sell.

Third, ready access to decent food here in Pointe Lévis has been a lifesaver for many—a fact confirmed by Dr. Senter, our expedition's physician. The importance of good food was enhanced when a gentleman named John Halsted, a New Jersey-born, pro-Patriot merchant, was expelled from Quebec.

Three days ago, in broad daylight, Mr. Halsted rowed across the river and volunteered to aid our cause. He immediately proved his worth by repairing and putting into operation the local gristmill. It is now running around the clock to convert a large store of good, recently harvested wheat into flour so our troops can have, for the first time in months, fresh bread!

For those who have never nearly starved to death, that passage in the Lord's Prayer, "Give us this day our daily bread . . ." is unlikely to have as much meaning as it does for those of us who have gone for weeks with nothing to eat but broth of boiled shoe leather.

Fourth, Pointe Lévis offers the narrowest cross-water transit to our objective—about a mile—directly across the Saint Lawrence River from our encampment. This is why, in the summer of 1759, British General James Wolfe launched his victorious siege against the French-held fortress of Quebec from Pointe Lévis.

But most importantly, all of us are acutely aware the enlistments of most of our troops expire at midnight on the last day of 1775. Any delay in bringing about the surrender of the British garrison guarding Quebec City increases the possibility we will not succeed before the expedition simply evaporates as troops go home. After the grueling travail we suffered to get this close, the thought of failure is unconscionable.

Colonel Arnold selected for his headquarters at Pointe Lévis, the snug, two-story cottage, part of the gristmill property, belonging to British Major Henry Caldwell—commander of the British Militia inside Quebec City.

After one of my many walks through the snow to help Major Febiger create a roster of those fit enough to fight when we cross the St. Lawrence, Colonel Arnold said as I entered headquarters, "Ensign Newman, if you must bring with you a blast of icy air each time you enter this place, please be kind enough to carry in a wet log for each of the four fireplaces. I want Major Caldwell, the Redcoat who owns this place, now peering at us through the frosted lens of his spyglass atop Cape Diamond, to see the steam from our chimneys—while he's freezing his 'arse' off."

At 8:00 a.m., in the midst of heavy snow blown horizontal by a bitter north wind off the river, Major Febiger sent messengers to our battalion and company commanders, summoning them for a 9:00 a.m. Council of War at Expedition Headquarters.

For those of us living and sleeping beneath tents in subfreezing weather, orders to report for a meeting with our Commanding Officer is deemed to be an invitation to warmth. As usual, Captain Morgan, 1st Lt. Humphrey, and I were the first to arrive. Dr. Senter and Chaplain Spring were but a few minutes behind.

Instead of Major Febiger, the expedition's Adjutant, it was Eleazer Oswald, Colonel Arnold's unpaid "aide," now serving as his "military secretary" who called the roll: "Lieutenant Colonel Greene, Major Meigs (now commanding our 2nd Battalion), Major Bigelow, Captain Ward, Captain Thayer, Captain Morgan, Captain Smith, Captain Hendricks, Captain Dearborn, Captain Topham, Captain Goodrich, Captain Hanchett, Captain Hubbard . . ."

As each field commander's name was called, "Aye" came the reply until it got to Captain Morgan. He responded, "Liberty or Death!" as did everyone after him.

Colonel Arnold then asked Chaplain Spring to open with a prayer and he did so by reading the 23rd Psalm.[2] He did not elaborate, nor did he need to. The psalm was a most appropriate prayer for the occasion.

As we have come to expect, Colonel Arnold got right to the point. "Two days ago I received by courier, a message from Brigadier General Montgomery, written on Sunday, October 29th from the British-held Fort St. John's. In General Montgomery's letter, he describes how he is now using heavy artillery delivered from Fort Ticonderoga on September 21st and October 5th to bombard Fort St. Johns—his last obstacle before Montreal.

"General Montgomery has pledged to join us at the gates of Quebec as soon as he subdues Montreal. He will be bringing heavy artillery from Ticonderoga with him. This is exactly the kind of weaponry we need to win this battle and this war—and what I recommended to General Schuyler and General Washington after I captured Ticonderoga last May."[3]

When Colonel Arnold said these words, I just happened to be looking at Captain Hanchett, seated across the table from Captains Goodrich and Hubbard. All three officers glanced at one another, and Hanchett shook his head. I resolved to bring this to Captain Morgan's attention.

Colonel Arnold continued, ". . . Given all we have endured since leaving Fort Western, I am disappointed Brigadier General Montgomery is not closer. But that, like the weather, is not something we can control.

"What we can do is get across the St. Lawrence River as soon as possible, isolate Quebec City from the rest of the countryside, and hold the place under siege until General Montgomery arrives with more troops, warm clothing, and some heavy artillery from Ticonderoga.

"To help us accomplish this mission, seated beside me is Mr. John Halsted, a merchant and a Patriot. Until he was expelled by the cowardly enemy across the river just days ago, he lived in a comfortable home in the Upper Town—not far from the Cape Diamond Bastion—the highest point you can see across the river. He tells us Carleton demanded all in the city unwilling to join the militia in its defense to leave. It is apparent the garrison is understaffed.

"Mr. Halsted has agreed to serve as our guide and pilot to get us safely across the river and identify vulnerable locations inside and outside the walls of Quebec. Since he has spent much more time in Quebec City than any of us, I have accepted his offer. Mr. Halsted, please give us your brief assessment of the enemy situation."

Halsted rose and, using a sketch map on an easel between him and Colonel Arnold, he spoke clearly, "There are now three armed Royal Navy vessels at anchor off Cape Diamond and two large, unarmed, supply ships, the *Elizabeth* and *Jacob*.

"The twenty-eight-gun frigate *Lizard* is the largest; the sloop *Hunter,* which will arrive in the next day or so, has ten guns; the schooner *Magdalen* arrived late last night carrying six guns, and the sloop *Charlotte* has six guns. All the small, hand-rowed cutters—there appear to be about ten of them serviceable for patrolling—have at least one bow-mounted swivel gun.

"As best I can tell, nearly all the naval artillery from the ships is being moved inside Quebec City's walls. The largest caliber pieces I have seen so far are the nine-pounders off the frigate. But there were at least five old French twelve-pounders mounted on the parapets of Diamond Bastion. I have seen them used for ceremonial salutes. I do not know if their carriages are fit for firing live rounds.

"As for getting across the river; I have made the one-mile ferry transit back and forth between here and Lower Town hundreds of times, but I am recommending to Colonel Arnold we make a night crossing from here to what is now called Wolfe's Cove, south-west of the city walls, where General Wolfe landed in September 1759.

It's a little bit longer than going straight across to the Lower Town, but much safer.

"If the count I received this morning is correct, we have forty birch-bark canoes and dugouts to move about 175 men at a time from here to Wolfe's Cove. If we start right after dusk with the wind and tides in our favor, we should be able to get about 550 men across the river before dawn.

"I have observed the enemy's nighttime patrols in their cutters. There are rarely more than three boats in the water at once. Their schedule seems to be haphazard for those who measure time on a watch. But those of us who have spent our lives on the water also measure time by the changing of the tides.

"It appears to me the sailors rowing the patrol cutters are choosing to head upriver on a rising tide—because it's easier to row upstream if the tide is behind you. If we want to avoid them, we need to leave here heading upriver before they head in that direction.

"We cannot take canoes and dugouts on the river in this kind of weather. They will founder. But we must move soon because the St. Lawrence will shortly be ice-choked, not frozen over, but impassable for canoes, dugouts, and even small boats like the cutters.

"I recommend as soon as the weather improves, we be ready to cross the river right after sunset on a rising tide. The moon is waning and rising later each night through the end of the month, but we dare not wait that long or we will be here until spring."

When Mr. Halsted finished, Colonel Arnold asked, "Any questions?"

Without the courtesy of standing to address our commander, Capt. Hanchett immediately said, "I don't have a question, but an observation. I think it's suicide to try to get across that river in the middle of any night. Half of our men aren't fit to fight even if we made it ashore on the other side. We have no idea how many well-armed, fully-trained Regulars and militia-men they have inside the walls . . ."

As Hanchett spoke, I watched Colonel Arnold. He didn't move except to turn his head toward the insubordinate captain. There was no apparent rise of color in the Colonel's cheeks. There was no change in his demeanor. But his eyes became like those of an owl watching a squirrel. He didn't squint. He didn't blink. He stared like a bird of prey about to swoop down to have dinner.

Hanchett wrapped up with, "I think we ought to put this idea to a vote."

At this point Colonel Arnold rose and, without taking his gaze from the captain's face, said very calmly, "We're not going to vote. If, after all we have endured, you do not wish to accompany us to accomplish our mission, by all means, defect like your cowardly battalion commander."

Then turning to the rest of us in the room, he asked, "Do any of you who are going with me to do our duty and carry out our orders, have any questions?"

There were none. After a moment of silence, Colonel Arnold concluded, "We will not be crossing the river tonight, but we will do so on the next night we have better weather. As of now we have twenty-seven serviceable bark canoes and ten rugged dugouts. We will continue to search for more of both—and more paddles.

"By this time tomorrow morning, please deliver to Major Febiger rosters of your units indicating those who are fit to fight and those who are not—and why not. Post sentries as usual tonight.

"If all goes as planned, before dark, Mr. Halsted will have baked six hundred loaves of bread. Each of your soldiers will get one loaf. If there are any loaves left, you and your officers may have one apiece. Any remaining will be delivered to Dr. Senter for the patients in his hospital."

And, as if he had just thought of it, Colonel Arnold ended the meeting, "With thanks to Captain Morgan, tonight's challenge is 'Liberty or' and the password is 'Death.'"

Pointe Lévis, Canada

Saturday, November 11th, 1775

The bread delivered last night was well received by all our Rifle-men. Captain Morgan, Lt. Humphrey, and I each saved half a loaf to enjoy this morning with some orange marmalade preserves Mr. Halsted presented to us last night.

We had just toasted slices of bread on the fire in the middle of our tent and were smearing marmalade on them with our scalping knives when Private Kilgannon arrived outside our tent and shouted above the wind, "Sirs, a British cutter from the sloop *Hunter* is approaching the cove where our canoes and dugouts are hidden. Corporal Sullivan wants to know if he should engage them."

We all jumped up as Captain Morgan yelled, "Hell, yes! How many are there?"

"At least a dozen, sir. They all appear to be armed. Even the four oarsmen."

"How many are with Sully?"

"Just the two of us with rifles and our four Indians, armed with muskets."

"Go help Sully. Tell him help is on the way!" As he grabbed his rifle and kit, he said to me, "Come with me, Ensign Newman."

He then turned to Lt. Humphrey and said, "William, alert Captains Hendricks and Smith. Get your ten-man quick reaction team and bring 'em up to that little knoll east of the cove, prepared to back us up." And on his way out the tent flap into the wind and snow, Capt. Morgan carefully set his piece of marmalade-coated toast on his backpack and said to us both, "That better be here when we get back."

The cove was about 200 yards from our perimeter and when we were about halfway there we heard a single shot. I couldn't tell with all the wind what it was, but the captain said, "Rifle. Outgoing."

A moment or two later there were a half dozen more shots, louder than the first. This time the captain said, "Muskets. Incoming," and began to sprint.

When we crested the little knoll above the cove, we could see a Royal Navy cutter being furiously rowed away from our shore—and a swimmer desperately trying to catch the long boat.

As we came up behind Cpl. Sullivan, two of his Indians fired at the swimmer and Sully shouted, "No! I said shoot at the boat—like this—" And from a kneeling position he cocked his rifle took aim, pulled the trigger, and the helmsman holding the rudder at the stern of the cutter pitched forward and fell among the rowers.

There followed a brief exchange of musket fire between the sailors in the boat and our Indians which was a waste of powder and shot, given the cutter was by now more than 200 yards away. Both Private Kilgannon and I fired our rifles once at the boat but without any apparent effect other than encouraging the oarsmen to row faster toward the British sloop *Hunter*.

During the musket melee, Captain Morgan was keeping his eye on the swimmer who somehow made it back to our shore and crept into a thick patch of reeds on the edge of the cove.

As 1st Lt. Humphrey and his ten Riflemen arrived, Captain Morgan and two of the Indians began searching for the swimmer as they walked along the shoreline. Suddenly, one of the Indians saw movement in the underbrush, pulled out his scalping knife and charged into the water.

Realizing we were about to lose a valuable prisoner of war, Captain Morgan tossed me his rifle and kit, jumped into the ice-crusted water, caught the Indian, motioned for him to put away his knife, and immediately thereafter a thoroughly soaked and nearly frozen, uniformed British sailor stood up and raised his hands.

At this, Lt. Humphrey and four Riflemen of his quick reaction team slid down from the crest of the knoll to take control of the prisoner and march him back to our encampment. He left five members of his quick reaction team to replace Corporal Sullivan, Private Kilgannon, and their four Indians as fresh guardians over our canoes and dugouts.

Though the entire Expeditionary Force seemed to be out and about, awaiting our return, we proceeded directly to Colonel Arnold's Headquarters with our prisoner. Major Febiger met us at the door of "the cottage" and after a mercifully brief parley, invited Captain Morgan, whose clothing was now frozen solid, 1st Lt. Humphrey, Corporal Sullivan, the nearly frozen British sailor, and me inside to stand by a fireplace while he went upstairs.

Less than five minutes later, time enough for the rear of Captain Morgan's hunting frock and leggin's to thaw and begin steaming, Colonel Arnold, Majors Meigs, Febiger, Messer's Oswald, Halsted, and Dr. Senter entered the room across the hall and sat at the table where we met yesterday.

Just before the prisoner was escorted into the room, Colonel Arnold said, "Captain Morgan, please have a seat at the table with us."

"Sir, with your permission I will stay right here in front of this fire. I appreciate your invitation, but my backside is more grateful for the warmth it is receiving right here."

By the end of a half-hour interrogation, we knew our captive was a Royal Navy Midshipman, the sixteen-year-old brother of Captain Thomas Mackenzie, the commanding officer of the sloop *Hunter*. The youngster admitted the cutter was sent to "determine if 'the rebels' are hiding small boats and canoes in the cove and if so, douse them with lantern oil and drop hand grenades on them to ensure destruction." Otherwise, he refused to answer any other questions.

When it became evident more information would not be forthcoming, Col. Arnold turned to Major Febiger and said, "Take him out and have him guarded across the hall near the fireplace for a few minutes."

After the door closed behind them, he said to Captain Morgan, "Well done, Daniel. He is potentially a very valuable acquisition."

Then turning to the rest of us he said, "We need a place to hold him where he won't escape or freeze. When we cross the river, we need to take him with us—and he needs to be healthy. Any ideas?"

"Yes, sir," Mr. Halsted replied. "Dr. Senter and I are billeted in the cabin next to the mill. There are two bedrooms—one larger than the other. We can both move into the small bedroom and put our prisoner and two guards in the other. There is only one fireplace. It's on the ground floor but it heats all the cabin very nicely."

To this, Major Meigs added, "If you wish, Colonel, I will have Captain Dearborn put a good sergeant from his company in charge of securing the lad and bringing him with us when we cross the river. It won't be hard to find volunteers for 'indoor duty' in this weather."

At this, Colonel Arnold stood and said, "Thank you, gentlemen, we have a solution. I am most grateful to all of you. Let us pray for better weather tomorrow. Dr. Senter, please examine our prisoner, ensure he is healthy, make the appropriate entries in your medical journal, and hope he stays that way."

As we prepared to leave, Captain Morgan said to Maj. Febiger, "Hans, if you don't mind, after you move our prisoner, I will remain in the room across the hall next to the fireplace long enough to dry the front of my clothing so it will be pleased to accompany the rear of my clothing before rejoining my comrades in my tent."

When our captain returned to our tent an hour later his clothing was dry, his rifle was clean, and his piece of marmalade-covered toast was right where he left it.

Pointe Lévis, Canada

Sunday, November 12th, 1775

Unfortunately, the weather this morning is, if anything, worse than it was yesterday. But, if the wind, snow, and white caps on the river ever abate, our prospects for getting across the St. Lawrence were enhanced this afternoon just after sunset when Natanis and his brother Sabatis delivered two more dugouts, and their braves brought to our cove three large birch-bark canoes and fifteen paddles. We now have forty-five vessels and at least four paddles for each.

The thirty-seven "volunteer" Indians Natanis and Sabatis recruited to serve as paddlers and guides are now encamped inside our perimeter near the trading post.

At 3:00 p.m. Colonel Arnold called for another commander's meeting. This one was shorter and less dramatic than yesterday's. The primary focus is on reconciling the rosters of each unit and ensuring we have full accountability for all our troops.

The rosters show we now have 597 of our original Expedition Force here, including Sgt. Grier's wife, Eliza, and the widow, Jemima Warner, whose husband perished in the wilderness. To this total we have added the Indians, and twenty-three French Canadians who have been distributed among the musket companies.

Doctor Senter has deemed only thirty-one of our number to be unfit for duty for various causes: injury, frostbite, dysentery, fever, vomiting, and "palsy." And Colonel Arnold has also decided to leave a sixty-man company here as a Rear Guard in case we need to retreat back across the river.

At the conclusion of the meeting, Colonel Arnold said, "Our local friends Natanis and Mr. Halsted tell me this storm will blow itself out by mid-morning. So, Major Febiger, how many will we be taking across the river with us tomorrow night?"

"Five hundred and sixty-six brave souls and one prisoner of war, sir."

Pointe Lévis, Canada

Monday, November 13th, 1775

Shortly after dawn this morning it was apparent the weather forecast was spot-on. The sky is clearing. The wind has dropped.

While it is still below freezing, it is noticeably warmer and there are no whitecaps on the river. Best of all, Mr. Halsted and his local bakers worked all night to produce 600 new loaves of bread.

At 11:00 a.m., Colonel Arnold summoned his commanders to meet at his HQ at noon. When all were seated he entered with Mr. Eleazer Oswald and Major Febiger and opened with: "This is our final Council of War on this side of the St. Lawrence River. Tonight, we are going across to liberate the City of Quebec from their British oppressors.

"Sunset tonight is at 4:03. By 5:30 it will be dark. The tide will be rising by 10:00 and a waning, slightly larger than half-moon, will start rising at about the same time. By 6:00 p.m. you need to have your units aligned in the sequence shown on the chart Major Febiger has prepared.

"Our first wave needs to be underway, heading upriver from the cove no later than 9:00 p.m. to get across before the British patrol boats start upriver from the Lower Town wharf. Major Febiger has a chart showing the sequence and timing for moving each division to the cove.

"I will be in the lead canoe, the large dugout with Captain Morgan, Natanis, Mr. Halsted, Ensign Newman, and Corporal Sullivan. The canoes immediately behind us will bring the rest of the Riflemen, then our Indian friends, and then the musket companies in subsequent waves. If all goes according to plan, we should have Patriots across to Wolfe's Cove and atop the Heights[4] before dawn."

By now the excitement in the room was palpable. Colonel Arnold, sensing his commanders are anxious to commence final preparations with their troops, raised his voice and said, "Cease fire on the chatter! Four important points to pass on to your men!

"First, everyone, including officers, must have a piece of white cloth on the back of their hat, hood, cape, or collar with the words 'Liberty or Death' on it.

"Second, do not load the last canoe in your wave. I want the last canoe in each wave to be available for rescue.

"Third, make sure everyone boarding has his firearm loaded—but not cocked!

"Fourth, remind your men if they are challenged by a British patrol boat, do not fire on them unless they have their swivel gun ready to fire on you or have already engaged your canoe.

"Are there any questions?"

This time Captain Hanchett had the good sense to stand and speak respectfully, "Sir, I do not see my company on Major Febiger's chart. Which wave are we in?"

Colonel Arnold replied, "For tonight, Captain Hanchett, your company will stay here to serve as our Rear Guard."

Our first wave—with 203 aboard—was loaded in the first forty-four canoes by 8:30 p.m. At precisely 9:00, on Colonel Arnold's whispered command, "Let's go!" the four strong Indians—two in the bow and two in the stern, silently pulled out of the cove and into the river. As predicted, it is near slack tide and there is almost no noticeable current. Behind us, another dugout silently follows in our wake.

We were better than half way across without incident when one of the old birch bark canoes broke in two, dumping Lieutenant Steele and four Riflemen into the icy water. The canoes behind them quickly picked them and their gear up one at a time—somehow without tipping over. But when the indomitable Lieutenant started climbing over the stern of the canoe, there was a loud sound of wood cracking. Instead of risking another breakup, he whispered, "I'll just hang on—keep going." And they did.

In little more than an hour from the time we departed Pointe Lévis, our first wave was all ashore and headed, single-file, up the same steep trail General Wolfe scaled with more than 4,000 British troops sixteen years ago—in the summer.

Once on top, Captain Morgan dispatched Lt. Heth, originally of Captain Stephenson's Virginia Rifle Company, and six Riflemen on a reconnaissance toward the wall, less than five hundred yards away.

Our second wave arrived at midnight without incident but with fewer canoes because Major Bigelow, responsible for loading at Pointe Lévis, began eliminating any vessels deemed to be unsafe. Still, three of the canoes in this wave leaked so badly they nearly foundered, soaking all eighteen men aboard and losing some muskets.

The third wave came in at 3:15 a.m.—but with only thirty-one canoes. As the troops disembarked and began scrambling up the hill, some of those from the second wave who were very wet started a fire in a nearby shed to warm up before the climb.

Lt. Humphrey rushed over and had them put it out but it was too late. Less than two minutes after our last canoe pushed off for the return trip to Pointe Lévis, a British cutter appeared out of the darkness, apparently so intent on investigating the light onshore they took no notice our dugout passing them within fifty yards of their port side.

The moon is now high enough—and they are close enough—there are a half-dozen of us with rifles and muskets in our hands watching. As the boat rows closer to us, a sailor removes a canvas from a swivel gun mounted on the bow of the longboat. He extracts a cork muzzle plug and we can see a glowing punk in the gunner's left hand. He blows on it before sticking it down the touchhole. But an instant before he can do so, we hear Colonel Arnold's voice scream, "Fire!"

The effect is as intended, except all four of the muskets fail to fire—likely because the powder in their flash pans is wet. The only weapons that do fire are Lieutenant Humphrey's and my rifles. The gunner pitches backward into the boat, the swivel gun's muzzle swings down into the water as the six oarsmen furiously row backward. A dozen or so other rifles and muskets open fire and two more sailors appear to be hit before the boat disappears into the mist.

Lt. Humphrey and I head immediately to the top of the cliff and arrive at Captain Morgan's position just as Lieutenant Heth's little patrol returns from exploring the city's western wall and Lt. Heth commences a hasty debrief. "We didn't see a single sentry anywhere outside the wall or on it. We were about 100 feet from St. John's gate when the shooting began.

"Based on what Mr. Halsted told us, we expected to hear church bells ringing and drummers waking the militia to their duty stations. But there was nothing. No watchmen. No sentinels. Then, maybe a minute later, St. John's gate opened and a single man walked out, took a leak against the wall, walked back inside, and closed the gate like it was his bedroom door."

"Could you hear if he barred the gate after he went back inside?" asked Captain Morgan.

"No, sir," Heth replied. "By that time we were just glad fifty dragoons hadn't ridden out to cut us down with their sabres instead of one guy looking for a place to pee."

Afterward, there were many who claimed the gate was not locked or blocked. That's not what any of us knew at the time and none of those who made those assertions were there.

What we did know at the time was we had 512 tough, resilient armed men just outside the west wall of an enemy-held city—and thus far, no indication anyone inside seemed to be aware of our presence.

After listening to Lt. Heth's report, Captain Morgan went a few yards where Colonel Arnold was telling Lieutenant Colonel Greene and Major Meigs where to position sentries. Nearby were Major Febiger, Messer's Oswald and Halsted, Chaplain Spring, and Dr. Senter. They all heard my captain say, "Sir, we still have nearly three hours until sunrise.[5] My Riflemen have six scaling ladders with us. Let me take them and our Indians over the wall. We will open the gates for the rest of our Patriots to pour in, and the city will be yours before breakfast."

I was surprised to hear the Colonel's whispered response: "Let me see or hear what our Comrades in Arms think." With that, Colonel Arnold asked all around him, "Who is in favor of Captain Morgan's plan to try and take the city tonight?"

Captain Morgan—the only "Aye" in the group—not even Colonel Arnold voted in favor—shrugged and said, "Very well, sir. Where do you want our Riflemen to go and what do you want them to do?"

We learned the next day, our arrival the night before went undetected and the St. John's Gate was open all night and manned by the one casual soldier Lt. Heth observed. Though I could tell this enraged Capt. Morgan, he spoke not a word about it.

Colonel Arnold decided to post nearly fifty Musket Company men as pickets where they can observe the walls and gates. He ordered our Riflemen to serve as the vanguard for moving the balance of the 512 rough men who made it across the river from Pointe Lévis to a place Mr. Halsted chose about a mile west of Quebec City.

The site he picked is the palatial estate of Major Henry Caldwell—commander of the British Militia—and owner of the gristmill on the other side of the river. We approached ready for the action we'd been craving only to find a few sleepy guards who meekly surrendered. Colonel Arnold made the Caldwell mansion his headquarters. The Rifle and Musket companies took up lodging in a perimeter of empty homes nearby.

West Wall of Quebec City, Canada
Tuesday, November 14th, 1775

By sunup, the British garrison was alerted to our presence and were prepared to engage an assault.

Awakened while still in Major Caldwell's feather bed, Colonel Arnold was informed one of our advance sentries was captured by a small band of the enemy and taken into the city.

Our sentry's capture convinced Col. Arnold the British were ready to engage in full battle Adjutant so we marched on the walls in a show of force we hoped would at least rally support from the civilian occupants. Beyond a few cheers and jeers from some gathered on the walls, nothing of consequence transpired. That is until young "gentleman volunteer" Matthais Ogden and a drummer were sent under a white flag to read the terms of the garrison's surrender to Lt. Governor Cramahé.

Standing next to Cramahé, the garrison's commander, Col. Allan Maclean responded with a wave of his hand which loosed a cannonball that landed close enough to Ogden to spray him and his drummer with frozen soil. Maclean was a seasoned and disciplined soldier with extensive experience in training and leading hardened troops. His experience played a significant role in what was to come for our mission. Having arrived back at Quebec after making a failed attempt to reinforce Carleton in Montreal just hours before Arnold's force crossed the St. Lawrence, he quickly reset the city's defense both militarily and by bringing the civilians in line.

West Wall of Quebec City, Canada
Wednesday, November 15th, 1775

To compound our troubles, an inventory of our arms and ammunition was bleak, yielding barely five rounds per man and a number of us without a musket and others not in firing condition. Captain Morgan is near the boiling point by now and takes his concerns to

Col. Arnold. As is his practice, his main complaint is on our behalf. The bread we received before leaving Pointe Lévis is long gone and Colonel Arnold has again put everyone on restricted rations.

Morgan's point for his commander was how his Rifle Company was bearing most of the load of intimidating those inside the walls and manning the pickets and patrols. When Arnold aggressively rebuffed Capt. Morgan's complaint, I thought I would see my captain strike a superior officer for the first time. A thought of his beloved Abigail must have flashed through his mind because he turned on his heel and rushed out. The next day Col. Arnold sent word that the Riflemen's rations were increased. With that order came his instructions for Morgan, Febiger, a small group of our Riflemen, Natanis, and Halsted to head west to reconnoiter the best and quickest route to Pointe-aux-Trembles.

West Wall of Quebec City, Canada
Saturday, November 18th, 1775

Col. Arnold received word Gen. Montgomery captured Montreal, garrisoned troops there, and was headed to Quebec with about 200 men. Perhaps more importantly, he instructed three armed schooners laden with more troops, artillery, clothing, supplies, and arms to follow him downriver.

With this news came a less encouraging report of Governor Carleton and his detachment escaping Montgomery's attack and heading to Quebec to fortify the British stand there.

We retreated up the St. Lawrence toward Montreal, to Pointe-aux-Trembles, out of reach from Quebec to await word about the advance of the Second Army. It was a sorrowful march by beleaguered, exhausted, and freezing men now only consisting of 550 functioning soldiers out of a total of the 597 who'd survived the trek from Boston.

When we arrived in the small village of Pointe-aux-Trembles, we noticed a ship on the St. Lawrence heading downstream toward Quebec. We discovered later the ship to be the brig *Fell* carrying

Governor Carleton to Quebec. One of General Montgomery's men told me the tale of how the governor slipped out of Montreal with a flotilla thinking he'd cleanly escaped. The wily General Montgomery previously posted artillery at Sorel, not far east of Montreal to form a blockade. Carleton donned peasant clothes and took a small boat he paddled with his hands to remain silent. He left the flotilla behind to take their chances and he was later picked up by the boat we saw moving down the river.

Pointe-aux-Trembles, Canada
Saturday, December 2nd, 1775

The morning after Gen. Montgomery arrives, being in the fittest condition, the Rifle Companies lead the return to Quebec to be followed by the main body the day after. A foot of snow lay on the ground as we approach Quebec, the frosting on the landscape and walls of the city give the vista an almost romantic appeal. That spell was broken before it could fully form.

We came upon the Redcoat pickets, who, not expecting our return so soon, are taken by surprise and captured.

General Montgomery, now in charge of the entire force of nearly a thousand men arrive in Quebec three days later. The supply ships having yet to arrive, we make several attempts to get Carleton to surrender.

Montgomery reorganized the assembled group of partial regiments to assure proper chain of command, accounting for the many losses already experienced, leaving Arnold's command mostly intact as it had arrived in Canada. One exception was his promotion of Aaron Burr to captain and making him his aide-de-camp. Burr's fellow volunteers, Eleazer Oswald and Matthias Ogden, remain in Col. Arnold's service.

Thanks to prisoners captured by our Riflemen, we know the Quebec garrison is in serious need of re-provisioning. We hope the combined British-Canadian force inside the walled city will be forced to lay down their arms. Rather, Carleton has the Quebec garrison fire on our messengers, probably a habit learned from Maclean.

Our resupply arrives several days later, the spoils of Carleton's narrow escape on the St. Lawrence. Reinforced and brought back to near battle fitness by shoes, winter clothing, and warm blankets, we span the Plains of Abraham west of Quebec. Montgomery arrayed our forces to cut off supplies of food and supplies into the city and prevent exit from the city by anyone other than women and children to further pressure the occupying troops into surrender.

December 16th, Dr. Senter records, "Pvt. Morton of 1st Infantry Battalion died from a grapeshot wound and widow Jemima Warner expired this morning after being struck by a shot from the city on December 11th." He added the following note: "When her husband, Pvt. James Warner, depleted by illness, fatigue, and hunger, died in the swamp below Lake Mégantic, she picked up his musket and marched with us to Quebec. She was as brave as any of the men."

We discover rather quickly the artillery General Montgomery brought with him has little effectiveness against the thick walls of the city. The enemy's larger caliber pieces being used by the garrison have greater range and effectiveness. To get our cannons close enough to lob rounds into the enemy makes them easy targets for the British.

ENDNOTE

1.   An example of *ex post facto* [or, "after-the-fact"] knowledge: In Journal #15, my contemporaneous entry for Thursday, November 9th states ". . . we ended our eight-week, 380-mile march. . . ." That's what I knew and believed at the time.

       But "after-the-fact" knowledge, gleaned later from other reports and measurements made on accurate maps of the portages and back-tracking yields a more precise figure for the distance most members of the Expedition covered: "about 300 miles."

2.   Psalm 23 King James Version (KJV)
      [1]The LORD is my shepherd; I shall not want.

[2] He maketh me to lie down in green pastures: he leadeth me beside the still waters.

[3] He restoreth my soul: he leadeth me in the paths of righteousness for his name's sake.

[4] Yea, though I walk through the valley of the shadow of death, I will fear no evil: for thou art with me; thy rod and thy staff they comfort me.

[5] Thou preparest a table before me in the presence of mine enemies: thou anointest my head with oil; my cup runneth over.

[6] Surely goodness and mercy shall follow me all the days of my life: and I will dwell in the house of the Lord for ever.

3.   Though Colonel Benedict Arnold and Ethan Allen had a lifelong dispute over who should be credited with seizing Fort Ticonderoga on 10 May 1775, there is no debate it was Col. Arnold who compiled the inventory of weapons, ammunition, and military stores captured at Ticonderoga. There is also no doubt Arnold discussed removing the military hardware—particularly the heavy artillery—for use by Patriot forces with Generals Montgomery, Schuyler, and Washington.

Every history of the American Revolution credits the remarkable feat Henry Knox achieved in bringing the heavy weaponry from Ticonderoga to Boston during the winter of 1775–76. Knox, using the "Arnold Inventory," selected sixty cannons, howitzers, and mortars to be transported by leaky barges, teams of draft horses, even crude ox-drawn sleds, on a ten-week, three-hundred-mile trek. The saga of how Knox and his men braved heavy snow and freezing cold while dragging weapons weighing as much as 6,000 pounds [the weight of a "24-pounder" cannon and carriage] across frozen rivers, through swamps, forests, and ascending and descending the Berkshire Mountains on the way to break the Boston stalemate in March of '76 is the stuff of legend.

Yet, the first time Patriot forces actually used Ticonderoga's heavy weapons in combat took place in September–October 1775 under the command of Brigadier General Richard Montgomery during the siege to capture Fort St. Johns. He used Ticonderoga weapons again to coerce the British surrender at Montreal and ultimately at Quebec.

4.   Better known as "The Plains of Abraham."

5.   Captain Morgan was off by a few minutes. His conversation with Colonel Arnold took place at 3:45 a.m. Sunrise in Quebec on the 14th of November was at 6:29 a.m.

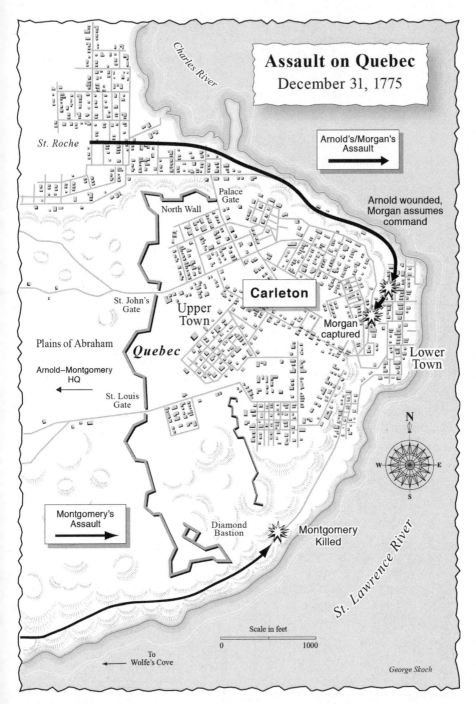

CHAPTER FOURTEEN

1775–1776: QUEBEC—
THE FORLORN
HOPE

Forlorn Hope: A body of combatants chosen to lead an assault against an enemy-held position where the risk of casualties is highest.

North Wall of Quebec City, Canada
Saturday, December 23rd, 1775

Our attacks on the city walls and Palace Gates area from the St. Charles River are having little effect. On the rare occasions the enemy show themselves, our Riflemen dispatch them, but we sustain losses as well from their cannons and volleys from the walls.

Resistance from the Redcoats inside Quebec is stalwart. Patriot artillery cannot be properly entrenched, inflicts little damage on the city, and is outgunned by superior British artillery pieces and placement.

The severity of our condition is measured with increased cold, infirmity, and death. Then, a smallpox outbreak among

Montgomery's New York troops further depletes our numbers. Every officer is aware that the term of service for nearly all of Arnold's troops expires at midnight, December 31st.

The Quebec Garrison remains on high alert and seemingly perpetual vigilance. The west wall cannot be penetrated by our small artillery nor scaled with enough troops to overwhelm the enemy. The final challenges to an assault are the narrow approaches around the western fortifications and high vantage points manned by the Redcoats and Canadian militia. There is no choice but to await another major snowstorm to cover our movement around the city. Since our return from Pointe-aux-Trembles, the weather has been clear though bone chillingly cold.

The Estate of Major Henry Caldwell/
General Montgomery's Headquarters

Monday, December 25th, 1775

General Montgomery has called a Council of War for his commanders to lay out his plan of attack to capture Quebec and fulfill Congressional directives to go on the offense. As is our habit, Col. Morgan, Lt. Humphrey, and I arrive before the other commanders and their staffs. Major Febiger met us at the door and ushered us into the parlor to join General Montgomery, Col. Arnold, Aaron Burr, and others from the general's staff.

General Montgomery presented the plan he and Colonel Arnold composed using the latest intelligence and advice from Mr. Halsted. Mr. Halsted has been most influential in the decision to circle the city from north and south and attack through Lower Town where much of the populations' stores are warehoused. Colonel Arnold's so-called "Kennebec Corps," now down to fewer than 500 battle-ready men including sixty Canadian and Indian volunteers, and forty men from Captain Lamb's artillery company will move to the north and east through the St. Roche suburb and along the St. Charles River. One small cannon lashed to a sled is to be brought with Lamb's men.

Col. Arnold and twenty-five volunteers will form our Forlorn Hope, those taking the highest risk of initial engagement with the enemy. Our Riflemen and Capt. Lamb's artillery detachment with a sled-mounted cannon are to follow closely behind them with scaling ladders. We will be armed with spontoons in addition to our rifles. Captain Lamb's artillery company and their sled-mounted cannon will follow us. Bringing up the rear of this assault force will be Col. Greene and Major Meigs leading the second New England battalion.

In an effort to create a diversion, two faux attacks against Upper Town are to be conducted. Captain Jacob Brown, leading a detachment of Massachusetts troops using scaling ladders and much noise, will strike at the wall near Cape Diamond. The other, a company of about 200 recently recruited Canadians led by Colonel Livingston will make a similar attack at St. John's Gate. To further distract and confuse our enemy, Lieutenant Wool's battery of five mortars in St. Roche, detached from Captain Lamb's Independent New York Artillery Company, will start lobbing bombs into the city as the two assault forces advance toward their objectives.

Because much of the clothing our men are wearing came from the British supply ships captured outside Sorel, everyone is instructed to pin patches of white cloth to their hats with the words, "Liberty or Death" written on them. Killing our own in the chaos of urban battle is always a threat, even when we all wear the same uniforms.

For the final part of the plan, General Montgomery said he will form on the Plains of Abraham near the St. Lawrence with four battalions of New York troops and move along the river road to the east and north past Diamond Bastion and link-up with Colonel Arnold in Lower Town. Once the two forces are joined, they will move west together to take the Upper Town and secure the city. Another small gun on a sled will go with Montgomery.

If all goes as we hope, this is still a very complicated and extremely dangerous assault. And the storm we need to cover our movements will slow us and make communications among and even within units, very challenging at best.

As General Montgomery prepared to dismiss us, Col. Arnold leaned into the general's ear after which he asked Reverend Spring to pray. Our chaplain jumped to his feet, we all bowed our heads and he intoned:

> Our sovereign God who loves us and ever purposes for our good, we seek Your Providence in these terrible efforts we are about to undertake for our cause of liberty. We know we shall not all live through this battle, so we now commit our lives to Your keeping in life and death. May we ask You to grant the least loss of life possible on both sides of this conflict in accomplishing our mission. This we pray in the name of the risen Savior. Amen.

The attending "amens" were low and solemn, but firm. I may be off on a word or two in recalling this prayer, but I shall never forget it.

St. Roche, Quebec, Canada
Sunday, December 31st, 1775

On Saturday evening, December 30th, the weather finally turned in our favor. The sky was devoid of stars and an increasingly powerful wind from the northeast started mounting in the afternoon. By dark it was snowing so hard we could barely see five yards in any direction. At 6:00 p.m. General Montgomery held a brief council of war and announced to all: "If this weather holds, we attack tonight."

Our long and brutal campaign is nearly over. Since departing Cambridge on September 11th, we have endured more than we thought humanly possible. In a few hours, more than three months after passing in review for General Washington we will assemble in a different place and formations to carry out the mission he gave us.

At 2:00 a.m. Col. Arnold and his twenty-five-man Forlorn Hope are leaning into the howling wind and snow, stomping their feet to keep blood flowing in the sub-freezing temperature. They—and all the rest of us—see the signal to launch the attack—five flares launched into the sky by Massachusetts Captain Brown, posted in defilade on the Plains of Abraham, not far from General Montgomery.

Seconds later, Colonel Arnold waves to those of us behind him, and says, "Pass the word back, Follow me?"[1]

Since the moment we launched the assault—and in its aftermath—we have learned many things we didn't know at the time were already working against us.

First, the storm we needed to conceal our movement was also a warning to Gov. Carleton and his second in command, Allan Maclean. As the snow started, Maclean predicted, "The rebels will come tonight." Hours before Capt. Brown fired the five flares, the garrison was preparing for us.

The British knew our artillery was unable to breach their west walls, so they left them lightly defended and positioned most of their garrison to the north and south sides of the city in anticipation of the very kind of double envelopment attack we have planned. So, when Captain Brown and Colonel Livingston launched their feints at Diamond Bastion and St. John's Gate, the intended distractions were totally ineffective.

We might still have succeeded, had General Montgomery's attack from the south prevailed. His long column was first held up just past Cape Diamond by two rows of heavy abatis that took far longer for the pioneers to chop through than expected.

At 7:00 a.m., the general and a handful of his men finally made their way through a narrow gap hacked through the abatis. But then—despite heavy, blowing snow—they see a fortified house about fifty yards ahead with apertures for muskets and cannons.

No smoke or sound issued from the place, no sign of footprints in the snow—getting deeper by the minute. The general assembled a handful of his officers and men, and a dozen or so slowly crept forward—a forlorn hope led by a general officer.

Unbeknownst to Montgomery and his New Yorkers, there were thirty armed British and Canadian militiamen and a handful of Royal Navy sailors with four light artillery pieces loaded with grapeshot inside. These inexperienced British defenders silently watched until Montgomery and his advance party were less than twenty yards away. Only then did the militia captain inside the structure yell, "Fire!"

The devastating salvo of grapeshot and musket balls immediately killed General Montgomery, three other officers, and nine New York soldiers. The next field grade officer to come upon the gruesome scene was Lieutenant Colonel Campbell, the division's quartermaster who was not equipped for battlefield leadership.

Within minutes of the carnage, Campbell ordered a retreat. Diminutive Aaron Burr more than a foot shorter than the general tried to carry his commander off the field but collapsed under the general's weight and was forced to withdraw. It was from Mr. Burr I got this account.

Col. Arnold and his northern attackers were totally unaware of the catastrophe that just occurred a half mile to their south.

Arnold's column initially moved slowly and unobserved from St. Roche but soon came under heavy musket fire from the city walls to their right.

We were about 100 yards behind his Forlorn Hope party when he sent a messenger back telling us to "close up" on his position. We did so and found them stopped by heavy fire coming from the bluff above their position near the water. Col. Arnold was struck in the leg by a musket ball and though he tried moving to press the attack, his leg wound soon had him unable to walk. Reverend

Spring and a Riflemen, one under each arm, assisted their commander all the way back to Dr. Senter's hospital.

When Colonel Arnold was wounded, Lt. Col. Green, Majors Bigelow and Meigs were about 200 yards behind us. The lead element of our column had already made a "right turn" on Rue du Sault-au-Matelot.[1] Captain Morgan, not wanting to lose momentum in the attack by waiting for the New Englanders to "close up," used his thunderous battlefield voice to rally the Americans around him and led us forward.

We immediately encountered a tall and strong barricade blocking our entrance into the city. Captain Morgan's Riflemen and Lamb's detachment were the only members of Arnold's force in the Lower Town to have brought scaling ladders with them. He wasted no time attacking the barrier by firing through its gun loopholes and throwing up the scaling ladders to get our men over the wall.

When a soldier hesitated in mounting a scaling ladder, Morgan pushed him aside, quickly ascended, and leaped over the wall and fell on a cannon, landing on his back—causing terrible pain. In fact, the fall atop the cannon may well have saved his life for he was able to use the gun and its carriage to avoid thrusting bayonets until the rest of us got over the wall.

It would have helped to have had Captain Lamb's cannon to breach the wall, but the sled to which it was attached became hopelessly stuck in the ice near the water and they could not retrieve it in the open under fire.

After getting our company over the rampart, we found the defenders less than enthusiastic about any further contest with us. They surrendered and were removed from the site by a few of Captain Lamb's men.

As the prisoners were being moved north down the narrow Rue du Sault-au-Matelot, Lieutenant Colonel Greene's New England battalion arrived. We quickly moved ahead, only to run into a second large barricade, this one even taller and thicker than the last.

Using the same tactics as before, we placed scaling ladders against the wall, but our initial assault was repelled by British regulars positioned about 100 feet behind the barricade with bayonets affixed. As soon as a Patriot head emerged above the wall, it was hit with a volley of musket fire.

At this point in the fight, Lieutenant Colonel Greene intervened and urged Captain Morgan to hold off on another effort to get over the top of the second barrier until General Montgomery arrived with reinforcements.

Like so much else in war, we didn't know what we didn't know. By 7:30 a.m. as Captain Morgan was organizing a second Forlorn Hope to follow him over the second barricade, we didn't know General Montgomery was already dead.

Nor were we aware the British had reinforced the other side of the barricade with more than 400 troops composed of Regulars, sailors, Canadian militia, and Royal Highland Emigrants, many with fixed bayonets. Two light artillery pieces were also placed on a platform ten yards behind the barrier to fire grapeshot across the top of the rampart. It was a grapeshot from one of these guns that hit the brave Capt. Lamb in the face.

And while the sky had brightened somewhat, the howling blizzard was unabated, reducing visibility to ten yards or so.

The tight quarters on the street, the short distance between attackers and defenders and the reduced visibility of the howling storm eliminated any advantage for our rifles. We not only had no bayonets, but it also took us longer to re-charge our firearms than the musketeers.

As we were positioning four ladders for Captain Morgan's Forlorn Hope, none of us can see the defenders on the other side of the second barrier breaking down doors and clamoring up to the second-story windows to engage any of us who manage to make our way to the top of the barricade.

Captain Morgan shouted, "Follow me, men, Quebec is ours!" and scrambled up the ladder. As he and the first five or six of our

Riflemen appeared over the top of the barricade, the defenders' cannons and muskets erupted, killing all but Captain Morgan who miraculously fell over backward, landing at our feet with new holes in his hat and hunting shirt. Lt. Humphrey and I bent to help him to his feet.

Suddenly, as our Forlorn Hope party is reloading our rifles, a dozen enemy troops rush through a sally port[2] with muskets at the ready, bayonets fixed. An officer, holding a pistol demands, "Drop your weapons! Surrender or die."

At this, Captain Morgan grabs my reloaded rifle and shoots the officer through the head.

As the British troops dragged their dead officer back through the portal to the other side of the barricade, all hell breaks loose.

Until this point in the battle I saw so many of my friends in front, beside, and behind me killed and wounded, I was quite convinced my prayers for protection[3] were being answered. They were. But not the way I expected.

Second Barricade, Rue du Sault-au-Matelot,
Lower Town, Quebec City, Canada

7:30 a.m., Sunday, December 31st, 1775

I didn't see the man who shot me.

I did see the men who, within a matter of minutes, killed Captain Hendricks, wounded Lieutenant Steele, and killed my friend, 1st Lt. William Humphrey. They were all hit by fire from the second-story shooters we didn't even know were there until they opened fire.

William and I were positioning a scaling ladder against the barricade so Captain Morgan could lead yet another Forlorn Hope over the barricade when a British ball fired from just a few feet over our heads struck William in the chest and he dropped into the snow.

I grabbed him and dragged him back about fifty feet where I thought he would be safer and propped him in the shelter of a doorway beneath a weathered sign, "Duquesne Fur Company."

As I bent over him with my back to the barrier, I was hit from behind, knocking me face down atop William. For an instant it felt like I was hit twice—once under my right arm and by another projectile on the right side of my head. I tried to rise off William and realized my right arm would not work and I was becoming very weak.

As I began to lose consciousness, I remember saying out loud, "Dear Lord Jesus, save me." And then, black.

I later learned the Quebec "Battle in the Blizzard" was over by 9:00 a.m., New Year's Eve, 1775. By then 454 of us had been killed or captured. I still thank God I was not among them.

Duquesne Fur Company, Rue du Sault-au-Matelot, Quebec City, Canada

Sunday, December 31ˢᵗ, 1775

My next conscious moment, I felt the door beside me open and two strong hands roll me off William's body and begin dragging me inside on my back by the collar of my dead brother's cloak.

It was dark. A single lantern on the far side of what seems to be a large room is the only light—too little for me to see who has come to my aid. But when my rescuer says in English with a slight French accent, "I am sorry for hurting you," I realize it is a woman. As she closes the door, I can see William's body, covered with snow and she asks, "Can you walk?"

"I will try. Please help me up."

She reaches down, sees all the blood on the right side of my clothing, and uses my left hand to pull me up to a sitting position.

She then goes behind me, kneels, puts her head beneath my left arm and gently as possible helps me stand.

As we start shuffling toward the lantern she says, "We must hide you. The British are coming down the street searching for American soldiers who have taken refuge in these buildings."

When we get to the far side of the large room, she opens another door and I can feel warmth.

To my surprise, the interior is a well-lighted, spacious, multi-room apartment with windows, paneled walls, carpets, and paintings on the walls. As we pass through a hallway into what appears to be an office or library, she asks, "If I place you on the chair near the desk, can you hold on for a moment?"

I can only nod my head at this point for fear of passing out. She gently sits me down and pulls the draperies over the windows. She then goes to a bookcase and pushes a book on the middle shelf. I can hear a quiet "click" and the bookcase pivots open to reveal another small room with a bed and a chair in it and says, "My father built this years ago for a time such as this."

As she helps me up and into bed, she says, "I will be right back after the search party leaves. I know you must be in pain." When I'm prone, she strikes a match, lights a lantern on the table next to the bed, and hands me a damp towel with the distinct scent of witch hazel. "Your head wound is beginning to bleed again. Hold this against it until I return. There is a cup of boiled water on the table and a chamber pot beneath the bed."

She goes to the rotating bookcase, points to a button on the wall and says, "I must clean up the drops of your blood leading from the front door to here. If the British take me away for questioning, this is how you open it." She then locked me inside.

Alone, I try to do an assessment of my injuries but am quickly overwhelmed with pain and fatigue. Just before I doze off, I look at my watch: 11:15. I recall thinking William and I were gunned down before 8:00 a.m.

I'm suddenly grateful not to have bled or frozen to death. And I say to myself, *Thank You, Lord, for keeping me alive and for . . .* Only then did it occur to me, I don't even know the name of the beautiful angel with the dark hair.

The heavy banging awakened me, disoriented. The first thing I did was check my watch and suddenly realize my vision is blurred. By closing my right eye, I can see the hands of my watch. It looks like 1:25. Is it afternoon or morning?

Now, there are voices getting closer.

Man's voice: (*A British officer?*) "Governor Carleton insists we thoroughly search every building for rebels, alive or dead. Did you provide refuge for the one at the front of the warehouse?"

Female voice: (*My dark-haired angel?*) "No, sir. He was there, dead when I first opened the door after all the shooting stopped. Will someone be coming to claim his body?"

Man's voice: "Yes. We're sending rebel prisoners under guard to fetch their dead comrades as soon as possible. Probably this afternoon. Looks to me like looters have already been through his pockets. We're arresting looters. Somebody got his shoes, gloves, and hat. Was it you?"

Female voice: "No sir. This is a Christian home."

Man's voice: "Oh yeah, we know all about you half-breed Indian Christians. Is your father here?"

Female voice: "No sir, but now the shooting has stopped, I hope he will be here tonight."

Man's voice: "Where is he?"

Female voice: "He is on his way back here from Fort Niagara."

Male voice: "Whose side is he on today?"

. Female voice: "You must know, sir, he's been loyal to the Crown since the Treaty of Paris."

Male voice: "Oh, sure. (*loudly*) Sergeant Wilcox! Find anything out there?"

"No sir, nothing out in the warehouse but eleven bales of furs. The bills of lading on all of 'em say 'Consigned to Hudson Bay Company.' You want us to check the roof, sir?"

Male voice: "No. We can see the roof from the building across the street."

Male voice: (*quieter*) "Now little princess, if you get lonely tonight, just come see me and I'll keep you warm."

I heard the door separating the warehouse and the apartment close.

A few minutes later the bookcase clicks and pivots open. She enters carrying a lantern, a large green bottle full of a clear liquid, and a small orange-colored glass bottle with a cork stopper and says cheerfully, "Good to see you are still alive. My name is Marie Sirois. What is your name?"

"Nathanael Newman."

"Good. Nathanael. That's a good Christian name. Are you a believer?"

"Yes. And you?"

"Certainly. And we can talk about all that and more after we get you cleaned up so we know how badly you are hurt." At this, she takes the stopper out of one of the bottle, pours some of it into the cup of boiled water, and says, "Please drink this. It's laudanum. It will ease your pain so we can try walking again. I will be back in a few minutes after it takes effect so we can try getting you up. I'm going to stoke the stove in the bathing room."

I had no idea what she was talking about. She was back in fifteen minutes and by then the laudanum had taken effect and I was relatively pain free. Helping me as she had before, we shuffled to a door at the end of the hall. When she opened it, I was stunned.

There in a very warm, well lighted, beautifully tiled room is what appears to be the bottom half of a beautifully crafted, wooden cask—about the size that would hold at least a tun of good wine or spirits.[4] A woodstove near the eastern wall is glowing red and a large iron pot atop one of the burners is steaming.

She helps me sit on a wooden chair beside the large cask which I can now see, is better than half full of warm water and says, "You do not seem to be bleeding right now, but we need to remove your clothing so I can see your wounds. May I cut off your cloak?"

"Marie, is there any way we can do this without destroying this cloak? It belonged to my brother who was killed near Concord, Massachusetts, last April. It has served me well. If there is any way we can save it, I would be grateful."

She looked straight at me and for the first time, I noticed her green eyes. Then, she said, "Nathanael, I will try to do as you wish. But you will have to tell me when the price you are paying in pain is greater than the value of something you cannot take with you where we all want to go."

It took ten minutes of excruciating pain for her to remove the cloak in one piece. In the process she dipped several towels into the cask beside us, soaking them with warm water, softening clotted blood. Once the cloak was off, she said, "I must cut off your wool vest and your hunting shirt. There is no way you can raise your right arm to remove them." She used shears to cut them straight up my back and gently pulled them off my front to make them easier to repair. From my vest she removed my pocket watch and set it on a table beside the towels.

She was silent for a few minutes, examining my wounds while gently wiping away caked blood with warm, wet towels, moistened in what she called "the tub," beside us.

Finally, she said, "There is an entry wound in your right arm-pit. It appears the projectile traveled upwards through your shoulder and exited your neck between your collarbone and trapezius muscle then struck your skull immediately in front of your right ear.

"The ball—or whatever it is—seems to be lodged beneath your scalp about two inches above your right ear. There is so much swelling around it I don't think it would be wise to do anything with it tonight because it may have broken your skull. I cannot tell how much damage has been done inside your shoulder.

"Given what I can observe about the trajectory of the projectile, it seems to have missed your lung and your carotid artery. The good news is, there is no longer much external bleeding. If I'm right and there is no internal bleeding, you should be alive in the morning. Now, Nathanael, how are you feeling?"

I told the truth. "Marie, I'm not in much pain; a bit dizzy; my right eye doesn't seem to focus well; a little nauseous—that all may be the laudanum. But what I'm really feeling is absolutely amazed. How do you know all this?"

She smiled and said, "My father is or was a very wise and wealthy man. He encouraged my desire to become a physician so he took me with him on many of his business trips from when I was a little girl, wherever I could meet some of the best doctors in Europe.

"I have not yet been admitted to a medical college on this continent, but I have learned enough to know I don't know everything. Still, I try to use what I have learned to help others as best I can. And one of the things I know for certain right now, Nathanael Newman, is you smell bad and need a bath."

I have never met anyone like this before. She is brilliant and she is beautiful. I don't know how to respond and ask, "What is a bath?"

She chuckles and says, "A bath is when you take off your filthy clothing, get into a 'tub' like the one next to you, wash your body and your clothing with Castile soap, rinse off, drain the water, dry off, hang up your clothing to dry, go to bed, and get up in the morning feeling and smelling better."

My immediate response is, "That sounds good, but I can't do that with you in this room!"

She laughed again and said, "Well, you are in no shape to do it without me in the room, so let's get on with it."

With her help, we did exactly that. She removed my leggin's and socks, helped me remove my britches, aided me up the step into what she called her "tub," helped me sit on the seat inside, poured a half cup of what she called "scented, hemp oil Castile soap" into the warm water, and used a sponge to gently wash my wounds.

She then handed me the sponge and said, "Use this to wash 'below' with your left hand while I wash your clothing." She moved around to use a "washboard" built into the sidewall of the tub. She then rinsed the clothing in a sink and hung them up on a wooden rack on the wall.

Finally, she said, "Use your foot to feel the drain-plug in the center of the tub and flip it up with your toes."

I did as instructed and the water started to drain. "Now, hang on to the edge of the tub with your left hand and stand up." She then took a bucket half full of clean water, added to it hot water from the pot on the stove, stood on the step, and poured it over my head.

After helping me towel dry, she assisted me in putting on a pair of her father's trousers and placed my watch in the left front pocket. She used a roll of white linen ticking to wrap my head wound and bandaged the exit wound on the top of my shoulder with a wad of the same material. She then pulled one of her father's soft cotton shirts on my left arm and gently draped the right arm over my right shoulder to hold the bandage in place.

Finally, she helped me up, guided me down the hallway to her father's bedroom and assisted me into his bed, covered me with a sheet and warm blankets, and said, "I pray you rest well and beg our Lord to heal you, Nathanael."

I was asleep in minutes.

Duquesne Fur Company, Rue du Sault-au-Matelot, Quebec City, Canada
Monday, January 1st, 1776

When I awakened on New Year's Day, she was asleep on a beautiful beaver fur mat on the floor beside my bed. She was covered by a sheet and a very light-colored mink blanket. By the light of the lantern on the table beside the bed I checked my watch: 4:45.

For better than three weeks this is how we have lived. Each morning she goes out to buy bread and vegetables from a bakery and a grocer down the hill. Rationing means there is very little good meat available though there appears to be an abundance of chicken and occasionally some very good fish.

When she returns, she checks my wounds, blots up any seepage, and changes the dressings. Though the swelling in my neck and head make it painful to chew and swallow, Marie is a magnificent cook and makes delicious soups, so my strength is returning and we have enjoyed many hours talking about every possible subject.

This morning, in the midst of a January blizzard that rivals the one on the day I was wounded, she asked me what an "Adjutant" does in our military. After I explained it to her, she got up, went into her father's office and returned with a beautiful leather-bound journal with more than 100 pages of lined paper, a silver pen with a gold nib and an inkwell and said, "Here is your next 'Official Journal' for our new expedition."

That night, before bed, I began making entries in "Volume 17" of my chronicle.

Duquesne Fur Company, Rue du Sault-au-Matelot, Quebec City, Canada

Thursday, February 1st, 1776

My brilliant, beautiful "Doctor Marie" told me this morning my temperature is slightly over 100 degrees and it has been slowly going up every day for a week. Her concern is for an infection in my head since "the small amount of seepage coming from your shoulder wounds do not smell."

"Tomorrow, I want to see what I can do about finding me some help with this."

"How?" I ask.

"Well, on my very brief visit to the bakery this morning, the only other person in the shop was an Indian named Natanis. He fits the description of the Natanis you told me was one of your allies and he happens to be an old, dear friend to my father and me. He said Governor Carlton released him a week after the New Year's Eve battle. Natanis carries with him a carte blanche[5] letter signed by the Governor. He showed it to me. It even has on it the Governor's Royal and personal seals. That means Natanis can go anywhere he wants."

At this point in our conversation, Marie reached out and put her hand on top of mine and continued, "Nathanael, if you trust him, I would like to see if Natanis can find us a doctor who can help with whatever kind of infection you have. I don't want to lose my favorite patient."

I didn't move my hand away, but I said, "Let's think and pray about this overnight and decide in the morning."

Her response was "Good." Tonight, for the first time since she saved my life, Marie didn't sleep beside my bed. She slept beside me.

Duquesne Fur Company, Rue du Sault-au-Matelot, Quebec City, Canada
Friday, March 1st, 1776

Marie's idea about connecting with Natanis has proven to be brilliant.

First, our Indian friend found in a nearby village, her father's retired doctor, Armand Foucault, a physician unquestionably loyal to Marie and her dad.

Second, at Natanis's urging, Dr. Foucault brought with him his surgical kit. In less than an hour, with Marie serving as his assistant, he sliced open my scalp and removed from my skull, a lead .75-caliber ball, undoubtedly from a British Brown Bess musket.

Third, after the surgery on my head he examined my shoulder, confirmed Marie's diagnosis it is likely not infected. After gently moving my right arm around some, he said (in French so, Marie translated), "You may very well be correct about this miraculously being only soft tissue damage. I do not feel or hear any 'crepitation' in the joint."

He then gave Marie two small bottles with cork stoppers: one, a salve to put daily on the incision he left open and the other three open wounds so they will drain. His guidance for the other bottle, tincture of arnica, was apparently funny because they both laughed.

After Doctor Foucault departed, I asked her why she didn't translate the second prescription and she said, "His instructions were to gently massage arnica into your shoulder but not into your bullet holes. He said arnica will relieve pain and stiffness but don't do it for too long because beautiful young women giving massages to handsome young men often brings on stiffness in other places."

Duquesne Fur Company, Rue du Sault-au-Matelot,
Quebec City, Canada

Friday, March 29th, 1776

Reconnecting with Natanis has not only resulted in my shoulder and head being nearly completely healed, it has also resulted in a plan for us to change our situation completely.

Natanis told Marie he is in contact with Lieutenant Archibald Steele who believes he has found a way to escape Prisoner of War confinement. According to Natanis, Lt. Steele's wounded hand has nearly healed—though he is missing three fingers.

Steele wants to escape as soon as possible and has convinced those who will come with him not to try rejoining Colonel Arnold because all the American units in Canada now have dozens dying every week from smallpox.

Instead, Steele and his comrades want to get across the St. Lawrence and make their way back to civilization the way we came.

Duquesne Fur Company, Rue du Sault-au-Matelot,
Quebec City, Canada

Monday, April 1st, 1776

At the bakery this morning, Natanis informed Marie, unless she says "no" at the bakery on Tuesday morning, April, 2nd, Lt. Steele and four Pennsylvania Riflemen will come here to the warehouse on Tuesday night, shortly after dark. Natanis will be here to guide us down to the river where Indians with good canoes will be waiting, ready to transport us across the river to Pointe Lévis.

This information prompts a nearly all-day conversation between Marie and me about the wisdom of this plan. The question: Is this the right thing to do?

There is no doubt in my mind about my future. If I stay here, I will for certain eventually be caught by the British—an event undoubtedly with a very bad outcome for me and very likely for Marie as well for sequestering me.

Yet, for her to leave with me, as she insists she wants, means she will be giving up a very comfortable life—particularly in contrast with most if not all her neighbors.

She repeatedly asserts, "Nathanael, if you are going, I am going with you."

"What about your father?" I ask. "The day the British officer asked where your father was you said, he was 'at Fort Niagara . . .' and that same night, when you were giving me my first 'bath,' you said he 'is *or was*' a very wise and wealthy man.

"From our hundreds of conversations these past three months you know everything about my family. Yet, I know almost nothing about yours."

She shook her head, locked eyes with me, and said, "Listen carefully, my dear Nathanael.

"My father, Pierre Phillipe Sirois was born Catholic in Lyon, France in 1720. He came to Canada in 1739 and quickly became a very successful fur trapper. In 1744 he founded Duquesne Fur Company. Within five years DFC was the most successful venture of its kind in 'New France.'

"By 1750 my father had dozens of trading posts, large and small, across Canada, New York, and Pennsylvania, all the way to the Ohio Valley. DFC had offices in Montreal, Quebec, New York, Boston, Norfolk, Paris, London, Lisbon, and Rotterdam. The company had a half dozen ships and more money than most of us can imagine.

"In 1756, when my father was thirty-six, in an Oneida Indian ceremony, he married my mother, Catherine, age nineteen, the daughter of a very powerful Oneida Bear Clan warrior and sachem with whom my father was doing a lot of business.

"That same year, France and Great Britain went to war and a British Army unit raided one of my father's Oneida trading posts near the New York-Pennsylvania border where my mother and her father were visiting. My grandfather and sister, who was still a baby, were killed, and my mother was wounded.

"My father brought my mother back here, built this warehouse, and pledged then he would always despise the British. I was born here in 1758.

"My parents and I traveled frequently to Europe to promote my father's fur business. In those travels both my parents learned the languages, spoken and written, of the countries we visited.

"We were in Lisbon when a Portuguese trader who had been to Japan, showed my father plans he brought home for a 'bath,' almost identical to the one in which we have been bathing.

"That's how my parents learned about using half of a very large cask for a 'tub,' gravity-fed cisterns on the roof as a water source, and the benefits of regular bathing—all practically unheard of in Europe and this continent. You told me your father is an architect. If I can find the drawings for this one, I will take them with us so you can give them to your father, and he will forever be known as 'Inventor of the Modern American bath room.'

"In 1766, the 10th anniversary of their 'Oneida Wedding Ceremony' my mother and father reaffirmed their wedding vows in a Christian ceremony performed by Presbyterian missionary Samuel Kirkland.[6]

"In the aftermath of the Treaty of Paris in 1763 ending the 'Seven Years War' between Great Britain and France, business became much more challenging for all the French-owned companies in Canada, including Duquesne Fur Company.

"In 1773, my father signed an agreement with the Hudson Bay Company to do a five-year 'buy out' of Duquesne Fur Company to be concluded no later than January 1st, 1778. Part of the contract is this warehouse, which remains the property of Duquesne Fur Company so long as DFC keeps its commitment to sell furs only to HBC.

"HBC failed to make its required payment to DFC on January 1st, 1775. After communicating through lawyers for months, my parents sailed from here to London on April 19th, the very day your brother was killed at Concord in Massachusetts.

"Since they arrived in London, I have received only two letters from them, one in June last year and a second last September. I have sent them a letter each month since they departed but have received no answers. I have no idea if they are alive or where they are.

"The British now rule Canada with the iron fist of martial law and I have no idea whether they are intercepting our correspondence. I need to get to one of our DFC offices where I can send and receive communications—hopefully with my parents—but at the very least with our many DFC lawyers.

"Going overseas right now is not a good idea for many reasons. The best thing I can do is get to New York City or Norfolk, Virginia. I have five thousand in Spanish silver dollar coins and an equal amount in British pound sterling coins in my father's office safe. I need to get that specie out of Quebec as soon as I can.

"That's one reason why I'm hoping and praying you will take me with you tomorrow night, Nathanael. Now, what else do you need to know about my family, dear one?"

I was, as I so often have been—to this very moment—stunned by Marie Sirois. Right from the first day when she saved my life, it was apparent she—or at least her family—had wealth. My father is an architect for affluent American families. But what Marie has shown me—and said over the last three months—is extraordinary.

All I could say in response to her query, "What else do you need to know about my family, dear one?" was with a question of my own: "How can I help you?"

She was still looking at me with those fascinating green eyes, her chin cupped in her right hand. She spoke very quietly, "We have talked about this enough. If you are leaving here—and you should—I am going with you.

"I want to spend the rest of my life with you. You have said the same thing about me. I care more about you than any of the material things here or anywhere else.

"Let's pack up and be ready to leave with Natanis and Lieutenant Steele tomorrow night. Do you agree?"

"Yes."

"Good," she said with that beautiful smile. "Because I may be pregnant with your child."

Newburyport, Massachusetts
Saturday, April 27th, 1776

Unlike our trip from Massachusetts to Quebec and all that's happened since we arrived, our return was in every way the opposite, even though it didn't begin that way.

As planned, Natanis arrived at the Personnel Door of the Duquesne Fur Company warehouse with two of his Indian guides precisely at 8:00 p.m. on Tuesday, April 2nd. An hour later, Lieutenant Archibald Steele, Ensign David Valinski, Sgt. Dennis Azato, and Corporals Joshua Smallbone, Michael Aitken, and Charles Holton arrived at the same portal.

That number, six, was two more than we expected. It was supposed to be Lt. Steele plus three. The other problem, the contents of the safe in Marie's father's office, was also numerical. Marie told me "ten thousand in Spanish dollars and pounds sterling." But

I failed to figure out what that would weigh. As it turns out it's more than sixty pounds.

Natanis's answer when I explained the situation to him (without letting on what we were bringing that weighed so much) is classic: "No problem."

And it really was not a problem. Our trip back was so fast I'm still surprised when I look at the brief entries made in Journal 17 compared to my previous record:

9:00 a.m., Wednesday, April 3rd, 1776: Departed Pointe Lévis on horseback.

7:00 a.m., Thursday, April 4th, 1776: Departed Sartigan on horseback.

5:00 p.m., Tuesday, April 9th, 1776: Cleared top of River Chaudière. Met by Natanis's friends with mounts for all.

4:30 p.m., Saturday, April 13th, 1776: Encamped on east bank of Lake Mégantic. Light rain with snow flurries.

3:00 p.m., Wednesday, April 17th, 1776: Completed traverse of Height of Land by horseback. Lt. Steele seems much fatigued. Tiny sliver of waning moon.

4:50 p.m. Saturday April 20th, 1776: We arrive at Natanis's home on a beautiful early spring afternoon on banks of Dead River. Days getting noticeably longer and much warmer. Natanis has one of his Indians bring us some venison for dinner. Marie, wearing a traditional Oneida Indian one-piece dress, is the star attraction.

5:15 p.m. Wednesday, April 24th, 1776: Entire party arrives Fort Halifax via canoes rowed by Indians. Mr. Calvin Coolidge meets us with wagons to carry us down to Fort Western. He confirms rumors we have heard that British fled Boston when Col. Knox arrived with artillery from Boston.

3:00 p.m. Friday, April 26th, 1776: Entire Party arrives Fort Western, now abandoned as Arnold Expedition Rear Base. We press on to Gardinerston where Mr. Reuben Colburn has entire town turn out to "Welcome the 'Famine Proof' Quebec survivors home." Natanis and his Indians bid us a tearful goodbye and head back up the Kennebec River. Based on the poor condition of Lt. Steele, Mr. Coburn books passage on a vessel tonight to Newburyport for Lt. Steele, Marie, Ensign Valinski, Sgt. Azato, Cpl. Holton, and me.

2:30 p.m. Saturday, April 27th, 1776: We arrive Newburyport to another grand welcome. Mr. Tracy of the local Committee of Safety comes aboard and volunteers to take Lt. Steele to the hospital after assuring him the smallpox epidemic has run its course.

As I was helping Lt. Steele down the gangway to the dock, I asked him, "Is the hardest part your wounded hand?"

"No, the hardest part of this whole affair for me was lying in the snow at the second barricade on Sault-au-Matelot watching Captain Morgan being forced to surrender. Did you see that?"

"No, I was wounded and pulled from the street before that."

"We were completely overrun. His back was against the wall with nothing more than a short sword to wield. With twenty British muskets pointed at his chest, a Redcoat officer repeatedly demanded his sword, to which the captain said, "Come and take it if you have the nerve."

"Did they kill my captain?"

"He saw a priest among those gathered round and said to him, 'I give my sword to you; but not a scoundrel of these cowards shall take it out of my hands!' Of all the men I've known in this war, none exceed Captain Morgan in my eyes."

I knew then my adventures with Daniel Morgan were not at an end.

Marie and I accept an offered carriage ride to Wolfe's Tavern.

Over dinner, we discuss our options. Everyone we have talked to since arriving at Gardinerston has told us there is little point in going on to Cambridge since the entire Continental Army is now in New York. It's a place where her father's company has offices.

Marie and I are talking about just that when in walks—or more accurately limps—Sgt. Steven Cady, the dragoon commander with whom I spent so much time here before the Arnold Expedition departed for Canada. He is not in uniform.

I rose, introduced him to Marie, invited him to join us for dinner, and asked him how he was injured.

"After the Arnold Expedition departed Newburyport, my squad of dragoons was assigned to the Life Guards, a new unit, mostly Marylanders, who have the responsibility for protecting His Excellency, General Washington, from harm."

Two weeks ago, as General Washington's headquarters staff was preparing to move down the turnpike toward New York City, my squad was ordered to reconnoiter the route, and a group of about fifty Tory bastards ambushed us. I took one of their musket balls in my left leg. Worse though, it passed straight through my calf and killed my great stallion. I'm now on thirty days of leave, waiting for the hole to heal."

At this I pulled out of my pocket the .75-caliber ball Dr. Foucault cut out of my head, showed it to him and said, "Was it one like this?" and showed it to him, and he nodded.

When Marie excused herself to "go out back," we bantered about where we were heading. She returned to the table just as Sgt. Cady said, "Sir, I recommend you take leave and you and your lady go back to Virginia for a while 'till the New York situation stabilizes. If you need any help getting there, I'm willing to help."

At this, Marie surprised us by interjecting, "That sounds like a good idea."

In the space of five minutes Sergeant Cady and I worked out a contract for him to rent a phaeton or a chaise, two good horses, and take us back where this all started.

Winchester, Virginia

Thursday, May 7ᵗʰ, 1776

Sgt. Cady pulled the reins back and shouted, "Whoah!" at the gate in front of our house.

Pieter and Lotte came running from their cottage, and Casey started her little "Spaniel dance" as I climbed down to help Marie out of the little cabin in which we had spent the last ten days—excluding the nights when we encamped in some delightful inns and taverns.

They were unloading our baggage when Rev. Thruston rode up on his well-lathered stallion shouting, "Welcome home, Nathanael! Welcome home!"

He dismounted, handed Pieter his reins, spun around, embraced me, and said, "You are an answer to my prayers!"

Then, with his hands on my shoulders, he pushed me out to the full length of his arms and looked me over head-to-toe for a full minute and said, "You have been wounded!"

"Yes, sir. But thanks be to God, not too badly. I am alive because of my doctor."

At this, I beckoned to Marie and Lotte. Her arm around Marie's waist, Lotte walked with her back to the gate. When they were beside us, I put my good left arm on her shoulders and said, "Reverend Thruston, this is Marie, my physician. She is an angel, sent by our Lord to save my life in Quebec. When can you make us husband and wife?"

His response was perfect. "Well, I suppose I can do it right now. We have witnesses, water in the trough, wine in your house. How about rings? Did either of you bring rings?"

At this, Marie laughed and said, "Oh, well, if we must wait until tomorrow, it will give me a chance to clean up a bit. That's not too bad, since we have been a month getting here.

"A month!" proclaimed Rev. Thruston. "That's more time than most married couples spend together in a year. What did you talk about?"

She paused to see if I was going to respond and when I didn't, she said, "I talked about a wedding and having children. All he talks about is how quickly he and Captain Morgan can get together to drive those red-breasted bâtards[7] out of America."

At this, Sgt. Cady, seated in the driver's seat of the carriage said, "May I stay for both?"

ENDNOTES

1.   Rue du Sault-au-Matelot, rough translation: "Street of the sailor's leap" [or, "fall"]

2.   Sally port: A heavy door in a gate or barricade designed to open only toward the attackers so defenders can emerge and counter-attack.

3.   Ephesians 6:10–18 King James Version (KJV)

[10]Finally, my brethren, be strong in the LORD, and in the power of his might.

[11]Put on the whole armour of God, that ye may be able to stand against the wiles of the devil.

[12]For we wrestle not against flesh and blood, but against principalities, against powers, against the rulers of the darkness of this world, against spiritual wickedness in high places.

[13]Wherefore take unto you the whole armour of God, that ye may be able to withstand in the evil day, and having done all, to stand.

[14]Stand therefore, having your loins girt about with truth, and having on the breastplate of righteousness;

[15]And your feet shod with the preparation of the gospel of peace;

[16]Above all, taking the shield of faith, wherewith ye shall be able to quench all the fiery darts of the wicked.

[17]And take the helmet of salvation, and the sword of the Spirit, which is the word of God:

[18]Praying always with all prayer and supplication in the Spirit, and watching thereunto with all perseverance and supplication for all saints.

4.   Tun: an archaic (but still used) term for the measurement of volume. In the eighteenth century, a hand-made wooden cask, built by a "cooper" (or cask-maker) of oak staves and iron "hoops," to ship a tun of liquid (usually wine or "spirits" such as rum) would hold 216 imperial gallons (260 U.S. gallons).

The "bath tub" Nathanael is looking at (a "half cask") is about four feet in diameter at its bottom and nearly six feet in in diameter at its "mid" (or in this case, "top"). It is about three and a half feet high and likely holds about 120 gallons of water plus a person.

On the bottom there is a brass drain fitting connected to a ceramic pipe beneath the floor allowing waste-water to gravity-drain from the cask, through a ceramic-pottery clay pipe, over the ledge behind the warehouse into the St. Lawrence River.

5.   Carte blanche: Complete freedom to act as one wishes or thinks best.

6.   Samuel Kirkland was a Presbyterian missionary to the Oneida peoples living in Northern New York. He graduated with a divinity degree in 1765 from the College of New Jersey [now, Princeton University]. Kirkland's "Study Master" was Rev. John Witherspoon—the same professor [and college president] who became Study Master to young James Madison, now known as "father of our Constitution." All three men—Kirkland, Witherspoon, and Madison—were unabashedly pro-independence in their political perspectives as were most all the Oneida tribal leaders.

7.   French for "bastards."

POSTSCRIPT

Those you now know who affected the lives of Daniel Morgan and Nathanael Newman for good or ill

Samuel Adams – Prolific polemicist of the Revolution, he was a key leader of anti-British Massachusetts radicals, founder of Secret Committees of Correspondence, delegate to Continental Congress (1774–81), signer of Declaration of Independence, and governor of Massachusetts (1794–97). Died, October 2, 1803.

Ethan Allen – Explorer, farmer, firebrand who served in the French and Indian War and American Revolution. He attained the rank of colonel in the Continental Army, advocated Vermont becoming an independent colony, state, country, and even part of Canada. Allen was held as POW in England after a failed attempt to capture Montreal in 1775. Died, February 12, 1789.

Benedict Arnold – Promoted to Brigadier General after Quebec disaster, had serial victories over British at Valcour Island, NY (October, 1776), Danbury, CT (April, 1777), Fort Stanwix, NY (August, 1777), and Saratoga, NY, where he was with Morgan and wounded again (September 19–October 7, 1777). Promoted

255

to Major Gen. and given command of forces defending Philadelphia (June, 1778). Initiated intrigues with British to defect (May
9, 1779) and did so (September 24, 1779). Treason compounded
by heinous crime of leading British troops killing hundreds of
Americans in Virginia (December, 1780–May 20, 1781) and Connecticut (September, 1781). Died, June 14, 1801.

Timothy Bigelow – Ardent Patriot and initially a farrier. He
was a delegate to the Massachusetts Provincial Congress, member
of Sam Adams's Secret Committee of Correspondence. Bigelow
was a major in Massachusetts Militia at Lexington and Concord
(April 19, 1775), captured at Quebec, New Year's Eve (1775),
POW in Canada, and paroled in a prisoner exchange along with
Morgan. He was promoted to colonel, Continental Line (February
8, 1777), and was Commanding Officer of 15th Massachusetts at
Saratoga (October 7, 1777). He served with Washington at Valley
Forge (1777–78), West Point, Monmouth, NJ (June 28, 1778), and
Yorktown, VA (October 19, 1781). After the war, Officer in
Charge, Springfield Arsenal, Massachusetts. Died, March 31,
1790.

Aaron Burr – After Quebec, briefly served on Washington's
staff, was commissioned Lieutenant Colonel (January 4, 1777),
spent winter at Valley Forge (1777–78), commanded a brigade at
battle of Monmouth (June 28, 1778), and was critical of Washington after battle. Burr resigned from the army (March 3, 1779),
opened New York law office with Alexander Hamilton (1783),
appointed New York Attorney General (1789), elected to U.S.
Senate (1791), ran unsuccessfully for President (1796), elected
Vice President (1800), and mortally wounded Alexander Hamilton
in a duel (July 11, 1804). Died, September 14, 1836.

Reuben Colburn – After the Arnold Expedition reached
Pointe Lévis across from Quebec, Colburn and his crew of boat
builders returned to Maine. He continued to build boats and support the American Revolution throughout the war. He was later a
delegate to the unsuccessful Falmouth Convention dedicated to
the statehood of Maine. He was financially ruined by the War of
1812 and died September 16, 1818.

Roger Enos – Court martialed for disobeying orders and removing his command from the Quebec Expedition. The only witnesses to testify were officers who retreated with him. He was acquitted and returned to service as a lieutenant colonel, commanding the 16th Connecticut Militia Regiment that served with no particular distinction in the Hudson Valley in 1778. After retiring from the Connecticut Militia in 1780, he moved to Vermont where he was appointed a Major General in the Vermont militia. He was alleged to have engaged with the "Haldimand Cabal"— Vermont activists (including Ethan Allen)—advocating Vermont becoming an independent colony, state, country, and even part of Canada. He died in Vermont on October 6, 1808.

Hans Christian Febiger – Captured by the British in Quebec on New Year's Eve, 1775; held as a POW until paroled in a prisoner exchange (January, 1777), promoted to Lieutenant Colonel, assigned to Colonel Daniel Morgan's 11th Virginia Regiment (February, 1777) where together they served in the Philadelphia Campaign (summer of 1777). Febiger was promoted to colonel (September 26, 1777), he took command of the 2nd Virginia Regiment and was a key leader in major battles at Germantown (October 4, 1777), Monmouth (June 28, 1778), and Stony Point, NY where in a night attack his troops captured the entire British command (July 16, 1779). He was at the final major engagement of the war when Cornwallis surrendered the British Army at Yorktown, VA (October 19, 1781). He retired from the Continental Army (January 1, 1783), was elected Treasurer of Pennsylvania (1789), a post he held until his death. Remained a close friend of Daniel Morgan until he died (September 20, 1796).

Horatio Gates – Late in 1777 he was nominated to be the president of the Board of War but didn't take up the task until January 1778. From that position, Gates pushed his final unsuccessful attempt to replace George Washington as Commander-in-Chief. After the war he took up politics in New York where he died in 1806.

Christopher Greene – Became renowned for his brilliant defense of Fort Mercer in the 1777 Battle of Red Bank, NJ. He later led a regiment of black soldiers from Rhode Island when they made their mark on Revolutionary War history in the 1778 Battle of Rhode Island. He died May 1781 during the Battle of Pine's Bridge. His death at the hands of Loyalists was likely due to his leadership of African American troops.

Nathanael Greene – Considered one of General Washington's most loyal and skilled officers, he was given command of the Southern Continental Army in October 1780. He used Rifleman styled warfare to inflict significant losses on Cornwallis's army which became pivotal in tipping the war in the Patriot's favor. Greene's military service spanned almost the entire war after which he settled into being a successful farmer in Georgia. Died, June 19, 1786.

Eliza, wife of Sgt. Joseph Grier – Was one of two wives who accompanied their husbands on Benedict Arnold's trek to Quebec. She was admired by other soldiers in Grier's unit for her strength and endurance. She survived the journey, but as one soldier's diary records, "a woman belonging to the Pennsylvania troops was killed today by accident—a soldier carelessly snapped his musket which proved to be loaded."

Benjamin Harrison – Was a member of the Continental Congress from 1774 until 1777. He signed the Declaration of Independence. As a delegate of the Virginia State Convention, he helped ratify the United States Constitution. He died at his home, *Berkeley*, in Charles City County, VA on April 24, 1791.

Patrick Henry – Was perhaps unparalleled in his passion for the independence of the Colonies from the British Crown. He worked to build the military defense of his native Virginia, but his highest and best work was in building what was to become the United States of America through legislation and his commanding oratorical and writing skills. Henry died June 6, 1799. Thomas Jefferson told Daniel Webster in 1824, "It is not now easy to say what we should have done without Patrick Henry. He was far before all in maintaining the spirit of the Revolution."

William Heth – Ascended to the rank of colonel during the Revolutionary War and thereafter went into Virginia politics. Colonel Heth succumbed to apoplexy suddenly in April 1807.

William Howe – Was one of the central characters in the anti-Revolution British military efforts. Though he always held a modicum of sympathy for the Colonial cause, he was highly successful in opposing General Washington's army. After Burgoyne's defeat in Saratoga in 1777 and his inability to rout Washington from Pennsylvania, the Crown expressed their loss of confidence in him. He resigned in April of 1778 and returned to England where he later rose to full general and served in a number of commands during the French Revolution. Died, July 12, 1814.

Henry Knox – His artillery command proved decisive in forcing the British out of Boston (March 17, 1776) and subsequent the battles of Monmouth (June 28, 1778) and at Yorktown (October 19, 1781) effectively ending the Revolutionary War. He was appointed the first Secretary of War under the Articles of Confederation and was brought into President George Washington's cabinet in the same role under the newly ratified U.S. Constitution in 1789. Died of infection caused by a chicken bone lodged in his throat (October 25, 1806).

John Lamb – After being released from captivity in Quebec in early 1776, Lamb went back to the Continental Army and rose to the rank of brigadier general and was given command of all artillery after the British surrender. He was permanently disfigured and lost an eye when he was severely wounded in Quebec. His service during the Revolutionary War was personally commended by General George Washington. Died, May 31, 1800.

Charles Lee – Ardent George Washington detractor which resulted in his being surrounded by much controversy and many duel challenges. One of the pistol contests left him wounded and unable to engage the next challenger in line. He returned home to Virginia in 1779, where he later received word of his expulsion

from the Continental Army (January 10, 1780). Moved to Philadelphia where he died (October 2, 1782).

Francis Lightfoot Lee – Was an early ally of Patrick Henry,
and his passion for American liberty drove his unwavering commitment as he was part of the Continental Congress from its start.
He retired from Congress in 1779 to his home in Virginia where
he died in 1797.

Richard Henry Lee – On June 7, 1776 Lee stood before the
Continental Congress and declared:

*Resolved: that these United Colonies are, and of right ought
to be, free and independent States, that they are absolved from all
allegiance to the British Crown, and that all political connection
between them and the state of Great Britain is, and ought to be
totally dissolved.*

Though a powerful force in the formation of the new United
States of America, he became an ardent opponent of a "strong
central government" which led to his push for the Bill of Rights.
Died, June 19, 1794.

Angus McDonald – Appointed by George Washington as a
lieutenant colonel in command of Virginia's militia in 1777. He
served with distinction until his death on August 19, 1778, at his
home near Winchester, VA. His death was attributed to being
given the wrong dose of a medicine.

Return Jonathan Meigs – Captured and made British POW
in Quebec (December 31, 1775), paroled (May 16, 1776),
exchanged (January 19, 1777), promoted to colonel and given
command of the 6th Connecticut Regiment of light infantry (May
12, 1777). He led the raid at Sag Harbor New York, burned British
ships, captured ninety prisoners with no U.S. losses (May 24,
1777). At the age of sixty-one, President Jefferson appointed him
Indian Agent to the Cherokee Nation (1801). He faithfully filled
that duty until his death from pneumonia, January 28, 1823.

Abigail Curry Morgan – Married Daniel on March 30, 1773
and is credited with being integral to her husband changing from

the raucous and rough wagoneer into a man driven to be respectable, and she taught him to read and write using the Bible. Abigail outlived Daniel Morgan by fourteen years and died May 20, 1816, in Russellville, Kentucky.

Daniel Morgan – Added to his legend after being paroled from Quebec by going on to serve George Washington and the Patriot cause in other pivotal battles. The injury he sustained falling atop a British cannon at the first "barricade" in Quebec plagued him the rest of his life. He died at his daughter's home in Winchester, VA on July 6, 1802.

Pastor John Peter Gabriel Muhlenberg – Rose to the rank of major general and was one of the most dedicated and accomplished leaders of the American Revolution. After descending from his pulpit in Virginia, he recruited an entire regiment from his congregation and the Shenandoah Valley, he was involved in most of the important battles of the war from Charleston in 1776 to Yorktown in 1781. Died, 1807.

John Murray/Lord Dunmore – The year 1775 proved to be the start of bad things for Dunmore: he and his troops were defeated in the Battle of Great Bridge on December 9 and he retaliated with an artillery barrage from his fleet off Norfolk early in 1776 which resulted in the city burning. He left for Great Britain on New Year's Day 1777, where he supported the interests of Loyalist Virginians. He tried returning to further prosecute the war, but Cornwallis's surrender at Yorktown diverted his plans. Died, February 25, 1809.

Natanis – Identified in August 1775 as a "Norridgewock" and "Abenaki" Indian by Dennis Getchell and Samuel Berry, two scouts hired by Reuben Colburn to conduct a reconnaissance of the route Arnold intended to take to Quebec. They found Natanis living alone in his house on a beautiful stretch of the Dead River—and immediately realized he could speak fluent English, apparently from Christian missionaries.

Other Indians and settlers in the region who knew of Natanis and his brother, Sabatis, claimed he was in the employ of the

British—which Natanis freely admitted. Nevertheless, he agreed to accompany them to the font of the River Chaudière. Hearing rumors of a British-allied Mohawk war party near the French-Canadian settlement at Sartigan, they wisely returned to deliver their report to Colburn.

When Arnold learned of this "British spy," Arnold ordered Lieutenant Steele—preparing to depart Fort Western on his scouting mission, "If you find this villain, kill him." Steele never saw the Indian until he reached Sartigan in November where the Indian volunteered to enlist in "Arnold's Corps of Patriots."

Natanis proved to be invaluable. He helped locate canoes and dugouts to cross the St. Lawrence, recruited local Indians as guides, "paddlers," and fighters, navigated the Corps to "Wolfe's Cove," was wounded in the wrist during the New Year's Eve fight, was captured and made a POW by the British, but released in less than a week by British Governor-General Carlton.

Natanis wasn't through yet. He organized the prison break for Lieutenant Steele and his five comrades, and aided them, Marie Sirois, and Ensign Nathanael Newman in their escape all the way back to Gardinerston, Maine.

In September–October 1777 he was on the Saratoga battlefield, serving as a scout and fighter with Daniel Morgan.

Natanis was last seen in August 1779, helping the American survivors of the ill-fated Penobscot Campaign make their way safely back to Boston. How, where, or when he died is not yet known.

Paul Revere – A Boston silversmith and a founding member of Sam Adams's secret committee, observed and reported movements of British troops. Revere was also instrumental in the production of gunpowder for the Continental Army, and fabricated courier balls. Following the war, Revere returned to his silversmith trade and expanded his work in metals. In 1800, he became the first American to successfully roll copper into sheets which became useful, for among other things, sheathing the hulls of ships. Died, May 10, 1818.

Philip Schuyler – Prepared the Continental Army for the 1777 stand against Burgoyne at Saratoga but was replaced by General Gates before the battle began. After resigning from the army in 1779, he served in the New York State Senate through the 1780s where he supported the ratification of the United States Constitution. He represented New York in the first United States Congress. He lost his seat in the 1791 Senatorial election to Aaron Burr. Died, November 18, 1804.

Dr. Isaac Senter – Was taken prisoner during the failed attack on Quebec where he continued to care for the casualties among his troops. He was released after several months and he returned to Cranston, Rhode Island. Senter served as Surgeon-General of Rhode Island from 1776–1778 when he was elected to the Rhode Island General Assembly. In 1779 he retired from Continental service and died at the early age of forty-six in 1799.

Rev. Samuel Spring – Cared for Arnold and the others in the Quebec party spiritually and physically until Arnold's transfer to Ticonderoga. He left army service in 1777. He pastored in Newburyport, MA, where he also published many works, including controversial pieces on the death of Washington and the duel between Aaron Burr and Alexander Hamilton. Died, March 4, 1819.

Archibald Steele – The escaped POW rejoined Washington's army in New Jersey. Due to his poor health, General Washington wisely promoted him to colonel and appointed him Deputy Quartermaster General in May, 1777. He served in that branch until his discharge in 1821 at the age of seventy-nine. Died, October 19, 1832.

Hugh Stephenson – In June 1776 a new force was formed by Congress as most of the Rifle Company enlistments were coming to an end. Hugh Stephenson was promoted to colonel in command of the Maryland and Virginia Rifle Regiment. Stephenson died later that same year of camp fever.

Charles Mynn Thruston – Head of the Frederick County Secret Committee of Safety, George Washington asked Thruston to recruit a new Virginia Regiment in 1776. He could not achieve the recruitment goal, so he volunteered to serve as a Company Commander with the Continental Army in New Jersey. He served in battle at Trenton (December 26, 1776), and at the Battle of Punk Hill (March 8, 1777) he was badly wounded resulting in the amputation of an arm. He never returned to the ministry. After the war, he served as a county judge and was elected to the Virginia House of Delegates, representing Frederick County from 1782–1788. In 1808 he moved to Louisiana where he resided until his death on March 21, 1812 (age 73).

Baron Cameron Thomas, the sixth Lord Fairfax – Lord Fairfax, the only British peer residing in the thirteen colonies (since 1747), professed to be Loyalist during the Revolutionary War. But he also maintained a secret friendship with George Washington and provided quiet support for the Patriot cause. His ruse prevented threats, retribution, or hostility against him by either Tories or rebels. Yet, in the Virginia Act of 1779, the Commonwealth of Virginia seized title to all of his unsettled land (originally more than five million acres granted to his family by the British Crown in 1649). He was at his home, *Greenway Court* in the Shenandoah Valley, when Cornwallis surrendered the British Army at Yorktown (October 19, 1781) and still there, unmolested, when he died on December 7, 1881.

Nathanael Tracy – Wealthy merchant and ship owner; headed the Newburyport, Massachusetts secret Committee of Safety and Correspondence; aided the Arnold Expedition in preparing for deployment; assisted survivors and escapees from Quebec (1775–76). His merchant fleet totaled more than 100 vessels. Received first letter of marque issued by Congress (1776). His twenty-four cruisers captured 120 "prizes" but in 1777 he lost a privateer and more than ninety of his merchant ships to storms and the Royal Navy. Financially devastated by the war, he died in what some described to be "genteel poverty" on September 20, 1796.

Jemima, wife of Pvt. James Warner – She held her husband until he died of an unknown sickness after he dropped from the ranks marching to Quebec, unable to walk. She then picked up his rifle and caught up with the column. She made it to Quebec only to die from a ball fired from the city.

George Washington – Resigned his commission as Commander-in-Chief on December 23, 1783. In 1789 he was coaxed from his beloved farm to serve as America's first president. After much pleading, he agreed to serve a second term in 1793. Though he was again urged to continue in the presidency for a third term, he retired to Mount Vernon in early 1797. In the second week of December 1799, he contracted a severe illness. On his deathbed shortly before he passed, he told his doctor, James Craik, "Doctor, I die hard, but I am not afraid to go." He died Saturday, December 14, 1799.

Isaac Zane – Raised a Quaker in Philadelphia, came to Virginia in early 1760s and acquired Marlboro Works and considerable real estate in the Shenandoah Valley. Member of the Frederick County Secret Committee of Safety. To the chagrin of some, he lived openly with his mistress, Elizabeth McFarland. Elected to the House of Burgesses in 1773. He later joined Thomas Jefferson on a Convention committee to develop their colony's armed defense. He was appointed by Governor Jefferson as brigadier general in the Virginia Militia at the end of the war, he retired to his beloved Shenandoah Valley. He died at home August 10, 1795.

ACKNOWLEDGMENTS

Daniel Morgan and his Riflemen won so many battles during the American Revolution because they worked as a team. Their legendary feats required they be able to count on one another, day in and day out. The difficult and often dangerous things they accomplished required the same kind of solidarity of purpose, pursuit of a common goal, and fellowship I experienced as a U.S. Marine.

Completing this book required that same kind of teamwork—and demands my gratitude.

In the 1980s, I was befriended by a WWII veteran, former Congressman, and at the time, Secretary of the Army, John O. Marsh. He was the first to encourage me to start this project. My only regret is not having done so sooner or worked faster so I could have handed him a copy of what he started long ago and before he left us to be with our Lord in February this year.

It still would not be started—and certainly not finished—but for all the research—first by Katie Roberts and subsequently by the wonderful folks Nathan Stalvey leads at Clarke County Historical Association; the librarians at Anderson House, Headquarters for The Society of the Cincinnati; the countless Park Rangers at the battlefields and places the Riflemen and others in this book fought, traversed, and lived; even my guide in Quebec who was kind enough to speak English instead of French!

As they have since the last century, Bob Barnett and Michael O'Connor at Williams & Connolly have once again ensured the words I write—like the rounds fired by Morgan's Riflemen—are on target. Their work with Anthony Ziccardi's team at Post Hill Press has forged an alliance as important to this mission as the one we had with France during the Revolution!

The maps used by Daniel Morgan's Riflemen on the way to their first fight in the American Revolution were wholly inadequate. But the ones George Skoch prepared for this book are spot-on! It has been an absolute pleasure to work with George as a cartographer and artist on the magnificent maps and end sheets in this book.

Many of the characters inside this work—including Morgan—suffered from wounds and the privation of war in service to our country. Describing all they endured is a reminder of the extraordinary work Tom Kilgannon and his team at Freedom Alliance do every day to help the current members of our Armed Forces, Veterans, and their families. That's why they are in this book.

Every military operation—like those Morgan's Riflemen engaged in during the Revolution—have scores of participants who must perform tasks essential to the mission for it to be accomplished. And those tasks require organization, teamwork, and leadership, not just management. This book is no different.

My dear friend and Samurai Word Warrior, Gary Terashita, Associate Publisher of Fidelis Books is just such a leader. His tireless work and the team he has assembled to accomplish the mission of getting this book into your hands or on a tablet for you to read is spectacular:

Gary's lovely wife Kim, proofreader extraordinaire, has caught my every "glitch."

Steve Chisholm at Xcel Graphic Services created the stunning interior design.

Amanda Varian has somehow done all the copyediting with incredible speed and accuracy.

Calvin Coolidge at Arclight, LLC, has solved every info-tech challenge.

Josh Smallbone at Smallbone Management has found a way to manage all my travel.

Duane Ward's logistics team at Premiere Centre, as they have so many times for nearly thirty years, is ensuring my books get where they need to be.

My Real American Heroes Productions team has arranged to keep our production schedule on track despite me: Dave Valinski, Dennis Azato, and Mike Aitken.

Most importantly—thank you Betsy, mother of our four children, grandmother of our eighteen grandchildren. For more than half a century you have been my mate, my muse, my most fervent advocate, my greatest inspiration, and my best friend. You are still the most fun I've ever had!

Oliver North
Narnia Farm
Clarke County, Virginia
September 2019

OTHER BOOKS BY OLIVER NORTH

Non-fiction

Under Fire: An American Story

War Stories: Operation Iraqi Freedom

War Stories II: Heroism in the Pacific

War Stories III: The Heroes Who Defeated Hitler

American Heroes: In the Fight Against Radical Islam

American Heroes in Special Operations

American Heroes on the Homefront:
The Hearts of Heroes

Fiction

Mission Compromised

Jericho Sanction

Assassins

Heroes Proved

Counterfeit Lies

Freedom Alliance
Healing the Wounds of War

Like the heroes you've read about in *The Rifleman*, there are thousands of modern-day heroes who have answered the call to serve our country and Freedom Alliance helps them and their families recover from the wounds of war.

Freedom Alliance cares for the sons and daughters of heroes who have sacrificed life or limb by providing college scholarships to their children.

Freedom Alliance also helps combat wounded servicemembers and their families thrive through a broad array of support efforts such as recreational therapy, emergency financial assistance, all-terrain wheelchairs, loan-free vehicles, and mortgage-free homes.

Freedom Alliance is a nonprofit 501(c)(3) charitable organization dedicated to advancing the American heritage of freedom by honoring and encouraging military service, defending the sovereignty of the United States, and promoting a strong national defense.

For more information, please contact:

Freedom Alliance
22570 Markey Court, Suite 240
Dulles, Virginia 20166
(703) 444-7940
Freedomalliance.org

Follow Us on Social Media:

Facebook.com/freedomalliance.org
Twitter.com/freedomalliance
Instagram.com/freedom.alliance
Linkedin.com/freedomalliance

Tools of the R

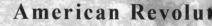

American Revolut

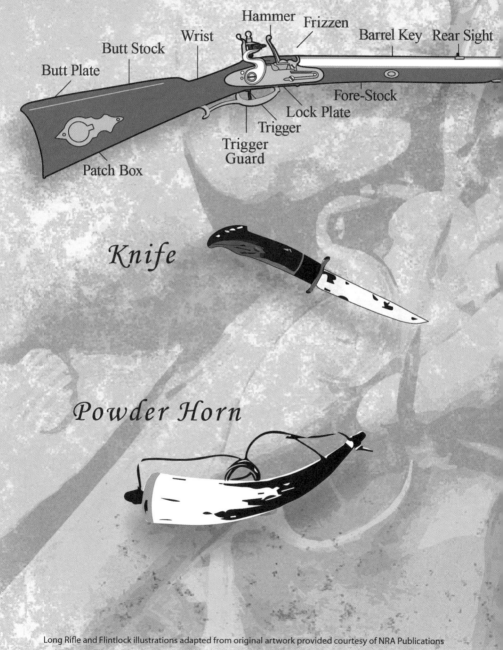

Butt Plate

Butt Stock

Wrist

Hammer Frizzen

Barrel Key Rear Sight

Fore-Stock

Lock Plate

Trigger

Trigger
Guard

Patch Box

Knife

Powder Horn

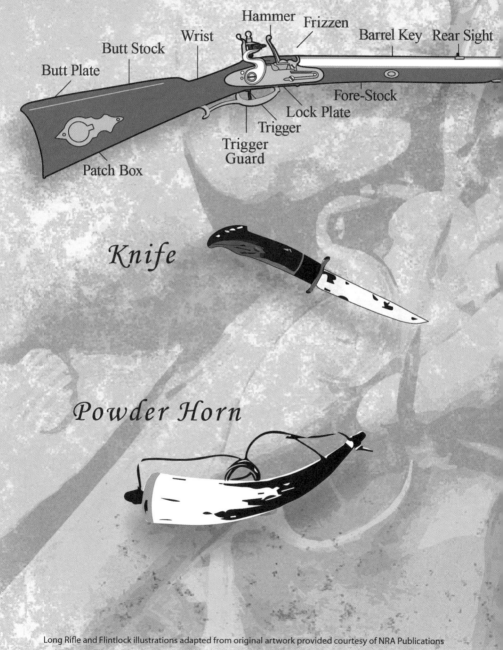